David Harum

Edward Noyes Westcott

Contents

DAVID HARUM

BY

Edward Noyes Westcott

INTRODUCTION.

The's as much human nature in some folks as th' is in others, if not more.--DAVID HARUM.

One of the most conspicuous characteristics of our contemporary native fiction is an increasing tendency to subordinate plot or story to the bold and realistic portrayal of some of the types of American life and manners. And the reason for this is not far to seek. The extraordinary mixing of races which has been going on here for more than a century has produced an enormously diversified human result; and the products of this "hybridization" have been still further differentiated by an environment that ranges from the Everglades of Florida to the glaciers of Alaska. The existence of these conditions, and the great literary opportunities which they contain, American writers long ago perceived; and, with a generally true appreciation of artistic values, they have created from them a gallery of brilliant *genre* pictures which to-day stand for the highest we have yet attained in the art of fiction.

Thus it is that we have (to mention but a few) studies of Louisiana and her people by Mr. Cable; of Virginia and Georgia by Thomas Nelson Page and Joel Chandler Harris; of New England by Miss Jewett and Miss Wilkins; of the Middle West by Miss French (Octave Thanet); of the great Northwest by Hamlin Garland; of Canada and the land of the *habitans* by Gilbert Parker; and finally, though really first in point of time, the Forty-niners and their successors by Bret Harte. This list might be indefinitely extended, for it is growing daily, but it is long enough as it stands to show that every section of our country has, or soon will have, its own painter and historian, whose works will live and become a permanent part of our literature in just the degree that they are artistically true. Some of these writers have already produced many books, while others have gained general recognition and even fame by the vividness and power of a single study, like Mr. Howe with The Story of a Country Town. But each one, it will be noticed, has chosen for his field of work that part of our country wherein he passed the early and formative years of his life; a natural selection that is, perhaps, an unconscious affirmation of David Harum's aphorism: "Ev'ry hoss c'n do a thing better 'n' spryer if he's ben broke to it as a colt."

In the case of the present volume the conditions are identical with those just mentioned. Most of the scenes are laid in central New York, where the author, Edward Noyes Westcott, was born, September 24, 1847, and where he died of consumption, March 31, 1898. Nearly all his life was passed in his native city of Syracuse, and although banking and not authorship was the occupation of his active years, yet his sensitive and impressionable temperament had become so saturated with the local atmosphere, and his retentive memory so charged with facts, that when at length he took up the pen he was able to create in David Harum a character so original, so true, and so strong, yet withal so delightfully quaint and humorous, that we are at once compelled to admit that here is a new and permanent addition to the long list of American literary portraits.

The book is a novel, and throughout it runs a love story which is characterized by sympathetic treatment and a constantly increasing interest; but the title role is taken by the old country banker, David Harum: dry, quaint, somewhat illiterate, no doubt, but possessing an amazing amount of knowledge not found in printed books, and holding fast to the cheerful belief that there is nothing wholly bad or useless in this world. Or, in his own words: "A reasonable amount of fleas is good for a dog-- they keep him f'm broodin' on bein' a dog." This horse-trading country banker and reputed Shylock, but real philanthropist, is an accurate portrayal of a type that exists in the rural districts of central New York to-day. Variations of him may be seen daily, driving about in their road wagons or seated in their "bank parlors," shrewd, sharp-tongued, honest as the sunlight from most points of view, but in a horse trade much inclined to follow the rule laid down by Mr. Harum himself for such transactions: "Do unto the other feller the way he'd like to do unto you--an' do it fust."

The genial humor and sunny atmosphere which pervade these pages are in dramatic contrast with the circumstances under which they were written. The book was finished while the author lay upon his deathbed, but, happily for the reader, no trace of his sufferings appears here. It was not granted that he should live to see his work in its present completed form, a consummation he most earnestly desired; but it seems not unreasonable to hope that the result of his labors will be appreciated, and that David Harum will endure.

FORBES HEERMANS.

SYRACUSE, N.Y., *August 20, 1898.*

DAVID HARUM.
CHAPTER I.

David poured half of his second cup of tea into his saucer to lower its temperature to the drinking point, and helped himself to a second cut of ham and a third egg. Whatever was on his mind to have kept him unusually silent during the evening meal, and to cause certain wrinkles in his forehead suggestive of perplexity or misgiving, had not impaired his appetite. David was what he called "a good feeder."

Mrs. Bixbee, known to most of those who enjoyed the privilege of her acquaintance as "Aunt Polly," though nieces and nephews of her blood there were none in Homeville, Freeland County, looked curiously at her brother, as, in fact, she had done at intervals during the repast; and concluding at last that further forbearance was uncalled for, relieved the pressure of her curiosity thus:

"Guess ye got somethin' on your mind, hain't ye? You hain't hardly said aye, yes, ner no sence you set down. Anythin' gone 'skew?"

David lifted his saucer, gave the contents a precautionary blow, and emptied it with sundry windy suspirations.

"No," he said, "nothin' hain't gone exac'ly wrong, 's ye might say--not yet; but I done that thing I was tellin' ye of to-day."

"Done what thing?" she asked perplexedly.

"I telegraphed to New York," he replied, "fer that young feller to come on--the young man General Wolsey wrote me about. I got a letter from him to-day, an' I made up my mind 'the sooner the quicker,' an' I telegraphed him to come 's soon 's he could."

"I forgit what you said his name was," said Aunt Polly.

"There's his letter," said David, handing it across the table. "Read it out 'loud."

"You read it," she said, passing it back after a search in her pocket; "I must 'a' left my specs in the settin'-room."

The letter was as follows:

"DEAR SIR: I take the liberty of addressing you at the instance of General Wolsey, who spoke to me of the matter of your communication to him, and was kind enough to say that he would write you in my behalf. My acquaintance with him has been in the nature of a social rather than a business one, and I fancy that he can only recommend me on general grounds. I will say, therefore, that I have had some experience with accounts, but not much practice in them for nearly three years. Nevertheless, unless the work you wish done is of an intricate nature, I think I shall be able to accomplish it with such posting at the outset as most strangers would require. General Wolsey told me that you wanted some one as soon as possible. I have nothing to prevent me from starting at once if you desire to have me. A telegram addressed to me at the office of the Trust Company will reach me promptly.

"Yours very truly,

"JOHN K. LENOX."

"Wa'al," said David, looking over his glasses at his sister, "what do you think on't?"

"The' ain't much brag in't," she replied thoughtfully.

"No," said David, putting his eyeglasses back in their case, "th' ain't no brag ner no promises; he don't even say he'll do his best, like most fellers would. He seems to have took it fer granted that I'll take it fer granted, an' that's what I like about it. Wa'al," he added, "the thing's done, an' I'll be lookin' fer him to-morrow mornin' or evenin' at latest."

Mrs. Bixbee sat for a moment with her large, light blue, and rather prominent eyes fixed on her brother's face, and then she said, with a slight undertone of anxiety, "Was you cal'latin' to have that young man from New York come here?"

"I hadn't no such idee," he replied, with a slight smile, aware of what was passing in her mind. "What put that in your head?"

"Wa'al," she answered, "you know the' ain't scarcely anybody in the village that takes boarders in the winter, an' I was wonderin' what he would do."

"I s'pose he'll go to the Eagle," said David. "I dunno where else, 'nless it's to the Lake House."

"The Eagil!" she exclaimed contemptuously. "Land sakes! Comin' here from New York! He won't stan' it there a week."

"Wa'al," replied David, "mebbe he will an' mebbe he won't, but I don't see what else the' is for it, an' I guess 'twon't kill him for a spell The fact is--" he was proceeding when Mrs. Bixbee interrupted him.

"I guess we'd better adjourn t' the settin'-room an' let Sairy clear off the tea-things," she said, rising and going into the kitchen.

"What was you sayin'?" she asked, as she presently found her brother in the apartment designated, and seated herself with her mending-basket in her lap.

"The fact is, I was sayin'," he resumed, sitting with hand and forearm resting on a round table, in the centre of which was a large kerosene lamp, "that my notion was, fust off, to have him come here, but when I come to think on't I changed my mind. In the fust place, except that he's well recommended, I don't know nothin' about him; an' in the second, you'n I are pretty well set in our ways, an' git along all right just as we be. I may want the young feller to stay, an' then agin I may not-- we'll see. It's a good sight easier to git a fishhook in 'n 'tis to git it out. I expect he'll find it putty tough at first, but if he's a feller that c'n be drove out of bus'nis by a spell of the Eagle Tavern, he ain't the feller I'm lookin' fer--though I will allow," he added with a grimace, "that it'll be a putty hard test. But if I want to say to him, after tryin' him a spell, that I guess me an' him don't seem likely to hitch, we'll both take it easier if we ain't livin' in the same house. I guess I'll take a look at the Trybune," said David, unfolding that paper.

Mrs. Bixbee went on with her needlework, with an occasional side glance at her brother, who was immersed in the gospel of his politics. Twice or thrice she opened her lips as if to address him, but apparently some restraining thought interposed. Finally, the impulse to utter her mind culminated. "Dave," she said, "d' you know what Deakin Perkins is sayin' about ye?"

David opened his paper so as to hide his face, and the corners of his mouth twitched as he asked in return, "Wa'al, what's the deakin sayin' now?"

"He's sayin'," she replied, in a voice mixed of indignation and apprehension, "thet you sold him a balky horse, an' he's goin' to hev the law on ye." David's shoulders shook behind the sheltering page, and his mouth expanded in a grin.

"Wa'al," he replied after a moment, lowering the paper and looking gravely at his companion over his glasses, "next to the deakin's religious experience, them of lawin' an' horse-tradin' air his strongest p'ints, an' he works the hull on 'em to once sometimes."

The evasiveness of this generality was not lost on Mrs. Bixbee, and she pressed the point with, "Did ye? an' will he?"

"Yes, an' no, an' mebbe, an' mebbe not," was the categorical reply.

"Wa'al," she answered with a snap, "mebbe you call that an answer. I s'pose if you don't want to let on you won't, but I do believe you've ben playin' some trick on the deakin, an' won't own up. I do wish," she added, "that if you hed to git rid of a balky horse onto somebody you'd hev picked out somebody else."

"When you got a balker to dispose of," said David gravely, "you can't alwus pick an' choose. Fust come, fust served." Then he went on more seriously: "Now I'll tell ye. Quite a while ago--in fact, not long after I come to enjoy the priv'lidge of the deakin's acquaintance--we hed a deal. I wasn't jest on my guard, knowin' him to be a deakin an' all that, an' he lied to me so splendid that I was took in, clean over my head, he done me so brown I was burnt in places, an' you c'd smell smoke 'round me fer some time."

"Was it a horse?" asked Mrs. Bixbee gratuitously.

"Wa'al," David replied, "mebbe it *had* ben some time, but at that partic'lar time the only thing to determine that fact was that it wa'n't nothin' else."

"Wa'al, I declare!" exclaimed Mrs. Bixbee, wondering not more at the deacon's turpitude than at the lapse in David's acuteness, of which she had an immense opinion, but commenting only on the former. "I'm 'mazed at the deakin."

"Yes'm," said David with a grin, "I'm quite a liar myself when it comes right down to the hoss bus'nis, but the deakin c'n give me both bowers ev'ry hand. He done it so slick that I had to laugh when I come to think it over--an' I had witnesses to the hull confab, too, that he didn't know of, an' I c'd 've showed him up in great shape if I'd had a mind to."

"Why didn't ye?" said Aunt Polly, whose feelings about the deacon were undergoing a revulsion.

"Wa'al, to tell ye the truth, I was so completely skunked that I hadn't a word to say. I got rid o' the thing fer what it was wuth fer hide an' taller, an' stid of squealin' 'round the way you say he's doin', like a stuck pig, I kep' my tongue between my teeth an' laid to git even some time."

"You ort to 've hed the law on him," declared Mrs. Bixbee, now fully converted. "The old scamp!"

"Wa'al," was the reply, "I gen'all prefer to settle out of court, an' in this partic'lar case, while I might 'a' ben willin' t' admit that I hed ben did up, I didn't feel much like swearin' to it. I reckoned the time 'd come when mebbe I'd git the laugh on the deakin, an' it did, an' we're putty well settled now in full."

"You mean this last pufformance?" asked Mrs. Bixbee. "I wish you'd quit beatin' about the bush, an' tell me the hull story."

"Wa'al, it's like this, then, if you **will** hev it. I was over to Whiteboro a while ago on a little matter of worldly bus'nis, an' I seen a couple of fellers halter-exercisin' a hoss in the tavern yard. I stood 'round a spell watchin' 'em, an' when he come to a standstill I went an' looked him over, an' I liked his looks fust rate.

"'Fer sale?' I says.

"'Wa'al,' says the chap that was leadin' him, 'I never see the hoss that wa'n't if the price was right.'

"'Your'n?' I says.

"'Mine an' his'n,' he says, noddin' his head at the other feller.

"'What ye askin' fer him?' I says.

"'One-fifty,' he says.

"I looked him all over agin putty careful, an' once or twice I kind o' shook my head 's if I didn't quite like what I seen, an' when I got through I sort o' half turned away without sayin' anythin', 's if I'd seen enough.

"'The' ain't a scratch ner a pimple on him,' says the feller, kind o' resentin' my looks. 'He's sound an' kind, an' 'll stand without hitchin', an' a lady c'n drive him 's well 's a man.'"

"'I ain't got anythin' agin him,' I says, 'an' prob'ly that's all true, ev'ry word on't; but one-fifty's a consid'able price fer a hoss these days. I hain't no pressin' use fer another hoss, an', in fact,' I says, 'I've got one or two fer sale myself.'

"'He's wuth two hunderd jest as he stands,' the feller says. 'He hain't had no trainin', an' he c'n draw two men in a road-wagin better'n fifty.'

"Wa'al, the more I looked at him the better I liked him, but I only says, 'Jes' so, jes' so, he may be wuth the money, but jest as I'm fixed now he ain't wuth it to *me*, an' I hain't got that much money with me if he was,' I says. The other feller hadn't said nothin' up to that time, an' he broke in now. 'I s'pose you'd take him fer a gift, wouldn't ye?' he says, kind o' sneerin'.

"'Wa'al, yes,' I says, 'I dunno but I would if you'd throw in a pound of tea an' a halter.'

"He kind o' laughed an' says, 'Wa'al, this ain't no gift enterprise, an' I guess we ain't goin' to trade, but I'd like to know,' he says, 'jest as a matter of curios'ty, what you'd say he *was* wuth to ye?'

"'Wa'al,' I says, 'I come over this mornin' to see a feller that owed me a trifle o' money. Exceptin' of some loose change, what he paid me 's all I got with me,' I says, takin' out my wallet. 'That wad's got a hunderd an' twenty-five into it, an' if you'd sooner have your hoss an' halter than the wad,' I says, 'why, I'll bid ye good-day.'

"'You're offerin' one-twenty-five fer the hoss an' halter?' he says.

"'That's what I'm doin',' I says.

"'You've made a trade,' he says, puttin' out his hand fer the money an' handin' the halter over to me."

"An' didn't ye suspicion nuthin' when he took ye up like that?" asked Mrs. Bixbee.

"I did smell woolen some," said David, "but I had the *hoss* an' they had the *money*, an', as fur 's I c'd see, the critter was all right. Howsomever, I says to 'em: 'This here's all right, fur 's it's gone, but you've talked putty strong 'bout this hoss. I don't know who you fellers be, but I c'n find out,' I says. Then the fust feller that done the talkin' 'bout the hoss put in an' says, 'The' hain't ben one word said to you about this hoss that wa'n't gospel truth, not one word.' An' when I come to think on't afterward," said David with a half laugh, "it mebbe wa'n't *gospel* truth, but it was good enough *jury* truth. I guess this ain't over 'n' above interestin' to ye, is it?" he asked after a pause, looking doubtfully at his sister.

"Yes, 'tis," she asserted. "I'm lookin' forrered to where the deakin comes in, but you jest tell it your own way."

"I'll git there all in good time," said David, "but some of the point of the story'll be lost if I don't tell ye what come fust."

"I allow to stan' it 's long 's you can," she said encouragingly, "seein' what work I had gettin' ye started. Did ye find out anythin' 'bout them fellers?"

"I ast the barn man if he knowed who they was, an' he said he never seen 'em till the yestiddy before, an' didn't know 'em f'm Adam. They come along with a couple of hosses, one drivin' an' t'other leadin'--the one I bought. I ast him if they knowed who I was, an' he said one on 'em ast him, an' he told him. The feller said to him, seein' me drive up: 'That's a putty likely-lookin' hoss. Who's drivin' him?' An' he says to the feller: 'That's Dave Harum, f'm over to Homeville. He's a great feller fer hosses,' he says."

"Dave," said Mrs. Bixbee, "them chaps jest laid fer ye, didn't they?"

"I reckon they did," he admitted; "an' they was as slick a pair as was ever drawed to," which expression was lost upon his sister. David rubbed the fringe of yellowish-gray hair which encircled his bald pate for a moment.

"Wa'al," he resumed, "after the talk with the barn man, I smelt woolen stronger'n ever, but I didn't say nothin', an' had the mare hitched an' started back. Old Jinny drives with one hand, an' I c'd watch the new one all right, an' as we come along I begun to think I wa'n't stuck after all. I never see a hoss travel evener an' nicer, an' when we come to a good level place I sent the old mare along the best she knew, an' the new one never broke his gait, an' kep' right up 'ithout 'par'ntly half tryin'; an' Jinny don't take most folks' dust neither. I swan! 'fore I got home I reckoned I'd jest as good as made seventy-five anyway."

CHAPTER II.

"Then the' wa'n't nothin' the matter with him, after all," commented Mrs. Bixbee in rather a disappointed tone.

"The meanest thing top of the earth was the matter with him," declared David, "but I didn't find it out till the next afternoon, an' then I found it out good. I hitched him to the open buggy an' went 'round by the East road, 'cause that ain't so much travelled. He went along all right till we got a mile or so out of the village, an' then I slowed him down to a walk. Wa'al, sir, scat my ----! He hadn't walked more'n a rod 'fore he come to a dead stan'still. I clucked an' git-app'd, an' finely took the gad to him a little; but he only jest kind o' humped up a little, an' stood like he'd took root."

"Wa'al, now!" exclaimed Mrs. Bixbee.

"Yes'm," said David; "I was stuck in ev'ry sense of the word."

"What d'ye do?"

"Wa'al, I tried all the tricks I knowed--an' I could lead him--but when I was in the buggy he wouldn't stir till he got good an' ready; 'n' then he'd start of his own accord an' go on a spell, an'--"

"Did he keep it up?" Mrs. Bixbee interrupted.

"Wa'al, I s'd say he did. I finely got home with the critter, but I thought one time I'd either hev to lead him or spend the night on the East road. He balked five sep'rate times, varyin' in length, an' it was dark when we struck the barn."

"I should hev thought you'd a wanted to kill him," said Mrs. Bixbee; "an' the fellers that sold him to ye, too."

"The' *was* times," David replied, with a nod of his head, "when if he'd a fell down dead I wouldn't hev figgered on puttin' a band on my hat, but it don't never pay to git mad with a hoss; an' as fur 's the feller I bought him of, when I remembered how he told me he'd stand without hitchin', I swan! I had to laugh. I did, fer a fact. 'Stand without hitchin'!' He, he, he!"

"I guess you wouldn't think it was so awful funny if you hadn't gone an' stuck that horse onto Deakin Perkins--an' I don't see how you done it."

"Mebbe that *is* part of the joke," David allowed, "an' I'll tell ye th' rest on't. Th' next day I hitched the new one to th' dem'crat wagin an' put in a lot of straps an' rope, an' started off fer the East road agin. He went fust rate till we come to about the place where we had the fust trouble, an', sure enough, he balked agin. I leaned over an' hit him a smart cut on the off shoulder, but he only humped a little, an' never lifted a foot. I hit him another lick, with the selfsame result. Then I got down an' I strapped that animal so't he couldn't move nothin' but his head an' tail, an' got back into the buggy. Wa'al, bom-by, it may 'a' ben ten minutes, or it may 'a' ben more or less--it's slow work settin' still behind a balkin' hoss--he was ready to go on his own account, but he couldn't budge. He kind o' looked around, much as to say, 'What on earth's the matter?' an' then he tried another move, an' then another, but no go. Then I got down an' took the hopples off an' then climbed back into the buggy, an' says 'Cluck, to him, an' off he stepped as chipper as could be, an' we went joggin' along all right mebbe two mile, an' when I slowed up, up he come agin. I gin him another clip in the same place on the shoulder, an' I got down an' tied him up agin, an' the same thing happened as before, on'y it didn't take him quite so long to make up his mind about startin', an' we went some further without a hitch. But I had to go through the pufformance the third time before he got it into his head that if he didn't go when *I* wanted he couldn't go when *he* wanted, an' that didn't suit him; an' when he felt the whip on his shoulder it meant bus'nis."

"Was that the end of his balkin'?" asked Mrs. Bixbee.

"I had to give him one more go-round," said David, "an' after that I didn't have no more trouble with him. He showed symptoms at times, but a touch of the whip on the shoulder alwus fetched him. I alwus carried them straps, though, till the last two or three times."

"Wa'al, what's the deakin kickin' about, then?" asked Aunt Polly. "You're jest sayin' you broke him of balkin'."

"Wa'al," said David slowly, "some hosses will balk with some folks an' not with others. You can't most alwus gen'ally tell."

"Didn't the deakin have a chance to try him?"

"He had all the chance he ast fer," replied David. "Fact is, he done most of the sellin', as well 's the buyin', himself."

"How's that?"

"Wa'al," said David, "it come about like this: After I'd got the hoss where I c'd handle him I begun to think I'd had some int'restin' an' valu'ble experience, an' it wa'n't scurcely fair to keep it all to myself. I didn't want no patent on't, an' I was willin' to let some other feller git a piece. So one mornin', week before last--let's see, week ago Tuesday it was, an' a mighty nice mornin' it was, too--one o' them days that kind o' lib'ral up your mind--I allowed to hitch an' drive up past the deakin's an' back, an' mebbe git somethin' to strengthen my faith, et cetery, in case I run

acrost him. Wa'al, 's I come along I seen the deakin putterin' 'round, an' I waved my
hand to him an' went by a-kitin'. I went up the road a ways an' killed a little time,
an' when I come back there was the deakin, as I expected. He was leanin' over the
fence, an' as I jogged up he hailed me, an' I pulled up.

"'Mornin', Mr. Harum,' he says.

"'Mornin', deakin,' I says. 'How are ye? an' how's Mis' Perkins these days?'

"'I'm fair,' he says; 'fair to middlin', but Mis' Perkins is ailin' some--as *usyul*'
he says."

"They do say," put in Mrs. Bixbee, "thet Mis' Perkins don't hev much of a time
herself."

"Guess she hez all the time the' is," answered David. "Wa'al," he went on, "we
passed the time o' day, an' talked a spell about the weather an' all that, an' finely I
straightened up the lines as if I was goin' on, an' then I says: 'Oh, by the way,' I says,
'I jest thought on't. I heard Dominie White was lookin' fer a hoss that 'd suit him.'
'I hain't heard,' he says; but I see in a minute he had--an' it really was a fact--an'
I says: 'I've got a roan colt risin' five, that I took on a debt a spell ago, that I'll sell
reasonable, that's as likely an' nice ev'ry way a young hoss as ever I owned. I don't
need him,' I says, 'an' didn't want to take him, but it was that or nothin' at the time
an' glad to git it, an' I'll sell him a barg'in. Now what I want to say to you, deakin,
is this: That hoss 'd suit the dominie to a tee in my opinion, but the dominie won't
come to me. Now if *you* was to say to him--bein' in his church an' all thet,' I says,
'that you c'd get him the right kind of a hoss, he'd believe you, an' you an' me 'd
be doin' a little stroke of bus'nis, an' a favor to the dominie into the bargain. The
dominie's well off,' I says, 'an' c'n afford to drive a good hoss.'"

"What did the deakin say?" asked Aunt Polly as David stopped for breath.

"I didn't expect him to jump down my throat," he answered; "but I seen him
prick up his ears, an' all the time I was talkin' I noticed him lookin' my hoss over,
head an' foot. 'Now I 'member,' he says, 'hearin' sunthin' 'bout Mr. White's lookin'
fer a hoss, though when you fust spoke on't it had slipped my mind. Of course,' he
says, 'the' ain't any real reason why Mr. White shouldn't deal with you direct, an'
yit mebbe I *could* do more with him 'n you could. But,' he says, 'I wa'n't cal'latin'
to go t' the village this mornin', an' I sent my hired man off with my drivin' hoss.
Mebbe I'll drop 'round in a day or two,' he says, 'an' look at the roan.'

"'You mightn't ketch me,' I says, 'an' I want to show him myself; an' more'n that,' I says, 'Dug Robinson's after the dominie. I'll tell ye,' I says, 'you jest git in 'ith me an' go down an' look at him, an' I'll send ye back or drive ye back, an' if you've got anythin' special on hand you needn't be gone three quarters of an hour,' I says."

"He come, did he?" inquired Mrs. Bixbee.

"He done *so*," said David sententiously. "Jest as I knowed he would, after he'd hem'd an' haw'd about so much, an' he rode a mile an' a half livelier 'n he done in a good while, I reckon. He had to pull that old broad-brim of his'n down to his ears, an' don't you fergit it. He, he, he, he! The road was jest *full* o' hosses. Wa'al, we drove into the yard, an' I told the hired man to unhitch the bay hoss an' fetch out the roan, an' while he was bein' unhitched the deakin stood 'round an' never took his eyes off'n him, an' I knowed I wouldn't sell the deakin no roan hoss *that* day, even if I wanted to. But when he come out I begun to crack him up, an' I talked hoss fer all I was wuth. The deakin looked him over in a don't-care kind of a way, an' didn't 'parently give much heed to what I was sayin'. Finely I says, 'Wa'al, what do you think of him?' 'Wa'al,' he says, 'he seems to be a likely enough critter, but I don't believe he'd suit Mr. White--'fraid not,' he says. 'What you askin' fer him?' he says. 'One-fifty,' I says, 'an' he's a cheap hoss at the money'; but," added the speaker with a laugh, "I knowed I might 's well of said a thousan'. The deakin wa'n't buyin' no roan colts that mornin'."

"What did he say?" asked Mrs. Bixbee.

"'Wa'al,' he says, 'wa'al, I guess you ought to git that much fer him, but I'm 'fraid he ain't what Mr. White wants.' An' then, 'That's quite a hoss we come down with,' he says. 'Had him long?' 'Jest long 'nough to git 'quainted with him,' I says. 'Don't you want the roan fer your own use?' I says. 'Mebbe we c'd shade the price a little.' 'No,' he says, 'I guess not. I don't need another hoss jest now.' An' then, after a minute he says: 'Say, mebbe the bay hoss we drove 'd come nearer the mark fer White, if he's all right. Jest as soon I'd look at him?' he says. 'Wa'al, I hain't no objections, but I guess he's more of a hoss than the dominie 'd care for, but I'll go an' fetch him out,' I says. So I brought him out, an' the deakin looked him all over. I see it was a case of love at fust sight, as the story-books says. 'Looks all right,' he says. 'I'll tell ye,' I says, 'what the feller I bought him of told me.' 'What's that?' says the deakin. 'He said to me,' I says, '"that hoss hain't got a scratch ner a pimple on him. He's sound an' kind, an' 'll stand without hitchin', an' a lady c'd drive him as well 's a man."'

"'That's what he said to me,' I says, 'an' it's every word on't true. You've seen whether or not he c'n travel,' I says, 'an', so fur 's I've seen, he ain't 'fraid of nothin'.' 'D'ye want to sell him?' the deakin says. 'Wa'al,' I says, 'I ain't offerin' him fer sale. You'll go a good ways,' I says, ''fore you'll strike such another; but, of course, he ain't the only hoss in the world, an' I never had anythin' in the hoss line I wouldn't sell at *some* price.' 'Wa'al,' he says, 'what d' ye ask fer him?' 'Wa'al,' I says, 'if my own brother was to ask me that question I'd say to him two hunderd dollars, cash down, an' I wouldn't hold the offer open an hour,' I says."

"My!" ejaculated Aunt Polly. "Did he take you up?"

"'That's more'n I give fer a hoss 'n a good while,' he says, shakin' his head, 'an' more'n I c'n afford, I'm 'fraid.' 'All right,' I says; 'I c'n afford to keep him'; but I knew I had the deakin same as the woodchuck had Skip. 'Hitch up the roan,' I says to Mike; 'the deakin wants to be took up to his house.' 'Is that your last word?' he says. 'That's what it is,' I says. 'Two hunderd, cash down.'"

"Didn't ye dast to trust the deakin?" asked Mrs. Bixbee.

"Polly," said David, "the's a number of holes in a ten-foot ladder." Mrs. Bixbee seemed to understand this rather ambiguous rejoinder.

"He must 'a' squirmed some," she remarked. David laughed.

"The deakin ain't much used to payin' the other feller's price," he said, "an' it was like pullin' teeth; but he wanted that hoss more'n a cow wants a calf, an' after a little more squimmidgin' he hauled out his wallet an' forked over. Mike come out with the roan, an' off the deakin went, leadin' the bay hoss."

"I don't see," said Mrs. Bixbee, looking up at her brother, "thet after all the' was anythin' you said to the deakin thet he could ketch holt on."

"The' wa'n't nothin'," he replied. "The only thing he c'n complain about's what I *didn't* say to him."

"Hain't he said anythin' to ye?" Mrs. Bixbee inquired.

"He, he, he, he! He hain't but once, an' the' wa'n't but little of it then."

"How?"

"Wa'al, the day but one after the deakin sold himself Mr. Stickin'-Plaster I had an arrant three four mile or so up past his place, an' when I was comin' back, along 'bout four or half past, it come on to rain like all possessed. I had my old umbrel'--though it didn't hender me f'm gettin' more or less wet--an' I sent the old mare along fer all she knew. As I come along to within a mile f'm the deakin's house I seen somebody in the road, an' when I come up closter I see it was the deakin himself, in trouble, an' I kind o' slowed up to see what was goin' on. There he was, settin' all humped up with his ole broad-brim hat slopin' down his back, a-sheddin' water like a roof. Then I seen him lean over an' larrup the hoss with the ends of the lines fer all he was wuth. It appeared he hadn't no whip, an' it wouldn't done him no good if he'd had. Wa'al, sir, rain or no rain, I jest pulled up to watch him. He'd larrup a spell, an' then he'd set back; an' then he'd lean over an' try it agin, harder'n ever. Scat my ----! I thought I'd die a-laughin'. I couldn't hardly cluck to the mare when I got ready to move on. I drove alongside an' pulled up. 'Hullo, deakin,' I says, 'what's the matter?' He looked up at me, an' I won't say he was the maddest man I ever see, but he was long ways the maddest-lookin' man, an' he shook his fist at me jest like one o' the unregen'rit. 'Consarn ye, Dave Harum!' he says, 'I'll hev the law on ye fer this.' 'What fer?' I says. 'I didn't make it come on to rain, did I?' I says. 'You know mighty well what fer,' he says. 'You sold me this ***damned beast***,' he says, 'an' he's balked with me ***nine*** times this afternoon, an' I'll fix ye for 't,' he says. 'Wa'al, deakin,' I says, 'I'm 'fraid the squire's office 'll be shut up 'fore you ***git*** there, but I'll take any word you'd like to send. You know I told ye,' I says, 'that he'd stand 'ithout hitchin'.' An' at that he only jest kind o' choked an' sputtered. He was so mad he couldn't say nothin', an' on I drove, an' when I got about forty rod or so I looked back, an' there was the deakin a-comin' along the road with as much of his shoulders as he could git under his hat an' ***leadin'*** his new hoss. He, he, he, he! Oh, my stars an' garters! Say, Polly, it paid me fer bein' born into this vale o' tears. It did, I declare for't!" Aunt Polly wiped her eyes on her apron.

"But, Dave," she said, "did the deakin really say--***that word***?"

"Wa'al," he replied, "if 'twa'n't that it was the puttiest imitation on't that ever I heard."

"David," she continued, "don't you think it putty mean to badger the deakin so't he swore, an' then laugh 'bout it? An' I s'pose you've told the story all over."

"Mis' Bixbee," said David emphatically, "if I'd paid good money to see a funny show I'd be a blamed fool if I didn't laugh, wouldn't I? That specticle of the deakin cost me consid'able, but it was more'n wuth it. But," he added, "I guess, the way the thing stands now, I ain't so much out on the hull."

Mrs. Bixbee looked at him inquiringly.

"Of course, you know Dick Larrabee?" he asked.

She nodded.

"Wa'al, three four days after the shower, an' the story 'd got aroun' some-- as *you* say, the deakin *is* consid'able of a talker--I got holt of Dick--I've done him some favors an' he natur'ly expects more--an' I says to him: 'Dick,' I says, 'I hear 't Deakin Perkins has got a hoss that don't jest suit him--hain't got knee-action enough at times,' I says, 'an' mebbe he'll sell him reasonable.' 'I've heerd somethin' about it,' says Dick, laughin'. 'One of them kind o' hosses 't you don't like to git ketched out in the rain with,' he says. 'Jes' so,' I says. 'Now,' I says, 'I've got a notion 't I'd like to own that hoss at a price, an' that mebbe *I* c'd git him home even if it did rain. Here's a hunderd an' ten,' I says, 'an' I want you to see how fur it'll go to buyin' him. If you git me the hoss you needn't bring none on't back. Want to try?' I says. 'All right,' he says, an' took the money. 'But,' he says, 'won't the deakin suspicion that it comes from you?' 'Wa'al,' I says, 'my portrit ain't on none o' the bills, an' I reckon *you* won't tell him so, out an' out,' an' off he went. Yistidy he come in, an' I says, 'Wa'al, done anythin'?' 'The hoss is in your barn,' he says. 'Good fer you!' I says. 'Did you make anythin'?' 'I'm satisfied,' he says. 'I made a ten-dollar note.' An' that's the net results on't," concluded David, "that I've got the hoss, an' he's cost me jest thirty-five dollars."

CHAPTER III.

Master Jacky Carling was a very nice boy, but not at that time in his career the safest person to whom to intrust a missive in case its sure and speedy delivery were a matter of importance. But he protested with so much earnestness and good will that it should be put into the very first post-box he came to on his way to school, and that nothing could induce him to forget it, that Mary Blake, his aunt, confidante and not unfrequently counsel and advocate, gave it him to post, and dismissed the matter from her mind. Unfortunately the weather, which had been very frosty, had changed in the night to a summer-like mildness. As Jacky opened the door, three or four of his school-fellows were passing. He felt the softness of the spring morning, and to their injunction to "Hurry up and come along!" replied with an entreaty to "Wait a minute till he left his overcoat" (all boys hate an overcoat), and plunged back into the house.

If John Lenox (John Knox Lenox) had received Miss Blake's note of condolence and sympathy, written in reply to his own, wherein, besides speaking of his bereavement, he had made allusion to some changes in his prospects and some necessary alterations in his ways for a time, he might perhaps have read between the lines something more than merely a kind expression of her sorrow for the trouble which had come upon him, and the reminder that he had friends who, if they could not do more to lessen his grief, would give him their truest sympathy. And if some days later he had received a second note, saying that she and her people were about to go away for some months, and asking him to come and see them before their departure, it is possible that very many things set forth in this narrative would not have happened.

*   *   *   *   *

Life had always been made easy for John Lenox, and his was not the temperament to interpose obstacles to the process. A course at Andover had been followed by two years at Princeton; but at the end of the second year it had occurred to him that practical life ought to begin for him, and he had thought it rather fine of himself to undertake a clerkship in the office of Rush & Co., where in the ensuing year and a half or so, though he took his work in moderation, he got a fair knowledge of accounts and the ways and methods of "the Street." But that period of it was enough. He found himself not only regretting the abandonment of his college career, but feeling that the thing for which he had given it up had been rather a waste of time. He came to the conclusion that, though he had entered college later than most, even now a further acquaintance with text-books and professors was more to be desired than with ledgers and brokers. His father (somewhat to his wonderment, and possibly a little to his chagrin) seemed rather to welcome the suggestion that he spend a couple of years in Europe, taking some lectures at Heidelberg or elsewhere, and traveling; and in the course of that time he acquired a pretty fair working acquaintance with German, brought his knowledge of French up to about the same point, and came back at the end of two years with a fine and discriminating taste in beer, and a scar over his left eyebrow which could be seen if attention were called to it.

He started upon his return without any definite intentions or for any special reason, except that he had gone away for two years and that the two years were up. He had carried on a desultory correspondence with his father, who had replied occasionally, rather briefly, but on the whole affectionately. He had noticed that during the latter part of his stay abroad the replies had been more than usually irregular, but had attributed no special significance to the fact. It was not until afterward that it occurred to him that in all their correspondence his father had never alluded in any way to his return.

On the passenger list of the Altruria John came upon the names of Mr. and Mrs. Julius Carling and Miss Blake.

"Blake, Blake," he said to himself. "Carling--I seem to remember to have known that name at some time. It must be little Mary Blake whom I knew as a small girl years ago, and, yes, Carling was the name of the man her sister married. Well, well, I wonder what she is like. Of course, I shouldn't know her from Eve now, or she me from Adam. All I can remember seems to be a pair of very slim and active legs, a lot of flying hair, a pair of brownish-gray or grayish-brown eyes, and that I thought her a very nice girl, as girls went. But it doesn't in the least follow that I might think so now, and shipboard is pretty close quarters for seven or eight days."

Dinner is by all odds the chief event of the day on board ship to those who are able to dine, and they will leave all other attractions, even the surpassingly interesting things which go on in the smoking-room, at once on the sound of the gong of promise. On this first night of the voyage the ship was still in smooth water at dinner time, and many a place was occupied which would know its occupant for the first, and very possibly for the last, time. The passenger list was fairly large, but not full. John had assigned to him a seat at a side table. He was hungry, having had no luncheon but a couple of biscuits and a glass of "bitter," and was taking his first mouthful of Perrier-Jouet, after the soup, and scanning the dinner card when the people at his table came in. The man of the trio was obviously an invalid of the nervous variety, and the most decided type. The small, dark woman who took the corner seat at his left was undoubtedly, from the solicitous way in which she adjusted a small shawl about his shoulders--to his querulous uneasiness--his wife. There was a good deal of white in the dark hair, brushed smoothly back from her face.

A tall girl, with a mass of brown hair under a felt traveling hat, took the corner seat at the man's right. That was all the detail of her appearance which the brief glance that John allowed himself revealed to him at the moment, notwithstanding the justifiable curiosity which he had with regard to the people with whom he was likely to come more or less in contact for a number of days. But though their faces, so far as he had seen them, were unfamiliar to him, their identity was made plain to him by the first words which caught his ear. There were two soups on the **menu**, and the man's mind instantly poised itself between them.

"Which soup shall I take?" he asked, turning with a frown of uncertainty to his wife.

"I should say the **consomme**, Julius," was the reply.

"I thought I should like the broth better," he objected.

"I don't think it will disagree with you," she said.

"Perhaps I had better have the **consomme**," he argued, looking with appeal to his wife and then to the girl at his right. "Which would you take, Mary?"

"I?" said the young woman; "I should take both in my present state of appetite.--Steward, bring both soups.--What wine shall I order for you, Julius? I want some champagne, and I prescribe it for you. After your mental struggle over the soup question you need a quick stimulant."

"Don't you think a red wine would be better for me?" he asked; "or perhaps some sauterne? I'm afraid that I sha'n't go to sleep if I drink champagne. In fact, I don't think I had better take any wine at all. Perhaps some ginger ale or Apollinaris water."

"No," she said decisively, "whatever you decide upon, you know that you'll think whatever I have better for you, and I shall want more than one glass, and Alice wants some, too. Oh, yes, you do, and I shall order a quart of champagne.--Steward"--giving her order--"please be as quick as you can."

John had by this fully identified his neighbors, and the talk which ensued between them, consisting mostly of controversies between the invalid and his family over the items of the bill of fare, every course being discussed as to its probable effect upon his stomach or his nerves--the question being usually settled with a whimsical high-handedness by the young woman--gave him a pretty good notion of their relations and the state of affairs in general. Notwithstanding Miss Blake's benevolent despotism, the invalid was still wrangling feebly over some last dish when John rose and went to the smoking room for his coffee and cigarette.

When he stumbled out in search of his bath the next morning the steamer was well out, and rolling and pitching in a way calculated to disturb the gastric functions of the hardiest. But, after a shower of sea water and a rub down, he found himself with a feeling for bacon and eggs that made him proud of himself, and he went in to breakfast to find, rather to his, surprise, that Miss Blake was before him, looking as fresh--well, as fresh as a handsome girl of nineteen or twenty and in perfect health could look. She acknowledged his perfunctory bow as he took his seat with a stiff little bend of the head; but later on, when the steward was absent on some order, he elicited a "Thank you!" by handing her something which he saw she wanted, and, one thing leading to another, as things have a way of doing where young and attractive people are concerned, they were presently engaged in an interchange of small talk, but before John was moved to the point of disclosing himself on the warrant of a former acquaintance she had finished her breakfast.

The weather continued very stormy for two days, and during that time Miss Blake did not appear at table. At any rate, if she breakfasted there it was either before or after his appearance, and he learned afterward that she had taken luncheon and dinner in her sister's room.

The morning of the third day broke bright and clear. There was a long swell upon the sea, but the motion of the boat was even and endurable to all but the most susceptible. As the morning advanced the deck began to fill with promenaders, and to be lined with chairs, holding wrapped-up figures, showing faces of all shades of green and gray.

John, walking for exercise, and at a wholly unnecessary pace, turning at a sharp angle around the deck house, fairly ran into the girl about whom he had been wondering for the last two days. She received his somewhat incoherent apologies, regrets, and self-accusations in such a spirit of forgiveness that before long they were supplementing their first conversation with something more personal and satisfactory; and when he came to the point of saying that half by accident he had found out her name, and begged to be allowed to tell her his own, she looked at him with a smile of frank amusement and said: "It is quite unnecessary, Mr. Lenox. I knew you instantly when I saw you at table the first night; but," she added mischievously, "I am afraid your memory for people you have known is not so good as mine."

"Well," said John, "you will admit, I think, that the change from a little girl in short frocks to a tall young woman in a tailor-made gown might be more disguising than what might happen with a boy of fifteen or so. I saw your name in the passenger list with Mr. and Mrs. Carling, and wondered if it could be the Mary Blake whom I really did remember, and the first night at dinner, when I heard your sister call Mr. Carling 'Julius,' and heard him call you 'Mary,' I was sure of you. But I hardly got a fair look at your face, and, indeed, I confess that if I had had no clew at all I might not have recognized you."

"I think you would have been quite excusable," she replied, "and whether you would or would not have known me is 'one of those things that no fellow can find out,' and isn't of supreme importance anyway. We each know who the other is now, at all events."

"Yes," said John, "I am happy to think that we have come to a conclusion on that point. But how does it happen that I have heard nothing of you all these years, or you of me, as I suppose?"

"For the reason, I fancy," she replied, "that during that period of short frocks with me my sister married Mr. Carling and took me with her to Chicago, where Mr. Carling was in business. We have been back in New York only for the last two or three years."

"It might have been on the cards that I should come across you in Europe," said John. "The beaten track is not very broad. How long have you been over?"

"Only about six months," she replied. "We have been at one or another of the German Spas most of the time, as we went abroad for Mr. Carling's health, and we are on our way home on about such an impulse as that which started us off--he thinks now that he will be better off there."

"I am afraid you have not derived much pleasure from your European experiences," said John.

"Pleasure!" she exclaimed. "If ever you saw a young woman who was glad and thankful to turn her face toward home, *I* am that person. I think that one of the heaviest crosses humanity has to bear is to have constantly to decide between two or more absolutely trivial conclusions in one's own affairs; but when one is called upon to multiply one's useless perplexities by, say, ten, life is really a burden.

"I suppose," she added after a pause, "you couldn't help hearing our discussions at dinner the other night, and I have wondered a little what you must have thought."

"Yes," he said, "I did hear it. Is it the regular thing, if I may ask?"

"Oh, yes," she replied, with a tone of sadness; "it has grown to be."

"It must be very trying at times," John remarked.

"It is, indeed," she said, "and would often be unendurable to me if it were not for my sense of humor, as it would be to my sister if it were not for her love, for Julius is really a very lovable man, and I, too, am very fond of him. But I must laugh sometimes, though my better nature should rather, I suppose, impel me to sighs.'"

"'A little laughter is much more worth,'" he quoted.

CHAPTER IV.

They were leaning upon the rail at the stern of the ship, which was going with what little wind there was, and a following sea, with which, as it plunged down the long slopes of the waves, the vessel seemed to be running a victorious race. The sea was a deep sapphire, and in the wake the sunlight turned the broken water to vivid emerald. The air was of a caressing softness, and altogether it was a day and scene of indescribable beauty and inspiration. For a while there was silence between them, which John broke at last.

"I suppose," he said, "that one would best show his appreciation of all this by refraining from the comment which must needs be comparatively commonplace, but really this is so superb that I must express some of my emotion even at the risk of lowering your opinion of my good taste, provided, of course, that you have one."

"Well," she said, laughing, "it may relieve your mind, if you care, to know that had you kept silent an instant longer I should have taken the risk of lowering your opinion of my good taste, provided, of course, that you have one, by remarking that this was perfectly magnificent."

"I should think that this would be the sort of day to get Mr. Carling on deck. This air and sun would brace him up," said John.

She turned to him with a laugh, and said: "That is the general opinion, or was two hours ago; but I'm afraid it's out of the question now, unless we can manage it after luncheon."

"What do you mean?" he asked with a puzzled smile at the mixture of annoyance and amusement visible in her face. "Same old story?"

"Yes," she replied, "same old story. When I went to my breakfast I called at my sister's room and said, '"Come, boys and girls, come out to play, the sun doth shine as bright as day,"' and when I've had my breakfast I'm coming to lug you both on deck. It's a perfectly glorious morning, and it will do you both no end of good after being shut up so long.' 'All right,' my sister answered, 'Julius has quite made up his mind to go up as soon as he is dressed. You call for us in half an hour, and we will be ready.'"

"And wouldn't he come?" John asked; "and why not?"

"Oh," she exclaimed with a laugh and a shrug of her shoulders, "shoes."

"Shoes!" said John. "What do you mean?"

"Just what I say," was the rejoinder. "When I went back to the room I found my brother-in-law sitting on the edge of the lounge, or what you call it, all dressed but his coat, rubbing his chin between his finger and thumb, and gazing with despairing perplexity at his feet. It seems that my sister had got past all the other dilemmas, but in a moment of inadvertence had left the shoe question to him, with the result that he had put on one russet shoe and one black one, and had laced them up before discovering the discrepancy."

"I don't see anything very difficult in that situation," remarked John.

"Don't you?" she said scornfully. "No, I suppose not, but it was quite enough for Julius, and more than enough for my sister and me. His first notion was to take off *both* shoes and begin all over again, and perhaps if he had been allowed to carry it out he would have been all right; but Alice was silly enough to suggest the obvious thing to him--to take off one, and put on the mate to the other--and then the trouble began. First he was in favor of the black shoes as being thicker in the sole, and then he reflected that they hadn't been blackened since coming on board. It seemed to him that the russets were more appropriate anyway, but the blacks were easier to lace. Had I noticed whether the men on board were wearing russet or black as a rule, and did Alice remember whether it was one of the russets or one of the blacks that he was saying the other day pinched his toe? He didn't quite like the looks of a russet shoe with dark trousers, and called us to witness that those he had on were dark; but he thought he remembered that it was the black shoe which pinched him. He supposed he could change his trousers--and so on, and so on, ***al fine***, ***de capo***, ***ad lib.***, sticking out first one foot and then the other, lifting them alternately to his knee for scrutiny, appealing now to Alice and now to me, and getting more hopelessly bewildered all the time. It went on that way for, it seemed to me, at least half an hour, and at last I said, 'Oh, come now, Julius, take off the brown shoe--it's too thin, and doesn't go with your dark trousers, and pinches your toe, and none of the men are wearing them--and just put on the other black one, and come along. We're all suffocating for some fresh air, and if you don't get started pretty soon we sha'n't get on deck to-day.' 'Get on deck!' he said, looking up at me with a puzzled expression, and holding fast to the brown shoe on his knee with both hands, as if he were afraid I would take it away from him by main strength-- 'get on deck! Why--why--I believe I'd better not go out this morning, don't you?'"

"And then?" said John after a pause.

"Oh," she replied, "I looked at Alice, and she shook her head as much to say, 'It's no use for the present,' and I fled the place."

"M'm!" muttered John. "He must have been a nice traveling companion. Has it been like that all the time?"

"Most of it," she said, "but not quite all, and this morning was rather an exaggeration of the regular thing. But getting started on a journey was usually pretty awful. Once we quite missed our train because he couldn't make up his mind whether to put on a light overcoat or a heavy one. I finally settled the question for him, but we were just too late."

"You must be a very amiable person," remarked John.

"Indeed, I am not," she declared, "but Julius is, and it's almost impossible to be really put out with him, particularly in his condition. I have come to believe that he can not help it, and he submits to my bullying with such sweetness that even my impatience gives way."

"Have you three people been alone together all the time?" John asked.

"Yes," she replied, "except for four or five weeks. We visited some American friends in Berlin, the Nollises, for a fortnight, and after our visit to them they traveled with us for three weeks through South Germany and Switzerland. We parted with them at Metz only about three weeks since."

"How did Mr. Carling seem while you were all together?" asked John, looking keenly at her.

"Oh," she replied, "he was more like himself than I have seen him for a long time--since he began to break down, in fact."

He turned his eyes from her face as she looked up at him, and as he did not speak she said suggestively, "You are thinking something you don't quite like to say, but I think I know pretty nearly what it is."

"Yes?" said John, with a query.

"You think he has had too much feminine companionship, or had it too exclusively. Is that it? You need not be afraid to say so."

"Well," said John, "if you put it 'too exclusively,' I will admit that there was something of the sort in my mind, and," he added, "if you will let me say so, it must at times have been rather hard for him to be interested or amused--that it must have--that is to say--"

"Oh, *say* it!" she exclaimed. "It must have been very *dull* for him. Is that it?"

"'Father,'" said John with a grimace, "'I can not tell a lie!'"

"Oh," she said, laughing, "your hatchet isn't very sharp. I forgive you. But really," she added, "I know it has been. You will laugh when I tell you the one particular resource we fell back upon."

"Bid me to laugh, and I will laugh," said John.

"Euchre!" she said, looking at him defiantly. "Two-handed euchre! We have played, as nearly as I can estimate, fifteen hundred games, in which he has held both bowers and the ace of trumps--or something equally victorious--I should say fourteen hundred times. Oh!" she cried, with an expression of loathing, "may I never, never, never see a card again as long as I live!" John laughed without restraint, and after a petulant little *moue* she joined him.

"May I light up my pipe?" he said. "I will get to leeward."

"I shall not mind in the least," she assented.

"By the way," he asked, "does Mr. Carling smoke?"

"He used to," she replied, "and while we were with the Nollises he smoked every day, but after we left them he fell back into the notion that it was bad for him."

John filled and lighted his pipe in silence, and after a satisfactory puff or two said: "Will Mr. Carling go in to dinner to-night?"

"Yes," she replied, "I think he will if it is no rougher than at present."

"It will probably be smoother," said John. "You must introduce me to him--"

"Oh," she interrupted, "of course, but it will hardly be necessary, as Alice and I have spoken so often to him of you--"

"I was going to say," John resumed, "that he may possibly let me take him off your hands a little, and after dinner will be the best time. I think if I can get him into the smoking room that a cigar and--and--something hot with a bit of lemon peel and so forth later on may induce him to visit with me for a while, and pass the evening, or part of it."

"You want to be an angel!" she exclaimed. "Oh, I--we--shall be so obliged. I know it's just what he wants--some *man* to take him in hand."

"I'm in no hurry to be an angel," said John, laughing, and, with a bow, "It's better sometimes to be *near* the rose than to *be* the rose, and you are proposing to overpay me quite. I shall enjoy doing what I proposed, if it be possible."

Their talk then drifted off into various channels as topics suggested themselves until the ship's bell sounded the luncheon hour. Miss Blake went to join her sister and brother-in-law, but John had some bread and cheese and beer in the smoking room. It appeared that the ladies had better success than in the morning, for he saw them later on in their steamer chairs with Mr. Carling, who was huddled in many wraps, with the flaps of his cap down over his ears. All the chairs were full--his own included (as happens to easy-tempered men)--and he had only a brief colloquy with the party. He noticed, however, that Mr. Carling had on the russet shoes, and wondered if they pinched him. In fact, though he couldn't have said exactly why, he rather hoped that they did. He had just that sympathy for the nerves of two-and-fifty which is to be expected from those of five-and-twenty--that is, very little.

When he went in to dinner the Carlings and Miss Blake had been at table some minutes. There had been the usual controversy about what Mr. Carling would drink with his dinner, and he had decided upon Apollinaris water. But Miss Blake, with an idea of her own, had given an order for champagne, and was exhibiting some consternation, real or assumed, at the fact of having a whole bottle brought in with the cork extracted--a customary trick at sea.

"I hope you will help me out," she said to John as he bowed and seated himself. "'Some one has blundered,' and here is a whole bottle of champagne which must be drunk to save it. Are you prepared to help turn my, or somebody's, blunder into hospitality?"

"I am prepared to make any sacrifice," said John, laughing, "in the sacred cause."

"No less than I expected of you," she said. "***Noblesse oblige!*** Please fill your glass."

"Thanks," said John. "Permit me," and he filled her own as well.

As the meal proceeded there was some desultory talk about the weather, the ship's run, and so on; but Mrs. Carling was almost silent, and her husband said but little more. Even Miss Blake seemed to have something on her mind, and contributed but little to the conversation. Presently Mr. Carling said, "Mary, do you think a mouthful of wine would hurt me?"

"Certainly not," was the reply. "It will do you good," reaching over for his glass and pouring the wine.

"That's enough, that's enough!" he protested as the foam came up to the rim of the glass. She proceeded to fill it up to the brim and put it beside him, and later, as she had opportunity, kept it replenished.

As the dinner concluded, John said to Mr. Carling: "Won't you go up to the smoking room with me for coffee? I like a bit of tobacco with mine, and I have some really good cigars and some cigarettes--if you prefer them--that I can vouch for."

As usual, when the unexpected was presented to his mind, Mr. Carling passed the perplexity on to his women-folk. At this time, however, his dinner and the two glasses of wine which Miss Blake had contrived that he should swallow had braced him up, and John's suggestion was so warmly seconded by the ladies that, after some feeble protests and misgivings, he yielded, and John carried him off.

"I hope it won't upset Julius," said Mrs. Carling doubtfully.

"It won't do anything of the sort," her sister replied. "He will get through the evening without worrying himself and you into fits, and, if Mr. Lenox succeeds, you won't see anything of him till ten o'clock or after, and not then, I hope. Mind, you're to be sound asleep when he comes in--snore a little if necessary--and let him get to bed without any talk at all."

"Why do you say 'if Mr. Lenox succeeds'?" asked Mrs. Carling.

"It was his suggestion," Miss Blake answered. "We had been talking about Julius, and he finally told me he thought he would be the better of an occasional interval of masculine society, and I quite agreed with him. You know how much he enjoyed being with George Nollis, and how much like himself he appeared."

"That is true," said Mrs. Carling.

"And you know that just as soon as he got alone again with us two women he began backing and filling as badly as ever. I believe Mr. Lenox is right, and that Julius is just petticoated to death between us."

"Did Mr. Lenox say that?" asked Mrs. Carling incredulously.

"No," said her sister, laughing, "he didn't make use of precisely that figure, but that was what he thought plainly enough."

"What do you think of Mr. Lenox?" said Mrs. Carling irrelevantly. "Do you like him? I thought that he looked at you very admiringly once or twice to-night," she added, with her eyes on her sister's face.

"Well," said Mary, with a petulant toss of the head, "except that I've had about an hour's talk with him, and that I knew him when we were children--at least when I was a child--he is a perfect stranger to me, and I do wish," she added in a tone of annoyance, "that you would give up that fad of yours, that every man who comes along is going to--to--be a nuisance."

"He seems very pleasant," said Mrs. Carling, meekly ignoring her sister's reproach.

"Oh, yes," she replied indifferently, "he's pleasant enough. Let us go up and have a walk on deck. I want you to be sound asleep when Julius comes in."

CHAPTER V.

John found his humane experiment pleasanter than he expected. Mr. Carling, as was to be anticipated, demurred a little at the coffee, and still more at the ciga-rette; but having his appetite for tobacco aroused, and finding that no alarming symptoms ensued, he followed it with a cigar and later on was induced to go the length of "Scotch and soda," under the pleasant effect of which--and John's sympa-thetic efforts--he was for the time transformed, the younger man being surprised to find him a man of interesting experience, considerable reading, and, what was most surprising, a jolly sense of humor and a fund of anecdotes which he related extremely well. The evening was a decided success, perhaps the best evidence of it coming at the last, when, at John's suggestion that they supplement their modest potations with a "night-cap," Mr. Carling cheerfully assented upon the condition that they should "have it with him"; and as he went along the deck after saying "Good night," John was positive that he heard a whistled tune.

The next day was equally fine, but during the night the ship had run into the swell of a storm, and in the morning there was more motion than the weaker ones could relish. The sea grew quieter as the day advanced. John was early, and finished his breakfast before Miss Blake came in. He found her on deck about ten o'clock. She gave him her hand as they said good morning, and he turned and walked by her side.

"How is your brother-in-law this morning?" he inquired.

"Oh," she said, laughing, "he's in a mixture of feeling very well and feeling that he ought not to feel so, but, as they are coming up pretty soon, it would appear that the misgivings are not overwhelming. He came in last night, and retired without saying a word. My sister pretended to be asleep. She says he went to sleep at once, and that she was awake at intervals and knows that he slept like a top. He won't make any very sweeping admissions, however, but has gone so far as to concede that he had a very pleasant evening--which is going a long way for him--and to say that you are a very agreeable young man. There! I didn't intend to tell you that, but you have been so good that perhaps so much as a second-hand compliment is no more than your due."

"Thank you very much," said John. "Mr. Carling is evidently a very discrimi-nating person. Really it wasn't good of me at all. I was quite the gainer, for he en-tertained me more than I did him. We had a very pleasant evening, and I hope we shall have more of them, I do, indeed. I got an entirely different impression of him," he added.

"Yes," she said, "I can imagine that you did. He can be very agreeable, and he is really a man of a great deal of character when he is himself. He has been goodness itself to me, and has managed my affairs for years. Even to-day his judgment in business matters is wonderfully sound. If it had not been for him," she continued, "I don't know but I should have been a pauper. My father left a large estate, but he died very suddenly, and his affairs were very much spread out and involved and had to be carried along. Julius put himself into the breach, and not only saved our fortunes, but has considerably increased them. Of course, Alice is his wife, but I feel very grateful to him on my own account. I did not altogether appreciate it at the time, but now I shudder to think that I might have had either to 'fend for myself' or be dependent."

"I don't think that dependence would have suited your book," was John's comment as he took in the lines of her clear-cut face.

"No," she replied, "and I thank heaven that I have not had to endure it. I am not," she added, "so impressed with what money procures for people as what it saves them from."

"Yes," said John, "I think your distinction is just. To possess it is to be free from some of the most disagreeable apprehensions certainly, but I confess, whether to my credit or my shame I don't know, I have never thought much about it. I certainly am not rich positively, and I haven't the faintest notion whether I may or not be prospectively. I have always had as much as I really needed, and perhaps more, but I know absolutely nothing about the future." They were leaning over the rail on the port side.

"I should think," she said after a moment, looking at him thoughtfully, "that it was, if you will not think me presuming, a matter about which you might have some justifiable curiosity."

"Oh, not at all," he assured her, stepping to leeward and producing a cigar. "I have had some stirrings of late. And please don't think me an incorrigible idler. I spent nearly two years in a down-town office and earned--well, say half my salary. In fact, my business instincts were so strong that I left college after my second year for that purpose, but seeing no special chance of advancement in the race for wealth, and as my father seemed rather to welcome the idea, I broke off and went over to Germany. I haven't been quite idle, though I should be puzzled, I admit, to find a market for what I have to offer to the world. Would you be interested in a schedule of my accomplishments."

"Oh," she said, "I should be charmed, but as I am every moment expecting the advent of my family, and as I am relied upon to locate them and tuck them up, I'm afraid I shall not have time to hear it."

"No," he said, laughing, "it's quite too long."

She was silent for some moments, gazing down into the water, apparently debating something in her mind, and quite unconscious of John's scrutiny. Finally she turned to him with a little laugh. "You might begin on your list, and if I am called away you can finish it at another time."

"I hope you didn't think I was speaking in earnest," he said.

"No," she replied, "I did not think you really intended to unpack your wares, but, speaking seriously--and at the risk, I fear, that you may think me rather 'cheeky,' if I may be allowed that expression--I know a good many men in America, and I think that without an exception they are professional men or business men, or, being neither--and I know but few such--have a competence or more; and I was wondering just now after what you told me what a man like you would or could do if he were thrown upon his own resources. I'm afraid that is rather frank for the acquaintance of a day, isn't it?" she asked with a slight flush, "but it really is not so personal as it may sound to you."

"My dear Miss Blake," he replied, "our acquaintance goes back at least ten years. Please let that fact count for something in your mind. The truth is, I have done some wondering along that same line myself without coming to any satisfactory conclusion. I devoutly hope I may not be so thrown absolutely, for the truth is I haven't a marketable commodity. 'A little Latin, and less Greek,' German and French enough to read and understand and talk--on the surface of things--and what mathematics, history, et cetera, I have not forgotten. I know the piano well enough to read and play an accompaniment after a fashion, and I have had some good teaching for the voice, and some experience in singing, at home and abroad. In fact, I come nearer to a market there, I think, than in any other direction perhaps. I have given some time to fencing in various schools, and before I left home Billy Williams would sometimes speak encouragingly of my progress with the gloves. There! That is my list, and not a dollar in it from beginning to end, I'm afraid."

"Who is Billy Williams?" she asked.

"Billy," said John, "is the very mild-mannered and gentlemanlike 'bouncer' at the Altman House, an ex-prize-fighter, and about the most accomplished member of his profession of his day and weight, who is employed to keep order and, if necessary, to thrust out the riotous who would disturb the contemplations of the lovers of art that frequent the bar of that hotel." It was to be seen that Miss Blake was not particularly impressed by this description of Billy and his functions, upon which she made no comment.

"You have not included in your list," she remarked, "what you acquired in the down-town office you told me of."

"No, upon my word I had forgotten that, and it's about the only thing of use in the whole category," he answered. "If I were put to it, and could find a place, I think I might earn fifty dollars a month as a clerk or messenger, or something. Hullo! here are your people."

He went forward with his companion and greeted Mrs. Carling and her husband, who returned his "Good morning" with a feeble smile, and submitted to his ministrations in the matter of chair and rugs with an air of unresisting invalidism, which was almost too obvious, he thought. But after luncheon John managed to induce him to walk for a while, to smoke a cigarette, and finally to brave the perils of a sherry and bitters before dinner. The ladies had the afternoon to themselves. John had no chance of a further visit with Mary during the day, a loss only partially made good to him by a very approving smile and a remark which she made to him at dinner, that he must be a lineal descendant of the Samaritan. Mr. Carling submitted himself to him for the evening. Indeed, it came about that for the rest of the voyage he had rather more of the company of that gentleman, who fairly attached himself to him, than, under all the circumstances, he cared for; but the gratitude of the ladies was so cordial that he felt paid for some sacrifices of his inclinations. And there was an hour or so every morning--for the fine weather lasted through--which he spent with Mary Blake, with increasing interest and pleasure, and he found himself inwardly rejoicing over a mishap to the engine which, though of no very great magnitude, would retard the passage by a couple of days.

There can hardly be any conditions more favorable to the forming of acquaintanceships, friendships, and even more tender relations than are afforded by the life on board ship. There is opportunity, propinquity, and the community of interest which breaks down the barriers of ordinary reserve. These relations, to be sure, are not always of the most lasting character, and not infrequently are practically ended before the parties thereto are out of the custom-house officer's hands and fade into nameless oblivion, unless one happens to run across the passenger list among one's souvenirs. But there are exceptions. If at this time the question had been asked our friend, even by himself, whether, to put it plainly, he were in love with Mary Blake, he would, no doubt, have strenuously denied it; but it is certain that if any one had said or intimated that any feature or characteristic of hers was faulty or suscep- tible of any change for the better, he would have secretly disliked that person, and entertained the meanest opinion of that person's mental and moral attributes. He would have liked the voyage prolonged indefinitely, or, at any rate, as long as the provisions held out.

It has been remarked by some one that all mundane things come to an end sooner or later, and, so far as my experience goes, it bears out that statement. The engines were successfully repaired, and the ship eventually came to anchor outside the harbor about eleven o'clock on the night of the last day. Mary and John were standing together at the forward rail. There had been but little talk between them, and only of a desultory and impersonal character. As the anchor chains rattled in the hawse-pipes, John said, "Well, that ends it."

"What ends what?" she asked.

"The voyage, and the holiday, and the episode, and lots of things," he replied. "We have come to anchor."

"Yes," she said, "the voyage is over, that is true; but, for my part, if the last six months can be called a holiday, its end is welcome, and I should think you might be glad that your holiday is over, too. But I don't quite understand what you mean by 'the episode and lots of things.'"

There was an undertone in her utterance which her companion did not quite comprehend, though it was obvious to him.

"The episode of--of--our friendship, if I may call it so," he replied.

"I call it so," she said decisively. "You have certainly been a friend to *all* of us. This episode is over to be sure, but is there any more than that?"

"Somebody says that 'friendship is largely a matter of streets,'" said John gloomily. "To-morrow you will go your way and I shall go mine."

"Yes," she replied, rather sharply, "that is true enough; but if that cynical quotation of yours has anything in it, it's equally true, isn't it, that friendship is a matter of cabs, and street cars, and the elevated road? Of course, we can hardly be expected to look you up, but Sixty-ninth Street isn't exactly in California, and the whole question lies with yourself. I don't know if you care to be told so, but Julius and my sister like you very much, and will welcome you heartily always."

"Thanks, very much!" said John, staring straight out in front of him, and forming a determination that Sixty-ninth Street would see but precious little of *him*. She gave a side glance at him as he did not speak further. There was light enough to see the expression of his mouth, and she read his thought almost in words. She had thought that she had detected a suggestion of sentimentality on his part which she intended to keep strictly in abeyance, but in her intention not to seem to respond to it she had taken an attitude of coolness and a tone which was almost sarcastic, and now perceived that, so far as results were apparent, she had carried matters somewhat further than she intended. Her heart smote her a little, too, to think that he was hurt. She really liked him very much, and contritely recalled how kind and thoughtful and unselfish he had been, and how helpful, and she knew that it had been almost wholly for her. Yes, she was willing--and glad--to think so. But while she wished that she had taken a different line at the outset, she hated desperately to make any concession, and the seconds of their silence grew into minutes. She stole another glance at his face. It was plain that negotiations for harmony would have to begin with her. Finally she said in a quiet voice:

"'Thanks, very much,' is an entirely polite expression, but it isn't very responsive."

"I thought it met your cordiality quite half way," was the rejoinder. "Of course, I am glad to be assured of Mr. and Mrs. Carling's regard, and that they would be glad to see me, but I think I might have been justified in hoping that you would go a little further, don't you think?"

He looked at her as he asked the question, but she did not turn her head. Presently she said in a low voice, and slowly, as if weighing her words:

"Will it be enough if I say that I shall be very sorry if you do not come?" He put his left hand upon her right, which was resting on the rail, and for two seconds she let it stay.

"Yes," he said, "thanks--very--much!"

"I must go now," she said, turning toward him, and for a moment she looked searchingly in his face. "Good night," she said, giving him her hand, and John looked after her as she walked down the deck, and he knew how it was with him.

CHAPTER VI.

John saw Miss Blake the next morning in the saloon among the passengers in line for the customs official. It was an easy conjecture that Mr. Carling's nerves were not up to committing himself to a "declaration" of any sort, and that Miss Blake was undertaking the duty for the party. He did not see her again until he had had his luggage passed and turned it over to an expressman. As he was on his way to leave the wharf he came across the group, and stopped to greet them and ask if he could be of service, and was told that their houseman had everything in charge, and that they were just going to their carriage, which was waiting. "And," said Miss Blake, "if you are going up town, we can offer you a seat."

"Sha'n't I discommode you?" he asked. "If you are sure I shall not, I shall be glad to be taken as far as Madison Avenue and Thirty-third Street, for I suppose that will be your route."

"Quite sure," she replied, seconded by the Carlings, and so it happened that John went directly home instead of going first to his father's office. The weather was a chilly drizzle, and he was glad to be spared the discomfort of going about in it with hand-bag, overcoat, and umbrella, and felt a certain justification in concluding that, after two years, a few hours more or less under the circumstances would make but little difference. And then, too, the prospect of half or three-quarters of an hour in Miss Blake's company, the Carlings notwithstanding, was a temptation to be welcomed. But if he had hoped or expected, as perhaps would have been not unnatural, to discover in that young woman's air any hint or trace of the feeling she had exhibited, or, perhaps it should be said, to a degree permitted to show itself, disappointment was his portion. Her manner was as much in contrast with that of the last days of their voyage together as the handsome street dress and hat in which she was attired bore to the dress and headgear of her steamer costume, and it almost seemed to him as if the contrasts bore some relation to each other. After the question of the carriage windows--whether they should be up or down, either or both, and how much--had been settled, and, as usual in such dilemmas, by Miss Blake, the drive up town was comparatively a silent one. John's mind was occupied with sundry reflections and speculations, of many of which his companion was the subject, and to some extent in noting the changes in the streets and buildings which an absence of two years made noticeable to him.

Mary looked steadily out of window, lost in her own thoughts save for an occasional brief response to some casual comment or remark of John's. Mr. Carling had muffled himself past all talking, and his wife preserved the silence which was characteristic of her when unurged.

John was set down at Thirty-third Street, and, as he made his adieus, Mrs. Carling said, "Do come and see us as soon as you can, Mr. Lenox"; but Miss Blake simply said "Good-by" as she gave him her hand for an instant, and he went on to his father's house.

He let himself in with the latch-key which he had carried through all his absence, but was at once encountered by Jeffrey, who, with his wife, had for years constituted the domestic staff of the Lenox household.

"Well, Jeff," said John, as he shook hands heartily with the old servant, "how are you? and how is Ann? You don't look a day older, and the climate seems to agree with you, eh?"

"You're welcome home, Mr. John," replied Jeffrey, "and thank you, sir. Me and Ann is very well, sir. It's a pleasure to see you again and home. It is, indeed."

"Thank you, Jeff," said John. "It's rather nice to be back. Is my room ready?"

"Yes, sir," said Jeffrey, "I think it's all right, though we thought that maybe it 'd be later in the day when you got here, sir. We thought maybe you'd go to Mr. Lenox's office first."

"I did intend to," said John, mounting the stairs, followed by Jeffrey with his bag, "but I had a chance to drive up with some friends, and the day is so beastly that I took advantage of it. How is my father?" he asked after entering the chamber, which struck him as being so strangely familiar and so familiarly strange.

"Well, sir," said Jeffrey, "he's much about the same most ways, and then again he's different, too. Seeing him every day, perhaps I wouldn't notice so much; but if I was to say that he's kind of quieter, perhaps that'd be what I mean, sir."

"Well," said John, smiling, "my father was about the quietest person I ever knew, and if he's grown more so--what do you mean?"

"Well, sir," replied the man, "I notice at table, sir, for one thing. We've been alone here off and on a good bit, sir, and he used always to have a pleasant word or two to say to me, and may be to ask me questions and that, sir; but for a long time lately he hardly seems to notice me. Of course, there ain't any need of his saying anything, because I know all he wants, seeing I've waited on him so long, but it's different in a way, sir."

"Does he go out in the evening to his club?" asked John.

"Very rarely, sir," said Jeffrey. "He mostly goes to his room after dinner, an' oftentimes I hear him walking up an' down, up an' down, and, sir," he added, "you know he often used to have some of his friends to dine with him, and that ain't happened in, I should guess, for a year."

"Have things gone wrong with him in any way?" said John, a sudden anxiety overcoming some reluctance to question a servant on such a subject.

"You mean about business, and such like?" replied Jeffrey. "No, sir, not so far as I know. You know, Mr. John, sir, that I pay all the house accounts, and there hasn't never been no--no shortness, as I might say, but we're living a bit simpler than we used to--in the matter of wine and such like--and, as I told you, we don't have comp'ny no more."

"Is that all?" asked John, with some relief.

"Well, sir," was the reply, "perhaps it's because Mr. Lenox is getting older and don't care so much about such things, but I have noticed that he hasn't had anything new from the tailor in a long time, and really, sir, though perhaps I oughtn't to say it, his things is getting a bit shabby, sir, and he used to be always so partic'lar."

John got up and walked over to the window which looked out at the rear of the house. The words of the old servant disquieted him, notwithstanding that there was nothing so far that could not be accounted for without alarm. Jeffrey waited for a moment and then asked:

"Is there anything I can do for you, Mr. John? Will you be having luncheon here, sir?"

"No, thank you, Jeff," said John; "nothing more now, and I will lunch here. I'll come down and see Ann presently."

"Thank you, sir," said Jeffrey, and withdrew.

The view from the back windows of most city houses is not calculated to arouse enthusiasm at the best of times, and the day was singularly dispiriting: a sky of lead and a drizzling rain, which emphasized the squalor of the back yards in view. It was all very depressing. Jeffrey's talk, though inconclusive, had stirred in John's mind an uneasiness which was near to apprehension. He turned and walked about the familiar room, recognizing the well-known furniture, his mother's picture over the mantel, the bookshelves filled with his boyhood's accumulations, the well-remembered pattern of the carpet, and the wall-paper--nothing was changed. It was all as he had left it two years ago, and for the time it seemed as if he had merely dreamed the life and experiences of those years. Indeed, it was with difficulty that he recalled any of them for the moment. And then suddenly there came into his mind the thought that he was at the beginning of a new epoch--that on this day his boyhood ended, for up to then he had been but a boy. The thought was very vivid. It had come, the time when he must take upon himself the responsibilities of his own life, and make it for himself; the time which he had looked forward to as to come some day, but not hitherto at any particular moment, and so not to be very seriously considered.

It has been said that life had always been made easy for him, and that he had accepted the situation without protest. To easy-going natures the thought of any radical change in the current of affairs is usually unwelcome, but he was too young to find it really repugnant; and then, too, as he walked about the room with his hands in his pockets, it was further revealed to him that he had recently found a motive and impulse such as he had never had before. He recalled the talk that he had had with the companion of his voyage. He thought of her as one who could be tender to misfortune and charitable to incapacity, but who would have nothing but scorn for shiftlessness and malingering; and he realized that he had never cared for anything as for the good opinion of that young woman. No, there should be for him no more sauntering in the vales and groves, no more of loitering or dallying. He would take his place in the working world, and perhaps--some day--

A thought came to him with the impact of a blow: What could he do? What work was there for him? How could he pull his weight in the boat? All his life he had depended upon some one else, with easy-going thoughtlessness. Hardly had it ever really occurred to him that he might have to make a career for himself. Of business he had thought as something which he should undertake some time, but it was always a business ready made to his hand, with plenty of capital not of his own acquiring--something for occupation, not of necessity. It came home to him that his father was his only resource, and that of his father's affairs he knew next to nothing.

In addition to his affection for him, he had always had an unquestioning confidence in his father. It was his earliest recollection, and he still retained it to almost a childish extent. There had always been plenty. His own allowance, from time to time increased, though never extravagant, had always been ample, and on the one occasion when he had grievously exceeded it the excess had been paid with no more protest than a gentle "I think you ought not to have done this." The two had lived together when John was at home without ostentation or any appearance of style, but with every essential of luxury. The house and its furnishings were old-fashioned, but everything was of the best, and when three or four of the elder man's friends would come to dine, as happened occasionally, the contents of the cellar made them look at each other over their glasses. Mr. Lenox was very reticent in all matters relating to himself, and in his talks with his son, which were mostly at the table, rarely spoke of business matters in general, and almost never of his own. He had read well, and was fond of talking of his reading when he felt in the vein of talking, which was not always; but John had invariably found him ready with comment and sympathy upon the topics in which he himself had interest, and there was a strong if undemonstrative affection between the father and son.

It was not strange, perhaps, all things considered, that John had come even to nearly six-and-twenty with no more settled intentions; that his boyhood should have been so long. He was not at all of a reckless disposition, and, notwithstanding the desultory way in which he had spent time, he had strong mental and moral fiber, and was capable of feeling deeply and enduringly. He had been desultory, but never before had he had much reason or warning against it. But now, he reflected, a time had come. Work he must, if only for work's sake, and work he would; and there was a touch of self-reproach in the thought of his father's increasing years and of his lonely life. He might have been a help and a companion during those two years of his not very fruitful European sojourn, and he would lose no time in finding out what there was for him to do, and in setting about it.

CHAPTER VII.

The day seemed very long. He ate his luncheon, having first paid a visit to Ann, who gave him an effusive welcome. Jeffrey waited, and during the meal they had some further talk, and among other things John said to him, "Does my father dress for dinner nowadays?"

"No, sir," was the reply, "I don't know when I've seen your father in his evenin' clothes, sir. Not for a long time, and then maybe two or three times the past year when he was going out to dinner, but not here, sir. Maybe it'll be different now you're back again, sir."

After luncheon John's luggage arrived, and he superintended the unpacking, but that employment was comparatively brief. The day dragged with him. Truly his home-coming was rather a dreary affair. How different had been yesterday, and the day before, and all those days before when he had so enjoyed the ship life, and most of all the daily hour or more of the companionship which had grown to be of such surpassing interest to him, and now seemed so utterly a thing of the past.

Of course, he should see her again. (He put aside a wonder if it would be within the proprieties on that evening or, at latest, the next.) But, in any case, "the episode," as he had said to her, was done, and it had been very pleasant--oh, yes, very dear to him. He wondered if she was finding the day as interminable as it seemed to him, and if the interval before they saw each other again would seem as long as his impatience would make it for him. Finally, the restless dullness became intolerable. He sallied forth into the weather and went to his club, having been on non-resident footing during his absence, and, finding some men whom he knew, spent there the rest of the afternoon.

His father was at home and in his room when John got back.

"Well, father," he said, "the prodigal has returned."

"He is very welcome," was the reply, as the elder man took both his son's hands and looked at him affectionately. "You seem very well."

"Yes," said John; "and how are you, sir?"

"About as usual, I think," said Mr. Lenox.

They looked at each other for a moment in silence. John thought that his father seemed thinner than formerly, and he had instantly observed that a white beard covered the always hitherto smooth-shaven chin, but he made no comment.

"The old place appears very familiar," he remarked. "Nothing is changed or even moved, as I can see, and Ann and Jeff are just the same old sixpences as ever."

"Yes," said his father, "two years make less difference with old people and their old habits than with young ones. You will have changed more than we have, I fancy."

"Do we dress for dinner?" asked John, after some little more unimportant talk.

"Yes," said his father, "in honor of the occasion, if you like. I haven't done it lately," he added, a little wearily.

   *   *   *   *   *

"I haven't had such a glass of wine since I left home," John remarked as they sat together after dinner.

"No," said his father, looking thoughtfully at his glass, "it's the old 'Mouton,' and pretty nearly the last of it; it's very old and wants drinking," he observed as he held his glass up to get the color. "It has gone off a bit even in two years."

"All right," said John cheerfully, "we'll drink it to save it, if needs be." The elder man smiled and filled both glasses.

There had been more or less talk during the meal, but nothing of special moment. John sat back in his chair, absently twirling the stem of his glass between thumb and fingers. Presently he said, looking straight before him at the table: "I have been thinking a good deal of late--more than ever before, positively, in fact-- that whatever my prospects may be," (he did not see the momentary contraction of his father's brow) "I ought to begin some sort of a career in earnest. I'm afraid," he continued, "that I have been rather unmindful, and that I might have been of some use to you as well as myself if I had stayed at home instead of spending the last two years in Europe."

"I trust," said his father, "that they have not been entirely without profit."

"No," said John, "perhaps not wholly, but their cash value would not be large,

I'm afraid."

"All value is not to be measured in dollars and cents," remarked Mr. Lenox. "If I could have acquired as much German and French as I presume you have, to say nothing of other things, I should look back upon the time as well spent at almost any cost. At your age a year or two more or less--you don't realize it now, but you will if you come to my age--doesn't count for so very much, and you are not too old," he smiled, "to begin at a beginning."

"I want to begin," said John.

"Yes," said his father, "I want to have you, and I have had the matter a good deal in my mind. Have you any idea as to what you wish to do?"

"I thought," said John, "that the most obvious thing would be to go into your office." Mr. Lenox reached over for the cigar-lamp. His cigar had gone out, and his hand shook as he applied the flame to it. He did not reply for a moment.

"I understand," he said at last. "It would seem the obvious thing to do, as you say, but," he clicked his teeth together doubtfully, "I don't see how it can be managed at present, and I don't think it is what I should desire for you in any case. The fact is," he went on, "my business has always been a sort of specialty, and, though it is still worth doing perhaps, it is not what it used to be. Conditions and methods have changed--and," he added, "I am too old to change with them."

"I am not," said John.

"In fact," resumed his father, ignoring John's assertion, "as things are going now, I couldn't make a place for you in my office unless I displaced Melig and made you my manager, and for many reasons I couldn't do that. I am too dependent on Melig. Of course, if you came with me it would be as a partner, but--"

"No," said John, "I should be a poor substitute for old Melig for a good while, I fancy."

"My idea would be," said Mr. Lenox, "that you should undertake a profession-- say the law. It is a fact that the great majority of men fail in business, and then most of them, for lack of training or special aptitude, fall into the ranks of clerks and subordinates. On the other hand, a man who has a profession--law, medicine, what not--even if he does not attain high rank, has something on which he can generally get along, at least after a fashion, and he has the standing. That is my view of the matter, and though I confess I often wonder at it in individual cases, it is my advice to you."

"It would take three or four years to put me where I could earn anything to speak of," said John, "even providing that I could get any business at the end of the time."

"Yes," said his father, "but the time of itself isn't of so much consequence. You would be living at home, and would have your allowance--perhaps," he suggested, "somewhat diminished, seeing that you would be here--"

"I can get on with half of it," said John confidently.

"We will settle that matter afterward," said Mr. Lenox.

They sat in silence for some minutes, John staring thoughtfully at the table, unconscious of the occasional scrutiny of his father's glance. At last he said, "Well, sir, I will do anything that you advise."

"Have you anything to urge against it?" asked Mr. Lenox.

"Not exactly on my own account," replied John, "though I admit that the three years or more seems a long time to me, but I have been drawing on you exclusively all my life, except for the little money I earned in Rush & Company's office, and--"

"You have done so, my dear boy," said his father gently, "with my acquiescence. I may have been wrong, but that is a fact. If in my judgment the arrangement may be continued for a while longer, and in the mean time you are making progress toward a definite end, I think you need have no misgivings. It gratifies me to have you feel as you do, though it is no more than I should have expected of you, for you have never caused me any serious anxiety or disappointment, my son."

Often in the after time did John thank God for that assurance.

"Thank you, sir," he said, putting down his hand, palm upward, on the table, and his eyes filled as the elder man laid his hand in his, and they gave each other a lingering pressure.

Mr. Lenox divided the last of the wine in the bottle between the two glasses, and they drank it in silence, as if in pledge.

"I will go in to see Carey & Carey in the morning, and if they are agreeable you can see them afterward," said Mr. Lenox. "They are not one of the great firms, but they have a large and good practice, and they are friends of mine. Shall I do so?" he asked, looking at his son.

"If you will be so kind," John replied, returning his look. And so the matter was concluded.

CHAPTER VIII.

This history will not concern itself to any extent with our friend's career as a law clerk, though, as he promised himself, he took it seriously and laboriously while it lasted, notwithstanding that after two years of being his own master, and the rather desultory and altogether congenial life he had led, he found it at first even more irksome than he had fancied. The novice penetrates but slowly the mysteries of the law, and, unless he be of unusual aptitude and imagination, the interesting and remunerative part seems for a long time very far off. But John stuck manfully to the reading, and was diligent in all that was put upon him to do; and after a while the days spent in the office and in the work appointed to him began to pass more quickly.

He restrained his impulse to call at Sixty-ninth Street until what seemed to him a fitting interval had elapsed; one which was longer than it would otherwise have been, from an instinct of shyness not habitual to him, and a distrustful apprehension that perhaps his advent was not of so much moment to the people there as to him. But their greeting was so cordial on every hand that Mrs. Carling's remark that they had been almost afraid he had forgotten them embarrassed while it pleased him, and his explanations were somewhat lame. Miss Blake, as usual, came to the rescue, though John's disconcert was not lessened by the suspicion that she saw through his inventions. He had conceived a great opinion of that young person's penetration.

His talk for a while was mostly with Mr. Carling, who was in a pleasant mood, being, like most nervous people, at his best in the evening. Mary made an occasional contributory remark, and Mrs. Carling, as was her wont, was silent except when appealed to. Finally, Mr. Carling rose and, putting out his hand, said: "I think I will excuse myself, if you will permit me. I have had to be down town to-day, and am rather tired." Mrs. Carling followed him, saying to John as she bade him good night: "Do come, Mr. Lenox, whenever you feel like it. We are very quiet people, and are almost always at home."

"Thank you, Mrs. Carling," responded John, with much sincerity. "I shall be most glad to. I am so quiet myself as to be practically noiseless."

The hall of the Carlings' house was their favorite sitting place in the evening. It ran nearly the whole depth of the house, and had a wide fireplace at the end. The further right hand portion was recessed by the stairway, which rose from about the middle of its length.

Miss Blake sat in a low chair, and John took its fellow at the other angle of the fireplace, which contained the smoldering remnant of a wood fire. She had a bit of embroidery stretched over a circular frame like a drum-head. Needlework was not a passion with her, but it was understood in the Carling household that in course of time a set of table doilies of elaborate devices in colored silks would be forthcoming. It has been deplored by some philosopher that custom does not sanction such little occupations for masculine hands. It would be interesting to speculate how many embarrassing or disastrous consequences might have been averted if at a critical point in a negotiation or controversy a needle had had to be threaded or a dropped stitch taken up before a reply was made, to say nothing of an excuse for averting features at times without confession of confusion.

The great and wise Charles Reade tells how his hero, who had an island, a treasure ship, and a few other trifles of the sort to dispose of, insisted upon Captain Fullalove's throwing away the stick he was whittling, as giving the captain an unfair advantage. The value of the embroidered doily as an article of table napery may be open to question, but its value, in an unfinished state, as an adjunct to discreet conversation, is beyond all dispute.

"Ought I to say good night?" asked John with a smile, as he seated himself on the disappearance of Mr. and Mrs. Carling.

"I don't see any reason," she replied. "It isn't late. Julius is in one of his periods of retiring early just now. By and by he will be sure to take up the idea again that his best sleep is after midnight. At present he is on the theory that it is before twelve o'clock."

"How has he been since your return?" John asked.

"Better in some ways, I think," she replied. "He seems to enjoy the home life in contrast with the traveling about and living in hotels; and then, in a moderate way, he is obliged to give some attention to business matters, and to come in contact with men and affairs generally."

"And you?" said John. "You find it pleasant to be back?"

"Yes," she said, "I do. As my sister said, we are quiet people. She goes out so little that it is almost not at all, and when I go it has nearly always to be with some one else. And then, you know that while Alice and I are originally New Yorkers, we have only been back here for two or three years. Most of the people, really, to whose houses we go are those who knew my father. But," she added, "it is a comfort not to be carrying about a traveling bag in one hand and a weight of responsibility in the other."

"I should think," said John, laughing, "that your maid might have taken the bag, even if she couldn't carry your responsibilities."

"No," she said, joining in his laugh, "that particular bag was too precious, and Eliza was one of my most serious responsibilities. She had to be looked after like the luggage, and I used to wish at times that she could be labeled and go in the van. How has it been with you since your return? and," as she separated a needleful of silk from what seemed an inextricable tangle, "if I may ask, what have you been doing? I was recalling," she added, putting the silk into the needle, "some things you said to me on the Altruria. Do you remember?"

"Perfectly," said John. "I think I remember every word said on both sides, and I have thought very often of some things you said to me. In fact, they had more influence upon my mind than you imagined."

She turned her work so that the light would fall a little more directly upon it.

"Really?" she asked. "In what way?"

"You put in a drop or two that crystallized the whole solution," he answered. She looked up at him inquiringly.

"Yes," he said, "I always knew that I should have to stop drifting some time, but there never seemed to be any particular time. Some things you said to me set the time. I am under 'full steam a-head' at present. Behold in me," he exclaimed, touching his breast, "the future chief of the Supreme Court of the United States, of whom you shall say some time in the next brief interval of forty years or so, 'I knew him as a young man, and one for whom no one would have predicted such eminence!' and perhaps you will add, 'It was largely owing to me.'"

She looked at him with an expression in which amusement and curiosity were blended.

"I congratulate you," she said, laughing, "upon the career in which it appears I had the honor to start you. Am I being told that you have taken up the law?"

"Not quite the whole of it as yet," he said; "but when I am not doing errands for the office I am to some extent taken up with it," and then he told her of his talk with his father and what had followed. She overcame a refractory kink in her silk before speaking.

"It takes a long time, doesn't it, and do you like it?" she asked.

"Well," said John, laughing a little, "a weaker word than 'fascinating' would describe the pursuit, but I hope with diligence to reach some of the interesting features in the course of ten or twelve years."

"It is delightful," she remarked, scrutinizing the pattern of her work, "to encounter such enthusiasm."

"Isn't it?" said John, not in the least wounded by her sarcasm.

"Very much so," she replied, "but I have always understood that it is a mistake to be too sanguine."

"Perhaps I'd better make it fifteen years, then," he said, laughing. "I should have a choice of professions by that time at any rate. You know the proverb that 'At forty every man is either a fool or a physician.'" She looked at him with a smile. "Yes," he said, "I realize the alternative." She laughed a little, but did not reply.

"Seriously," he continued, "I know that in everything worth accomplishing there is a lot of drudgery to be gone through with at the first, and perhaps it seems the more irksome to me because I have been so long idly my own master. However," he added, "I shall get down to it, or up to it, after a while, I dare say. That is my intention, at any rate."

"I don't think I have ever wished that I were a man," she said after a moment, "but I often find myself envying a man's opportunities."

"Do not women have opportunities, too?" he said. "Certainly they have greatly to do with the determination of affairs."

"Oh, yes," she replied, "it is the usual answer that woman's part is to influence somebody. As for her own life, it is largely made for her. She has, for the most part, to take what comes to her by the will of others."

"And yet," said John, "I fancy that there has seldom been a great career in which some woman's help or influence was not a factor."

"Even granting that," she replied, "the career was the man's, after all, and the fame and visible reward. A man will sometimes say, 'I owe all my success to my wife, or my mother, or sister,' but he never really believes it, nor, in fact, does any one else. It is *his* success, after all, and the influence of the woman is but a circumstance, real and powerful though it may be. I am not sure," she added, "that woman's influence, so called, isn't rather an overrated thing. Women like to feel that they have it, and men, in matters which they hold lightly, flatter them by yielding, but I am doubtful if a man ever arrives at or abandons a settled course or conviction through the influence of a woman, however exerted."

"I think you are wrong," said John, "and I feel sure of so much as this: that a man might often be or do for a woman's sake that which he would not for its sake or his own."

"That is quite another thing," she said. "There is in it no question of influence; it is one of impulse and motive."

"I have told you to-night," said John, "that what you said to me had influenced me greatly."

"Pardon me," she replied, "you employed a figure which exactly defined your condition. You said I supplied the drop which caused the solution to crystallize-- that is, to elaborate your illustration, that it was already at the point of saturation with your own convictions and intentions."

"I said also," he urged, "that you had set the time for me. Is the idea unpleasant to you?" he asked after a moment, while he watched her face. She did not at once reply, but presently she turned to him with slightly heightened color and said, ignoring his question:

"Would you rather think that you had done what you thought right because you so thought, or because some one else wished to have you? Or, I should say, would you rather think that the right suggestion was another's than your own?"

He laughed a little, and said evasively: "You ought to be a lawyer, Miss Blake. I should hate to have you cross-examine me unless I were very sure of my evidence."

She gave a little shrug of her shoulders in reply as she turned and resumed her embroidery. They talked for a while longer, but of other things, the discussion of woman's influence having been dropped by mutual consent.

After John's departure she suspended operations on the doily, and sat for a while gazing reflectively into the fire. She was a person as frank with herself as with others, and with as little vanity as was compatible with being human, which is to say that, though she was not without it, it was of the sort which could be gratified but not flattered--in fact, the sort which flattery wounds rather than pleases. But despite her apparent skepticism she had not been displeased by John's assertion that she had influenced him in his course. She had expressed herself truly, believing that he would have done as he had without her intervention; but she thought that he was sincere, and it was pleasant to her to have him think as he did.

Considering the surroundings and conditions under which she had lived, she had had her share of the acquaintance and attentions of agreeable men, but none of them had ever got with her beyond the stage of mere friendliness. There had never been one whose coming she had particularly looked forward to, or whose going she had deplored. She had thought of marriage as something she might come to, but she had promised herself that it should be on such conditions as were, she was aware, quite improbable of ever being fulfilled. She would not care for a man because he was clever and distinguished, but she felt that he must be those things, and to have, besides, those qualities of character and person which should attract her. She had known a good many men who were clever and to some extent distinguished, but none who had attracted her personally. John Lenox did not strike her as being particularly clever, and he certainly was not distinguished, nor, she thought, ever very likely to be; but she had had a pleasure in being with him which she had never experienced in the society of any other man, and underneath some boyish ways she divined a strength and steadfastness which could be relied upon at need. And she admitted to herself that during the ten days since her return, though she had unsparingly snubbed her sister's wonderings why he did not call, she had speculated a good deal upon the subject herself, with a sort of resentful feeling against both herself and him that she should care--

Her face flushed as she recalled the momentary pressure of his hand upon hers on that last night on deck. She rang for the servant, and went up to her room.

CHAPTER IX.

It is not the purpose of this narrative to dwell minutely upon the events of the next few months. Truth to say, they were devoid of incidents of sufficient moment in themselves to warrant chronicle. What they led up to was memorable enough.

As time went on John found himself on terms of growing intimacy with the Carling household, and eventually it came about that if there passed a day when their door did not open to him it was *dies non*.

Mr. Carling was ostensibly more responsible than the ladies for the frequency of our friend's visits, and grew to look forward to them. In fact, he seemed to re-gard them as paid primarily to himself, and ignored an occasional suggestion on his wife's part that it might not be wholly the pleasure of a chat and a game at cards with him that brought the young man so often to the house. And when once she ventured to concern him with some stirrings of her mind on the subject, he rather testily (for him) pooh-poohed her misgivings, remarking that Mary was her own mistress, and, so far as he had ever seen, remarkably well qualified to regulate her own affairs. Had she ever seen anything to lead her to suppose that there was any particular sentiment existing between Lenox and her sister?

"No," said Mrs. Carling, "perhaps not exactly, but you know how those things go, and he always stays after we come up when she is at home." To which her hus-band vouchsafed no reply, but began a protracted wavering as to the advisability of leaving the steam on or turning it off for the night, which was a cold one--a di-lemma which, involving his personal welfare or comfort at the moment, permitted no consideration of other matters to share his mind.

*   *   *   *   *

Mrs. Carling had not spoken to her sister upon the subject. She thought that that young woman, if she were not, as Mr. Carling said, "remarkably well qualified to regulate her own affairs," at least held the opinion that she was, very strongly.

The two were devotedly fond of each other, but Mrs. Carling was the elder by twenty years, and in her love was an element of maternal solicitude to which her sister, while giving love for love in fullest measure, did not fully respond. The elder would have liked to share every thought, but she was neither so strong nor so clever as the girl to whom she had been almost as a mother, and who, though perfectly truthful and frank when she was minded to express herself, gave, as a rule, little satisfaction to attempts to explore her mind, and on some subjects was capable of meeting such attempts with impatience, not to say resentment--a fact of which her sister was quite aware. But as time went on, and the frequency of John's visits and attentions grew into a settled habit, Mrs. Carling's uneasiness, with which perhaps was mingled a bit of curiosity, got the better of her reserve, and she determined to get what satisfaction could be obtained for it.

They were sitting in Mrs. Carling's room, which was over the drawing-room in the front of the house. A fire of cannel blazed in the grate.

A furious storm was whirling outside. Mrs. Carling was occupied with some sort of needlework, and her sister, with a writing pad on her lap, was composing a letter to a friend with whom she carried on a desultory and rather one-sided cor-respondence. Presently she yawned slightly, and, putting down her pad, went over to the window and looked out.

"What a day!" she exclaimed. "It seems to get worse and worse. Positively you can't see across the street. It's like a western blizzard."

"It is, really," said Mrs. Carling; and then, moved by the current of thought which had been passing in her mind of late, "I fancy we shall spend the evening by ourselves to-night."

"That would not be so unusual as to be extraordinary, would it?" said Mary.

"Wouldn't it?" suggested Mrs. Carling in a tone that was meant to be slightly quizzical.

"We are by ourselves most evenings, are we not?" responded her sister, without turning around. "Why do you particularize to-night?"

"I was thinking," answered Mrs. Carling, bending a little closer over her work, "that even Mr. Lenox would hardly venture out in such a storm unless it were ab-solutely necessary."

"Oh, yes, to be sure, Mr. Lenox; very likely not," was Miss Blake's comment, in a tone of indifferent recollection.

"He comes here very often, almost every night, in fact," remarked Mrs. Carling, looking up sideways at her sister's back.

"Now that you mention it," said Mary dryly, "I have noticed something of the sort myself."

"Do you think he ought to?" asked her sister, after a moment of silence.

"Why not?" said the girl, turning to her questioner for the first time. "And why should I think he should or should not? Doesn't he come to see Julius, and on Julius's invitation? I have never asked him--but once," she said, flushing a little as she recalled the occasion and the wording of the invitation.

"Do you think," returned Mrs. Carling, "that his visits are wholly on Julius's account, and that he would come so often if there were no other inducement? You know," she continued, pressing her point timidly but persistently, "he always stays after we go upstairs if you are at home, and I have noticed that when you are out he always goes before our time for retiring."

"I should say," was the rejoinder, "that that was very much the proper thing. Whether or not he comes here too often is not for me to say--I have no opinion on the subject. But, to do him justice, he is about the last man to wait for a tacit dismissal, or to cause you and Julius to depart from what he knows to be your regular habit out of politeness to him. He is a person of too much delicacy and good breeding to stay when--if--that is to say--" She turned again to the window without completing her sentence, and, though Mrs. Carling thought she could complete it for her, she wisely forbore. After a moment of silence, Mary said in a voice devoid of any traces of confusion:

"You asked me if I thought Mr. Lenox would come so often if there were no object in his coming except to see Julius. I can only say that if Julius were out of the question I think he would come here but seldom; but," she added, as she left the window and resumed her seat, "I do not quite see the object of this discussion, and, indeed, I am not quite sure of what we are discussing. Do you object," she asked, looking curiously at her sister and smiling slightly, "to Mr. Lenox's coming here as he does, and if so, why?" This was apparently more direct than Mrs. Carling was quite prepared for. "And if you do," Mary proceeded, "what is to be done about it? Am I to make him understand that it is not considered the proper thing? or will you? or shall we leave it to Julius?"

Mrs. Carling looked up into her sister's face, in which was a smile of amused penetration, and looked down again in visible embarrassment.

The young woman laughed as she shook her finger at her.

"Oh, you transparent goose!" she cried. "What did he say?"

"What did who say?" was the evasive response.

"Julius," said Mary, putting her finger under her sister's chin and raising her face. "Tell me now. You've been talking with him, and I insist upon knowing the truth, the whole truth, and nothing but the truth. So there!"

"Well," she admitted hesitatingly, "I said to him something like what I have to you, that it seemed to me that Mr. Lenox came very often, and that I did not believe it was all on his account, and that he" (won't somebody please invent another pronoun?) "always stayed when you were at home--"

"--and," broke in her sister, "that you were afraid my young affections were being engaged, and that, after all, we didn't know much if anything about the young man, or, perhaps, that he was forming a hopeless attachment, and so on."

"No," said Mrs. Carling, "I didn't say that exactly. I--"

"Didn't you, really?" said Mary teasingly. "One ought to be explicit in such cases, don't you think? Well, what did Julius say? Was he very much concerned?" Mrs. Carling's face colored faintly under her sister's raillery, and she gave a little embarrassed laugh.

"Come, now," said the girl relentlessly, "what did he say?"

"Well," answered Mrs. Carling, "I must admit that he said 'Pooh!' for one thing, and that you were your own mistress, and, so far as he had seen, you were very well qualified to manage your own affairs."

Her sister clapped her hands. "Such discrimination have I not seen," she exclaimed, "no, not in Israel! What else did he say?" she demanded, with a dramatic gesture. "Let us know the worst."

Mrs. Carling laughed a little. "I don't remember," she admitted, "that he said anything more on the subject. He got into some perplexity about whether the steam should be off or on, and after that question was settled we went to bed." Mary laughed outright.

"So Julius doesn't think I need watching," she said.

"Mary," protested her sister in a hurt tone, "you don't think I ever did or could watch you? I don't want to pry into your secrets, dear," and she looked up with tears in her eyes. The girl dropped on her knees beside her sister and put her arms about her neck.

"You precious old lamb!" she cried, "I know you don't. You couldn't pry into anybody's secrets if you tried. You couldn't even try. But I haven't any, dear, and I'll tell you every one of them, and, rather than see a tear in your dear eyes, I would tell John Lenox that I never wanted to see him again; and I don't know what you have been thinking, but I haven't thought so at all" (which last assertion made even Mrs. Carling laugh), "and I know that I have been teasing and horrid, and if you won't put me in the closet I will be good and answer every question like a nice little girl." Whereupon she gave her sister a kiss and resumed her seat with an air of abject penitence which lasted for a minute. Then she laughed again, though there was a watery gleam in her own eyes. Mrs. Carling gave her a look of great love and admiration.

"I ought not to have brought up the subject," she said, "knowing as I do how you feel about such discussions, but I love you so much that sometimes I can't help--"

"Alice," exclaimed the girl, "please have the kindness to call me a selfish P--I--G. It will relieve my feelings."

"But I do not think you are," said Mrs. Carling literally.

"But I am at times," declared Mary, "and you deserve not only to have, but to be shown, all the love and confidence that I can give you. It's only this, that sometimes your solicitude makes you imagine things that do not exist, and you think I am withholding my confidence; and then, again, I am enough like other people that I don't always know exactly what I do think. Now, about this matter--"

"Don't say a word about it, dear," her sister interrupted, "unless you would rather than not."

"I wish to," said Mary. "Of course I am not oblivious of the fact that Mr. Lenox comes here very often, nor that he seems to like to stay and talk with me, because, don't you know, if he didn't he could go when you do, and I don't mind admitting that, as a general thing, I like to have him stay; but, as I said to you, if it weren't for Julius he would not come here very often."

"Don't you think," said Mrs. Carling, now on an assured footing, "that if it were not for you he would not come so often?"

Perhaps Mary overestimated the attraction which her brother-in-law had for

Mr. Lenox, and she smiled slightly as she thought that it was quite possible. "I suppose," she went on, with a little shrug of the shoulders, "that the proceeding is not strictly conventional, and that the absolutely correct thing would be for him to say good night when you and Julius do, and that there are those who would regard my permitting a young man in no way related to me to see me very often in the evening without the protection of a duenna as a very unbecoming thing."

"I never have had such a thought about it," declared Mrs. Carling.

"I never for a moment supposed you had, dear," said Mary, "nor have I. We are rather unconventional people, making very few claims upon society, and upon whom 'society' makes very few."

"I am rather sorry for that on your account," said her sister.

"You needn't be," was the rejoinder. "I have no yearnings in that direction which are not satisfied with what I have." She sat for a minute or two with her hands clasped upon her knee, gazing reflectively into the fire, which, in the growing darkness of the winter afternoon, afforded almost the only light in the room. Presently she became conscious that her sister was regarding her with an air of expectation, and resumed: "Leaving the question of the conventions out of the discussion as settled," she said, "there is nothing, Alice, that you need have any concern about, either on Mr. Lenox's account or mine."

"You like him, don't you?" asked Mrs. Carling.

"Yes," said Mary frankly, "I like him very much. We have enough in common to be rather sympathetic, and we differ enough not to be dull, and so we get on very well. I never had a brother," she continued, after a momentary pause, "but I feel toward him as I fancy I should feel toward a brother of about my own age, though he is five or six years older than I am."

"You don't think, then," said Mrs. Carling timidly, "that you are getting to care for him at all?"

"In the sense that you use the word," was the reply, "not the least in the world. If there were to come a time when I really believed I should never see him again, I should be sorry; but if at any time it were a question of six months or a year, I do not think my equanimity would be particularly disturbed."

"And how about him?" suggested Mrs. Carling. There was no reply.

"Don't you think he may care for you, or be getting to?"

Mary frowned slightly, half closing her eyes and stirring a little uneasily in her chair.

"He hasn't said anything to me on the subject," she replied evasively.

"Would that be necessary?" asked her sister.

"Perhaps not," was the reply, "if the fact were very obvious."

"Isn't it?" persisted Mrs. Carling, with unusual tenacity.

"Well," said the girl, "to be quite frank with you, I have thought once or twice that he entertained some such idea--that is--no, I don't mean to put it just that way. I mean that once or twice something has occurred to give me that idea. That isn't very coherent, is it? But even if it be so," she went on after a moment, with a wave of her hands, "what of it? What does it signify? And if it does signify, what can I do about it?"

"You have thought about it, then?" said her sister.

"As much as I have told you," she answered. "I am not a very sentimental person, I think, and not very much on the lookout for such things, but I know there is such a thing as a man's taking a fancy to a young woman under circumstances which bring them often together, and I have been led to believe that it isn't necessarily fatal to the man even if nothing comes of it. But be that as it may," she said with a shrug of her shoulders, "what can I do about it? I can't say to Mr. Lenox, 'I think you ought not to come here so much,' unless I give a reason for it, and I think we have come to the conclusion that there is no reason except the danger--to put it in so many words--of his falling in love with me. I couldn't quite say that to him, could I?"

"No, I suppose not," acquiesced Mrs. Carling faintly.

"No, I should say not," remarked the girl. "If he were to say anything to me in the way of--declaration is the word, isn't it?--it would be another matter. But there is no danger of that."

"Why not, if he is fond of you?" asked her sister.

"Because," said Mary, with an emphatic nod, "I won't let him," which assertion was rather weakened by her adding, "and he wouldn't, if I would."

"I don't understand," said her sister.

"Well," said Mary, "I don't pretend to know all that goes on in his mind; but allowing, or rather conjecturing, that he does care for me in the way you mean, I haven't the least fear of his telling me so, and one of the reasons is this, that he is wholly dependent upon his father, with no other prospect for years to come."

"I had the idea somehow," said Mrs. Carling, "that his father was very well-to-do. The young man gives one the impression of a person who has always had everything that he wanted."

"I think that is so," said Mary, "but he told me one day, coming over on the steamer, that he knew nothing whatever of his own prospects or his father's affairs. I don't remember--at least, it doesn't matter--how he came to say as much, but he did, and afterward gave me a whimsical catalogue of his acquirements and accomplishments, remarking, I remember, that 'there was not a dollar in the whole list'; and lately, though you must not fancy that he discusses his own affairs with me, he has now and then said something to make me guess that he was somewhat troubled about them."

"Is he doing anything?" asked Mrs. Carling.

"He told me the first evening he called here," said Mary, "that he was studying law, at his father's suggestion; but I don't remember the name of the firm in whose office he is."

"Why doesn't he ask his father about his prospects?" said Mrs. Carling.

Mary laughed. "You seem to be so much more interested in the matter than I am," she said, "why don't you ask him yourself?" To which unjustifiable rejoinder her sister made no reply.

"I don't see why he shouldn't," she remarked.

"I think I understand," said Mary. "I fancy from what he has told me that his father is a singularly reticent man, but one in whom his son has always had the most implicit confidence. I imagine, too, that until recently, at any rate, he has taken it for granted that his father was wealthy. He has not confided any misgivings to me, but if he has any he is just the sort of person not to ask, and certainly not to press a question with his father."

"It would seem like carrying delicacy almost too far," remarked Mrs. Carling.

"Perhaps it would," said her sister, "but I think I can understand and sympathize with it."

Mrs. Carling broke the silence which followed for a moment or two as if she were thinking aloud. "You have plenty of money," she said, and colored at her inadvertence. Her sister looked at her for an instant with a humorous smile, and then, as she rose and touched the bell button, said, "That's another reason."

CHAPTER X.

I think it should hardly be imputed to John as a fault or a shortcoming that he did not for a long time realize his father's failing powers. True, as has been stated, he had noted some changes in appearance on his return, but they were not great enough to be startling, and, though he thought at times that his father's manner was more subdued than he had ever known it to be, nothing really occurred to arouse his suspicion or anxiety. After a few days the two men appeared to drop into their accustomed relation and routine, meeting in the morning and at dinner; but as John picked up the threads of his acquaintance he usually went out after dinner, and even when he did not his father went early to his own apartment.

From John's childhood he had been much of the time away from home, and there had never, partly from that circumstance and partly from the older man's natural and habitual reserve, been very much intimacy between them. The father did not give his own confidence, and, while always kind and sympathetic when appealed to, did not ask his son's; and, loving his father well and loyally, and trusting him implicitly, it did not occur to John to feel that there was anything wanting in the relation. It was as it had always been. He was accustomed to accept what his father did or said without question, and, as is very often the case, had always regarded him as an old man. He had never felt that they could be in the same equation. In truth, save for their mutual affection, they had little in common; and if, as may have been the case, his father had any cravings for a closer and more intimate relation, he made no sign, acquiescing in his son's actions as the son did in his, without question or suggestion. They did not know each other, and such cases are not rare, more is the pity.

But as time went on even John's unwatchful eye could not fail to notice that all was not well with his father. Haggard lines were multiplying in the quiet face, and the silence at the dinner table was often unbroken except by John's unfruitful efforts to keep some sort of a conversation in motion. More and more frequently it occurred that his father would retire to his own room immediately after dinner was over, and the food on his plate would be almost untouched, while he took more wine than had ever been his habit. John, retiring late, would often hear him stirring uneasily in his room, and it would be plain in the morning that he had spent a wakeful, if not a sleepless, night. Once or twice on such a morning John had suggested to his father that he should not go down to the office, and the suggestion had been met with so irritable a negative as to excite his wonder.

         *   *   *   *   *

It was a day in the latter part of March. The winter had been unusually severe, and lingered into spring with a heart-sickening tenacity, occasional hints of clemency and promise being followed by recurrences which were as irritating as a personal affront.

John had held to his work in the office, if not with positive enthusiasm, at least with industry, and thought that he had made some progress. On the day in question the managing clerk commented briefly but favorably on something of his which was satisfactory, and, such experiences being rare, he was conscious of a feeling of mild elation. He was also cherishing the anticipation of a call at Sixty-ninth Street, where, for reasons unnecessary to recount, he had not been for a week. At dinner that night his father seemed more inclined than for a long time to keep up a conversation which, though of no special import, was cheerful in comparison with the silence which had grown to be almost the rule, and the two men sat for a while over the coffee and cigars. Presently, however, the elder rose from the table, saying pleasantly, "I suppose you are going out to-night."

"Not if you'd like me to stay in," was the reply. "I have no definite engagement."

"Oh, no," said Mr. Lenox, "not at all, not at all," and as he passed his son on the way out of the room he put out his hand and taking John's, said, "Good night."

As John stood for a moment rather taken aback, he heard his father mount the stairs to his room. He was puzzled by the unexpected and unusual occurrence, but finally concluded that his father, realizing how taciturn they had become of late, wished to resume their former status, and this view was confirmed to his mind by the fact that they had been more companionable than usual that evening, albeit that nothing of any special significance had been said.

As has been stated, a longer interval than usual had elapsed since John's last visit to Sixty-ninth Street, a fact which had been commented on by Mr. Carling, but not mentioned between the ladies. When he found himself at that hospitable house on that evening, he was greeted by Miss Blake alone.

"Julius did not come down to-night, and my sister is with him," she said, "so you will have to put up with my society--unless you'd like me to send up for Alice. Julius is strictly *en retraite*, I should say."

"Don't disturb her, I beg," protested John, laughing, and wondering a bit at the touch of coquetry in her speech, something unprecedented in his experience of her, "if you are willing to put up with my society. I hope Mr. Carling is not ill?"

They seated themselves as she replied: "No, nothing serious, I should say. A bit of a cold, I fancy; and for a fortnight he has been more nervous than usual. The changes in the weather have been so great and so abrupt that they have worn upon his nerves. He is getting very uneasy again. Now, after spending the winter, and when spring is almost at hand, I believe that if he could make up his mind where to go he would be for setting off to-morrow."

"Really?" said John, in a tone of dismay.

"Quite so," she replied with a nod.

"But," he objected, "it seems too late or too early. Spring may drop in upon us any day. Isn't this something very recent?"

"It has been developing for a week or ten days," she answered, "and symptoms have indicated a crisis for some time. In fact," she added, with a little vexed laugh, "we have talked of nothing for a week but the advantages and disadvantages of Florida, California, North Carolina, South Carolina, and Virginia at large; besides St. Augustine, Monterey, Santa Barbara, Aiken, Asheville, Hot Springs, Old Point Comfort, Bermuda, and I don't know how many other places, not forgetting Atlantic City and Lakewood, and only not Barbadoes and the Sandwich Islands because nobody happened to think of them. Julius," remarked Miss Blake, "would have given a forenoon to the discussion of the two latter places as readily as to any of the others."

"Can't you talk him along into warm weather?" suggested John, with rather a mirthless laugh. "Don't you think that if the weather were to change for good, as it's likely to do almost any time now, he might put off going till the usual summer flitting?"

"The change in his mind will have to come pretty soon if I am to retain my mental faculties," she declared. "He might possibly, but I am afraid not," she said, shaking her head. "He has the idea fixed in his mind, and considerations of the weather here, while they got him started, are not now so much the question. He has the moving fever, and I am afraid it will have to run its course. I think," she said, after a moment, "that if I were to formulate a special anathema, it would be, 'May traveling seize you!'"

"Or restlessness," suggested John.

"Yes," she said, "that's more accurate, perhaps, but it doesn't sound quite so smart. Julius is in that state of mind when the only place that seems desirable is somewhere else."

"Of course you will have to go," said John mournfully.

"Oh, yes," she replied, with an air of compulsory resignation. "I shall not only have to go, of course, but I shall probably have to decide where in order to save my mind. But it will certainly be somewhere, so I might as well be packing my trunks."

"And you will be away indefinitely, I suppose?"

"Yes, I imagine so."

"Dear me!" John ejaculated in a dismal tone.

They were sitting as described on a former occasion, and the young woman was engaged upon the second (perhaps the third, or even the fourth) of the set of doilies to which she had committed herself. She took some stitches with a composed air, without responding to her companion's exclamation.

"I'm awfully sorry," he said presently, leaning forward with his elbows on his knees, his hands hanging in an attitude of unmistakable dejection, and staring fixedly into the fire.

"I am very sorry myself," she said, bending her head a little closer over her work. "I think I like being in New York in the spring better than at any other time; and I don't at all fancy the idea of living in my trunks again for an indefinite period."

"I shall miss you horribly," he said, turning his face toward her.

Her eyes opened with a lift of the brows, but whether the surprise so indicated was quite genuine is a matter for conjecture.

"Yes," he declared desperately, "I shall, indeed."

"I should fancy you must have plenty of other friends," she said, flushing a little, "and I have wondered sometimes whether Julius's demands upon you were not more confident than warrantable, and whether you wouldn't often rather have gone elsewhere than to come here to play cards with him." She actually said this as if she meant it.

"Do you suppose--" he exclaimed, and checked himself. "No," he said, "I have come because--well, I've been only too glad to come, and--I suppose it has got to be a habit," he added, rather lamely. "You see, I've never known any people in the way I have known you. It has seemed to me more like home life than anything I've ever known. There has never been any one but my father and I, and you can have no idea what it has been to me to be allowed to come here as I have, and--oh, you must know--" He hesitated, and instantly she advanced her point.

Her face was rather white, and the hand which lay upon the work in her lap trembled a little, while she clasped the arm of the chair with the other; but she broke in upon his hesitation with an even voice:

"It has been very pleasant for us all, I'm sure," she said, "and, frankly, I'm sorry that it must be interrupted for a while, but that is about all there is of it, isn't it? We shall probably be back not later than October, I should say, and then you can renew your contests with Julius and your controversies with me."

Her tone and what she said recalled to him their last night on board the ship, but there was no relenting on this occasion. He realized that for a moment he had been on the verge of telling the girl that he loved her, and he realized, too, that she had divined his impulse and prevented the disclosure; but he registered a vow that he would know before he saw her again whether he might consistently tell her his love, and win or lose upon the touch.

Miss Blake made several inaccurate efforts to introduce her needle at the exact point desired, and when that endeavor was accomplished broke the silence by saying, "Speaking of 'October,' have you read the novel? I think it is charming."

"Yes," said John, with his vow in his mind, but not sorry for the diversion, "and I enjoyed it very much. I thought it was immensely clever, but I confess that I didn't quite sympathize with the love affairs of a hero who was past forty, and I must also confess that I thought the girl was, well--to put it in plain English--a fool."

Mary laughed, with a little quaver in her voice. "Do you know," she said, "that sometimes it seems to me that I am older than you are?"

"I know you're awfully wise," said John with a laugh, and from that their talk drifted off into the safer channels of their usual intercourse until he rose to say good night.

"Of course, we shall see you again before we go," she said as she gave him her hand.

"Oh," he declared, "I intend regularly to haunt the place."

CHAPTER XI.

When John came down the next morning his father, who was, as a rule, the most punctual of men, had not appeared. He opened the paper and sat down to wait. Ten minutes passed, fifteen, twenty. He rang the bell. "Have you heard my father this morning?" he said to Jeffrey, remembering for the first time that he himself had not.

"No, sir," said the man. "He most generally coughs a little in the morning, but I don't think I heard him this morning, sir."

"Go up and see why he doesn't come down," said John, and a moment later he followed the servant upstairs, to find him standing at the chamber door with a frightened face.

"He must be very sound asleep, sir," said Jeffrey. "He hasn't answered to my knockin' or callin', sir." John tried the door. He found the chain bolt on, and it opened but a few inches. "Father!" he called, and then again, louder. He turned almost unconsciously to Jeffrey, and found his own apprehensions reflected in the man's face. "We must break in the door," he said. "Now, together!" and the bolt gave way.

His father lay as if asleep. "Go for the doctor at once! Bring him back with you. Run!" he cried to the servant. Custom and instinct said, "Send for the doctor," but he knew in his heart that no ministrations would ever reach the still figure on the bed, upon which, for the moment, he could not look. It was but a few minutes (how long such minutes are!) before the doctor came--Doctor Willis, who had brought John into the world, and had been a lifelong friend of both father and son. He went swiftly to the bed without speaking, and made a brief examination, while John watched him with fascinated eyes; and as the doctor finished, the son dropped on his knees by the bed, and buried his face in it. The doctor crossed the room to Jeffrey, who was standing in the door with an awe-stricken face, and in a low voice gave him some directions. Then, as the man departed, he first glanced at the kneeling figure and then looked searchingly about the room. Presently he went over to the grate in which were the ashes of an extinct fire, and, taking the poker, pressed down among them and covered over a three or four ounce vial. He had found what he was looking for.

     *   *   *   *   *

There is no need to speak of the happenings of the next few days, nor is it necessary to touch at any length upon the history of some of the weeks and months which ensued upon this crisis in John Lenox's life, a time when it seemed to him that everything he had ever cared for had been taken. And yet, with that unreason which may perhaps be more easily understood than accounted for, the one thing upon which his mind most often dwelt was that he had had no answer to his note to Mary Blake. We know what happened to her missive. It turned up long afterward in the pocket of Master Jacky Carling's overcoat; so long afterward that John, so far as Mary was concerned, had disappeared altogether. The discovery of Jacky's dereliction explained to her, in part at least, why she had never seen him or heard from him after that last evening at Sixty-ninth Street. The Carlings went away some ten days later, and she did, in fact, send another note to his house address, asking him to see them before their departure; but John had considered himself fortunate in getting the house off his hands to a tenant who would assume the lease if given possession at once, and had gone into the modest apartment which he occupied during the rest of his life in the city, and so the second communication failed to reach him. Perhaps it was as well. Some weeks later he walked up to the Carlings' house one Sunday afternoon, and saw that it was closed, as he had expected. By an impulse which was not part of his original intention--which was, indeed, pretty nearly aimless--he was moved to ring the doorbell; but the maid, a stranger to him, who opened the door could tell him nothing of the family's whereabouts, and Mr.

Betts (the house man in charge) was "hout." So John retraced his steps with a feeling of disappointment wholly disproportionate to his hopes or expectations so far as he had defined them to himself, and never went back again.

     *   *   *   *   *

He has never had much to say of the months that followed.

It came to be the last of October. An errand from the office had sent him to General Wolsey, of the Mutual Trust Company, of whom mention has been made by David Harum. The general was an old friend of the elder Lenox, and knew John well and kindly. When the latter had discharged his errand and was about to go, the general said: "Wait a minute. Are you in a hurry? If not, I want to have a little talk with you."

"Not specially," said John.

"Sit down," said the general, pointing to a chair. "What are your plans? I see you are still in the Careys' office, but from what you told me last summer I conclude that you are there because you have not found anything more satisfactory."

"That is the case, sir," John replied. "I can't be idle, but I don't see how I can keep on as I am going now, and I have been trying for months to find something by which I can earn a living. I am afraid," he added, "that it will be a longer time than I can afford to wait before I shall be able to do that out of the law."

"If you don't mind my asking," said the general, "what are your resources? I don't think you told me more than to give me to understand that your father's affairs were at a pretty low ebb. Of course, I do not wish to pry into your affairs--"

"Not at all," John interposed; "I am glad to tell you, and thank you for your interest. I have about two thousand dollars, and there is some silver and odds and ends of things stored. I don't know what their value might be--not very much, I fancy--and there were a lot of mining stocks and that sort of thing which have no value so far as I can find out--no available value, at any rate. There is also a tract of half-wild land somewhere in Pennsylvania. There is coal on it, I believe, and some timber; but Melig, my father's manager, told me that all the large timber had been cut. So far as available value is concerned, the property is about as much of an asset as the mining stock, with the disadvantage that I have to pay taxes on it."

"H'm," said the general, tapping the desk with his eyeglasses. "H'm--well, I should think if you lived very economically you would have about enough to carry you through till you can be admitted, provided you feel that the law is your voca-tion," he added, looking up.

"It was my father's idea," said John, "and if I were so situated that I could go on with it, I would. But I am so doubtful with regard to my aptitude that I don't feel as if I ought to use up what little capital I have, and some years of time, on a doubtful experiment, and so I have been looking for something else to do."

"Well," said the general, "if you were very much interested--that is, if you were anxious to proceed with your studies--I should advise you to go on, and at a pinch I should be willing to help you out; but, feeling as you do, I hardly know what to advise. I was thinking of you," he went on, "before you came in, and was intending to send for you to come in to see me." He took a letter from his desk.

"I got this yesterday," he said. "It is from an old acquaintance of mine by the name of Harum, who lives in Homeville, Freeland County. He is a sort of a banker there, and has written me to recommend some one to take the place of his manager or cashier whom he is sending away. It's rather a queer move, I think, but then," said the general with a smile, "Harum is a queer customer in some ways of his own. There is his letter. Read it for yourself."

The letter stated that Mr. Harum had had some trouble with his cashier and wished to replace him, and that he would prefer some one from out of the village who wouldn't know every man, woman, and child in the whole region, and "blab everything right and left." "I should want," wrote Mr. Harum, "to have the young man know something about bookkeeping and so on, but I should not insist upon his having been through a trainer's hands. In fact, I would rather break him in myself, and if he's willing and sound and no vice, I can get him into shape. I will pay a thou-sand to start on, and if he draws and travels all right, may be better in the long run," etc. John handed back the letter with a slight smile, which was reflected in the face of the general. "What do you think of it?" asked the latter.

"I should think it might be very characteristic," remarked John.

"Yes," said the general, "it is, to an extent. You see he writes pretty fair English, and he can, on occasion, talk as he writes, but usually, either from habit or choice, he uses the most unmitigated dialect. But what I meant to ask you was, what do you think of the proposal?"

"You mean as an opportunity for *me*?" asked John.

"Yes," said General Wolsey, "I thought of you at once."

"Thank you very much," said John. "What would be your idea?"

"Well," was the reply, "I am inclined to think I should write to him if I were you, and I will write to him about you if you so decide. You have had some office experience, you told me--enough, I should say, for a foundation, and I don't believe that Harum's books and accounts are very complicated."

John did not speak, and the general went on: "Of course, it will be a great change from almost everything you have been used to, and I dare say that you may find the life, at first at least, pretty dull and irksome. The stipend is not very large, but it is large for the country, where your expenses will be light. In fact, I'm rather surprised at his offering so much. At any rate, it is a living for the present, and may lead to something better. The place is a growing one, and, more than that, Harum is well off, and keeps more irons in the fire than one, and if you get on with him you may do well."

"I don't think I should mind the change so much," said John, rather sadly. "My present life is so different in almost every way from what it used to be, and I think I feel it in New York more even than I might in a country village; but the venture seems a little like burning my bridges."

"Well," replied the general, "if the experiment should turn out a failure for any reason, you won't be very much more at a loss than at present, it seems to me, and, of course, I will do anything I can should you wish me to be still on the lookout for you here."

"You are exceedingly kind, sir," said John earnestly, and then was silent for a moment or two. "I will make the venture," he said at length, "and thank you very much."

"You are under no special obligations to the Careys, are you?" asked the general.

"No, I think not," said John with a laugh. "I fancy that their business will go on without me, after a fashion," and he took his leave.

CHAPTER XII.

And so it came about that certain letters were written as mentioned in a previous chapter, and in the evening of a dripping day early in November John Lenox found himself, after a nine hours' journey, the only traveler who alighted upon the platform of the Homeville station, which was near the end of a small lake and about a mile from the village. As he stood with his bag and umbrella, at a loss what to do, he was accosted by a short and stubby individual with very black eyes and hair and a round face, which would have been smooth except that it had not been shaved for a day or two. "Goin' t' the village?" he said.

"Yes," said John, "that is my intention, but I don't see any way of getting there."

"Carry ye over fer ten cents," said the man. "Carryall's right back the deepo. Got 'ny baggidge?"

"Two trunks," said John.

"That'll make it thirty cents," said the native. "Where's your checks? All right; you c'n jest step 'round an' git in. Mine's the only rig that drew over to-night."

It was a long clumsy affair, with windows at each end and a door in the rear, but open at the sides except for enamel cloth curtains, which were buttoned to the supports that carried a railed roof extending as far forward as the dashboard. The driver's seat was on a level with those inside. John took a seat by one of the front windows, which was open but protected by the roof.

His luggage having been put on board, they began the journey at a walk, the first part of the road being rough and swampy in places, and undergoing at intervals the sort of repairs which often prevails in rural regions--namely, the deposit of a quantity of broken stone, which is left to be worn smooth by passing vehicles, and is for the most part carefully avoided by such whenever the roadway is broad enough to drive round the improvement. But the worst of the way having been accomplished, the driver took opportunity, speaking sideways over his shoulder, to allay the curiosity which burned within him, "Guess I never seen you before." John was tired and hungry, and generally low in his mind.

"Very likely not," was his answer. Mr. Robinson instantly arrived at the determination that the stranger was "stuck up," but was in no degree cast down thereby.

"I heard Chet Timson tellin' that the' was a feller comin' f'm N'York to work in Dave Harum's bank. Guess you're him, ain't ye?"

No answer this time: theory confirmed.

"My name's Robinson," imparted that individual. "I run the prince'ple liv'ry to Homeville."

"Ah!" responded the passenger.

"What d'you say your name was?" asked Mr. Robinson, after he had steered his team around one of the monuments to public spirit.

"It's Lenox," said John, thinking he might concede something to such deserving perseverance, "but I don't remember mentioning it."

"Now I think on't, I guess you didn't," admitted Mr. Robinson. "Don't think I ever knowed anybody of the name," he remarked. "Used to know some folks name o' Lynch, but they couldn't 'a' ben no relations o' your'n, I guess." This conjecture elicited no reply.

"Git up, goll darn ye!" he exclaimed, as one of the horses stumbled, and he gave it a jerk and a cut of the whip. "Bought that hoss of Dave Harum," he confided to his passenger. "Fact, I bought both on 'em of him, an' dum well stuck I was, too," he added.

"You know Mr. Harum, then," said John, with a glimmer of interest. "Does he deal in horses?"

"Wa'al, I guess I make eout to know him," asserted the "prince'ple liv'ryman," "an' he'll git up 'n the middle o' the night any time to git the best of a hoss trade. Be you goin' to work fer him?" he asked, encouraged to press the question. "Goin' to take Timson's place?"

"Really," said John, in a tone which advanced Mr. Robinson's opinion to a rooted conviction, "I have never heard of Mr. Timson."

"He's the feller that Dave's lettin' go," explained Mr. Robinson. "He's ben in the bank a matter o' five or six year, but Dave got down on him fer some little thing or other, an' he's got his walkin' papers. He says to me, says he, 'If any feller thinks he c'n come up here f'm N'York or anywheres else, he says, 'an' do Dave Harum's work to suit him, he'll find he's bit off a dum sight more'n he c'n chaw. He'd better keep his gripsack packed the hull time,' Chet says."

"I thought I'd sock it to the cuss a little," remarked Mr. Robinson in recounting the conversation subsequently; and, in truth, it was not elevating to the spirits of our friend, who found himself speculating whether or no Timson might not be right.

"Where you goin' to put up?" asked Mr. Robinson after an interval, having failed to draw out any response to his last effort.

"Is there more than one hotel?" inquired the passenger.

"The's the Eagle, an' the Lake House, an' Smith's Hotel," replied Jehu.

"Which would you recommend?" asked John.

"Wa'al," said Robinson, "I don't gen'ally praise up one more'n another. You see, I have more or less dealin' with all on 'em."

"That's very diplomatic of you, I'm sure," remarked John, not at all diplomatically. "I think I will try the Eagle."

Mr. Robinson, in his account of the conversation, said in confidence--not wishing to be openly invidious--that "he was dum'd if he wa'n't almost sorry he hadn't recommended the Lake House."

It may be inferred from the foregoing that the first impression which our friend made on his arrival was not wholly in his favor, and Mr. Robinson's conviction that he was "stuck up," and a person bound to get himself "gen'ally disliked," was elevated to an article of faith by his retiring to the rear of the vehicle, and quite out of ordinary range. But they were nearly at their journey's end, and presently the carryall drew up at the Eagle Hotel.

It was a frame building of three stories, with a covered veranda running the length of the front, from which two doors gave entrance--one to the main hall, the other to the office and bar combined. This was rather a large room, and was also to be entered from the main hall.

John's luggage was deposited, Mr. Robinson was settled with, and took his departure without the amenities which might have prevailed under different conditions, and the new arrival made his way into the office.

Behind the bar counter, which faced the street, at one end of which was a small high desk and at the other a glazed case containing three or four partly full boxes of forlorn-looking cigars, but with most ambitious labels, stood the proprietor, manager, clerk, and what not of the hostelry, embodied in the single person of Mr. Amos Elright, who was leaning over the counter in conversation with three or four loungers who sat about the room with their chairs tipped back against the wall.

A sketch of Mr. Elright would have depicted a dull "complected" person of a tousled baldness, whose dispirited expression of countenance was enhanced by a chin whisker. His shirt and collar gave unmistakable evidence that pajamas or other night-gear were regarded as superfluities, and his most conspicuous garment as he appeared behind the counter was a cardigan jacket of a frowsiness beyond compare. A greasy neck scarf was embellished with a gem whose truthfulness was without pretence. The atmosphere of the room was accounted for by a remark which was made by one of the loungers as John came in. "Say, Ame," the fellow drawled, "I guess the' was more skunk cabbidge 'n pie plant 'n usual 'n that last lot o' cigars o' your'n, wa'n't the'?" to which insinuation "Ame" was spared the necessity of a rejoinder by our friend's advent.

"Wa'al, guess we c'n give ye a room. Oh, yes, you c'n register if you want to. Where is the dum thing? I seen it last week somewhere. Oh, yes," producing a thin book ruled for accounts from under the counter, "we don't alwus use it," he remarked--which was obvious, seeing that the last entry was a month old.

John concluded that it was a useless formality. "I should like something to eat," he said, "and desire to go to my room while it is being prepared; and can you send my luggage up now?"

"Wa'al," said Mr. Elright, looking at the clock, which showed the hour of half-past nine, and rubbing his chin perplexedly, "supper's ben cleared off some time ago."

"I don't want very much," said John; "just a bit of steak, and some stewed potatoes, and a couple of boiled eggs, and some coffee." He might have heard the sound of a slap in the direction of one of the sitters.

"I'm 'fraid I can't 'commodate ye fur's the steak an' things goes," confessed the landlord. "We don't do much cookin' after dinner, an' I reckon the fire's out anyway. P'r'aps," he added doubtfully, "I c'd hunt ye up a piece o' pie 'n some doughnuts, or somethin' like that."

He took a key, to which was attached a huge brass tag with serrated edges, from a hook on a board behind the bar--on which were suspended a number of the like--lighted a small kerosene lamp, carrying a single wick, and, shuffling out from behind the counter, said, "Say, Bill, can't you an' Dick carry the gentleman's trunks up to 'thirteen?'" and, as they assented, he gave the lamp and key to one of them and left the room. The two men took a trunk at either end and mounted the stairs, John following, and when the second one came up he put his fingers into his waistcoat pocket suggestively.

"No," said the one addressed as Dick, "that's all right. We done it to oblige Ame."

"I'm very much obliged to you, though," said John.

"Oh, that's all right," remarked Dick as they turned away.

John surveyed the apartment. There were two small-paned windows overlooking the street, curtained with bright "Turkey-red" cotton; near to one of them a small wood stove and a wood box, containing some odds and ends of sticks and bits of bark; a small chest of drawers, serving as a washstand; a malicious little looking-glass; a basin and ewer, holding about two quarts; an earthenware mug and soap-dish, the latter containing a thin bit of red translucent soap scented with sassafras; an ordinary wooden chair and a rocking-chair with rockers of divergent aims; a yellow wooden bedstead furnished with a mattress of "excelsior" (calculated to induce early rising), a dingy white spread, a gray blanket of coarse wool, a pair of cotton sheets which had too obviously done duty since passing through the hands of the laundress, and a pair of flabby little pillows in the same state, in respect to their cases, as the sheets. On the floor was a much used and faded ingrain carpet, in one place worn through by the edge of a loose board. A narrow strip of unpainted pine nailed to the wall carried six or seven wooden pegs to serve as wardrobe. Two diminutive towels with red borders hung on the rail of the washstand, and a battered tin slop jar, minus a cover, completed the inventory.

"Heavens, what a hole!" exclaimed John, and as he performed his ablutions (not with the sassafras soap) he promised himself a speedy flitting. There came a knock at the door, and his host appeared to announce that his "tea" was ready, and to conduct him to the dining-room--a good-sized apartment, but narrow, with a long table running near the center lengthwise, covered with a cloth which bore the marks of many a fray. Another table of like dimensions, but bare, was shoved up against the wall. Mr. Elright's ravagement of the larder had resulted in a triangle of cadaverous apple pie, three doughnuts, some chunks of soft white cheese, and a plate of what are known as oyster crackers.

"I couldn't git ye no tea," he said. "The hired girls both gone out, an' my wife's gone to bed, an' the' wa'n't no fire anyway."

"I suppose I could have some beer," suggested John, looking dubiously at the banquet.

"We don't keep no ale," said the proprietor of the Eagle, "an' I guess we're out o' lawger. I ben intendin' to git some more," he added.

"A glass of milk?" proposed the guest, but without confidence.

"Milkman didn't come to-night," said Mr. Elright, shuffling off in his carpet slippers, worn out in spirit with the importunities of the stranger. There was water on the table, for it had been left there from supper time. John managed to consume a doughnut and some crackers and cheese, and then went to his room, carrying the water pitcher with him, and, after a cigarette or two and a small potation from his flask, to bed. Before retiring, however, he stripped the bed with the intention of turning the sheets, but upon inspection thought better of it, and concluded to leave them as they were. So passed his first night in Homeville, and, as he fondly promised himself, his last at the Eagle Hotel.

When Bill and Dick returned to the office after "obligin' Ame," they stepped with one accord to the counter and looked at the register. "Why, darn it," exclaimed Bill, "he didn't sign his name, after all."

"No," said Dick, "but I c'n give a putty near guess who he is, all the same."

"Some drummer?" suggested Bill.

"Naw," said Richard scornfully. "What 'd a drummer be doin' here this time o' year? That's the feller that's ousted Chet Timson, an' I'll bet ye the drinks on't. Name's Linx or Lenx, or somethin' like that. Dave told me."

"So that's the feller, is it?" said Bill. "I guess he won't stay 'round here long. I guess you'll find he's a little too toney fer these parts, an' in pertic'ler fer Dave Harum. Dave'll make him feel 'bout as comf'table as a rooster in a pond. Lord," he exclaimed, slapping his leg with a guffaw, "'d you notice Ame's face when he said he didn't want much fer supper, only beefsteak, an' eggs, an' tea, an' coffee, an' a few little things like that? I thought I'd split."

"Yes," said Dick, laughing, "I guess the' ain't nothin' the matter with Ame's heart, or he'd 'a' fell down dead.--Hullo, Ame!" he said when the gentleman in question came back after ministering to his guest, "got the Prince o' Wales fixed up all right? Did ye cut that pickled el'phant that come last week?"

"Huh!" grunted Amos, whose sensibilities had been wounded by the events of the evening, "I didn't cut no el'phant ner no cow, ner rob no hen roost neither, but I guess he won't starve 'fore mornin'," and with that he proceeded to fill up the stove and shut the dampers.

"That means 'git,' I reckon," remarked Bill as he watched the operation.

"Wa'al," said Mr. Elright, "if you fellers think you've spent enough time droolin' 'round here swapping lies, I think *I'll* go to bed," which inhospitable and injurious remark was by no means taken in bad part, for Dick said, with a laugh:

"Well, Ame, if you'll let me run my face for 'em, Bill 'n I'll take a little somethin' for the good o' the house before we shed the partin' tear." This proposition was not declined by Mr. Elright, but he felt bound on business principles not to yield with too great a show of readiness.

"Wa'al, I don't mind for this once," he said, going behind the bar and setting out a bottle and glasses, "but I've gen'ally noticed that it's a damn sight easier to git somethin' *into* you fellers 'n 't is to git anythin' *out* of ye."

CHAPTER XIII.

The next morning at nine o'clock John presented himself at Mr. Harum's banking office, which occupied the first floor of a brick building some twenty or twenty-five feet in width. Besides the entrance to the bank, there was a door at the south corner opening upon a stairway leading to a suite of two rooms on the second floor.

The banking office consisted of two rooms--one in front, containing the desks and counters, and what may be designated as the "parlor" (as used to be the case in the provincial towns) in the rear, in which were Mr. Harum's private desk, a safe of medium size, the necessary assortment of chairs, and a lounge. There was also a large Franklin stove.

The parlor was separated from the front room by a partition, in which were two doors, one leading into the inclosed space behind the desks and counters, and the other into the passageway formed by the north wall and a length of high desk, topped by a railing. The teller's or cashier's counter faced the street opposite the entrance door. At the left of this counter (viewed from the front) was a high-standing desk, with a rail. At the right was a glass-inclosed space of counter of the same height as that portion which was open, across which latter the business of paying and receiving was conducted.

As John entered he saw standing behind this open counter, framed, as it were, between the desk on the one hand, and the glass inclosure on the other, a person whom he conjectured to be the "Chet" (short for Chester) Timson of whom he had heard. This person nodded in response to our friend's "Good morning," and anticipated his inquiry by saying:

"You lookin' for Dave?"

"I am looking for Mr. Harum," said John. "Is he in the office?"

"He hain't come in yet," was the reply. "Up to the barn, I reckon, but he's liable to come in any minute, an' you c'n step into the back room an' wait fer him," indicating the direction with a wave of his hand.

Business had not begun to be engrossing, though the bank was open, and John had hardly seated himself when Timson came into the back room and, taking a chair where he could see the counter in the front office, proceeded to investigate the stranger, of whose identity he had not the smallest doubt. But it was not Mr. Timson's way to take things for granted in silence, and it must be admitted that his curiosity in this particular case was not without warrant. After a scrutiny of John's face and person, which was not brief enough to be unnoticeable, he said, with a directness which left nothing in that line to be desired, "I reckon you're the new man Dave's ben gettin' up from the city."

"I came up yesterday," admitted John.

"My name's Timson," said Chet.

"Happy to meet you," said John, rising and putting out his hand. "My name is Lenox," and they shook hands--that is, John grasped the ends of four limp fingers. After they had subsided into their seats, Chet's opaquely bluish eyes made another tour of inspection, in curiosity and wonder.

"You alwus lived in the city?" he said at last.

"It has always been my home," was the reply.

"What put it in your head to come up here?" with another stare.

"It was at Mr. Harum's suggestion," replied John, not with perfect candor; but he was not minded to be drawn out too far.

"D'ye know Dave?"

"I have never met him." Mr. Timson looked more puzzled than ever.

"Ever ben in the bankin' bus'nis?"

"I have had some experience of such accounts in a general way."

"Ever keep books?"

"Only as I have told you," said John, smiling at the little man.

"Got any idee what you'll have to do up here?" asked Chet.

"Only in a general way."

"Wa'al," said Mr. Timson, "I c'n tell ye; an', what's **more**, I c'n tell ye, young man, 't you hain't no idee of what you're undertakin', an' ef you don't wish you was back in New York 'fore you git through I ain't no guesser."

"That is possible," said John readily, recalling his night and his breakfast that morning.

"Yes, sir," said the other. "Yes, *sir*; if you do what I've had to do, you'll do the hull darned thing, an' nobody to help you but Pele Hopkins, who don't count fer a row o' crooked pins. As fer's Dave's concerned," asserted the speaker with a wave of his hands, "he don't know no more about bankin' 'n a cat. He couldn't count a thousan' dollars in an hour, an', as for addin' up a row o' figures, he couldn't git it twice alike, I don't believe, if he was to be hung for't."

"He must understand the meaning of his own books and accounts, I should think," remarked John.

"Oh," said Chet scornfully, "anybody c'd do that. That's easy 'nough; but as fur 's the real bus'nis is concerned, he don't have nothin' to do with it. It's all ben left to me: chargin' an' creditin', postin', individule ledger, gen'ral ledger, bill-book, discount register, tickler, for'n register, checkin' off the N'York accounts, drawin' off statemunts f'm the ledgers an' bill-book, writin' letters--why, the' ain't an hour 'n the day in bus'nis hours some days that the's an hour 't I ain't busy 'bout somethin'. No, sir," continued Chet, "Dave don't give himself no trouble about the bus'nis.

All he does is to look after lendin' the money, an' seein' that it gits paid when the time comes, an' keep track of how much money the' is here an' in N'York, an' what notes is comin' due--an' a few things like that, that don't put pen to paper, ner take an hour of his time. Why, a man'll come in an' want to git a note done, an' it'll be 'All right,' or, 'Can't spare the money to-day,' all in a minute. He don't give it no thought at all, an' he ain't 'round here half the time. Now," said Chet, "when I work fer a man I like to have him 'round so 't I c'n say to him: 'Shall I do it so? or shall I do it *so*? shall I? or sha'n't I?' an' then when I make a mistake--'s anybody's liable to--he's as much to blame 's I be."

"I suppose, then," said John, "that you must have to keep Mr. Harum's private accounts also, seeing that he knows so little of details. I have been told that he is interested in a good many matters besides this business."

"Wa'al," replied Timson, somewhat disconcerted, "I suppose he must keep 'em himself in *some* kind of a fashion, an' I don't know a thing about any outside matters of his'n, though I suspicion he has got quite a few. He's got some books in that safe" (pointing with his finger) "an' he's got a safe in the vault, but if you'll believe *me*"--and the speaker looked as if he hardly expected it--"I hain't never so much as seen the inside of either one on 'em. No, sir," he declared, "I hain't no more idee of what's in them safes 'n you have. He's close, Dave Harum is," said Chet with a convincing motion of the head; "on the hull, the clostest man I ever see. I believe," he averred, "that if he was to lay out to keep it shut that lightnin' might strike him square in the mouth an' it wouldn't go in an eighth of an inch. An' yet," he added, "he c'n talk by the rod when he takes a notion."

"Must be a difficult person to get on with," commented John dryly.

"I couldn't stan' it no longer," declared Mr. Timson with the air of one who had endured to the end of virtue, "an' I says to him the other day, 'Wa'al,' I says, 'if I can't suit ye, mebbe you'd better suit yourself.'"

"Ah!" said John politely, seeing that some response was expected of him; "and what did he say to that?"

"He ast me," replied Chet, "if I meant by that to throw up the situation. 'Wa'al,' I says 'I'm sick enough to throw up most anythin',' I says, 'along with bein' found fault with fer nothin'.'"

"And then?" queried John, who had received the impression that the motion to adjourn had come from the other side of the house.

"Wa'al," replied Chet, not quite so confidently, "he said somethin' about my requirin' a larger spear of action, an' that he thought I'd do better on a mile track--some o' his hoss talk. That's another thing," said Timson, changing the subject. "He's all fer hosses. He'd sooner make a ten-dollar note on a hoss trade than a hunderd right here 'n this office. Many's the time right in bus'nis hours, when I've wanted to ask him how he wanted somethin' done, he'd be busy talkin' hoss, an' wouldn't pay no attention to me more'n 's if I wa'n't there."

"I am glad to feel," said John, "that you can not possibly have any unpleasant feeling toward me, seeing that you resigned as you did."

"Cert'nly not, cert'nly not," declared Timson, a little uneasily. "If it hadn't 'a' ben you, it would 'a' had to ben somebody else, an' now I seen you an' had a talk with you--Wa'al, I guess I better git back into the other room. Dave's liable to come in any minute. But," he said in parting, "I will give ye piece of advice: You keep enough laid by to pay your gettin' back to N'York. You may want it in a hurry," and with this parting shot the rejected one took his leave.

*   *   *   *   *

The bank parlor was lighted by a window and a glazed door in the rear wall, and another window on the south side. Mr. Harum's desk was by the rear, or west, window, which gave view of his house, standing some hundred feet back from the street. The south, or side, window afforded a view of his front yard and that of an adjoining dwelling, beyond which rose the wall of a mercantile block. Business was encroaching upon David's domain. Our friend stood looking out of the south window. To the left a bit of Main Street was visible, and the naked branches of the elms and maples with which it was bordered were waving defiantly at their rivals over the way, incited thereto by a northwest wind.

We invariably form a mental picture of every unknown person of whom we think at all. It may be so faint that we are unconscious of it at the time, or so vivid that it is always recalled until dissipated by seeing the person himself, or his likeness. But that we do so make a picture is proved by the fact that upon being confronted by the real features of the person in question we always experience a certain amount of surprise, even when we have not been conscious of a different conception of him.

Be that as it may, however, there was no question in John Lenox's mind as to the identity of the person who at last came briskly into the back office and interrupted his meditations. Rather under the middle height, he was broad-shouldered and deep-chested, with a clean-shaven, red face, with--not a mole--but a slight protuberance the size of half a large pea on the line from the nostril to the corner of the mouth; bald over the crown and to a line a couple of inches above the ear, below that thick and somewhat bushy hair of yellowish red, showing a mingling of gray; small but very blue eyes; a thick nose, of no classifiable shape, and a large mouth with the lips so pressed together as to produce a slightly downward and yet rather humorous curve at the corners. He was dressed in a sack coat of dark "pepper-and-salt," with waistcoat and trousers to match. A somewhat old-fashioned standing collar, flaring away from the throat, was encircled by a red cravat, tied in a bow under his chin. A diamond stud of perhaps two carats showed in the triangle of spotless shirt front, and on his head was a cloth cap with ear lappets. He accosted our friend with, "I reckon you must be Mr. Lenox. How are you? I'm glad to see you," tugging off a thick buckskin glove, and putting out a plump but muscular hand.

John thanked him as they shook hands, and "hoped he was well."

"Wa'al," said Mr. Harum, "I'm improvin' slowly. I've got so 'st I c'n set up long enough to have my bed made. Come last night, I s'pose? Anybody to the deepo to bring ye over? This time o' year once 'n a while the' don't nobody go over for passengers."

John said that he had had no trouble. A man by the name of Robinson had brought him and his luggage.

"E-up!" said David with a nod, backing up to the fire which was burning in the grate of the Franklin stove, "'Dug' Robinson. 'D he do the p'lite thing in the matter of questions an' gen'ral conversation?" he asked with a grin. John laughed in reply to this question.

"Where'd you put up?" asked David, John said that he passed the night at the Eagle Hotel. Mr. Harum had seen Dick Larrabee that morning and heard what he had to say of our friend's reception, but he liked to get his information from original sources.

"Make ye putty comf'table?" he asked, turning to eject a mouthful into the fire.

"I got along pretty well under the circumstances," said John.

Mr. Harum did not press the inquiry. "How'd you leave the gen'ral?" he inquired.

"He seemed to be well," replied John, "and he wished to be kindly remembered to you."

"Fine man, the gen'ral," declared David, well pleased. "Fine man all 'round. Word's as good as his bond. Yes, sir, when the gen'ral gives his warrant, I don't care whether I see the critter or not. Know him much?"

"He and my father were old friends, and I have known him a good many years," replied John, adding, "he has been very kind and friendly to me."

"Set down, set down," said Mr. Harum, pointing to a chair. Seating himself, he took off his cap and dropped it with his gloves on the floor. "How long you ben here in the office?" he asked.

"Perhaps half an hour," was the reply.

"I meant to have ben here when you come," said the banker, "but I got hendered about a matter of a hoss I'm looking at. I guess I'll shut that door," making a move toward the one into the front office.

"Allow me," said John, getting up and closing it.

"May's well shut the other one while you're about it. Thank you," as John resumed his seat. "I hain't got nothin' very private, but I'm 'fraid of distractin' Timson's mind. Did he int'duce himself?"

"Yes," said John, "we introduced ourselves and had a few minutes conversation."

"Gin ye his hull hist'ry an' a few relations throwed in?"

"There was hardly time for that," said John, smiling.

"Rubbed a little furn'ture polish into my char'cter an' repitation?" insinuated Mr. Harum.

"Most of our talk was on the subject of his duties and responsibilities," was John's reply. ("Don't cal'late to let on any more'n he cal'lates to," thought David to himself.)

"Allowed he run the hull shebang, didn't he?"

"He seemed to have a pretty large idea of what was required of one in his place," admitted the witness.

"Kind o' friendly, was he?" asked David.

"Well," said John, "after we had talked for a while I said to him that I was glad to think that he could have no unpleasant feeling toward me, seeing that he had given up the place of his own preference, and he assured me that he had none."

David turned and looked at John for an instant, with a twinkle in his eye. The younger man returned the look and smiled slightly. David laughed outright.

"I guess you've seen folks before," he remarked.

"I have never met any one exactly like Mr. Timson, I think," said our friend with a slight laugh.

"Fortunitly them kind is rare," observed Mr. Harum dryly, rising and going to his desk, from a drawer of which he produced a couple of cigars, one of which he proffered to John, who, for the first time in his life, during the next half hour regretted that he was a smoker. David sat for two or three minutes puffing diligently, and then took the weed out of his mouth and looked contemplatively at it.

"How do you like that cigar?" he inquired.

"It burns very nicely," said the victim. Mr. Harum emitted a cough which was like a chuckle, or a chuckle which was like a cough, and relapsed into silence again. Presently he turned his head, looked curiously at the young man for a moment, and then turned his glance again to the fire.

"I've ben wonderin' some," he said, "pertic'lerly since I see you, how 't was 't you wanted to come up here to Homeville. Gen'l Wolsey gin his warrant, an' so I reckon you hadn't ben gettin' into no scrape nor nothin'," and again he looked sharply at the young man at his side.

"Did the general say nothing of my affairs?" the latter asked.

"No," replied David, "all 't he said was in a gen'ral way that he'd knowed you an' your folks a good while, an' he thought you'd be jest the feller I was lookin' fer. Mebbe he reckoned that if you wanted your story told, you'd ruther tell it yourself."

CHAPTER XIV.

Whatever might have been John's repugnance to making a confidant of the man whom he had known but for half an hour, he acknowledged to himself that the other's curiosity was not only natural but proper. He could not but know that in appearance and manner he was in marked contrast with those whom the man had so far seen. He divined the fact that his coming from a great city to settle down in a village town would furnish matter for surprise and conjecture, and felt that it would be to his advantage with the man who was to be his employer that he should be perfectly and obviously frank upon all matters of his own which might be properly mentioned. He had an instinctive feeling that Harum combined acuteness and suspiciousness to a very large degree, and he had also a feeling that the old man's confidence, once gained, would not be easily shaken. So he told his hearer so much of his history as he thought pertinent, and David listened without interruption or comment, save an occasional "E-um'm."

"And here I am," John remarked in conclusion.

"Here you *be*, fer a fact," said David. "Wa'al, the's worse places 'n Homeville--after you git used to it," he added in qualification. "I ben back here a matter o' thirteen or fourteen year now, an' am gettin' to feel my way 'round putty well; but not havin' ben in these parts fer putty nigh thirty year, I found it ruther lonesome to start with, an' I guess if it hadn't 'a' ben fer Polly I wouldn't 'a' stood it. But up to the time I come back she hadn't never ben ten mile away f'm here in her hull life, an' I couldn't budge her. But then," he remarked, "while Homeville aint a metrop'lis, it's some a diff'rent place f'm what it used to be--in some *ways*. Polly's my sister," he added by way of explanation.

"Well," said John, with rather a rueful laugh, "if it has taken you all that time to get used to it the outlook for me is not very encouraging, I'm afraid."

"Wa'al," remarked Mr. Harum, "I'm apt to speak in par'bles sometimes. I guess you'll git along after a spell, though it mayn't set fust rate on your stomech till you git used to the diet. Say," he said after a moment, "if you'd had a couple o' thousan' more, do you think you'd 'a' stuck to the law bus'nis?"

"I'm sure I don't know," replied John, "but I am inclined to think not. General Wolsey told me that if I were very anxious to go on with it he would help me, but after what I told him he advised me to write to you."

"He did, did he?"

"Yes," said John, "and after what I had gone through I was not altogether sorry to come away."

"Wa'al," said Mr. Harum thoughtfully, "if I was to lose what little I've got, an' had to give up livin' in the way I was used to, an' couldn't even keep a hoss, I c'n allow 't I might be willin' fer a change of scene to make a fresh start in. Yes, sir, I guess I would. Wa'al," looking at his watch, "I've got to go now, an' I'll see ye later, mebbe. You feel like takin' holt to-day?"

"Oh, yes," said John with alacrity.

"All right," said Mr. Harum. "You tell Timson what you want, an' make him show you everythin'. He understands, an' I've paid him for't. He's agreed to stay any time in reason 't you want him, but I guess," he added with a laugh, "'t you c'n pump him dry 'n a day or two. It haint rained wisdom an' knowlidge in his part o' the country fer a consid'able spell."

David stood for a moment drawing on his gloves, and then, looking at John with his characteristic chuckle, continued:

"Allowed he'd ben drawin' the hull load, did he? Wa'al, sir, the truth on't is 't he never come to a hill yet, 'f 't wa'n't more 'n a foot high, but what I had to git out an' push; nor never struck a turn in the road but what I had to take him by the head an' lead him into it." With which Mr. Harum put on his overcoat and cap and departed.

    *   *   *   *   *

Mr. Timson was leaning over the counter in animated controversy with a man on the outside who had evidently asserted or quoted (the quotation is the usual weapon: it has a double barb and can be wielded with comparative safety) something of a wounding effect.

"No, sir," exclaimed Chet, with a sounding slap on the counter, "no, sir! The' ain't one word o' truth in't. I said myself, 'I won't stan' it,' I says, 'not f'm you ner nobody else,' I says, 'an' what's more,' says I--" The expression in the face of Mr. Timson's tormentor caused that gentleman to break off and look around. The man on the outside grinned, stared at John a moment, and went out, and Timson turned and said, as John came forward, "Hello! The old man picked ye to pieces all he wanted to?"

"We are through for the day, I fancy," said our friend, smiling, "and if you are ready to begin my lessons I am ready to take them. Mr. Harum told me that you would be good enough to show me what was necessary."

"All right," said Mr. Timson readily enough, and so John began his first day's work in David's office. He was surprised and encouraged to find how much his experience in Rush & Company's office stood him in hand, and managed to acquire in a comparatively short time a pretty fair comprehension of the system which prevailed in "Harum's bank," notwithstanding the incessant divagations of his instructor.

It was decided between Timson and our friend that on the following day the latter should undertake the office work under supervision, and the next morning John was engaged upon the preliminaries of the day's business when his employer came in and seated himself at his desk in the back room. After a few minutes, in which he was busy with his letters, he appeared in the doorway of the front room. He did not speak, for John saw him, and, responding to a backward toss of the head, followed him into the "parlor," and at an intimation of the same silent character shut the doors. Mr. Harum sat down at his desk, and John stood awaiting his pleasure.

"How 'd ye make out yestidy?" he asked. "Git anythin' out of old tongue-tied?" pointing with his thumb toward the front room.

"Oh, yes," said John, smiling, as he recalled the unceasing flow of words which had enveloped Timson's explanations.

"How much longer do you think you'll have to have him 'round?" asked Mr. Harum.

"Well," said John, "of course your customers are strangers to me, but so far as the routine of the office is concerned I think I can manage after to-day. But I shall have to appeal to you rather often for a while until I get thoroughly acquainted with my work."

"Good fer you," said David. "You've took holt a good sight quicker 'n I thought ye would, an' I'll spend more or less time 'round here fer a while, or be where you c'n reach me. It's like this," he continued; "Chet's a helpless kind of critter, fer all his braggin' an' talk, an' I ben feelin' kind o' wambly about turnin' him loose--though the Lord knows," he said with feeling, "'t I've had bother enough with him to kill a tree. But anyway I wrote to some folks I know up to Syrchester to git something fer him to do, an' I got a letter to send him along, an' mebbe they'd give him a show.

See?"

"Yes, sir," said John, "and if you are willing to take the chances of my mistakes I will undertake to get on without him."

"All right," said the banker, "we'll call it a heat--and, say, don't let on what I've told you. I want to see how long it'll take to git all over the village that he didn't ask no odds o' nobody. Hadn't ben out o' a job three days 'fore the' was a lot o' chances, an' all 't he had to do was to take his pick out o' the lot on 'em."

"Really?" said John.

"Yes, sir," said David. "Some folks is gaited that way. Amusin', ain't it?--Hullo, Dick! Wa'al?"

"Willis'll give two hunderd fer the sorr'l colt," said the incomer, whom John recognized as one of the loungers in the Eagle bar the night of his arrival.

"E-um'm!" said David. "Was he speakin' of any pertic'ler colt, or sorril colts in gen'ral? I hain't got the only one the' is, I s'pose."

Dick merely laughed. "Because," continued the owner of the "sorril colt," "if Steve Willis wants to lay in sorril colts at two hunderd a piece, I ain't goin' to gain-say him, but you tell him that two-forty-nine ninety-nine won't buy the one in my barn." Dick laughed again.

John made a move in the direction of the front room.

"Hold on a minute," said David. "Shake hands with Mr. Larrabee."

"Seen ye before," said Dick, as they shook hands. "I was in the barroom when you come in the other night," and then he laughed as at the recollection of some-thing very amusing.

John flushed a little and said, a bit stiffly, "I remember you were kind enough to help about my luggage."

"Excuse me," said Dick, conscious of the other's manner. "I wa'n't laughin' at you, that is, not in pertic'ler. I couldn't see your face when Ame offered ye pie an' doughnuts instid of beefsteak an' fixins. I c'd only guess at that; but Ame's face was enough fer me," and Dick went off into another cachinnation.

David's face indicated some annoyance. "Oh, shet up," he exclaimed. "You'd keep that yawp o' your'n goin', I believe, if it was the judgment day."

"Wa'al," said Dick with a grin, "I expect the' might be some fun to be got out o' *that*, if a feller wa'n't worryin' too much about his own skin; an' as fur's I'm concerned----" Dick's further views on the subject of that momentous occasion were left unexplained. A significant look in David's face caused the speaker to break off and turn toward the door, through which came two men, the foremost a hulking, shambling fellow, with an expression of repellent sullenness. He came forward to within about ten feet of David's desk, while his companion halted near the door. David eyed him in silence.

"I got this here notice this mornin'," said the man, "sayin' 't my note 'd be due to-morrer, an' 'd have to be paid."

"Wa'al," said David, with his arm over the back of his chair and his left hand resting on his desk, "that's so, ain't it?"

"Mebbe so," was the fellow's reply, "fur 's the comin' due 's concerned, but the payin' part 's another matter."

"Was you cal'latin' to have it renewed?" asked David, leaning a little forward.

"No," said the man coolly, "I don't know 's I want to renew it fer any pertic'ler time, an' I guess it c'n run along fer a while jest as 't is." John looked at Dick Larrabee. He was watching David's face with an expression of the utmost enjoyment. David twisted his chair a little more to the right and out from the desk.

"You think it c'n run along, do ye?" he asked suavely. "I'm glad to have your views on the subject. Wa'al, I guess it kin, too, until *to-morro'* at four o'clock, an' after that you c'n settle with lawyer Johnson or the sheriff." The man uttered a disdainful laugh.

"I guess it'll puzzle ye some to c'lect it," he said. Mr. Harum's bushy red eyebrows met above his nose.

"Look here, Bill Montaig," he said, "I know more 'bout this matter 'n you think for. I know 't you ben makin' your brags that you'd fix me in this deal. You allowed that you'd set up usury in the fust place, an' if that didn't work I'd find you was execution proof anyways. That's so, ain't it?"

"That's about the size on't," said Montaig, putting his feet a little farther apart. David had risen from his chair.

"You didn't talk that way," proceeded the latter, "when you come whinin' 'round here to git that money in the fust place, an' as I reckon some o' the facts in the case has slipped out o' your mind since that time, I guess I'd better jog your mem'ry a little."

It was plain from the expression of Mr. Montaig's countenance that his confidence in the strength of his position was not quite so assured as at first, but he maintained his attitude as well as in him lay.

"In the fust place," David began his assault, "*I* didn't **lend** ye the money. I borr'ed it for ye on my indorsement, an' charged ye fer doin' it, as I told ye at the time; an' another thing that you appear to forgit is that you signed a paper statin' that you was wuth, in good and available pusson'ls, free an' clear, over five hunderd dollars, an' that the statement was made to me with the view of havin' me indorse your note fer one-fifty. Rec'lect that?" David smiled grimly at the look of disconcert which, in spite of himself, appeared in Bill's face.

"I don't remember signin' no paper," he said doggedly.

"Jest as like as not," remarked Mr. Harum. "What *you* was thinkin' of about that time was gittin' that **money**."

"I'd like to see that paper," said Bill, with a pretence of incredulity.

"You'll see it when the time comes," asserted David, with an emphatic nod. He squared himself, planting his feet apart, and, thrusting his hands deep in his coat pockets, faced the discomfited yokel.

"Do you think, Bill Montaig," he said, with measureless contempt, "that I didn't know who I was dealin' with? that I didn't know what a low-lived, roost-robbin' skunk you was? an' didn't know how to protect myself agin such an'muls as you be? Wa'al, I did, an' don't you stop thinkin' 'bout it--an'," he added, shaking his finger at the object of his scorn, "*you'll pay that note* or I'll put ye where the dogs won't bite ye," and with that he turned on his heel and resumed his seat. Bill stood for a minute with a scowl of rage and defeat in his lowering face.

"Got any further bus'nis with me?" inquired Mr. Harum. "Anythin' more 't I c'n oblige ye about?" There was no answer.

"I asked you," said David, raising his voice and rising to his feet, "if you had any further bus'nis with me."

"I dunno's I have," was the sullen response.

"All right," said David. "That bein' the case, an' as I've got somethin' to do beside wastin' my time on such wuthless pups as you be, I'll thank you to git out. There's the door," he added, pointing to it.

"He, he, he, he, ho, ho, ha, h-o-o-o-o-o!" came from the throat of Dick Larrabee. This was too much for the exasperated Bill, and he erred (to put it mildly) in raising his arm and advancing a step toward his creditor. He was not swift enough to take the second, however, for David, with amazing quickness, sprang upon him, and twisting him around, rushed him out of the door, down the passage, and out of the front door, which was obligingly held open by an outgoing client, who took in the situation and gave precedence to Mr. Montaig. His companion, who so far had taken no part, made a motion to interfere, but John, who stood nearest to him, caught him by the collar and jerked him back, with the suggestion that it would be better to let the two have it out by themselves. David came back rather breathless and very red in the face, but evidently in exceeding good humor.

"Scat my ----!" he exclaimed. "Hain't had such a good tussle I dunno when."

"Bill's considered ruther an awk'ard customer," remarked Dick. "I guess he hain't had no such handlin' fer quite a while."

"Sho!" exclaimed Mr. Harum. "The' ain't nothin' to him but wind an' meanness. Who was that feller with him?"

"Name 's Smith, I believe," replied Dick. "Guess Bill brought him along fer a witness, an' I reckon he seen all he wanted to. I'll bet *his* neck's achin' some," added Mr. Larrabee with a laugh.

"How's that?" asked David.

"Well, he made a move to tackle you as you was escortin' Bill out, an' Mr. Lenox there caught him in the collar an' gin him a jerk that'd 'a' landed him on his back," said Dick, "if," turning to John, "you hadn't helt holt of him. You putty nigh broke his neck. He went off--he, he, he, he, ho!--wrigglin' it to make sure."

"I used more force than was necessary, I'm afraid," said Billy Williams's pupil, "but there wasn't much time to calculate."

"Much obliged," said David with a nod.

"Not at all," protested John, laughing. "I have enjoyed a great deal this morning."

"It *has* ben ruther pleasant," remarked David with a chuckle, "but you mustn't cal'late on havin' such fun ev'ry mornin'."

John went into the business office, leaving the banker and Dick.

"Say," said the latter when they were alone, "that young man o' your'n 's quite a feller. He took care o' that big Smith chap with one hand; an' say, *you* c'n git round on your pins 'bout 's lively 's they make 'em, I guess. I swan!" he exclaimed, slapping his thigh and shaking with laughter, "the hull thing head-an'-shouldered any show I seen lately." And then for a while they fell to talking of the "sorril colt" and other things.

CHAPTER XV.

When John went back to the office after the noonday intermission it was manifest that something had happened to Mr. Timson, and that the something was of a nature extremely gratifying to that worthy gentleman. He was beaming with satisfaction and rustling with importance. Several times during the afternoon he appeared to be on the point of confiding his news, but in the face of the interruptions which occurred, or which he feared might check the flow of his communication, he managed to restrain himself till after the closing of the office. But scarcely were the shutters up (at the willing hands of Peleg Hopkins) when he turned to John and, looking at him sharply, said, "Has Dave said anythin' 'bout my leavin'?"

"He told me he expected you would stay as long as might be necessary to get me well started," said John non-committally, mindful of Mr. Harum's injunction.

"Jest like him," declared Chet. "Jest like him for all the world; but the fact o' the matter is 't I'm goin' to-morro'. I s'pose he thought," reflected Mr. Timson, "thet he'd ruther you'd find it out yourself than to have to break it to ye, 'cause then, don't ye see, after I was gone he c'd lay the hull thing at my door."

"Really," said John, "I should have said that he ought to have told me."

"Wa'al," said Chet encouragingly, "mebbe you'll git along somehow, though I'm 'fraid you'll have more or less trouble; but I told Dave that as fur 's I c'd see, mebbe you'd do 's well 's most anybody he c'd git that didn't know any o' the customers, an' hadn't never done any o' this kind o' work before."

"Thank you very much," said John. "And so you are off to-morrow, are you?"

"Got to be," declared Mr. Timson. "I'd 'a' liked to stay with you a spell longer, but the's a big concern f'm out of town that as soon as they heard I was at libe'ty wrote for me to come right along up, an' I s'pose I hadn't ought to keep 'em waitin'."

"No, I should think not," said John, "and I congratulate you upon having located yourself so quickly."

"Oh!" said Mr. Timson, with ineffable complacency, "I hain't give myself no worry; I hain't lost no sleep. I've allowed all along that Dave Harum'd find out that he wa'n't the unly man that needed my kind o' work, an' I ain't meanin' any disrispect to you when I say 't--"

"Just so," said John. "I quite understand. Nobody could expect to take just the place with him that you have filled. And, by the way," he added, "as you are going in the morning, and I may not see you again, would you kindly give me the last balance sheets of the two ledgers and the bill-book. I suppose, of course, that they are brought down to the first of the month, and I shall want to have them."

"Oh, yes, cert'nly, of course--wa'al I guess Dave's got 'em," replied Chet, looking considerably disconcerted, "but I'll look 'em up in the mornin'. My train don't go till ten o'clock, an' I'll see you 'bout any little last thing in the mornin'--but I guess I've got to go now on account of a lot of things. You c'n shut up, can't ye?"

Whereupon Mr. Timson made his exit, and not long afterward David came in. By that time everything had been put away, the safe and vault closed, and Peleg had departed with the mail and his freedom for the rest of the day.

"Wa'al," said Mr. Harum, lifting himself to a seat on the counter, "how've you made out? All O.K.?"

"Yes," replied John, "I think so."

"Where's Chet?"

"He went away some few minutes ago. He said he had a good many things to attend to as he was leaving in the morning."

"E-um'm!" said David incredulously. "I guess 't won't take him long to close up his matters. Did he leave ev'rything in good shape? Cash all right, an' so on?"

"I think so," said John. "The cash is right I am sure."

"How 'bout the books?"

"I asked him to let me have the balance sheets, and he said that you must have them, but that he would come in in the morning and--well, what he said was that he would see me in the morning, and, as he put it, look after any little last thing."

"E-um'm!" David grunted. "He won't do no such a thing. We've seen the last of him, you bet, an' a good riddance. He'll take the nine o'clock to-night, that's what he'll do. Drawed his pay, I guess, didn't he?"

"He said he was to be paid for this month," answered John, "and took sixty dollars. Was that right?"

"Yes," said David, nodding his head absently. "What was it he said about them statements?" he inquired after a moment.

"He said he guessed you must have them."

"E-um'm!" was David's comment. "What'd he say about leavin'?"

John laughed and related the conversation as exactly as he could.

"What'd I tell ye," said Mr. Harum, with a short laugh. "Mebbe he won't go till to-morro', after all," he remarked. "He'll want to put in a leetle more time tellin' how he was sent for in a hurry by that big concern f'm out of town 't he's goin' to."

"Upon my word, I can't understand it," said John, "knowing that you can contradict him."

"Wa'al," said David, "he'll allow that if he gits in the fust word, he'll take the pole. It don't matter anyway, long 's he's gone. I guess you an' me c'n pull the load, can't we?" and he dropped down off the counter and started to go out. "By the way," he said, halting a moment, "can't you come in to tea at six o'clock? I want to make ye acquainted with Polly, an' she's itchin' to see ye."

"I shall be delighted," said John.

    *   *   *   *   *

"Polly," said David, "I've ast the young feller to come to tea, but don't you say the word 'Eagle,' to him. You c'n show your ign'rance 'bout all the other kinds of birds an' animals you ain't familiar with," said the unfeeling brother, "but leave eagles alone."

"What you up to now?" she asked, but she got no answer but a laugh.

From a social point of view the entertainment could not be described as a very brilliant success. Our friend was tired and hungry. Mr. Harum was unusually taciturn, and Mrs. Bixbee, being under her brother's interdict as regarded the subject which, had it been allowed discussion, might have opened the way, was at a loss for generalities. But John afterward got upon terms of the friendliest nature with that kindly soul.

CHAPTER XVI.

Some weeks after John's assumption of his duties in the office of David Harum, Banker, that gentleman sat reading his New York paper in the "wing settin'-room," after tea, and Aunt Polly was occupied with the hemming of a towel. The able editorial which David was perusing was strengthening his conviction that all the intelligence and virtue of the country were monopolized by the Republican party, when his meditations were broken in upon by Mrs. Bixbee, who knew nothing and cared less about the Force Bill or the doctrine of protection to American industries.

"You hain't said nothin' fer quite a while about the bank," she remarked. "Is Mr. Lenox gittin' along all right?"

"Guess he's gittin' into condition as fast as c'd be expected," said David, between two lines of his editorial.

"It must be awful lonesome fer him," she observed, to which there was no reply.

"Ain't it?" she asked, after an interval.

"Ain't what?" said David, looking up at her.

"Awful lonesome," she reiterated.

"Guess nobody ain't ever very lonesome when you're 'round an' got your breath," was the reply. "What you talkin' about?"

"I ain't talkin' about you, 't any rate," said Mrs. Bixbee. "I was sayin' it must be awful lonesome fer Mr. Lenox up here where he don't know a soul hardly, an' livin' at that hole of a tavern."

"I don't see 't you've any cause to complain long's he don't," said David, hoping that it would not come to his sister's ears that he had, for reasons of his own, discouraged any attempt on John's part to better his quarters, "an' he hain't ben very lonesome daytimes, I guess, so fur, 'thout he's ben makin' work fer himself to kill time."

"What do you mean?"

"Wa'al," said David, "we found that Chet hadn't done more 'n to give matters a lick an' a promise in most a year. He done just enough to keep up the day's work an' no more an' the upshot on't is that John's had to put in consid'able time to git things straightened out."

"What a shame!" exclaimed Aunt Polly.

"Keeps him f'm bein' lonesome," remarked her brother with a grin.

"An' he hain't had no time to himself!" she protested. "I don't believe you've made up your mind yet whether you're goin' to like him, an' I don't believe he'll **stay** anyway."

"I've told more 'n forty-leven times," said Mr. Harum, looking up over his paper, "that I thought we was goin' to make a hitch of it, an' he cert'nly hain't said nuthin' 'bout leavin', an' I guess he won't fer a while, tavern or no tavern. He's got a putty stiff upper lip of his own, I reckon," David further remarked, with a short laugh, causing Mrs. Bixbee to look up at him inquiringly, which look the speaker answered with a nod, saying, "Me an' him had a little go-round to-day."

"You hain't had no **words**, hev ye?" she asked anxiously.

"Wa'al, we didn't have what ye might call **words**. I was jest tryin' a little experiment with him."

"Humph," she remarked, "you're alwus tryin' exper'ments on somebody, an' you'll be liable to git ketched at it some day."

"Exceptin' on you," said David. "You don't think I'd try any experiments on you, do ye?"

"Me!" she cried. "You're at me the hull endurin' time, an' you know it."

"Wa'al, but Polly," said David insinuatingly, "you don't know how int'restin' you **be**."

"Glad you think so," she declared, with a sniff and a toss of the head. "What you ben up to with Mr. Lenox?"

"Oh, nuthin' much," replied Mr. Harum, making a feint of resuming his reading.

"Be ye goin' to tell me, or--air ye too *'shamed* on't?" she added with a little laugh, which somewhat turned the tables on her teasing brother.

"Wa'al, I laid out to try an' read this paper," he said, spreading it out on his lap, "but," resignedly, "I guess 't ain't no use. Do you know what a count'fit bill is?" he asked.

"I dunno 's I ever see one," she said, "but I s'pose I do. They're agin the law, ain't they?"

"The's a number o' things that's agin the law," remarked David dryly.

"Wa'al?" ejaculated Mrs. Bixbee after a moment of waiting.

"Wa'al," said David, "the' ain't much to tell, but it's plain I don't git no peace till you git it out of me. It was like this: The young feller's took holt everywhere else right off, but handlin' the money bothered him consid'able at fust. It was slow work, an' I c'd see it myself; but he's gettin' the hang on't now. Another thing I expected he'd run up agin was count'fits. The' ain't so very many on 'em round now-a-days, but the' is now an' then one. He allowed to me that he was liable to get stuck at fust, an' I reckoned he would. But I never said nuthin' about it, nor ast no questions until to-day; an' this afternoon I come in to look 'round, an' I says to him, 'What luck have you had with your money? Git any bad?' I says. 'Wa'al,' he says, colorin' up a little, 'I don't know how many I may have took in an' paid out agin without knowin' it,' he says, 'but the' was a couple sent back from New York out o' that package that went down last Friday.'"

"'What was they?' I says.

"'A five an' a ten,' he says.

"'Where be they?' I says.

"'They're in the draw there--they're ruther int'restin' objects of study,' he says, kind o' laughin' on the wrong side of his mouth.

"'Countin' 'em in the cash?' I says, an' with that he kind o' reddened up agin. 'No, sir,' he says, 'I charged 'em up to my own account, an' I've kept 'em to compare with.'

"'You hadn't ought to done that,' I says.

"'You think I ought to 'a' put 'em in the fire at once?' says he.

"'No,' I says, 'that wa'n't what I meant. Why didn't you mix 'em up with the other money, an' let 'em go when you was payin' out? Anyways,' I says, 'you charge 'em up to profit an' loss if you're goin' to charge 'em to anythin', an' let me have 'em,' I says.

"'What'll you do with 'em?' he says to me, kind o' shuttin' his jaws together.

"'I'll take care on 'em,' I says. 'They mayn't be good enough to send down to New York,' I says, 'but they'll go around here all right--jest as good as any other,' I says, 'long 's you keep 'em movin'.'"

"David Harum!" cried Polly, who, though not quite comprehending some of the technicalities of detail, was fully alive to the turpitude of the suggestion. "I hope to gracious he didn't think you was in earnest. Why, s'pose they was passed around, wouldn't somebody git stuck with 'em in the long run? You know they would." Mrs. Bixbee occasionally surprised her brother with unexpected penetration, but she seldom got much recognition of it.

"I see by the paper," he remarked, "that the' was a man died in Pheladelphy one day last week," which piece of barefaced irrelevancy elicited no notice from Mrs. Bixbee.

"What more did he say?" she demanded.

"Wa'al," responded Mr. Harum with a laugh, "he said that he didn't see why I should be a loser by his mistakes, an' that as fur as the bills was concerned they belonged to him, an' with that," said the narrator, "Mister Man gits 'em out of the draw an' jest marches into the back room an' puts the dum things int' the fire."

"He done jest right," declared Aunt Polly, "an' you know it, don't ye now?"

"Wa'al," said David, "f'm his standpoint--f'm his standpoint, I guess he did, an'," rubbing his chin with two fingers of his left hand, "it's a putty dum good standpoint too. I've ben lookin'," he added reflectively, "fer an honest man fer quite a number o' years, an' I guess I've found him; yes'm, I guess I've found him."

"An' be you goin' to let him lose that fifteen dollars?" asked the practical Polly, fixing her brother with her eyes.

"Wa'al," said David, with a short laugh, "what c'n I do with such an obst'nit critter 's he is? He jest backed into the britchin', an' I couldn't do nothin' with him." Aunt Polly sat over her sewing for a minute or two without taking a stitch.

"I'm sorry you done it," she said at last.

"I dunno but I did make ruther a mess of it," admitted Mr. Harum.

CHAPTER XVII.

It was the 23d of December, and shortly after the closing hour. Peleg had departed and our friend had just locked the vault when David came into the office and around behind the counter.

"Be you in any hurry?" he asked.

John said he was not, whereupon Mr. Harum hitched himself up onto a high office stool, with his heels on the spindle, and leaned sideways upon the desk, while John stood facing him with his left arm upon the desk.

"John," said David, "do ye know the Widdo' Cullom?"

"No" said John, "but I know who she is--a tall, thin woman, who walks with a slight stoop and limp. I noticed her and asked her name because there was something about her looks that attracted my attention--as though at some time she might have seen better days."

"That's the party," said David. "She has seen better days, but she's eat an' drunk sorro' mostly fer goin' on thirty year, an' darned little else good share o' the time, I reckon."

"She has that appearance certainly," said John.

"Yes sir," said David, "she's had a putty tough time, the widdo' has, an' yet," he proceeded after a momentary pause, "the' was a time when the Culloms was some o' the king-pins o' this hull region. They used to own quarter o' the county, an' they lived in the big house up on the hill where Doc Hays lives now. That was considered to be the finest place anywheres 'round here in them days. I used to think the Capitol to Washington must be somethin' like the Cullom house, an' that Billy P. (folks used to call him Billy P. 'cause his father's name was William an' his was William Parker), an' that Billy P. 'd jest 's like 's not be president. I've changed my mind some on the subject of presidents since I was a boy."

Here Mr. Harum turned on his stool, put his right hand into his sack-coat pocket, extracted therefrom part of a paper of "Maple Dew," and replenished his left cheek with an ample wad of "fine-cut." John took advantage of the break to head off what he had reason to fear might turn into a lengthy digression from the matter in hand by saying, "I beg pardon, but how does it happen that Mrs. Cullom is in such circumstances? Has the family all died out?"

"Wa'al," said David, "they're most on 'em dead, all on 'em, in fact, except the widdo's son Charley, but as fur 's the family 's concerned, it more 'n *died* out--it *gin* out! 'D ye ever hear of Jim Wheton's calf? Wa'al, Jim brought three or four veals into town one spring to sell. Dick Larrabee used to peddle meat them days. Dick looked 'em over an' says, 'Look here, Jim,' he says, 'I guess you got a "deakin" in that lot,' he says. 'I dunno what you mean,' says Jim. 'Yes, ye do, goll darn ye!' says Dick, 'yes, ye do. You didn't never kill that calf, an' you know it. That calf died, that's what that calf done. Come, now, own up,' he says. 'Wa'al,' says Jim, 'I didn't **kill** it, an' it didn't **die** nuther--it jest kind o' **gin out**.'"

John joined in the laugh with which the narrator rewarded his own effort, and David went on: "Yes, sir, they jest petered out. Old Billy, Billy P.'s father, inheritid all the prop'ty--never done a stroke of work in his life. He had a collidge education, went to Europe, an' all that', an' before he was fifty year old he hardly ever come near the old place after he was growed up. The land was all farmed out on shares, an' his farmers mostly bamboozled him the hull time. He got consid'able income, of course, but as things went along and they found out how slack he was they kept bitin' off bigger chunks all the time, an' sometimes he didn't git even the core. But all the time when he wanted money--an' he wanted it putty often I tell ye--the easiest way was to stick on a morgidge; an' after a spell it got so 't he'd have to give a morgidge to pay the int'rist on the other morgidges."

"But," said John, "was there nothing to the estate but land?"

"Oh, yes," said David, "old Billy's father left him some consid'able pers'nal, but after that was gone he went into the morgidge bus'nis as I tell ye. He lived mostly up to Syrchester and around, an' when he got married he bought a place in Syrchester and lived there till Billy P. was about twelve or thirteen year old, an' he was about fifty. By that time he'd got 'bout to the end of his rope, an' the' wa'n't nothin' for it but to come back here to Homeville an' make the most o' what the' was left--an' that's what he done, let alone that he didn't make the most on't to any pertic'ler extent. Mis' Cullom, his wife, wa'n't no help to him. She was a city woman an' didn't take to the country no way, but when she died it broke old Billy up wus 'n ever. She peaked an' pined, an' died when Billy P. was about fifteen or so. Wa'al, Billy P. an' the old man wrastled along somehow, an' the boy went to collidge fer a year or so. How they ever got along 's they did I dunno. The' was a story that some far-off relation left old Billy some money, an' I guess that an' what they got off'm what farms was left carried 'em along till Billy P. was twenty-five or so, an' then he up an' got married. That was the crownin' stroke," remarked David. "She was one o' the village girls--respectable folks, more 'n ordinary good lookin' an' high steppin', an' had had some schoolin'. But the old man was prouder 'n a cock-turkey, an' thought nobody wa'n't quite good enough fer Billy P., an' all along kind o' reckoned that he'd marry some money an' git a new start. But when he got married--on the quiet, you know, cause he knowed the old man would kick--wa'al, that killed the trick, an' the old man into the bargain. It took the gumption all out of him, an' he didn't live a year. Wa'al, sir, it was curious, but, 's I was told, putty much the hull village sided with the old man. The Culloms was kind o' kings in them days, an' folks wa'n't so one-man's-good's-anotherish as they be now. They thought Billy P. done wrong, though they didn't have nothin' to say 'gainst the girl neither--an' she's very much respected, Mis' Cullom is, an' as fur's I'm concerned, I've alwus guessed she kept Billy P. goin' full as long 's any one could. But 't wa'n't no use--that is to say, the sure thing come to pass. He had a nom'nal title to a good deal o' prop'ty, but the equity in most on't if it had ben to be put up wa'n't enough to pay fer the papers. You see, the' ain't never ben no real cash value in farm prop'ty in these parts. The' ain't ben hardly a dozen changes in farm titles, 'cept by inher'tance or foreclosure, in thirty years. So Billy P. didn't make no effort. Int'rist's one o' them things that keeps right on nights an' Sundays. He jest had the deeds made out and handed 'em over when the time came to settle. The' was some village lots though that was clear, that fetched him in some money from time to time until they was all gone but one, an' that's the one Mis' Cullom lives on now. It was consid'able more'n a lot--in fact, a putty sizable place. She thought the sun rose an' set where Billy P. was, but she took a crotchit in her head, and wouldn't ever sign no papers fer that, an' lucky fer him too. The' was a house on to it, an' he had a roof over his head anyway when he died six or seven years after he married, an' left her with a boy to raise. How she got along all them years till Charley got big enough to help, I swan! I don't know. She took in sewin' an' washin', an' went out to cook an' nurse, an' all that, but I reckon the' was now an' then times when they didn't overload their stomechs much, nor have to open the winders to cool off. But she held onto that prop'ty of her'n like a pup to a root. It was putty well out when Billy P. died, but the village has growed up to it. The's some good lots could be cut out on't, an' it backs up to the river where the current's enough to make a mighty good power fer a 'lectric light. I know some fellers that are talkin' of startin' a plant here, an' it ain't out o' sight that they'd pay a good price fer the river front, an' enough land to build on. Fact on't is, it's got to be a putty valu'ble piece o' prop'ty, more 'n she cal'lates on, I reckon."

Here Mr. Harum paused, pinching his chin with thumb and index finger, and mumbling his tobacco. John, who had listened with more attention than interest--wondering the while as to what the narrative was leading up to--thought something might properly be expected of him to show that he had followed it, and said, "So Mrs. Cullom has kept this last piece clear, has she?"

"No," said David, bringing down his right hand upon the desk with emphasis, "that's jest what she hain't done, an' that's how I come to tell ye somethin' of the story, an' more on't 'n you've cared about hearin', mebbe."

"Not at all," John protested. "I have been very much interested."

"You have, have you?" said Mr. Harum. "Wa'al, I got somethin' I want ye to do. Day after to-morro' 's Chris'mus, an' I want ye to drop Mis' Cullom a line, somethin' like this, 'That Mr. Harum told ye to say that that morgidge he holds, havin' ben past due fer some time, an' no int'rist havin' ben paid fer, let me see, more'n a year, he wants to close the matter up, an' he'll see her Chris'mus mornin' at the bank at nine o'clock, he havin' more time on that day; but that, as fur as he can see, the bus'nis won't take very long'--somethin' like that, you understand?"

"Very well, sir," said John, hoping that his employer would not see in his face the disgust and repugnance he felt as he surmised what a scheme was on foot, and recalled what he had heard of Harum's hard and unscrupulous ways, though he had to admit that this, excepting perhaps the episode of the counterfeit money, was the first revelation to him personally. But this seemed very bad to him.

"All right," said David cheerfully, "I s'pose it won't take you long to find out what's in your stockin', an' if you hain't nothin' else to do Chris'mus mornin' I'd like to have you open the office and stay 'round a spell till I git through with Mis' Cullom. Mebbe the' 'll be some papers to fill out or witniss or somethin'; an' have that skeezicks of a boy make up the fires so'st the place'll be warm."

"Very good, sir," said John, hoping that the interview was at an end.

But the elder man sat for some minutes apparently in a brown study, and occasionally a smile of sardonic cunning wrinkled his face. At last he said: "I've told ye so much that I may as well tell ye how I come by that morgidge. 'Twont take but a minute, an' then you can run an' play," he added with a chuckle.

"I trust I have not betrayed any impatience," said John, and instantly conscious of his infelicitous expression, added hastily, "I have really been very much interested."

"Oh, no," was the reply, "you hain't **betrayed** none, but I know old fellers like me gen'rally tell a thing twice over while they're at it. Wa'al," he went on, "it was like this. After Charley Cullom got to be some grown he helped to keep the pot a-bilin', 'n they got on some better. 'Bout seven year ago, though, he up an' got married, an' then the fat ketched fire. Finally he allowed that if he had some money he'd go West 'n take up some land, 'n git along like pussly 'n a flower gard'n. He ambitioned that if his mother 'd raise a thousan' dollars on her place he'd be sure to take care of the int'rist, an' prob'ly pay off the princ'ple in almost no time. Wa'al, she done it, an' off he went. She didn't come to me fer the money, because--I dunno--at any rate she didn't, but got it of 'Zeke Swinney.

"Wa'al, it turned out jest 's any fool might 've predilictid, fer after the first year, when I reckon he paid it out of the thousan', Charley never paid no int'rist. The second year he was jest gettin' goin', an' the next year he lost a hoss jest as he was cal'latin' to pay, an' the next year the grasshoppers smote him, 'n so on; an' the outcome was that at the end of five years, when the morgidge had one year to run, Charley'd paid one year, an' she'd paid one, an' she stood to owe three years' int'rist. How old Swinney come to hold off so was that she used to pay the cuss ten dollars or so ev'ry six months 'n git no credit fer it, an' no receipt an' no witniss, 'n he knowed the prop'ty was improving all the time. He may have had another reason, but at any rate he let her run, and got the shave reg'lar. But at the time I'm tellin' you about he'd begun to cut up, an' allowed that if she didn't settle up the int'rist he'd foreclose, an' I got wind on't an' I run across her one day an' got to talkin' with her, an' she gin me the hull narration. 'How much do you owe the old critter?' I says. 'A hunderd an' eighty dollars,' she says, 'an' where I'm goin' to git it,' she says, 'the Lord only knows.' 'An' He won't tell ye, I reckon,' I says. Wa'al, of course I'd known that Swinney had a morgidge because it was a matter of record, an' I knowed him well enough to give a guess what his game was goin' to be, an' more'n that I'd had my eye on that piece an' parcel an' I figured that he wa'n't any likelier a citizen 'n I was." ("Yes," said John to himself, "where the carcase is the vultures are gathered together.")

"'Wa'al,' I says to her, after we'd had a little more talk, 's'posen you come 'round to my place to-morro' 'bout 'leven o'clock, an' mebbe we c'n cipher this thing out.

I don't say positive that we kin,' I says, 'but mebbe, mebbe.' So that afternoon I sent over to the county seat an' got a description an' had a second morgidge drawed up fer two hundred dollars, an' Mis' Cullom signed it mighty quick. I had the morgidge made one day after date, 'cause, as I said to her, it was in the nature of a temp'rary loan, but she was so tickled she'd have signed most anythin' at that pertic'ler time. 'Now,' I says to her, 'you go an' settle with old Step-an'-fetch-it, but don't you say a word where you got the money,' I says. 'Don't ye let on nothin'--stretch that con- science o' your'n if nes'sary,' I says, 'an' be pertic'ler if he asks you if Dave Harum give ye the money you jest say, "No, he didn't." That wont be no lie,' I says, 'because I aint *givin'* it to ye,' I says. Wa'al, she done as I told her. Of course Swinney suspi- cioned fust off that I was mixed up in it, but she stood him off so fair an' square that he didn't know jest what *to* think, but his claws was cut fer a spell, anyway.

"Wa'al, things went on fer a while, till I made up my mind that I ought to re- lieve Swinney of some of his anxieties about worldly bus'nis, an' I dropped in on him one mornin' an' passed the time o' day, an' after we'd eased up our minds on the subjects of each other's health an' such like I says, 'You hold a morgidge on the Widder Cullom's place, don't ye?' Of course he couldn't say nothin' but 'yes.' 'Does she keep up the int'rist all right?' I says. 'I don't want to be pokin' my nose into your bus'nis,' I says, 'an' don't tell me nothin' you don't want to.' Wa'al, he knowed Dave Harum was Dave Harum, an' that he might 's well spit it out, an' he says, 'Wa'al, she didn't pay nothin' fer a good while, but last time she forked over the hull amount. 'But I hain't no notion,' he says, 'that she'll come to time agin.' 'An' s'posin' she don't,' I says, 'you'll take the prop'ty, won't ye?' 'Don't see no other way,' he says, an' lookin' up quick, 'unless you over-bid me,' he says. 'No,' I says, 'I ain't buyin' no real estate jest now, but the thing I come in fer,' I says, 'leavin' out the pleasure of havin' a talk with you, was to say that I'd take that morgidge off'm your hands.'

"Wa'al, sir, he, he, he, he! Scat my ----! At that he looked at me fer a minute with his jaw on his neck, an' then he hunched himself, 'n drawed in his neck like a mud turtle. 'No,' he says, 'I ain't sufferin' fer the money, an' I guess I'll keep the mor- gidge. It's putty near due now, but mebbe I'll let it run a spell. I guess the secur'ty's good fer it.' 'Yes,' I says, 'I reckon you'll let it run long enough fer the widder to pay the taxes on't once more anyhow; I guess the secur'ty's good enough to take that resk; but how 'bout *my* secur'ty?' I says. 'What d'you mean?' he says. 'I mean,' says

I, 'that I've got a second morgidge on that prop'ty, an' I begin to tremble fer my secur'ty. You've jest told me,' I says, 'that you're goin' to foreclose an' I cal'late to protect myself, an' I *don't* cal'late,' I says, 'to have to go an' bid on that prop'ty, an' put in a lot more money to save my investment, unless I'm 'bleeged to--not *much*! an' you can jest sign that morgidge over to me, an' the sooner the quicker,' I says."

David brought his hand down on his thigh with a vigorous slap, the fellow of the one which, John could imagine, had emphasized his demand upon Swinney. The story, to which he had at first listened with polite patience merely, he had found more interesting as it went on, and, excusing himself, he brought up a stool, and mounting it, said, "And what did Swinney say to that?" Mr. Harum emitted a gurgling chuckle, yawned his quid out of his mouth, tossing it over his shoulder in the general direction of the waste basket, and bit off the end of a cigar which he found by slapping his waistcoat pockets. John got down and fetched him a match, which he scratched in the vicinity of his hip pocket, lighted his cigar (John declining to join him on some plausible pretext, having on a previous occasion accepted one of the brand), and after rolling it around with his lips and tongue to the effect that the lighted end described sundry eccentric curves, located it firmly with an upward angle in the left-hand corner of his mouth, gave it a couple of vigorous puffs, and replied to John's question.

"Wa'al, 'Zeke Swinney was a perfesser of religion some years ago, an' mebbe he is now, but what he said to me on this pertic'ler occasion was that he'd see me in hell fust, an' *then* he wouldn't.

"'Wa'al,' I says, 'mebbe you won't, mebbe you will, it's alwus a pleasure to meet ye,' I says, 'but in that case this morgidge bus'nis 'll be a question fer our executors,' I says, 'fer *you* don't never foreclose that morgidge, an' don't you fergit it,' I says.

"'Oh, you'd like to git holt o' that prop'ty yourself. I see what you're up to,' he says.

"'Look a-here, 'Zeke Swinney,' I says, 'I've got an int'rist in that prop'ty, an' I propose to p'tect it. You're goin' to sign that morgidge over to me, or I'll foreclose and surrygate ye,' I says, 'unless you allow to bid in the prop'ty, in which case we'll see whose weasel-skin's the longest. But I guess it won't come to that,' I says. 'You kin take your choice,' I says. 'Whether I want to git holt o' that prop'ty myself ain't neither here nor there. Mebbe I do, an' mebbe I don't, but anyways,' I says, '*you* don't git it, nor wouldn't ever, for if I can't make you sign over, I'll either do what I said or I'll back the widder in a defence fer usury. Put that in your pipe an' smoke it,' I says.

"'What do you mean?' he says, gittin' half out his chair.

"'I mean this,' I says, 'that the fust six months the widder couldn't pay she gin you ten dollars to hold off, an' the next time she gin you fifteen, an' that you've bled her fer shaves to the tune of sixty odd dollars in three years, an' then got your int'rist in full.'

"That riz him clean out of his chair," said David. "'She can't prove it,' he says, shakin' his fist in the air.

"'Oh, ho! ho!' I says, tippin' my chair back agin the wall. 'If Mis' Cullom was to swear how an' where she paid you the money, givin' chapter an' verse, and showin' her own mem'randums even, an' I was to swear that when I twitted you with gittin' it you didn't deny it, but only said that she couldn't *prove* it, how long do you think it 'ould take a Freeland County jury to find agin ye? I allow, 'Zeke Swinney,' I says, 'that you wa'n't born yestyd'y, but you ain't so old as you look, not by a dum sight!' an' then how I did laugh!

"Wa'al," said David, as he got down off the stool and stretched himself, yawning, "I guess I've yarned it enough fer one day. Don't fergit to send Mis' Cullom that notice, an' make it up an' up. I'm goin' to git the thing off my mind this trip."

"Very well, sir," said John, "but let me ask, did Swinney assign the mortgage without any trouble?"

"O Lord! yes," was the reply. "The' wa'n't nothin' else fer him to do. I had another twist on him that I hain't mentioned. But he put up a great show of doin' it to obleege me. Wa'al, I thanked him an' so on, an' when we'd got through I ast him if he wouldn't step over to the 'Eagil' an' take somethin', an' he looked kind o' shocked an' said he never drinked nothin'. It was 'gin his princ'ples, he said. Ho, ho, ho, ho! Scat my ----! Princ'ples!" and John heard him chuckling to himself all the way out of the office.

CHAPTER XVIII.

Considering John's relations with David Harum, it was natural that he should wish to think as well of him as possible, and he had not (or thought he had not) allowed his mind to be influenced by the disparaging remarks and insinuations which had been made to him, or in his presence, concerning his employer. He had made up his mind to form his opinion upon his own experience with the man, and so far it had not only been pleasant but favorable, and far from justifying the half-jeering, half-malicious talk that had come to his ears. It had been made manifest to him, it was true, that David was capable of a sharp bargain in certain lines, but it seemed to him that it was more for the pleasure of matching his wits against another's than for any gain involved. Mr. Harum was an experienced and expert horseman, who delighted above all things in dealing in and trading horses, and John soon discovered that, in that community at least, to get the best of a "hoss-trade" by almost any means was considered a venial sin, if a sin at all, and the standards of ordinary business probity were not expected to govern those transactions.

David had said to him once when he suspected that John's ideas might have sustained something of a shock, "A hoss-trade ain't like anythin' else. A feller may be straighter 'n a string in ev'rythin' else, an' never tell the truth--that is, the hull truth--about a hoss. I trade hosses with hoss-traders. They all think they know as much as I do, an' I dunno but what they do. They hain't learnt no diff'rent anyway, an' they've had chances enough. If a feller come to me that didn't think he knowed anythin' about a hoss, an' wanted to buy on the square, he'd git, fur's I knew, square treatment. At any rate I'd tell him all 't I knew. But when one o' them smart Alecks comes along and cal'lates to do up old Dave, why he's got to take his chances, that's all. An' mind ye," asserted David, shaking his forefinger impressively, "it ain't only them fellers. I've ben wuss stuck two three time by church members in good standin' than anybody I ever dealed with. Take old Deakin Perkins. He's a terrible feller fer church bus'nis; c'n pray an' psalm-sing to beat the Jews, an' in spiritual matters c'n read his title clear the hull time, but when it comes to hoss-tradin' you got to git up very early in the mornin' or he'll skin the eyeteeth out of ye. Yes, sir! Scat my

----! I believe the old critter *makes* hosses! But the deakin," added David, "he, he, he, he! the deakin hain't hardly spoke to me fer some consid'able time, the deakin hain't. He, he, he!

"Another thing," he went on, "the' ain't no gamble like a hoss. You may think you know him through an' through, an' fust thing you know he'll be cuttin' up a lot o' didos right out o' nothin'. It stands to reason that sometimes you let a hoss go all on the square--as you know him--an' the feller that gits him don't know how to hitch him or treat him, an' he acts like a diff'rent hoss, an' the feller allows you swindled him. You see, hosses gits used to places an' ways to a certain extent, an' when they're changed, why they're apt to act diff'rent. Hosses don't know but dreadful little, really. Talk about hoss sense--wa'al, the' ain't no such thing."

Thus spoke David on the subject of his favorite pursuit and pastime, and John thought then that he could understand and condone some things he had seen and heard, at which at first he was inclined to look askance. But this matter of the Widow Cullom's was a different thing, and as he realized that he was expected to play a part, though a small one, in it, his heart sank within him that he had so far cast his fortunes upon the good will of a man who could plan and carry out so heartless and cruel an undertaking as that which had been revealed to him that afternoon. He spent the evening in his room trying to read, but the widow's affairs persistently thrust themselves upon his thoughts. All the unpleasant stories he had heard of David came to his mind, and he remembered with misgiving some things which at the time had seemed regular and right enough, but which took on a different color in the light in which he found himself recalling them. He debated with himself whether he should not decline to send Mrs. Cullom the notice as he had been instructed, and left it an open question when he went to bed.

He wakened somewhat earlier than usual to find that the thermometer had gone up, and the barometer down. The air was full of a steady downpour, half snow, half rain, about the most disheartening combination which the worst climate in the world--that of central New York--can furnish. He passed rather a busy day in the office in an atmosphere redolent of the unsavory odors raised by the proximity of wet boots and garments to the big cylinder stove outside the counter, a compound of stale smells from kitchen and stable.

After the bank closed he dispatched Peleg Hopkins, the office boy, with the note for Mrs. Cullom. He had abandoned his half-formed intention to revolt, but had made the note not only as little peremptory as was compatible with a clear intimation of its purport as he understood it, but had yielded to a natural impulse in beginning it with an expression of personal regret--a blunder which cost him no little chagrin in the outcome.

Peleg Hopkins grumbled audibly when he was requested to build the fires on Christmas day, and expressed his opinion that "if there warn't Bible agin workin' on Chris'mus, the' 'd ort ter be"; but when John opened the door of the bank that morning he found the temperature in comfortable contrast to the outside air. The weather had changed again, and a blinding snowstorm, accompanied by a buffeting gale from the northwest, made it almost impossible to see a path and to keep it. In the central part of the town some tentative efforts had been made to open walks, but these were apparent only as slight and tortuous depressions in the depths of snow. In the outskirts, the unfortunate pedestrian had to wade to the knees.

As John went behind the counter his eye was at once caught by a small parcel lying on his desk, of white note paper, tied with a cotton string, which he found to be addressed, "Mr. John Lenox, Esq., Present," and as he took it up it seemed heavy for its size.

Opening it, he found a tiny stocking, knit of white wool, to which was pinned a piece of paper with the legend, "A Merry Christmas from Aunt Polly." Out of the stocking fell a packet fastened with a rubber strap. Inside were five ten-dollar gold pieces and a slip of paper on which was written, "A Merry Christmas from Your Friend David Harum." For a moment John's face burned, and there was a curious smarting of the eyelids as he held the little stocking and its contents in his hand. Surely the hand that had written "Your Friend" on that scrap of paper could not be the hand of an oppressor of widows and orphans. "This," said John to himself, "is what he meant when 'he supposed it wouldn't take me long to find out what was in my stocking.'"

*   *   *   *   *

The door opened and a blast and whirl of wind and snow rushed in, ushering the tall, bent form of the Widow Cullom. The drive of the wind was so strong that John vaulted over the low cash counter to push the door shut again. The poor woman was white with snow from the front of her old worsted hood to the bottom of her ragged skirt.

"You are Mrs. Cullom?" said John. "Wait a moment till I brush off the snow, and then come to the fire in the back room. Mr. Harum will be in directly, I expect."

"Be I much late?" she asked. "I made 's much haste 's I could. It don't appear to me 's if I ever see a blusteriner day, 'n I ain't as strong as I used to be. Seemed as if I never would git here."

"Oh, no," said John, as he established her before the glowing grate of the Franklin stove in the bank parlor, "not at all. Mr. Harum has not come in himself yet. Shall you mind if I excuse myself a moment while you make yourself as comfortable as possible?" She did not apparently hear him. She was trembling from head to foot with cold and fatigue and nervous excitement. Her dress was soaked to the knees, and as she sat down and put up her feet to the fire John saw a bit of a thin cotton stocking and her deplorable shoes, almost in a state of pulp. A snow-obliterated path led from the back door of the office to David's house, and John snatched his hat and started for it on a run. As he stamped off some of the snow on the veranda the door was opened for him by Mrs. Bixbee. "Lord sakes!" she exclaimed. "What on earth be you cavortin' 'round for such a mornin' 's this without no overcoat, an' on a dead run? What's the matter?"

"Nothing serious," he answered, "but I'm in a great hurry. Old Mrs. Cullom has walked up from her house to the office, and she is wet through and almost perished. I thought you'd send her some dry shoes and stockings, and an old shawl or blanket to keep her wet skirt off her knees, and a drop of whisky or something. She's all of a tremble, and I'm afraid she will have a chill."

"Certain! certain!" said the kind creature, and she bustled out of the room, returning in a minute or two with an armful of comforts. "There's a pair of bedroom slips lined with lamb's wool, an' a pair of woolen stockin's, an' a blanket shawl. This here petticut, 't ain't what ye'd call bran' new, but it's warm and comf'table, an' I don't believe she's got much of anythin' on 'ceptin' her dress, an' I'll git ye the whisky, but"--here she looked deprecatingly at John--"it ain't gen'ally known 't we keep the stuff in the house. I don't know as it's right, but though David don't hardly ever touch it he will have it in the house."

"Oh," said John, laughing, "you may trust my discretion, and we'll swear Mrs.

Cullom to secrecy."

"Wa'al, all right," said Mrs. Bixbee, joining in the laugh as she brought the bottle; "jest a minute till I make a passel of the things to keep the snow out. There, now, I guess you're fixed, an' you kin hurry back 'fore she ketches a chill."

"Thanks very much," said John as he started away. "I have something to say to you besides 'Merry Christmas,' but I must wait till another time."

When John got back to the office David had just preceded him.

"Wa'al, wa'al," he was saying, "but you be in a putty consid'able state. Hullo, John! what you got there? Wa'al, you air the stuff! Slips, blanket-shawl, petticut, stockin's--wa'al, you an' Polly ben puttin' your heads together, I guess. What's that? Whisky! Wa'al, scat my ----! I didn't s'pose wild hosses would have drawed it out o' Polly to let on the' was any in the house, much less to fetch it out. Jest the thing! Oh, yes ye are, Mis' Cullom--jest a mouthful with water," taking the glass from John, "jest a spoonful to git your blood a-goin', an' then Mr. Lenox an' me 'll go into the front room while you make yourself comf'table."

"Consarn it all!" exclaimed Mr. Harum as they stood leaning against the teller's counter, facing the street, "I didn't cal'late to have Mis' Cullom hoof it up here the way she done. When I see what kind of a day it was I went out to the barn to have the cutter hitched an' send for her, an' I found ev'rythin' topsy-turvy. That dum'd uneasy sorril colt had got cast in the stall, an' I ben fussin' with him ever since. I clean forgot all 'bout Mis' Cullom till jest now."

"Is the colt much injured?" John asked.

"Wa'al, he won't trot a twenty gait in some time, I reckon," replied David. "He's wrenched his shoulder some, an' mebbe strained his inside. Don't seem to take no int'rist in his feed, an' that's a bad sign. Consarn a hoss, anyhow! If they're wuth anythin' they're more bother 'n a teethin' baby. Alwus some dum thing ailin' 'em, an' I took consid'able stock in that colt too," he added regretfully, "an' I could 'a' got putty near what I was askin' fer him last week, an' putty near what he was wuth, an' I've noticed that most gen'ally alwus when I let a good offer go like that, some cussed thing happens to the hoss. It ain't a bad idee, in the hoss bus'nis anyway, to be willin' to let the other feller make a dollar once 'n a while."

After that aphorism they waited in silence for a few minutes, and then David called out over his shoulder, "How be you gettin' along, Mis' Cullom?"

"I guess I'm fixed," she answered, and David walked slowly back into the parlor, leaving John in the front office. He was annoyed to realize that in the bustle over Mrs. Cullom and what followed, he had forgotten to acknowledge the Christmas gift; but, hoping that Mr. Harum had been equally oblivious, promised himself to repair the omission later on. He would have preferred to go out and leave the two to settle their affair without witness or hearer, but his employer, who, as he had found, usually had a reason for his actions, had explicitly requested him to remain, and he had no choice. He perched himself upon one of the office stools and composed himself to await the conclusion of the affair.

CHAPTER XIX.

Mrs. Cullom was sitting at one corner of the fire, and David drew a chair opposite to her.

"Feelin' all right now? whisky hain't made ye liable to no disorderly conduct, has it?" he asked with a laugh.

"Yes, thank you," was the reply, "the warm things are real comfortin', 'n' I guess I hain't had licker enough to make me want to throw things. You got a kind streak in ye, Dave Harum, if you did send me this here note--but I s'pose ye know your own bus'nis," she added with a sigh of resignation. "I ben fearin' fer a good while 't I couldn't hold on t' that prop'ty, an' I don't know but what you might's well git it as 'Zeke Swinney, though I ben hopin' 'gainst hope that Charley 'd be able to do more 'n he has."

"Let's see the note," said David curtly. "H'm, humph, 'regret to say that I have been instructed by Mr. Harum'--wa'al, h'm'm, cal'lated to clear his own skirts anyway--h'm'm--'must be closed up without further delay' (John's eye caught the little white stocking which still lay on his desk)--wa'al, yes, that's about what I told Mr. Lenox to say fur's the bus'nis part's concerned--I might 'a' done my own regrettin' if I'd wrote the note myself." (John said something to himself.) "'T ain't the pleasantest thing in the world fer ye, I allow, but then you see, bus'nis is bus'nis."

John heard David clear his throat, and there was a hiss in the open fire. Mrs. Cullom was silent, and David resumed:

"You see, Mis' Cullom, it's like this. I ben thinkin' of this matter fer a good while. That place ain't ben no real good to ye sence the first year you signed that morgidge. You hain't scurcely more'n made ends meet, let alone the int'rist, an' it's ben simply a question o' time, an' who'd git the prop'ty in the long run fer some years. I reckoned, same as you did, that Charley 'd mebbe come to the front--but he hain't done it, an' 't ain't likely he ever will. Charley's a likely 'nough boy some ways, but he hain't got much 'git there' in his make-up, not more'n enough fer one anyhow, I reckon. That's about the size on't, ain't it?"

Mrs. Cullom murmured a feeble admission that she was "'fraid it was."

"Wa'al," resumed Mr. Harum, "I see how things was goin', an' I see that unless I played euchre, 'Zeke Swinney 'd git that prop'ty, an' whether I wanted it myself or not, I didn't cal'late he sh'd git it anyway. He put a spoke in my wheel once, an' I hain't forgot it. But that hain't neither here nor there. Wa'al," after a short pause, "you know I helped ye pull the thing along on the chance, as ye may say, that you an' your son 'd somehow make a go on't."

"You ben very kind, so fur," said the widow faintly.

"Don't ye say that, don't ye say that," protested David. "'T wa'n't no kindness. It was jest bus'nis: I wa'n't takin' no chances, an' I s'pose I might let the thing run a spell longer if I c'd see any use in't. But the' ain't, an' so I ast ye to come up this mornin' so 't we c'd settle the thing up without no fuss, nor trouble, nor lawyer's fees, nor nothin'. I've got the papers all drawed, an' John--Mr. Lenox--here to take the acknowlidgments. You hain't no objection to windin' the thing up this mornin', have ye?"

"I s'pose I'll have to do whatever you say," replied the poor woman in a tone of hopeless discouragement, "an' I might as well be killed to once, as to die by inch pieces."

"All right then," said David cheerfully, ignoring her lethal suggestion, "but before we git down to bus'nis an' signin' papers, an' in order to set myself in as fair a light 's I can in the matter, I want to tell ye a little story."

"I hain't no objection 's I know of," acquiesced the widow graciously.

"All right," said David, "I won't preach more 'n about up to the sixthly--How'd you feel if I was to light up a cigar? I hain't much of a hand at a yarn, an' if I git stuck, I c'n puff a spell. Thank ye. Wa'al, Mis' Cullom, you used to know somethin' about my folks. I was raised on Buxton Hill. The' was nine on us, an' I was the youngest o' the lot. My father farmed a piece of about forty to fifty acres, an' had a small shop where he done odd times small jobs of tinkerin' fer the neighbors when the' was anythin' to do. My mother was his second, an' I was the only child of that marriage. He married agin when I was about two year old, an' how I ever got raised 's more 'n I c'n tell ye. My sister Polly was 'sponsible more 'n any one, I guess, an' the only one o' the whole lot that ever gin me a decent word. Small farmin' ain't cal'lated to fetch out the best traits of human nature--an' keep 'em out--an' it seems to me sometimes that when the old man wa'n't cuffin' my ears he was lickin' me with a rawhide or a strap. Fur 's that was concerned, all his boys used to ketch it putty reg'lar till they got too big. One on 'em up an' licked him one night, an' lit out next day. I s'pose the old man's disposition was sp'iled by what some feller said farmin' was, 'workin' all day, an' doin' chores all night,' an' larrupin' me an' all the rest on us was about all the enjoyment he got. My brothers an' sisters--'ceptin' of Polly--was putty nigh as bad in respect of cuffs an' such like; an' my step-marm was, on the hull, the wust of all. She hadn't no childern o' her own, an' it appeared 's if I was jest pizen to her. 'T wa'n't so much slappin' an' cuffin' with her as 't was tongue. She c'd say things that 'd jest raise a blister like pizen ivy. I s'pose I *was* about as ord'nary, no-account-lookin', red-headed, freckled little cuss as you ever see, an' slinkin' in my manners. The air of our home circle wa'n't cal'lated to raise heroes in.

"I got three four years' schoolin', an' made out to read an' write an' cipher up to long division 'fore I got through, but after I got to be six year old, school or no school, I had to work reg'lar at anything I had strength fer, an' more too. Chores before school an' after school, an' a two-mile walk to git there. As fur 's clo'es was concerned, any old thing that 'd hang together was good enough fer me; but by the time the older boys had outgrowed their duds, an' they was passed on to me, the' wa'n't much left on 'em. A pair of old cowhide boots that leaked in more snow an' water 'n they kept out, an' a couple pairs of woolen socks that was putty much all darns, was expected to see me through the winter, an' I went barefoot f'm the time the snow was off the ground till it flew agin in the fall. The' wa'n't but two seasons o' the year with me--them of chilblains an' stun-bruises."

The speaker paused and stared for a moment into the comfortable glow of the fire, and then discovering to his apparent surprise that his cigar had gone out, lighted it from a coal picked out with the tongs.

"Farmin' 's a hard life," remarked Mrs. Cullom with an air of being expected to make some contribution to the conversation.

"An' yit, as it seems to me as I look back on't," David resumed pensively, "the wust on't was that nobody ever gin me a kind word, 'cept Polly. I s'pose I got kind o' used to bein' cold an' tired; dressin' in a snowdrift where it blowed into the attic, an' goin' out to fodder cattle 'fore sun-up; pickin' up stun in the blazin' sun, an' doin' all the odd jobs my father set me to, an' the older ones shirked onto me. That was the reg'lar order o' things; but I remember I never *did* git used to never pleasin' nobody. 'Course I didn't expect nothin' f'm my step-marm, an' the only way I ever knowed I'd done my stent fur 's father was concerned, was that he didn't say nothin'. But sometimes the older ones 'd git settin' 'round, talkin' an' laughin', havin' pop corn an' apples, an' that, an' I'd kind o' sidle up, wantin' to join 'em, an' some on 'em 'd say, 'What *you* doin' here? time you was in bed,' an' give me a shove or a cuff. Yes, ma'am," looking up at Mrs. Cullom, "the wust on't was that I was kind o' scairt the hull time. Once in a while Polly 'd give me a mossel o' comfort, but Polly wa'n't but little older 'n me, an' bein' the youngest girl, was chored most to death herself."

It had stopped snowing, and though the wind still came in gusty blasts, whirling the drift against the windows, a wintry gleam of sunshine came in and touched the widow's wrinkled face.

"It's amazin' how much trouble an' sorrer the' is in the world, an' how soon it begins," she remarked, moving a little to avoid the sunlight. "I hain't never ben able to reconcile how many good things the' be, an' how little most on us gits o' them. I hain't ben to meetin' fer a long spell 'cause I hain't had no fit clo'es, but I remember most of the preachin' I've set under either dwelt on the wrath to come, or else on the Lord's doin' all things well, an' providin'. I hope I ain't no wickeder 'n than the gen'ral run, but it's putty hard to hev faith in the Lord's providin' when you hain't got nothin' in the house but corn meal, an' none too much o' that."

"That's so, Mis' Cullom, that's so," affirmed David. "I don't blame ye a mite. 'Doubts assail, an' oft prevail,' as the hymn-book says, an' I reckon it's a sight easier to have faith on meat an' potatoes 'n it is on corn meal mush. Wa'al, as I was sayin'--I hope I ain't tirin' ye with my goin's on?"

"No," said Mrs. Cullom, "I'm engaged to hear ye, but nobody 'd suppose to see ye now that ye was such a f'lorn little critter as you make out."

"It's jest as I'm tellin' ye, an' more also, as the Bible says," returned David, and then, rather more impressively, as if he were leading up to his conclusion, "it come along to a time when I was 'twixt thirteen an' fourteen. The' was a cirkis billed to show down here in Homeville, an' ev'ry barn an' shed fer miles around had pictures stuck onto 'em of el'phants, an' rhinoceroses, an' ev'ry animul that went into the ark; an' girls ridin' bareback an' jumpin' through hoops, an' fellers ridin' bareback an' turnin' summersets, an' doin' turnovers on swings; an' clowns gettin' hoss-whipped, an' ev'ry kind of a thing that could be pictered out; an' how the' was to be a grand percession at ten o'clock, 'ith golden chariots, an' scripteral allegories, an' the hull bus'nis; an' the gran' performance at two o'clock; admission twenty-five cents, children under twelve, at cetery, an' so forth. Wa'al, I hadn't no more idee o' goin' to that cirkis 'n I had o' flyin' to the moon, but the night before the show somethin' waked me 'bout twelve o'clock. I don't know how 't was. I'd ben helpin' mend fence all day, an' gen'ally I never knowed nothin' after my head struck the bed till mornin'. But that night, anyhow, somethin' waked me, an' I went an' looked out the windo', an' there was the hull thing goin' by the house. The' was more or less moon, an' I see the el'phant, an' the big wagins--the drivers kind o' noddin' over the dashboards--an' the chariots with canvas covers--I don't know how many of 'em--an' the cages of the tigers an' lions, an' all. Wa'al, I got up the next mornin' at sun-up an' done my chores; an' after breakfust I set off fer the ten-acre lot where I was mendin' fence. The ten-acre was the farthest off of any, Homeville way, an' I had my dinner in a tin pail so't I needn't lose no time goin' home at noon, an', as luck would have it, the' wa'n't nobody with me that mornin'. Wa'al, I got down to the lot an' set to work; but somehow I couldn't git that show out o' my head nohow. As I said, I hadn't no more notion of goin' to that cirkis 'n I had of kingdom come. I'd never had two shillin' of my own in my hull life. But the more I thought on't the uneasier I got. Somethin' seemed pullin' an' haulin' at me, an' fin'ly I gin in. I allowed I'd see that percession anyway if it took a leg, an' mebbe I c'd git back 'ithout nobody missin' me. 'T any rate, I'd take the chances of a lickin' jest once--fer that's what it meant--an' I up an' put fer the village lickity-cut. I done them four mile lively, I c'n tell ye, an' the stun-bruises never hurt me once.

"When I got down to the village it seemed to me as if the hull population of

Freeland County was there. I'd never seen so many folks together in my life, an' fer a spell it seemed to me as if ev'rybody was a-lookin' at me an' sayin', 'That's old Harum's boy Dave, playin' hookey,' an' I sneaked 'round dreadin' somebody 'd give me away; but I fin'ly found that nobody wa'n't payin' any attention to me--they was there to see the show, an' one red-headed boy more or less wa'n't no pertic'ler account. Wa'al, putty soon the percession hove in sight, an' the' was a reg'lar stampede among the boys, an' when it got by, I run an' ketched up with it agin, an' walked alongside the el'phant, tin pail an' all, till they fetched up inside the tent. Then I went off to one side--it must 'a' ben about 'leven or half-past, an' eat my dinner--I had a devourin' appetite--an' thought I'd jest walk round a spell, an' then light out fer home. But the' was so many things to see an' hear--all the side-show pictures of Fat Women, an' Livin' Skelitons; an' Wild Women of Madygasker, an' Wild Men of Borneo; an' snakes windin' round women's necks; hand-orgins; fellers that played the 'cordion, an' mouth-pipes, an' drum an' cymbals all to once, an' such like--that I fergot all about the time an' the ten-acre lot, an' the stun fence, an' fust I knowed the folks was makin' fer the ticket wagin, an' the band begun to play inside the tent. Be I taxin' your patience over the limit?" said David, breaking off in his story and addressing Mrs. Cullom more directly.

"No, I guess not," she replied; "I was jest thinkin' of a circus I went to once," she added with an audible sigh.

"Wa'al," said David, taking a last farewell of the end of his cigar, which he threw into the grate, "mebbe what's comin' 'll int'rest ye more 'n the rest on't has. I was standin' gawpin' 'round, list'nin' to the band an' watchin' the folks git their tickets, when all of a suddin I felt a twitch at my hair--it had a way of workin' out of the holes in my old chip straw hat--an' somebody says to me, 'Wa'al, sonny, what you thinkin' of?' he says. I looked up, an' who do you s'pose it was? It was Billy P. Cullom! I knowed who he was, fer I'd seen him before, but of course he didn't know me. Yes, ma'am, it was Billy P., an' wa'n't he rigged out to kill!"

The speaker paused and looked into the fire, smiling. The woman started forward facing him, and clasping her hands, cried, "My husband! What'd he have on?"

"Wa'al," said David slowly and reminiscently, "near's I c'n remember, he had on a blue broad-cloth claw-hammer coat with flat gilt buttons, an' a double-breast-ed plaid velvet vest, an' pearl-gray pants, strapped down over his boots, which was of shiny leather, an' a high pointed collar an' blue stock with a pin in it (I remember wonderin' if it c'd be real gold), an' a yeller-white plug beaver hat."

At the description of each article of attire Mrs. Cullom nodded her head, with her eyes fixed on David's face, and as he concluded she broke out breathlessly, "Oh, yes! Oh, yes! David, he wore them very same clo'es, an' he took me to that very same show that very same night!" There was in her face a look almost of awe, as if a sight of her long-buried past youth had been shown to her from a coffin.

Neither spoke for a moment or two, and it was the widow who broke the silence. As David had conjectured, she was interested at last, and sat leaning forward with her hands clasped in her lap.

"Well," she exclaimed, "ain't ye goin' on? What did he say to ye?"

"Cert'nly, cert'nly," responded David, "I'll tell ye near 's I c'n remember, an' I c'n remember putty near. As I told ye, I felt a twitch at my hair, an' he said, 'What be you thinkin' about, sonny?' I looked up at him, an' looked away quick. 'I dunno,' I says, diggin' my big toe into the dust; an' then, I dunno how I got the spunk to, for I was shyer 'n a rat, 'Guess I was thinkin' 'bout mendin' that fence up in the ten-acre lot's much's anythin',' I says.

"'Ain't you goin' to the cirkis?' he says.

"'I hain't got no money to go to cirkises,' I says, rubbin' the dusty toes o' one foot over t' other, 'nor nothin' else,' I says.

"'Wa'al,' he says, 'why don't you crawl under the canvas?'

"That kind o' riled me, shy 's I was. 'I don't crawl under no canvases,' I says. 'If I can't go in same 's other folks, I'll stay out,' I says, lookin' square at him fer the fust time. He wa'n't exac'ly smilin', but the' was a look in his eyes that was the next thing to it."

"Lordy me!" sighed Mrs. Cullom, as if to herself. "How well I can remember that look; jest as if he was laughin' at ye, an' wa'n't laughin' at ye, an' his arm around your neck!"

David nodded in reminiscent sympathy, and rubbed his bald poll with the back of his hand.

"Wa'al," interjected the widow.

"Wa'al," said David, resuming, "he says to me, 'Would you like to go to the cirkis?' an' with that it occurred to me that I did want to go to that cirkis more'n anythin' I ever wanted to before--nor since, it seems to me. But I tell ye the truth, I was so far f'm expectin' to go't I really hadn't knowed I wanted to. I looked at him, an' then down agin, an' began tenderin' up a stun-bruise on one heel agin the other instep, an' all I says was, bein' so dum'd shy, 'I dunno,' I says. But I guess he seen in my face what my feelin's was, fer he kind o' laughed an' pulled out half-a-dollar an' says: 'D' you think you could git a couple o' tickits in that crowd? If you kin, I think I'll go myself, but I don't want to git my boots all dust,' he says. I allowed I c'd try; an' I guess them bare feet o' mine tore up the dust some gettin' over to the wagin. Wa'al, I had another scare gettin' the tickits, fer fear some one that knowed me 'd see me with a half-a-dollar, an' think I must 'a' stole the money. But I got 'em an' carried 'em back to him, an' he took 'em an' put 'em in his vest pocket, an' handed me a ten-cent piece, an' says, 'Mebbe you'll want somethin' in the way of refresh-ments fer yourself an' mebbe the el'phant,' he says, an' walked off toward the tent; an' I stood stun still, lookin' after him. He got off about a rod or so an' stopped an' looked back. 'Ain't you comin'?' he says.

"'Be I goin' with *you*?" I says.

"'Why not?' he says, "'nless you'd ruther go alone,' an' he put his finger an' thumb into his vest pocket. Wa'al, ma'am, I looked at him a minute, with his shiny hat an' boots, an' fine clo'es, an' gold pin, an' thought of my ragged ole shirt, an' cotton pants, an' ole chip hat with the brim most gone, an' my tin pail an' all. 'I ain't fit to,' I says, ready to cry--an'--wa'al, he jest laughed, an' says, 'Nonsense,' he says, 'come along. A man needn't be ashamed of his workin' clo'es,' he says, an' I'm dum'd if he didn't take holt of my hand, an' in we went that way together."

"How like him that was!" said the widow softly.

"Yes, ma'am, yes, ma'am, I reckon it was," said David, nodding.

"Wa'al," he went on after a little pause, "I was ready to sink into the ground with shyniss at fust, but that wore off some after a little, an' we two seen the hull show, I *tell* ye. We walked 'round the cages, an' we fed the el'phant--that is, he bought the stuff an' I fed him. I 'member--he, he, he!--'t he says, 'mind you git the right end,' he says, an' then we got a couple o' seats, an' the doin's begun."

CHAPTER XX.

The widow was looking at David with shining eyes and devouring his words. All the years of trouble and sorrow and privation were wiped out, and she was back in the days of her girlhood. Ah, yes! how well she remembered him as he looked that very day--so handsome, so splendidly dressed, so debonair; and how proud she had been to sit by his side that night, observed and envied of all the village girls.

"I ain't goin' to go over the hull show," proceeded David, "well 's I remember it. The' didn't nothin' git away from me that afternoon, an' once I come near to stickin' a piece o' gingerbread into my ear 'stid o' my mouth. I had my ten-cent piece that Billy P. give me, but he wouldn't let me buy nothin'; an' when the gingerbread man come along he says, 'Air ye hungry, Dave? (I'd told him my name), air ye hungry?' Wa'al, I was a growin' boy, an' I was hungry putty much all the time. He bought two big squares an' gin me one, an' when I'd swallered it, he says, 'Guess you better tackle this one too,' he says, 'I've dined.' I didn't exac'ly know what 'dined' meant, but--he, he, he, he!--I tackled it," and David smacked his lips in memory.

"Wa'al," he went on, "we done the hull programmy--gingerbread, lemon-ade--*pink* lemonade, an' he took some o' that--pop corn, peanuts, pep'mint candy, cin'mun candy--scat my ----! an' he payin' fer ev'rythin'--I thought he was jest made o' money! An' I remember how we talked about all the doin's; the ridin', an' jumpin', an' summersettin', an' all--fer he'd got all the shyniss out of me for the time--an' once I looked up at him, an' he looked down at me with that curious look in his eyes an' put his hand on my shoulder. Wa'al, now, I tell ye, I had a queer, crinkly feelin' go up an' down my back, an' I like to up an' cried."

"Dave," said the widow, "I kin see you two as if you was settin' there front of me. He was alwus like that. Oh, my! Oh, my! David," she added solemnly, while two tears rolled slowly down her wrinkled face, "we lived together, husban' an' wife, fer seven year, an' he never give me a cross word."

"I don't doubt it a mossel," said David simply, leaning over and poking the fire, which operation kept his face out of her sight and was prolonged rather unduly. Finally he straightened up and, blowing his nose as it were a trumpet, said:

"Wa'al, the cirkis fin'ly come to an end, an' the crowd hustled to git out 's if they was afraid the tent 'd come down on 'em. I got kind o' mixed up in 'em, an' somebody tried to git my tin pail, or I thought he did, an' the upshot was that I lost sight o' Billy P., an' couldn't make out to ketch a glimpse of him nowhere. An' *then* I kind o' come down to earth, kerchug! It was five o'clock, an' I had better 'n four mile to walk--mostly up hill--an' if I knowed anything 'bout the old man, an' I thought I ***did***, I had the all-firedist lickin' ahead of me 't I'd ever got, an' that was sayin' a good deal. But, boy 's I was, I had grit enough to allow 't was wuth it, an' off I put."

"Did he lick ye much?" inqured Mrs. Cullom anxiously.

"Wa'al," replied David, "he done his best. He was layin' fer me when I struck the front gate--I knowed it wa'n't no use to try the back door, an' he took me by the ear--most pulled it off--an' marched me off to the barn shed without a word. I never see him so mad. Seemed like he couldn't speak fer a while, but fin'ly he says, 'Where you ben all day?'

"'Down t' the village,' I says.

"'What you ben up to down there?' he says.

"'Went to the cirkis,' I says, thinkin' I might 's well make a clean breast on't.

"'Where 'd you git the money?' he says.

"'Mr. Cullom took me,' I says.

"'You lie,' he says. 'You stole the money somewheres, an' I'll trounce it out of ye, if I kill ye,' he says.

"Wa'al," said David, twisting his shoulders in recollection, "I won't harrer up your feelin's. 'S I told you, he done his best. I was willin' to quit long 'fore he was. Fact was, he overdone it a little, an' he had to throw water in my face 'fore he got through; an' he done that as thorough as the other thing. I was somethin' like a chickin jest out o' the cistern. I crawled off to bed the best I could, but I didn't lay on my back fer a good spell, I c'n tell ye."

"You poor little critter," exclaimed Mrs. Cullom sympathetically. "You poor little critter!"

"'T was more'n wuth it, Mis' Cullom," said David emphatically. "I'd had the most enjoy'ble day, I might say the only enjoy'ble day, 't I'd ever had in my hull life, an' I hain't never fergot it. I got over the lickin' in course of time, but I've ben enjoyin' that cirkis fer forty year. The' wa'n't but one thing to hender, an' that's this, that I hain't never ben able to remember--an' to this day I lay awake nights tryin' to--that I said 'Thank ye' to Billy P., an' I never seen him after that day."

"How's that?" asked Mrs. Cullom.

"Wa'al," was the reply, "that day was the turnin' point with me. The next night I lit out with what duds I c'd git together, an' as much grub 's I could pack in that tin pail; an' the next time I see the old house on Buxton Hill the' hadn't ben no Harums in it fer years."

Here David rose from his chair, yawned and stretched himself, and stood with his back to the fire. The widow looked up anxiously into his face. "Is that all?" she asked after a while.

"Wa'al, it is an' it ain't. I've got through yarnin' about Dave Harum at any rate, an' mebbe we'd better have a little confab on your matters, seein' 't I've got you 'way up here such a mornin' 's this. I gen'ally do bus'nis fust an' talkin' afterward," he added, "but I kind o' got to goin' an' kept on this time."

He put his hand into the breast pocket of his coat and took out three papers, which he shuffled in review as if to verify their identity, and then held them in one hand, tapping them softly upon the palm of the other, as if at a loss how to begin. The widow sat with her eyes fastened upon the papers, trembling with nervous apprehension. Presently he broke the silence.

"About this here morgidge o' your'n," he said, "I sent ye word that I wanted to close the matter up, an' seein' 't you're here an' come fer that purpose, I guess we'd better make a job on't. The' ain't no time like the present, as the sayin' is."

"I s'pose it'll hev to be as you say," said the widow in a shaking voice.

"Mis' Cullom," said David solemnly, "*you* know, an' I know, that I've got the repitation of bein' a hard, graspin', schemin' man. Mebbe I be. Mebbe I've ben hard done by all my hull life, an' have had to be; an' mebbe, now 't I've got ahead some, it's got to be second nature, an' I can't seem to help it. 'Bus'nis is bus'nis' ain't part of the golden rule, I allow, but the way it gen'ally runs, fur 's I've found out, is, 'Do unto the other feller the way he'd like to do unto you, an' do it fust.' But, if you want to keep this thing a-runnin' as it's goin' on now fer a spell longer, say one year, or two, or even three, you may, only I've got somethin' to say to ye 'fore ye elect."

"Wa'al," said the poor woman, "I expect it 'd only be pilin' up wrath agin' the day o' wrath. I can't pay the int'rist now without starvin', an' I hain't got no one to bid in the prop'ty fer me if it was to be sold."

"Mis' Cullom," said David, "I said I'd got somethin' more to tell ye, an' if, when I git through, you don't think I've treated you right, includin' this mornin's confab, I hope you'll fergive me. It's this, an' I'm the only person livin' that 's knowin' to it, an' in fact I may say that I'm the only person that ever was really knowin' to it. It was before you was married, an' I'm sure he never told ye, fer I don't doubt he fergot all about it, but your husband, Billy P. Cullom, that was, made a small investment once on a time, yes, ma'am, he did, an' in his kind of careless way it jest slipped his mind. The amount of cap'tal he put in wa'n't large, but the rate of int'rist was uncommon high. Now, he never drawed no dividends on't, an' they've ben 'cumulatin' fer forty year, more or less, at compound int'rist."

The widow started forward, as if to rise from her seat. David put his hand out gently and said, "Jest a minute, Mis' Cullom, jest a minute, till I git through. Part o' that cap'tal," he resumed, "consistin' of a quarter an' some odd cents, was invested in the cirkis bus'nis, an' the rest on't--the cap'tal, an' all the cash cap'tal that I started in bus'nis with--was the ten cents your husband give me that day, an' here," said David, striking the papers in his left hand with the back of his right, "*here* is the *dividends*! This here second morgidge, not bein' on record, may jest as well go onto the fire--it's gettin' low--an' here's a satisfaction piece which I'm goin' to execute now, that'll clear the thousan' dollar one. Come in here, John," he called out.

The widow stared at David for a moment speechless, but as the significance of his words dawned upon her, the blood flushed darkly in her face. She sprang to her feet and, throwing up her arms, cried out: "My Lord! My Lord! Dave! Dave Harum! Is it true?--tell me it's true! You ain't foolin' me, air ye, Dave? You wouldn't fool a poor old woman that never done ye no harm, nor said a mean word agin ye, would ye? Is it true? an' is my place clear? an' I don't owe nobody anythin'--I mean, no money? Tell it agin. Oh, tell it agin! Oh, Dave! it's too good to be true! Oh! Oh! Oh, *my*! an' here I be cryin' like a great baby, an', an'"--fumbling in her pocket--"I do believe I hain't got no hank'chif--Oh, thank ye," to John; "I'll do it up an' send it back to-morrer. Oh, what made ye do it, Dave?"

"Set right down an' take it easy, Mis' Cullom," said David soothingly, putting his hands on her shoulders and gently pushing her back into her chair. "Set right down an' take it easy.--Yes," to John, "I acknowledge that I signed that."

He turned to the widow, who sat wiping her eyes with John's handkerchief.

"Yes, ma'am," he said, "It's as true as anythin' kin be. I wouldn't no more fool ye, ye know I wouldn't, don't ye? than I'd--jerk a hoss," he asseverated. "Your place is clear now, an' by this time to-morro' the' won't be the scratch of a pen agin it. I'll send the satisfaction over fer record fust thing in the mornin'."

"But, Dave," protested the widow, "I s'pose ye know what you're doin'--?"

"Yes," he interposed, "I cal'late I do, putty near. You ast me why I done it, an' I'll tell ye if ye want to know. I'm payin' off an old score, an' gettin' off cheap, too. That's what I'm doin'! I thought I'd hinted up to it putty plain, seein' 't I've talked till my jaws ache; but I'll sum it up to ye if you like."

He stood with his feet aggressively wide apart, one hand in his trousers pocket, and holding in the other the "morgidge," which he waved from time to time in emphasis.

"You c'n estimate, I reckon," he began, "what kind of a bringin'-up I had, an' what a poor, mis'able, God-fersaken, scairt-to-death little forlorn critter I was; put upon, an' snubbed, an' jawed at till I'd come to believe myself--what was rubbed into me the hull time--that I was the most all-'round no-account animul that was ever made out o' dust, an' wa'n't ever likely to be no diff'rent. Lookin' back, it seems to me that--exceptin' of Polly--I never had a kind word said to me, nor a day's fun. Your husband, Billy P. Cullom, was the fust man that ever treated me human up to that time. He give me the only enjoy'ble time 't I'd ever had, an' I don't know 't anythin' 's ever equaled it since. He spent money on me, an' he give me money to spend--that had never had a cent to call my own--*an'*, Mis' Cullom, he took me by the hand, an' he talked to me, an' he gin me the fust notion 't I'd ever had that mebbe I wa'n't only the scum o' the earth, as I'd ben teached to believe. I told ye that that day was the turnin' point of my life. Wa'al, it wa'n't the lickin' I got, though that had somethin' to do with it, but I'd never have had the spunk to run away's I did if it hadn't ben for the heartenin' Billy P. gin me, an' never knowed it, an' never knowed it," he repeated mournfully. "I alwus allowed to pay some o' that debt back to him, but seein' 's I can't do that, Mis' Cullom, I'm glad an' thankful to pay it to his widdo'."

"Mebbe he knows, Dave," said Mrs. Cullom softly.

"Mebbe he does," assented David in a low voice.

Neither spoke for a time, and then the widow said: "David, I can't thank ye 's I ought ter--I don't know how--but I'll pray for ye night an' mornin' 's long 's I got breath. An', Dave," she added humbly, "I want to take back what I said about the Lord's providin'."

She sat a moment, lost in her thoughts, and then exclaimed, "Oh, it don't seem 's if I c'd wait to write to Charley!"

"I've wrote to Charley," said David, "an' told him to sell out there an' come home, an' to draw on me fer any balance he needed to move him. I've got somethin' in my eye that'll be easier an' better payin' than fightin' grasshoppers an' drought in Kansas."

"Dave Harum!" cried the widow, rising to her feet, "you ought to 'a' ben a king!"

"Wa'al," said David with a grin, "I don't know much about the kingin' bus'nis, but I guess a cloth cap 'n' a hoss whip 's more 'n my line than a crown an' scepter. An' now," he added, "'s we've got through 'th our bus'nis, s'pose you step over to the house an' see Polly. She's expectin' on ye to dinner. Oh, yes," replying to the look of deprecation in her face as she viewed her shabby frock, "you an' Polly c'n prink up some if you want to, but we can't take 'No' fer an answer Chris'mus day, clo'es or no clo'es."

"I'd really like ter," said Mrs. Cullom.

"All right then," said David cheerfully. "The path is swep' by this time, I guess, an' I'll see ye later. Oh, by the way," he exclaimed, "the's somethin' I fergot. I want to make you a proposition, ruther an onusual one, but seein' ev'rythin' is as 't is, perhaps you'll consider it."

"Dave," declared the widow, "if I could, an' you ast for it, I'd give ye anythin' on the face o' this mortal globe!"

"Wa'al," said David, nodding and smiling, "I thought that mebbe, long 's you got the int'rist of that investment we ben talkin' about, you'd let me keep what's left of the princ'pal. Would ye like to see it?"

Mrs. Cullom looked at him with a puzzled expression without replying.

David took from his pocket a large wallet, secured by a strap, and, opening it, extracted something enveloped in much faded brown paper. Unfolding this, he displayed upon his broad fat palm an old silver dime black with age.

"There's the cap'tal," he said.

CHAPTER XXI.

John walked to the front door with Mrs. Cullom, but she declined with such evident sincerity his offer to carry her bundle to the house that he let her out of the office and returned to the back room. David was sitting before the fire, leaning back in his chair with his hands thrust deep in his trousers pockets. He looked up as John entered and said, "Draw up a chair."

John brought a chair and stood by the side of it while he said, "I want to thank you for the Christmas remembrance, which pleased and touched me very deeply; and," he added diffidently, "I want to say how mortified I am--in fact, I want to apologize for--"

"Regrettin'?" interrupted David with a motion of his hand toward the chair and a smile of great amusement. "Sho, sho! Se' down, se' down. I'm glad you found somethin' in your stockin' if it pleased ye, an' as fur's that regret o' your'n was concerned--wa'al--wa'al, I liked ye all the better for't, I did fer a fact. He, he, he! Appearances was ruther agin me, wasn't they, the way I told it."

"Nevertheless," said John, seating himself, "I ought not to have--that is to say, I ought to have known--"

"How could ye," David broke in, "When I as good as told ye I was cal'latin' to rob the old lady? He, he, he, he! Scat my ----! Your face was a picture when I told ye to write that note, though I reckon you didn't know I noticed it."

John laughed and said, "You have been very generous all through, Mr. Har-um."

"Nothin' to brag on," he replied, "nothin' to brag on. Fur 's Mis' Cullom's matter was concerned, 't was as I said, jest payin' off an old score; an' as fur 's your stockin', it's really putty much the same. I'll allow you've earned it, if it'll set any easier on your stomach."

"I can't say that I have been overworked," said John with a slight laugh.

"Mebbe not," rejoined David, "but you hain't ben overpaid neither, an' I want ye to be satisfied. Fact is," he continued, "my gettin' you up here was putty consid'able of an experiment, but I ben watchin' ye putty close, an' I'm more'n satisfied. Mebbe Timson c'd beat ye at figurin' an' countin' money when you fust come, an' knowed more about the pertic'ler points of the office, but outside of that he was the biggist dumb-head I ever see, an' you know how he left things. He hadn't no tack, fer one thing. Outside of summin' up figures an' countin' money he had a faculty fer gettin' things t'other-end to that beat all. I'd tell him a thing, an' explain it to him two three times over, an' he'd say 'Yes, yes,' an', scat my ----! when it came to carryin' on't out, he hadn't sensed it a mite--jest got it which-end-t'other. An talk! Wa'al, I think it must 'a' ben a kind of disease with him. He really didn't mean no harm, mebbe, but he couldn't no more help lettin' out anythin' he knowed, or thought he knowed, than a settin' hen c'n help settin'. He kep' me on tenter-hooks the hull endurin' time."

"I should say he was honest enough, was he not?" said John.

"Oh, yes," replied David with a touch of scorn, "he was honest enough fur 's money matters was concerned; but he hadn't no tack, nor no sense, an' many a time he done more mischief with his gibble-gabble than if he'd took fifty dollars out an' out. Fact is," said David, "the kind of honesty that won't actually steal 's a kind of fool honesty that's common enough; but the kind that keeps a feller's mouth shut when he hadn't ought to talk 's about the scurcest thing goin'. I'll jest tell ye, fer example, the last mess he made. You know Purse, that keeps the gen'ral store? Wa'al, he come to me some months ago, on the quiet, an' said that he wanted to borro' five hunderd. He didn't want to git no indorser, but he'd show me his books an' give me a statement an' a chattel morgidge fer six months. He didn't want nobody to know 't he was anyway pushed fer money because he wanted to git some extensions, an' so on. I made up my mind it was all right, an' I done it. Wa'al, about a month or so after he come to me with tears in his eyes, as ye might say, an' says, 'I got somethin' I want to show ye,' an' handed out a letter from the house in New York he had some of his biggist dealin's with, tellin' him that they regretted"--here David gave John a nudge--"that they couldn't give him the extensions he ast for, an' that his paper must be paid as it fell due--some twelve hunderd dollars. 'Somebody 's leaked,' he says, 'an' they've heard of that morgidge, an' I'm in a putty scrape,' he says.

"'H'm'm,' I says, 'what makes ye think so?'

"'Can't be nothin' else,' he says; 'I've dealt with them people fer years an' never ast fer nothin' but what I got it, an' now to have 'em round up on me like this, it can't be nothin' but what they've got wind o' that chattel morgidge,' he says.

"'H'm'm,' I says. 'Any o' their people ben up here lately?' I says.

"'That's jest it,' he says. 'One o' their travellin' men was up here last week, an' he come in in the afternoon as chipper as you please, wantin' to sell me a bill o' goods, an' I put him off, sayin' that I had a putty big stock, an' so on, an' he said he'd see me agin in the mornin'--you know that sort of talk,' he says.

"'Wa'al,' I says, 'did he come in?'

"'No,' says Purse, 'he didn't. I never set eyes on him agin, an' more'n that,' he says, 'he took the first train in the mornin', an' now,' he says, 'I expect I'll have ev'ry last man I owe anythin' to buzzin' 'round my ears.'

"'Wa'al,' I says, 'I guess I see about how the land lays, an' I reckon you ain't fur out about the morgidge bein' at the bottom on't, an' the' ain't no way it c'd 'a' leaked out 'ceptin' through that dum'd chuckle-head of a Timson. But this is the way it looks to me--you hain't heard nothin' in the village, have ye?' I says.

"'No,' he says. 'Not *yit*,' he says.

"'Wa'al, ye won't, I don't believe,' I says, 'an' as fur as that drummer is concerned, you c'n bet,' I says, 'that he didn't nor won't let on to nobody but his own folks--not till *his* bus'nis is squared up, an' more 'n that,' I says, 'seein' that your trouble 's ben made ye by one o' my help, I don't see but what I'll have to see ye through,' I says. 'You jest give me the address of the New York parties, an' tell me what you want done, an' I reckon I c'n fix the thing so 't they won't bother ye. I don't believe,' I says, 'that anybody else knows anythin' yet, an' I'll shut up Timson's yawp so 's it'll stay shut.'"

"How did the matter come out?" asked John, "and what did Purse say?"

"Oh," replied David, "Purse went off head up an' tail up. He said he was everlastin'ly obliged to me, an'--he, he, he!--he said 't was more 'n he expected. You see I charged him what I thought was right on the 'rig'nal deal, an' he squimmidged some, an' I reckon he allowed to be putty well bled if I took holt agin; but I done as I agreed on the extension bus'nis, an' I'm on his paper for twelve hunderd fer nothin', jest because that nikum-noddy of a Timson let that drummer bamboozle him into talkin'. I found out the hull thing, an' the very day I wrote to the New York fellers fer Purse, I wrote to Gen'ral Wolsey to find me somebody to take Timson's place. I allowed I'd ruther have somebody that didn't know nobody, than such a clackin' ole he-hen as Chet."

"I should have said that it was rather a hazardous thing to do," said John, "to put a total stranger like me into what is rather a confidential position, as well as a responsible one."

"Wa'al," said David, "in the fust place I knew that the Gen'ral wouldn't recommend no dead-beat nor no skin, an' I allowed that if the raw material was O.K., I could break it in; an' if it wa'n't I should find it out putty quick. Like a young hoss," he remarked, "if he's sound an' kind, an' got gumption, I'd sooner break him in myself 'n not--fur's my use goes--an' if I can't, nobody can, an' I get rid on him. You understand?"

"Yes," said John with a smile.

"Wa'al," continued David, "I liked your letter, an' when you come I liked your looks. Of course I couldn't tell jest how you'd take holt, nor if you an' me 'd hitch. An' then agin, I didn't know whether you could stan' it here after livin' in a city all your life. I watched ye putty close--closter 'n you knowed of, I guess. I seen right off that you was goin' to fill your collar, fur's the work was concerned, an' though you didn't know nobody much, an' couldn't have no amusement to speak on, you didn't mope nor sulk, an' what's more--though I know I advised ye to stay there fer a spell longer when you spoke about boardin' somewhere else--I know what the Eagle tavern is in winter; summer, too, fer that matter, though it's a little better then, an' I allowed that air test 'd be final. He, he, he! Putty rough, ain't it?"

"It is, rather," said John, laughing. "I'm afraid my endurance is pretty well at an end. Elright's wife is ill, and the fact is, that since day before yesterday I have been living on what I could buy at the grocery--crackers, cheese, salt fish, canned goods, *et cetera*."

"Scat my ----!" cried David. "Wa'al! Wa'al! That's too dum'd bad! Why on earth--why, you must be **hungry**! Wa'al, you won't have to eat no salt herrin' to-day, because Polly 'n I are expectin' ye to dinner."

Two or three times during the conversation David had gone to the window overlooking his lawn and looked out with a general air of observing the weather, and at this point he did so again, coming back to his seat with a look of satisfaction, for which there was, to John, no obvious reason. He sat for a moment without speaking, and then, looking at his watch, said: "Wa'al, dinner 's at one o'clock, an' Polly's a great one fer bein' on time. Guess I'll go out an' have another look at that pesky colt. You better go over to the house 'bout quarter to one, an' you c'n make your t'ilet over there. I'm 'fraid if you go over to the Eagle it'll spoil your appetite. She'd think it might, anyway."

So David departed to see the colt, and John got out some of the books and busied himself with them until the time to present himself at David's house.

CHAPTER XXII.

"Why, Mis' Cullom, I'm real glad to see ye. Come right in," said Mrs. Bixbee as she drew the widow into the "wing settin' room," and proceeded to relieve her of her wraps and her bundle. "Set right here by the fire while I take these things of your'n into the kitchen to dry 'em out. I'll be right back"; and she bustled out of the room. When she came back Mrs. Cullom was sitting with her hands in her lap, and there was in her eyes an expression of smiling peace that was good to see.

Mrs. Bixbee drew up a chair, and seating herself, said: "Wa'al, I don't know when I've seen ye to git a chance to speak to ye, an' I was real pleased when David said you was goin' to be here to dinner. An' my! how well, you're lookin'--more like Cynthy Sweetland than I've seen ye fer I don't know when; an' yet," she added, looking curiously at her guest, "you 'pear somehow as if you'd ben cryin'."

"You're real kind, I'm sure," responded Mrs. Cullom, replying to the other's welcome and remarks *seriatim*; "I guess, though, I don't look much like Cynthy Sweetland, if I do feel twenty years younger 'n I did a while ago; an' I have ben cryin', I allow, but not fer sorro', Polly Harum," she exclaimed, giving the other her maiden name. "Your brother Dave comes putty nigh to bein' an angel!"

"Wa'al," replied Mrs. Bixbee with a twinkle, "I reckon Dave might hev to be fixed up some afore he come out in that pertic'ler shape, but," she added impressively, "es fur as bein' a *man* goes, he's 'bout 's good 's they make 'em. I know folks thinks he's a hard bargainer, an' close-fisted, an' some on 'em that ain't fit to lick up his tracks says more'n that. He's got his own ways, I'll allow, but down at bottom, an' all through, I know the' ain't no better man livin'. No, ma'am, the' ain't, an' what he's ben to me, Cynthy Cullom, nobody knows but me--an'--an'--mebbe the Lord--though I hev seen the time," she said tentatively, "when it seemed to me 't I knowed more about my affairs 'n He did," and she looked doubtfully at her companion, who had been following her with affirmative and sympathetic nods, and now drew her chair a little closer, and said softly: "Yes, yes, I know. I ben putty doubtful an' rebellious myself a good many times, but seems now as if He had had me in His mercy all the time." Here Aunt Polly's sense of humor asserted itself. "What's Dave ben up to now?" she asked.

And then the widow told her story, with tears and smiles, and the keen enjoyment which we all have in talking about ourselves to a sympathetic listener like Aunt Polly, whose interjections pointed and illuminated the narrative. When it was finished she leaned forward and kissed Mrs. Cullom on the cheek.

"I can't tell ye how glad I be for ye," she said; "but if I'd known that David held that morgidge, I could hev told ye ye needn't hev worried yourself a mite. He wouldn't never have taken your prop'ty, more'n he'd rob a hen-roost. But he done the thing his own way--kind o' fetched it round fer a Merry Chris'mus, didn't he? Curious," she said reflectively, after a momentary pause, "how he lays up things about his childhood," and then, with a searching look at the Widow Cullom, "you didn't let on, an' I didn't ask ye, but of course you've heard the things that some folks says of him, an' natchally they got some holt on your mind. There's that story about 'Lish, over to Whitcom--you heard somethin' about that, didn't ye?"

"Yes," admitted the widow, "I heard somethin' of it, I s'pose."

"Wa'al," said Mrs. Bixbee, "you never heard the hull story, ner anybody else really, but I'm goin' to tell it to ye--"

"Yes," said Mrs. Cullom assentingly.

Mrs. Bixbee sat up straight in her chair with her hands on her knees and an air of one who would see justice done.

"'Lish Harum," she began, "wa'n't only half-brother to Dave. He was hull-brother to me, though, but notwithstandin' that, I will say that a meaner boy, a meaner growin' man, an' a meaner man never walked the earth. He wa'n't satisfied to git the best piece an' the biggist piece--he hated to hev any one else git anythin' at all. I don't believe he ever laughed in his life, except over some kind o' suff'rin'-

-man or beast--an' what'd tickle him the most was to be the means on't. He took pertic'ler delight in abusin' an' tormentin' Dave, an' the poor little critter was jest as 'fraid as death of him, an' good reason. Father was awful hard, but he didn't go out of his way; but 'Lish never let no chance slip. Wa'al, I ain't goin' to give you the hull fam'ly hist'ry, an' I've got to go into the kitchen fer a while 'fore dinner, but what I started out fer 's this: 'Lish fin'ly settled over to Whitcom."

"Did he ever git married?" interrupted Mrs. Cullom.

"Oh, yes," replied Mrs. Bixbee, "he got married when he was past forty. It's curious," she remarked, in passing, "but it don't seem as if the' was ever yit a man so mean but he c'd find some woman was fool enough to marry him, an' she was a putty decent sort of a woman too, f'm all accounts, an' good lookin'. Wa'al, she stood him six or seven year, an' then she run off."

"With another man?" queried the widow in an awed voice. Aunt Polly nodded assent with compressed lips.

"Yes'm," she went on, "she left him an' went out West somewhere, an' that was the last of **her**; an' when her two boys got old enough to look after themselves a little, they quit him too, an' they wa'n't no way growed up neither. Wa'al, the long an' the short on't was that 'Lish got goin' down hill ev'ry way, health an' all, till he hadn't nothin' left but his disposition, an' fairly got onter the town. The' wa'n't nothin' for it but to send him to the county house, onless somebody 'd s'port him. Wa'al, the committee knew Dave was his brother, an' one on 'em come to see him to see if he'd come forwud an' help out, an' he seen Dave right here in this room, an' Dave made me stay an' hear the hull thing. Man's name was Smith, I remember, a peaked little man with long chin whiskers that he kep' clawin' at with his fingers. Dave let him tell his story, an' he didn't say nothin' fer a minute or two, an' then he says, 'What made ye come to me?' he says. 'Did he send ye?'

"'Wa'al,' says Smith, 'when it was clear that he couldn't do nuthin', we ast him if the' wa'n't nobody could put up fer him, an' he said you was his brother, an' well off, an' hadn't ought to let him go t' the poorhouse.'

"'He said that, did he?' says Dave.

"'Amountin' to that,' says Smith.

"'Wa'al,' says Dave, 'it's a good many years sence I see 'Lish, an' mebbe you know him better 'n I do. You known him some time, eh?'

"'Quite a number o' years,' says Smith.

"'What sort of a feller was he,' says Dave, 'when he was somebody? Putty good feller? good citizen? good neighber? lib'ral? kind to his fam'ly? ev'rybody like him? gen'ally pop'lar, an' all that?'

"'Wa'al,' says Smith, wigglin' in his chair an' pullin' out his whiskers three four hairs to a time, 'I guess he come some short of all that.'

"'E'umph!' says Dave, 'I guess he did! Now, honest,' he says, '*is* the' man, woman, or child in Whitcom that knows 'Lish Harum that's got a good word fer him? or ever knowed of his doin' or sayin' anythin' that hadn't got a mean side to it some way? Didn't he drive his wife off, out an' out? an' didn't his two boys hev to quit him soon 's they could travel? *An*',' says Dave, 'if any one was to ask you to figure out a pattern of the meanist human skunk you was capable of thinkin' of, wouldn't it--honest, now!' Dave says, 'honest, now--wouldn't it be 's near like 'Lish Harum as one buckshot 's like another?'"

"My!" exclaimed Mrs. Cullom. "What did Mr. Smith say to that?"

"Wa'al," replied Mrs. Bixbee, "he didn't say nuthin' at fust, not in so many words. He sot fer a minute clawin' away at his whiskers--an' he'd got both hands into 'em by that time--an' then he made a move as if he gin the hull thing up an' was goin'. Dave set lookin' at him, an' then he says, 'You ain't goin', air ye?'

"'Wa'al,' says Smith, 'feelin' 's you do, I guess my arrant here ain't goin' t' amount to nothin', an' I may 's well.'

"'No, you set still a minute,' says Dave. 'If you'll answer my question honest an' square, I've got sunthin' more to say to ye. Come, now,' he says.

"'Wa'al,' says Smith, with a kind of give-it-up sort of a grin, 'I guess you sized him up about right. I didn't come to see you on 'Lish Harum's account. I come fer the town of Whitcom.' An' then he spunked up some an' says, 'I don't give a darn,' he says, 'what comes of 'Lish, an' I don't know nobody as does, fur's he's person'ly concerned; but he's got to be a town charge less 'n you take 'm off our hands.'

"Dave turned to me an' says, jest as if he meant it, 'How 'd you like to have him here, Polly?'

"'Dave Harum!' I says, 'what be you thinkin' of, seein' what he is, an' alwus was, an' how he alwus treated you? Lord sakes!' I says, 'you ain't thinkin' of it!'

"'Not much,' he says, with an ugly kind of a smile, such as I never see in his face before, 'not much! Not under this roof, or any roof of mine, if it wa'n't more'n my cow stable--an',' he says, turnin' to Smith, 'this is what I want to say to you: You've done all right. I hain't no fault to find with you. But I want you to go back an' say to 'Lish Harum that you've seen me, an' that I told you that not one cent of my money nor one mossel o' my food would ever go to keep him alive one minute of time; that if I had an empty hogpen I wouldn't let him sleep in't overnight, much less to bunk in with a decent hog. You tell him that I said the poorhouse was his proper dwellin', barrin' the jail, an' that it 'd have to be a dum'd sight poorer house 'n I ever heard of not to be a thousan' times too good fer him.'"

"My!" exclaimed Mrs. Cullom again. "I can't really 'magine it of Dave."

"Wa'al," replied Mrs. Bixbee, "I told ye how set he is on his young days, an' no-body knows how cruel mean 'Lish used to be to him; but I never see it come out of him so ugly before, though I didn't blame him a mite. But I hain't told ye the upshot: 'Now,' he says to Smith, who set with his mouth gappin' open, 'you understand how I feel about the feller, an' I've got good reason for it. I want you to promise me that you'll say to him, word fer word, jest what I've said to you about him, an' I'll do this: You folks send him to the poorhouse, an' let him git jest what the rest on 'em gits--no more an' no less--as long 's he lives. When he dies you git him the tightest coffin you kin buy, to keep him f'm spilin' the earth as long as may be, an' then you send me the hull bill. But this has got to be between you an' me only. You c'n tell the rest of the committee what you like, *but* if you ever tell a livin' soul about this here understandin', an' I find it out, I'll never pay one cent, an' you'll be to blame. I'm willin', on them terms, to stan' between the town of Whitcom an' harm; but fer 'Lish Harum, not one sumarkee! Is it a barg'in?' Dave says.

"'Yes, sir,' says Smith, puttin' out his hand. 'An' I guess,' he says, 'f'm all 't I c'n gather, thet you're doin' all 't we could expect, an' more too,' an' off he put."

"How 'd it come out?" asked Mrs. Cullom.

"'Lish lived about two year," replied Aunt Polly, "an' Dave done as he agreed, but even then when he come to settle up, he told Smith he didn't want no more said about it 'n could be helped."

"Wa'al," said Mrs. Cullom, "it seems to me as if David did take care on him after all, fur 's spendin' money was concerned."

"That's the way it looks to me," said Mrs. Bixbee, "but David likes to think t'other. He meant to be awful mean, an' he was--as mean as he could--but the fact is, he didn't reelly know how. My sakes! Cynthy (looking at the clock), I'll hev to excuse myself fer a spell. Ef you want to do any fixin' up 'fore dinner, jest step into my bedroom. I've laid some things out on the bed, if you should happen to want any of 'em," and she hurried out of the room.

CHAPTER XXIII.

David's house stood about a hundred feet back from the street, facing the east. The main body of the house was of two stories (through which ran a deep bay in front), with mansard roof. On the south of the main body of the house were two stories of the "wing," in which were the "settin' room," Aunt Polly's room, and, above, David's quarters. Ten minutes or so before one o'clock John rang the bell at the front door.

"Sairy's busy," said Mrs. Bixbee apologetically as she let him in, "an' so I come to the door myself."

"Thank you very much," said John. "Mr. Harum told me to come over a little before one, but perhaps I ought to have waited a few minutes longer."

"No, it's all right," she replied, "for mebbe you'd like to wash an' fix up 'fore dinner, so I'll jest show ye where to," and she led the way upstairs and into the "front parlor bedroom."

"There," she said, "make yourself comf'table, an' dinner 'll be ready in about ten minutes."

For a moment John mentally rubbed his eyes. Then he turned and caught both of Mrs. Bixbee's hands and looked at her, speechless. When he found words he said: "I don't know what to say, nor how to thank you properly. I don't believe you know how kind this is."

"Don't say nothin' about it," she protested, but with a look of great satisfaction. "I done it jest t' relieve my mind, because ever sence you fust come, I ben worryin' over your bein' at that nasty tavern," and she made a motion to go.

"You and your brother," said John earnestly, still holding her hands, "have made me a gladder and happier man this Christmas day than I have been for a very long time."

"I'm glad on't," she said heartily, "an' I hope you'll be comf'table an' contented here. I must go now an' help Sairy dish up. Come down to the settin' room when you're ready," and she gave his hands a little squeeze.

"Aunt Po----, I beg pardon, Mrs. Bixbee," said John, moved by a sudden impulse, "do you think you could find it in your heart to complete my happiness by giving me a kiss? It's Christmas, you know," he added smilingly.

Aunt Polly colored to the roots of her hair. "Wa'al," she said, with a little laugh, "seein' 't I'm old enough to be your mother, I guess 't won't hurt me none," and as she went down the stairs she softly rubbed her lips with the side of her forefinger.

John understood now why David had looked out of the bank window so often that morning. All his belongings were in Aunt Polly's best bedroom, having been moved over from the Eagle while he and David had been in the office. A delightful room it was, in immeasurable contrast to his squalid surroundings at that hostelry. The spacious bed, with its snowy counterpane and silk patchwork "comf'table" folded on the foot, the bright fire in the open stove, the big bureau and glass, the soft carpet, the table for writing and reading standing in the bay, his books on the broad mantel, and his dressing things laid out ready to his hand, not to mention an ample supply of *dry* towels on the rack.

The poor fellow's life during the weeks which he had lived in Homeville had been utterly in contrast with any previous experience. Nevertheless he had tried to make the best of it, and to endure the monotony, the dullness, the entire lack of companionship and entertainment with what philosophy he could muster. The hours spent in the office were the best part of the day. He could manage to find occupation for all of them, though a village bank is not usually a scene of active bustle. Many of the people who did business there diverted him somewhat, and most of them seemed never too much in a hurry to stand around and talk the sort of thing that interested them. After John had got acquainted with his duties and the people he came in contact with, David gave less personal attention to the affairs of the bank; but he was in and out frequently during the day, and rarely failed to interest his cashier with his observations and remarks.

But the long winter evenings had been very bad. After supper, a meal which revolted every sense, there had been as many hours to be got through with as he found wakeful, an empty stomach often adding to the number of them, and the only resource for passing the time had been reading, which had often been well-nigh impossible for sheer physical discomfort. As has been remarked, the winter climate of the middle portion of New York State is as bad as can be imagined. His light was a kerosene lamp of half-candle power, and his appliance for warmth consisted of a small wood stove, which (as David would have expressed it) "took two men an' a boy" to keep in action, and was either red hot or exhausted.

As from the depths of a spacious lounging chair he surveyed his new surroundings, and contrasted them with those from which he had been rescued out of pure kindness, his heart was full, and it can hardly be imputed to him as a weakness that for a moment his eyes filled with tears of gratitude and happiness--no less.

Indeed, there were four happy people at David's table that Christmas day. Aunt Polly had "smartened up" Mrs. Cullom with collar and cuffs, and in various ways which the mind of man comprehendeth not in detail; and there had been some arranging of her hair as well, which altogether had so transformed and transfigured her that John thought that he should hardly have known her for the forlorn creature whom he had encountered in the morning. And as he looked at the still fine eyes, large and brown, and shining for the first time in many a year with a soft light of happiness, he felt that he could understand how it was that Billy P. had married the village girl.

Mrs. Bixbee was grand in black silk and lace collar fastened with a shell-cameo pin not quite as large as a saucer, and John caught the sparkle of a diamond on her plump left hand--David's Christmas gift--with regard to which she had spoken apologetically to Mrs. Cullom:

"I told David that I was ever so much obliged to him, but I didn't want a dimun' more'n a cat wanted a flag, an' I thought it was jest throwin' away money. But he would have it--said I c'd sell it an' keep out the poorhouse some day, mebbe."

David had not made much change in his usual raiment, but he was shaved to the blood, and his round red face shone with soap and satisfaction. As he tucked his napkin into his shirt collar, Sairy brought in the tureen of oyster soup, and he remarked, as he took his first spoonful of the stew, that he was "hungry 'nough t' eat a graven imidge," a condition that John was able to sympathize with after his two days of fasting on crackers and such provisions as he could buy at Purse's. It was, on the whole, he reflected, the most enjoyable dinner that he ever ate. Never was such a turkey; and to see it give way under David's skillful knife--wings, drumsticks, second joints, side bones, breast--was an elevating and memorable experience. And such potatoes, mashed in cream; such boiled onions, turnips, Hubbard squash, succotash, stewed tomatoes, celery, cranberries, "currant jell!" Oh! and to "top off" with, a mince pie to die for and a pudding (new to John, but just you try it some time) of steamed Indian meal and fruit, with a sauce of cream sweetened with shaved maple sugar.

"What'll you have?" said David to Mrs. Cullom, "dark meat? white meat?"

"Anything," she replied meekly, "I'm not partic'ler. Most any part of a turkey 'll taste good, I guess."

"All right," said David. "Don't care means a little o' both. I alwus know what to give Polly--piece o' the second jint an' the last-thing-over-the-fence. Nice 'n rich fer scraggly folks," he remarked. "How fer you, John?--little o' both, eh?" and he heaped the plate till our friend begged him to keep something for himself.

"Little too much is jest right," he asserted.

When David had filled the plates and handed them along--Sairy was for bringing in and taking out; they did their own helping to vegetables and "passin'"--he hesitated a moment, and then got out of his chair and started in the direction of the kitchen door.

"What's the matter?" asked Mrs. Bixbee in surprise. "Where you goin'?"

"Woodshed," said David.

"Woodshed!" she exclaimed, making as if to rise and follow.

"You set still," said David. "Somethin' I fergot."

"What on earth!" she exclaimed, with an air of annoyance and bewilderment. "What do you want in the woodshed? Can't you set down an' let Sairy git it for ye?"

"No," he asserted with a grin. "Sairy might sqush it. It must be putty meller by this time," And out he went.

"Manners!" ejaculated Mrs. Bixbee. "You'll think (to John) we're reg'ler heathin."

"I guess not," said John, smiling and much amused.

Presently Sairy appeared with four tumblers which she distributed, and was followed by David bearing a bottle. He seated himself and began a struggle to un-wire the same with an ice-pick. Aunt Polly leaned forward with a look of perplexed curiosity.

"What you got there?" she asked.

"Vewve Clikot's universal an' suv'rin remedy," said David, reading the label and bringing the corners of his eye and mouth almost together in a wink to John, "fer toothache, earache, burns, scalds, warts, dispepsy, fallin' o' the hair, windgall, ringbone, spavin, disapp'inted affections, an' pips in hens," and out came the cork with a "*wop*," at which both the ladies, even Mrs. Cullom, jumped and cried out.

"David Harum," declared his sister with conviction, "I believe thet that's a bottle of champagne."

"If it ain't," said David, pouring into his tumbler, "I ben swindled out o' four shillin'," and he passed the bottle to John, who held it up tentatively, looking at Mrs. Bixbee.

"No, thank ye," she said with a little toss of the head, "I'm a son o' temp'rence. I don't believe," she remarked to Mrs. Cullom, "thet that bottle ever cost *less* 'n a dollar." At which remarks David apparently "swallered somethin' the wrong way," and for a moment or two was unable to proceed with his dinner. Aunt Polly looked at him suspiciously. It was her experience that, in her intercourse with her brother, he often laughed utterly without reason--so far as she could see.

"I've always heard it was dreadful expensive," remarked Mrs. Cullom.

"Let me give you some," said John, reaching toward her with the bottle. Mrs. Cullom looked first at Mrs. Bixbee and then at David.

"I don't know," she said. "I never tasted any."

"Take a little," said David, nodding approvingly.

"Just a swallow," said the widow, whose curiosity had got the better of scruples. She took a swallow of the wine.

"How do ye like it?" asked David.

"Well," she said as she wiped her eyes, into which the gas had driven the tears, "I guess I could get along if I couldn't have it regular."

"Don't taste good?" suggested David with a grin.

"Well," she replied, "I never did care any great for cider, and this tastes to me about as if I was drinkin' cider an' snuffin' horseradish at one and the same time."

"How's that, John?" said David, laughing.

"I suppose it's an acquired taste," said John, returning the laugh and taking a mouthful of the wine with infinite relish. "I don't think I ever enjoyed a glass of wine so much, or," turning to Aunt Polly, "ever enjoyed a dinner so much," which statement completely mollified her feelings, which had been the least bit in the world "set edgeways."

"Mebbe your app'tite's got somethin' to do with it," said David, shoveling a knife-load of good things into his mouth. "Polly, this young man's ben livin' on crackers an' salt herrin' fer a week."

"My land!" cried Mrs. Bixbee with an expression of horror. "Is that reelly so? 'T ain't now, reelly?"

"Not quite so bad as that," John answered, smiling; "but Mrs. Elright has been ill for a couple of days and--well, I have been foraging around Purse's store a little."

"Wa'al, of all the mean shames!" exclaimed Aunt Polly indignantly. "David Harum, you'd ought to be ridic'lous t' allow such a thing."

"Wa'al, I never!" said David, holding his knife and fork straight up in either fist as they rested on the table, and staring at his sister. "I believe if the meetin'-house roof was to blow off you'd lay it onto me somehow. I hain't ben runnin' the Eagle tavern fer quite a consid'able while. You got the wrong pig by the ear as usual. Jest you pitch into him," pointing with his fork to John. "It's his funeral, if anybody's."

"Wa'al," said Aunt Polly, addressing John in a tone of injury, "I do think you might have let somebody know; I think you'd ortter 've known--"

"Yes, Mrs. Bixbee," he interrupted, "I did know how kind you are and would have been, and if matters had gone on so much longer I should have appealed to you, I should have indeed; but really," he added, smiling at her, "a dinner like this is worth fasting a week for."

"Wa'al," she said, mollified again, "you won't git no more herrin' 'nless you ask fer 'em."

"That is just what your brother said this morning," replied John, looking at David with a laugh.

CHAPTER XXIV.

The meal proceeded in silence for a few minutes. Mrs. Cullom had said but little, but John noticed that her diction was more conventional than in her talk with David and himself in the morning, and that her manner at the table was distinctly refined, although she ate with apparent appetite, not to say hunger. Presently she said, with an air of making conversation, "I suppose you've always lived in the city, Mr. Lenox?"

"It has always been my home," he replied, "but I have been away a good deal."

"I suppose folks in the city go to theaters a good deal," she remarked.

"They have a great many opportunities," said John, wondering what she was leading up to. But he was not to discover, for David broke in with a chuckle.

"Ask Polly, Mis' Cullom," he said. "She c'n tell ye all about the theater, Polly kin." Mrs. Cullom looked from David to Mrs. Bixbee, whose face was suffused.

"Tell her," said David, with a grin.

"I wish you'd shet up," she exclaimed. "I sha'n't do nothin' of the sort."

"Ne' mind," said David cheerfully, "*I'll* tell ye, Mis' Cullom."

"Dave Harum!" expostulated Mrs. Bixbee, but he proceeded without heed of her protest.

"Polly an' I," he said, "went down to New York one spring some years ago. Her nerves was some wore out 'long of diff'rences with Sairy about clearin' up the woodshed, an' bread risin's, an' not bein' able to suit herself up to Purse's in the qual'ty of silk velvit she wanted fer a Sunday-go-to-meetin' gown, an' I thought a spell off 'd do her good. Wa'al, the day after we got there I says to her while we was havin' breakfust--it was picked-up el'phant on toast, near 's I c'n remember, wa'n't it, Polly?"

"That's as near the truth as most o' the rest on't so fur," said Polly with a sniff.

"Wa'al, I says to her," he proceeded, untouched by her scorn, "'How'd you like to go t' the theater? You hain't never ben,' I says, 'an' now you're down here you may jest as well see somethin' while you got a chanst,' I says. Up to that *time*" he remarked, as it were in passing, "she'd ben somewhat pre*juced* 'ginst theaters, an'----"

"Wa'al," Mrs. Bixbee broke in, "I guess what we see that night was cal'lated----"

"You hold on," he interposed. "I'm tellin' this story. You had a chanst to an' wouldn't. Anyway," he resumed, "she allowed she'd try it once, an' we agreed we'd go somewheres that night. But somethin' happened to put it out o' my mind, an' I didn't think on't agin till I got back to the hotel fer supper. So I went to the feller at the news-stand an' says, 'Got any show-tickits fer to-night?'

"'Theater?' he says.

"'I reckon so,' I says.

"'Wa'al,' he says, 'I hain't got nothin' now but two seats fer 'Clyanthy.''

"'Is it a good show?' I says--'moral, an' so on? I'm goin' to take my sister, an' she's a little pertic'ler about some things,' I says. He kind o' grinned, the feller did. 'I've took my wife twice, an' she's putty pertic'ler herself,' he says, laughin.'"

"She must 'a' ben," remarked Mrs. Bixbee with a sniff that spoke volumes of her opinion of "the feller's wife." David emitted a chuckle.

"Wa'al," he continued, "I took the tickits on the feller's recommend, an' the fact of his wife's bein' so pertic'ler, an' after supper we went. It was a mighty hand-some place inside, gilded an' carved all over like the outside of a cirkis wagin, an' when we went in the orchestry was playin' an' the people was comin' in, an' after we'd set a few minutes I says to Polly, 'What do you think on't?' I says.

"'I don't see anythin' very unbecomin' so fur, an' the people looks respectable enough,' she says.

"'No jail birds in sight fur 's ye c'n see so fur, be they?' I says. He, he, he, he!"

"You needn't make me out more of a gump 'n I was," protested Mrs. Bixbee. "An' you was jest as----" David held up his finger at her.

"Don't you sp'ile the story by discountin' the sequil. Wa'al, putty soon the band struck up some kind of a dancin' tune, an' the curt'in went up, an' a girl come prancin' down to the footlights an' begun singin' an' dancin', an', scat my ----! to all human appearances you c'd 'a' covered ev'ry dum thing she had on with a post-age stamp." John stole a glance at Mrs. Cullom. She was staring at the speaker with wide-open eyes of horror and amazement.

"I guess I wouldn't go very *fur* into pertic'lers," said Mrs. Bixbee in a warning tone.

David bent his head down over his plate and shook from head to foot, and it was nearly a minute before he was able to go on. "Wa'al," he said, "I heard Polly give a kind of a gasp an' a snort, 's if some one 'd throwed water 'n her face. But she didn't say nothin', an', I swan! I didn't dast to look at her fer a spell; an' putty soon in come a hull crowd more girls that had left their clo'es in their trunks or somewhere, singin', an' dancin', an' weavin' 'round on the stage, an' after a few minutes I turned an' looked at Polly. He, he, he, he!"

"David Harum!" cried Mrs. Bixbee, "ef you're goin' to discribe any more o' them scand'lous goin's on I sh'll take my victuals into the kitchin. *I* didn't see no more of 'em," she added to Mrs. Cullom and John, "after that fust trollop appeared."

"I don't believe she did," said David, "fer when I turned she set there with her eys shut tighter 'n a drum, an' her mouth shut too so's her nose an' chin most come together, an' her face was red enough so 't a streak o' red paint 'd 'a' made a white mark on it. 'Polly,' I says, 'I'm afraid you ain't gettin' the wuth o' your money.'

"'David Harum,' she says, with her mouth shut all but a little place in the corner toward me, 'if you don't take me out o' this place, I'll go without ye,' she says.

"'Don't you think you c'd stan' it a little longer?' I says. 'Mebbe they've sent home fer their clo'es,' I says. He, he, he, he! But with that she jest give a hump to start, an' I see she meant bus'nis. When Polly Bixbee," said David impressively, "puts that foot o' her'n ***down*** somethin's got to sqush, an' don't you fergit it." Mrs. Bixbee made no acknowledgment of this tribute to her strength of character. John looked at David.

"Yes," he said, with a solemn bend of the head, as if in answer to a question, "I squshed. I says to her, 'All right. Don't make no disturbance more'n you c'n help, an' jest put your hank'chif up to your nose 's if you had the nosebleed,' an' we squeezed out of the seats, an' sneaked up the aisle, an' by the time we got out into the entry I guess my face was as red as Polly's. It couldn't 'a' ben no redder," he added.

"You got a putty fair color as a gen'ral thing," remarked Mrs. Bixbee dryly.

"Yes, ma'am; yes, ma'am, I expect that's so," he assented, "but I got an extry coat o' tan follerin' you out o' that theater. When we got out into the entry one o' them fellers that stands 'round steps up to me an' says, 'Ain't your ma feelin' well?' he says. 'Her feelin's has ben a trifle rumpled up,' I says, 'an' that gen'ally brings on the nosebleed,' an' then," said David, looking over Mrs. Bixbee's head, "the feller went an' leaned up agin the wall."

"David Harum!" exclaimed Mrs. Bixbee, "that's a downright *lie*. You never spoke to a soul, an'--an'--ev'rybody knows 't I ain't more 'n four years older 'n you be."

"Wa'al, you see, Polly," her brother replied in a smooth tone of measureless aggravation, "the feller wa'n't acquainted with us, an' he only went by appearances."

Aunt Polly appealed to John: "Ain't he enough to--to--I d' know what?"

"I really don't see how you live with him," said John, laughing.

Mrs. Cullom's face wore a faint smile, as if she were conscious that something amusing was going on, but was not quite sure what. The widow took things seriously for the most part, poor soul.

"I reckon you haven't followed theater-goin' much after that," she said to her hostess.

"No, ma'am," Mrs. Bixbee replied with emphasis, "you better believe I hain't. I hain't never thought of it sence without tinglin' all over. I believe," she asserted, "that David 'd 'a' stayed the thing out if it hadn't ben fer me; but as true 's you live, Cynthy Cullom, I was so 'shamed at the little 't I did see that when I come to go to bed I took my clo'es off in the dark."

David threw back his head and roared with laughter. Mrs. Bixbee looked at him with unmixed scorn. "If I couldn't help makin' a----" she began, "I'd----"

"Oh, Lord! Polly," David broke in, "be sure 'n wrap up when you go out. If you sh'd ketch cold an' your sense o' the ridic'lous sh'd strike in you'd be a dead-'n'-goner sure." This was treated with the silent contempt which it deserved, and David fell upon his dinner with the remark that "he guessed he'd better make up fer lost time," though as a matter of fact while he had done most of the talking he had by no means suspended another function of his mouth while so engaged.

For a time nothing more was said which did not relate to the replenishment of plates, glasses, and cups. Finally David cleaned up his plate with his knife blade and a piece of bread, and pushed it away with a sigh of fullness, mentally echoed by John.

"I feel 's if a child could play with me," he remarked. "What's comin' now, Polly?"

"The's a mince pie, an' Injun puddin' with maple sugar an' cream, an' ice cream," she replied.

"Mercy on us!" he exclaimed. "I guess I'll have to go an' jump up an' down on the verandy. How do you feel, John? I s'pose you got so used to them things at the Eagle 't you won't have no stomach fer 'em, eh? Wa'al, fetch 'em along. May 's well die fer the ole sheep 's the lamb, but, Polly Bixbee, if you've got designs on my life, I may 's well tell ye right now 't I've left all my prop'ty to the Institution fer Disappinted Hoss Swappers."

"That's putty near next o' kin, ain't it?" was the unexpected rejoinder of the injured Polly.

"Wa'al, scat my ----!" exclaimed David, hugely amused, "if Polly Bixbee hain't made a joke! You'll git yourself into the almanic, Polly, fust thing you know." Sairy brought in the pie and then the pudding.

"John," said David, "if you've got a pencil an' a piece o' paper handy I'd like to have ye take down a few of my last words 'fore we proceed to the pie an' puddin' bus'nis. Any more 'hoss-redish' in that bottle?" holding out his glass. "Hi! hi! that's enough. You take the rest on't," which John did, nothing loath.

David ate his pie in silence, but before he made up his mind to attack the pudding, which was his favorite confection, he gave an audible chuckle, which elicited Mrs. Bixbee's notice.

"What you gigglin' 'bout now?" she asked.

David laughed. "I was thinkin' of somethin' I heard up to Purse's last night," he said as he covered his pudding with the thick cream sauce. "Amri Shapless has ben gittin' married."

"Wa'al, I declare!" she exclaimed. "That ole shack! Who in creation could he git to take him?"

"Lize Annis is the lucky woman," replied David with a grin.

"Wa'al, if that don't beat all!" said Mrs. Bixbee, throwing up her hands, and even from Mrs. Cullom was drawn a "Well, I never!"

"Fact," said David, "they was married yestidy forenoon. Squire Parker done the job. Dominie White wouldn't have nothin' to do with it!"

"Squire Parker 'd ortter be 'shamed of himself," said Mrs. Bixbee indignantly.

"Don't you think that trew love had ought to be allowed to take its course?"

asked David with an air of sentiment.

"I think the squire'd ortter be 'shamed of himself," she reiterated. "S'pose them two old skinamulinks was to go an' have children?"

"Polly, you make me blush," protested her brother. "Hain't you got no respect fer the holy institution of matrimuny?--and--at cet'ry?" he added, wiping his whole face with his napkin.

"Much as you hev, I reckon," she retorted. "Of all the amazin' things in this world, the amazinist to me is the kind of people that gits married to each other in gen'ral; but this here performance beats ev'rything holler."

"Amri give a very good reason for't," said David with an air of conviction, and then he broke into a laugh.

"Ef you got anythin' to tell, tell it," said Mrs. Bixbee impatiently.

"Wa'al," said David, taking the last of his pudding into his mouth, "if you insist on't, painful as 't is. I heard Dick Larrabee tellin' 'bout it. Amri told Dick day before yestiday that he was thinkin' of gettin' married, an' ast him to go along with him to Parson White's an' be a witniss, an' I reckon a kind of moral support. When it comes to moral supportin'," remarked David in passing, "Dick's as good 's a professional, an' he'd go an' see his gran'mother hung sooner 'n miss anythin', an' never let his cigar go out durin' the performance. Dick said he congratilated Am on his choice, an' said he reckoned they'd be putty ekally yoked together, if nothin' else."

Here David leaned over toward Aunt Polly and said, protestingly, "Don't gi' me but jest a teasp'nful o' that ice cream. I'm so full now 't I can't hardly reach the table." He took a taste of the cream and resumed: "I can't give it jest as Dick did," he went on, "but this is about the gist on't. Him, an' Lize, an' Am went to Parson White's about half after seven o'clock an' was showed into the parler, an' in a minute he come in, an' after sayin' 'Good evenin'' all 'round, he says, 'Well, what c'n I do for ye?' lookin' at Am an' Lize, an' then at Dick.

"'Wa'al,' says Am, 'me an' Mis' Annis here has ben thinkin' fer some time as how we'd ought to git married.'

"'*Ought* to git married?' says Parson White, scowlin' fust at one an' then at t'other.

"'Wa'al,' says Am, givin' a kind o' shuffle with his feet, 'I didn't mean *ortter* exac'ly, but jest as *well*--kinder comp'ny,' he says. 'We hain't neither on us got nobody, an' we thought we might 's well.'

"'What have you got to git married on?' says the dominie after a minute. 'Anythin'?' he says.

"'Wa'al,' says Am, droppin' his head sideways an' borin' into his ear 'ith his middle finger, 'I got the promise mebbe of a job o' work fer a couple o' days next week.' 'H'm'm'm,' says the dominie, lookin' at him. 'Have *you* got anythin' to git married on?' the dominie says, turnin' to Lize. 'I've got ninety cents comin' to me fer some work I done last week,' she says, wiltin' down onto the sofy an' beginnin' to snivvle. Dick says that at that the dominie turned round an' walked to the other end of the room, an' he c'd see he was dyin' to laugh, but he come back with a straight face.

"'How old air you, Shapless?' he says to Am. 'I'll be fifty-eight or mebbe fifty-nine come next spring,' says Am.

"'How old air *you*?' the dominie says, turnin' to Lize. She wriggled a minute an' says, 'Wa'al, I reckon I'm all o' thirty,' she says."

"All o' thirty!" exclaimed Aunt Polly. "The woman 's most 's old 's I be."

David laughed and went on with, "Wa'al, Dick said at that the dominie give a kind of a choke, an' Dick he bust right out, an' Lize looked at him as if she c'd eat him. Dick said the dominie didn't say anythin' fer a minute or two, an' then he says to Am, 'I suppose you c'n find somebody that'll marry you, but I cert'inly won't, an' what possesses you to commit such a piece o' folly,' he says, 'passes my understandin'. What earthly reason have you fer wantin' to marry? On your own showin',' he says, 'neither one on you 's got a cent o' money or any settled way o' gettin' any.'

"'That's jest the very reason,' says Am, 'that's jest the *very reason*. I hain't got nothin', an' Mis' Annis hain't got nothin', an' we figured that we'd jest better git married an' settle down, an' make a good home fer us both,' an' if that ain't good reasonin'," David concluded, "I don't know what is."

"An' be they actually married?" asked Mrs. Bixbee, still incredulous of anything so preposterous.

"So Dick says," was the reply. "He says Am an' Lize come away f'm the dominie's putty down in the mouth, but 'fore long Amri braced up an' allowed that if he had half a dollar he'd try the squire in the mornin', an' Dick let him have it. I says to Dick, 'You're out fifty cents on that deal,' an' he says, slappin' his leg, 'I don't give a dum,' he says; 'I wouldn't 'a' missed it fer double the money.'"

Here David folded his napkin and put it in the ring, and John finished the cup of clear coffee which Aunt Polly, rather under protest, had given him. Coffee without cream and sugar was incomprehensible to Mrs. Bixbee.

CHAPTER XXV.

Two or three days after Christmas John was sitting in his room in the evening when there came a knock at the door, and to his "Come in" there entered Mr. Harum, who was warmly welcomed and entreated to take the big chair, which, after a cursory survey of the apartment and its furnishings, he did, saying, "Wa'al, I thought I'd come in an' see how Polly'd got you fixed; whether the baskit [casket?] was worthy of the jew'l, as I heard a feller say in a theater once."

"I was never more comfortable in my life," said John. "Mrs. Bixbee has been kindness itself, and even permits me to smoke in the room. Let me give you a cigar."

"Heh! You got putty well 'round Polly, I reckon," said David, looking around the room as he lighted the cigar, "an' I'm glad you're comf'table--I reckon 't is a shade better 'n the Eagle," he remarked, with his characteristic chuckle.

"I should say so," said John emphatically, "and I am more obliged than I can tell you."

"All Polly's doin's," asserted David, holding the end of his cigar critically under his nose. "That's a trifle better article 'n I'm in the habit of smokin'," he remarked.

"I think it's my one extravagance," said John semi-apologetically, "but I don't smoke them exclusively. I am very fond of good tobacco, and--"

"I understand," said David, "an' if I had my life to live over agin, knowin' what I do now, I'd do diff'rent in a number o' ways. I often think," he proceeded, as he took a pull at the cigar and emitted the smoke with a chewing movement of his mouth, "of what Andy Brown used to say. Andy was a curious kind of a customer 't I used to know up to Syrchester. He liked good things, Andy did, an' didn't scrimp himself when they was to be had--that is, when he had the go-an'-fetch-it to git 'em with. He used to say, 'Boys, whenever you git holt of a ten-dollar note you want to git it ***into*** ye or ***onto*** ye jest 's quick 's you kin. We're here to-day an' gone to-morrer,' he'd say, 'an' the' ain't no pocket in a shroud,' an' I'm dum'd if I don't think sometimes," declared Mr. Harum, "that he wa'n't very fur off neither. 'T any rate," he added with a philosophy unexpected by his hearer, "'s I look back, it ain't the money 't I've spent fer the good times 't I've had 't I regret; it's the good times 't I might 's well 've had an' didn't. I'm inclined to think," he remarked with an air of having given the matter consideration, "that after Adam an' Eve got bounced out of the gard'n they kicked themselves as much as anythin' fer not havin' cleaned up the hull tree while they was about it."

John laughed and said that that was very likely among their regrets.

"Trouble with me was," said David, "that till I was consid'able older 'n you be I had to scratch grav'l like all possessed, an' it's hard work now sometimes to git the idee out of my head but what the money's wuth more 'n the things. I guess," he remarked, looking at the ivory-backed brushes and the various toilet knick-knacks of cut-glass and silver which adorned John's bureau, and indicating them with a motion of his hand, "that up to about now you ben in the habit of figurin' the other way mostly."

"Too much so, perhaps," said John; "but yet, after all, I don't think I am sorry. I wouldn't spend the money for those things now, but I am glad I bought them when I did."

"Jess so, jess so," said David appreciatively. He reached over to the table and laid his cigar on the edge of a book, and, reaching for his hip pocket, produced a silver tobacco box, at which he looked contemplatively for a moment, opening and shutting the lid with a snap.

"There," he said, holding it out on his palm, "I was twenty years makin' up my mind to buy that box, an' to this day I can't bring myself to carry it all the time. Yes, sir, I wanted that box fer twenty years. I don't mean to say that I didn't spend the wuth of it foolishly times over an' agin, but I couldn't never make up my mind to put that amount o' money into that pertic'ler thing. I was alwus figurin' that some day I'd have a silver tobacco box, an' I sometimes think the reason it seemed so extrav'gant, an' I put it off so long, was because I wanted it so much. Now I s'pose you couldn't understand that, could ye?"

"Yes," said John, nodding his head thoughtfully, "I think I can understand it perfectly," and indeed it spoke pages of David's biography.

"Yes, sir," said David, "I never spent a small amount o' money but one other time an' got so much value, only I alwus ben kickin' myself to think I didn't do it sooner."

"Perhaps," suggested John, "you enjoyed it all the more for waiting so long."

"No," said David, "it wa'n't that--I dunno--'t was the feelin' 't I'd got there at last, I guess. Fur's waitin' fer things is concerned, the' is such a thing as waitin' too long. Your appetite 'll change mebbe. I used to think when I was a youngster that if ever I got where I c'd have all the custard pie I c'd eat that'd be all 't I'd ask fer. I used to imagine bein' baked into one an' eatin' my way out. Nowdays the's a good many things I'd sooner have than custard pie, though," he said with a wink, "I gen'ally do eat two pieces jest to please Polly."

John laughed. "What was the other thing?" he asked.

"Other thing I once bought?" queried David. "Oh, yes, it was the fust hoss I ever owned. I give fifteen dollars fer him, an' if he wa'n't a dandy you needn't pay me a cent. Crowbait wa'n't no name fer him. He was stun blind on the off side, an' couldn't see anythin' in pertic'ler on the nigh side--couldn't get nigh 'nough, I reckon--an' had most ev'rythin' wrong with him that c'd ail a hoss; but I thought he was a thoroughbred. I was 'bout seventeen year old then, an' was helpin' lock-tender on the Erie Canal, an' when the' wa'n't no boat goin' through I put in most o' my time cleanin' that hoss. If he got through 'th less 'n six times a day he got off cheap, an' once I got up an' give him a little attention at night. Yes, sir, if I got big money's wuth out o' that box it was mostly a matter of feelin'; but as fur 's that old plugamore of a hoss was concerned, I got it both ways, for I got my fust real start out of his old carkiss."

"Yes?" said John encouragingly.

"Yes, sir," affirmed David, "I cleaned him up, an' fed him up, an' almost got 'im so'st he c'd see enough out of his left eye to shy at a load of hay close by; an' fin'ly traded him off fer another record-breaker an' fifteen dollars to boot."

"Were you as enthusiastic over the next one as the first?" asked John, laughing.

"Wa'al," replied David, relighting his temporarily abandoned cigar against a protest and proffer of a fresh one--"wa'al, he didn't lay holt on my affections to quite the same extent. I done my duty by him, but I didn't set up with him nights. You see," he added with a grin, "I'd got some used to bein' a hoss owner, an' the edge had wore off some." He smoked for a minute or two in silence, with as much apparent relish as if the cigar had not been stale.

"Aren't you going on?" asked John at last

"Wa'al," he replied, pleased with his audience, "I c'd go on, I s'pose, fast enough an' fur enough, but I don't want to tire ye out. I reckon you never had much to do with canals?"

"No," said John, smiling, "I can't say that I have, but I know something about the subject in a general way, and there is no fear of your tiring me out."

"All right," proceeded David. "As I was sayin', I got another equine wonder an' fifteen dollars to boot fer my old plug, an' it wa'n't a great while before I was in the hoss bus'nis to stay. After between two an' three years I had fifty or sixty hosses an' mules, an' took all sorts of towin' jobs. Then a big towin' concern quit bus'nis, an' I bought their hull stock an' got my money back three four times over, an' by the time I was about twenty-one I had got ahead enough to quit the canal an' all its works fer good, an' go into other things. But there was where I got my livin' after I run away f'm Buxton Hill. Before I got the job of lock-tendin' I had made the trip to Albany an' back twice--'walkin' my passage,' as they used to call it, an' I made one trip helpin' steer, so 't my canal experience was putty thorough, take it all 'round."

"It must have been a pretty hard life," remarked John.

David took out his penknife and proceeded to impale his cigar upon the blade thereof. "No," he said, to John's proffer of the box, "this 'll last quite a spell yet. Wa'al," he resumed after a moment, in reply to John's remark, "viewin' it all by itself, it *was* a hard life. A thing is hard though, I reckon, because it's harder 'n somethin' else, or you think so. Most things go by comparin'. I s'pose if the gen'ral run of trotters never got better 'n three 'n a half that a hoss that c'd do it in three 'd be fast, but we don't call 'em so nowdays. I s'pose if at that same age you'd had to tackle the life you'd 'a' found it hard, an' the' was hard things about it--trampin' all night in the rain, fer instance; sleepin' in barns at times, an' all that; an' once the cap'n o' the boat got mad at somethin' an' pitched me head over heels into the canal. It was about the close of navigation an' the' was a scum of ice. I scrambled out somehow, but he wouldn't 'a' cared if I'd ben drownded. He was an exception, though. The canalers was a rough set in gen'ral, but they averaged fer disposition 'bout like the ord'nary run o' folks; the' was mean ones an' clever ones; them that would put upon ye, an' them that would treat ye decent. The work was hard an' the grub wasn't alwus much better 'n what you--he, he, he!--what you ben gettin' at the Eagle" (John was now by the way of rather relishing jokes on that subject); "but I hadn't ben raised in the lap o' luxury--not to any consid'able extent--not enough to stick my nose up much. The men I worked fer was rough, an' I got my share of cusses an' cuffs, an' once in a while a kick to keep up my spirit of perseverance; but, on the hull, I think I got more kindness 'n I did at home (leavin' Polly out), an' as fer gen'ral treatment, none on 'em c'd come up to my father, an' wuss yet, my oldest brother 'Lish. The cap'n that throwed me overboard was the wust, but alongside o' 'Lish he was a forty hosspower angil with a hull music store o' harps; an' even my father c'd 'a' given him cards an' spades; an' as fer the victuals" (here David dropped his cigar end and pulled from his pocket the silver tobacco box)--"as fer the vict-uals," he repeated, "they mostly averaged up putty high after what I'd ben used to. Why, I don't believe I ever tasted a piece of beefsteak or roast beef in my life till after I left home. When we had meat at all it was pork--boiled pork, fried pork, pigs' liver, an' all that, enough to make you 'shamed to look a pig in the face--an' fer the rest, potatoes, an' duff, an' johnny-cake, an' meal mush, an' milk emptins bread that you c'd smell a mile after it got cold. With 'leven folks on a small farm nuthin' c'd afford to be eat that c'd be sold, an' ev'rythin' that couldn't be sold had to be eat. Once in a while the' 'd be pie of some kind, or gingerbread; but with 'leven to eat 'em I didn't ever git more 'n enough to set me hankerin'."

"I must say that I think I should have liked the canal better," remarked John as David paused. "You were, at any rate, more or less free--that is, comparatively, I should say."

"Yes, sir, I did," said David, "an' I never see the time, no matter how rough things was, that I wished I was back on Buxton Hill. I used to want to see Polly putty bad once in a while, an' used to figure that if I ever growed up to be a man, an' had money enough, I'd buy her a new pair o' shoes an' the stuff fer a dress, an' sometimes my cal'lations went as fur 's a gold breastpin; but I never wanted to see none o' the rest on 'em, an' fer that matter, I never did. Yes, sir, the old ditch was better to me than the place I was borned in, an', as you say, I wa'n't nobody's slave, an' I wa'n't scairt to death the hull time. Some o' the men was rough, but they wa'n't cruel, as a rule, an' as I growed up a little I was putty well able to look out fer myself--wa'al, wa'al (looking at his watch), I guess you must 'a' had enough o' my meemores fer one sittin'.'"

"No, really," John protested, "don't go yet. I have a little proposal to make to you," and he got up and brought a bottle from the bottom of the washstand.

"Wa'al," said David, "fire it out."

"That you take another cigar and a little of this," holding up the bottle.

"Got any glasses?" asked David with practical mind.

"One and a tooth mug," replied John, laughing. "Glass for you, tooth mug for me. Tastes just as good out of a tooth mug."

"Wa'al," said David, with a comical air of yielding as he took the glass and held it out to John, "under protest, stric'ly under protest--sooner than have my clo'es torn. I shall tell Polly--if I should happen to mention it--that you threatened me with vi'lence. Wa'al, here's lookin' at ye," which toast was drunk with the solemnity which befitted it.

CHAPTER XXVI.

The two men sat for a while smoking in silence, John taking an occasional sip of his grog. Mr. Harum had swallowed his own liquor "raw," as was the custom in Homeville and vicinity, following the potation with a mouthful of water. Presently he settled a little farther down in his chair and his face took on a look of amused recollection.

He looked up and gave a short laugh. "Speakin' of canals," he said, as if the subject had only been casually mentioned, "I was thinkin' of somethin'."

"Yes?" said John.

"E-up," said David. "That old ditch f'm Albany to Buffalo was an almighty big enterprise in them days, an' a great thing fer the prosperity of the State, an' a good many better men 'n I be walked the ole towpath when they was young. Yes, sir, that's a fact. Wa'al, some years ago I had somethin' of a deal on with a New York man by the name of Price. He had a place in Newport where his fam'ly spent the summer, an' where he went as much as he could git away. I was down to New York to see him, an' we hadn't got things quite straightened out, an' he says to me, 'I'm goin' over to Newport, where my wife an' fam'ly is, fer Sunday, an' why can't you come with me,' he says, 'an' stay over till Monday? an' we c'n have the day to ourselves over this matter?' 'Wa'al,' I says, 'I'm only down here on this bus'nis, an' as I left a hen on, up home, I'm willin' to save the time 'stid of waitin' here fer you to git back, if you don't think,' I says, 'that it'll put Mis' Price out any to bring home a stranger without no notice.'

"'Wa'al,' he says, laughin', 'I guess she c'n manage fer once,' an' so I went along. When we got there the' was a carriage to meet us, an' two men in uniform, one to drive an' one to open the door, an' we got in an' rode up to the house--cottige, he called it, but it was built of stone, an' wa'n't only about two sizes smaller 'n the Fifth Avenue Hotel. Some kind o' doin's was goin' on, fer the house was blazin' with light, an' music was playin'.

"'What's on?' says Price to the feller that let us in.

"'Sir and Lady somebody 's dinin' here to-night, sir,' says the man.

"'Damn!' says Price, 'I fergot all about the cussed thing. Have Mr. Harum showed to a room,' he says, 'an' serve dinner in my office in a quarter of an hour, an' have somebody show Mr. Harum there when it's ready.'

"Wa'al," pursued David, "I was showed up to a room. The' was lace coverin's on the bed pillers, an' a silk an' lace spread, an' more dum trinkits an' bottles an' lookin'-glasses 'n you c'd shake a stick at, an' a bathroom, an' Lord knows what; an' I washed up, an' putty soon one o' them fellers come an' showed me down to where Price was waitin'. Wa'al, we had all manner o' things fer supper, an' champagne, an' so on, an' after we got done, Price says, 'I've got to ask you to excuse me, Harum,' he says. 'I've got to go an' dress an' show up in the drawin'-room,' he says. 'You smoke your cigar in here, an' when you want to go to your room jest ring the bell.'

"'All right,' I says. 'I'm 'bout ready to turn in anyway.'"

The narrator paused for a moment. John was rather wondering what it all had to do with the Erie Canal, but he said nothing.

"Wa'al, next mornin'," David resumed, "I got up an' shaved an' dressed, an' set 'round waitin' fer the breakfust bell to ring till nigh on to half-past nine o'clock. Bom-by the' came a knock at the door, an' I says, 'Come in,' an' in come one o' them fellers. 'Beg pah'din, sir,' he says. 'Did you ring, sir?'

"'No,' I says, 'I didn't ring. I was waitin' to hear the bell.'

"'Thank you, sir,' he says. 'An' will you have your breakfust now, sir?'

"'Where?' I says.

"'Oh,' he says, kind o' grinnin', 'I'll bring it up here, sir, d'rec'ly,' he says, an' went off. Putty soon come another knock, an' in come the feller with a silver tray covered with a big napkin, an' on it was a couple of rolls wrapped up in a napkin, a b'iled egg done up in another napkin, a cup an' saucer, a little chiney coffee-pot, a little pitcher of cream, some loaf sugar in a silver dish, a little pancake of butter, a silver knife, two little spoons like what the childern play with, a silver pepper duster an' salt dish, an' an orange. Oh, yes, the' was another contraption--a sort of a chiney wineglass. The feller set down the tray an' says, 'Anythin' else you'd like to have, sir?'

"'No,' I says, lookin' it over, 'I guess there's enough to last me a day or two,' an' with that he kind o' turned his face away fer a second or two. 'Thank you, sir,' he says. 'The second breakfast is at half-past twelve, sir,' an' out he put. Wa'al," David continued, "the bread an' butter was all right enough, exceptin' they'd fergot the salt in the butter, an' the coffee was all right; but when it come to the egg, dum'd if I wa'n't putty nigh out of the race; but I made up my mind it must be hard-b'iled, an' tackled it on that idee. Seems t' amuse ye," he said with a grin, getting up and helping himself. After swallowing the refreshment, and the palliating mouthful of water, he resumed his seat and his narrative.

"Wa'al, sir," he said, "that dum'd egg was about 's near raw as it was when i' was laid, an' the' was a crack in the shell, an' fust thing I knowed it kind o' c'lapsed, an' I give it a grab, an' it squirtid all over my pants, an' the floor, an' on my coat an' vest, an' up my sleeve, an' all over the tray. Scat my ----! I looked gen'ally like an ab'lition orator before the war. You never see such a mess," he added, with an expression of rueful recollection. "I believe that dum'd egg held more 'n a pint."

John fairly succumbed to a paroxysm of laughter.

"Funny, wa'n't it?" said David dryly.

"Forgive me," pleaded John, when he got his breath.

"Oh, that's all right," said David, "but it wa'n't the kind of emotion it kicked up in my breast at the time. I cleaned myself up with a towel well 's I could, an' thought I'd step out an' take the air before the feller 'd come back to git that tray, an' mebbe rub my nose in't."

"Oh, Lord!" cried John.

"Yes, sir," said David, unheeding, "I allowed 't I'd walk 'round with my mouth open a spell, an' git a little air on my stomech to last me till that second breakfust; an' as I was pokin' 'round the grounds I come to a sort of arbor, an' there was Price, smokin' a cigar.

"'Mornin', Harum; how you feelin'?' he says, gettin' up an' shakin' hands; an' as we passed the time o' day, I noticed him noticin' my coat. You see as they dried out, the egg spots got to showin' agin.

"'Got somethin' on your coat there,' he says.

"'Yes,' I says, tryin' to scratch it out with my finger nail.

"'Have a cigar?' he says, handin' one out.

"'Never smoke on an empty stomach,' I says.

"'What?' he says.

"'Bad fer the ap'tite,' I says, 'an' I'm savin' mine fer that second breakfust o' your'n.'

"'What!' he says, 'haven't you had anythin' to eat?' An' then I told him what I ben tellin' you. Wa'al, sir, fust he looked kind o' mad an' disgusted, an' then he laughed till I thought he'd bust, an' when he quit he says, 'Excuse me, Harum, it's too damned bad; but I couldn't help laughin' to save my soul. An' it's all my fault too,' he says. 'I intended to have you take your breakfust with me, but somethin' happened last night to upset me, an' I woke with it on my mind, an' I fergot. Now you jest come right into the house, an' I'll have somethin' got fer you that'll stay your stomach better 'n air,' he says.

"'No,' I says, 'I've made trouble enough fer one day, I guess,' an' I wouldn't go, though he urged me agin an' agin. 'You don't fall in with the customs of this region?' I says to him.

"'Not in that pertic'ler, at any rate,' he says. 'It's one o' the fool notions that my wife an' the girls brought home f'm Eurup. I have a good solid meal in the mornin', same as I alwus did,' he says."

Mr. Harum stopped talking to relight his cigar, and after a puff or two, "When I started out," he said, "I hadn't no notion of goin' into all the highways an' byways, but when I git begun one thing's apt to lead to another, an' you never c'n tell jest where I *will* fetch up. Now I started off to tell somethin' in about two words, an' I'm putty near as fur off as when I begun."

"Well," said John, "it's Saturday night, and the longer your story is the better I shall like it. I hope the second breakfast was more of a success than the first one," he added with a laugh.

"I managed to average up on the two meals, I guess," David remarked. "Wa'al," he resumed, "Price an' I set 'round talkin' bus'nis an' things till about twelve or a little after, mebbe, an' then he turned to me an' kind o' looked me over an' says, 'You an' me is about of a build, an' if you say so I'll send one of my coats an' vests up to your room an' have the man take yours an' clean 'em.'

"'I guess the' is ruther more egg showin' than the law allows,' I says, 'an' mebbe that 'd be a good idee; but the pants caught it the wust,' I says.

"'Mine'll fit ye,' he says.

"'What'll your wife say to seein' me airifyin' 'round in your git-up?' I says. He gin me a funny kind of look. 'My wife?' he says. 'Lord, she don't know more about my clo'es 'n you do.' That struck me as bein' ruther curious," remarked David. "Wouldn't it you?"

"Very," replied John gravely.

"Yes, sir," said David. "Wa'al, when we went into the eatin' room the table was full, mostly young folks, chatterin' an' laughin'. Price int'duced me to his wife, an' I set down by him at the other end of the table. The' wa'n't nothin' wuth mentionin'; nobody paid any attention to me 'cept now an' then a word from Price, an' I wa'n't fer talkin' anyway--I c'd have eat a raw dog. After breakfust, as they called it, Price an' I went out onto the verandy an' had some coffee, an' smoked an' talked fer an hour or so, an' then he got up an' excused himself to write a letter. 'You may like to look at the papers awhile,' he says. 'I've ordered the hosses at five, an' if you like I'll show you 'round a little.'

"'Won't your wife be wantin' 'em?' I says.

"'No, I guess she'll git along,' he says, kind o' smilin'.

"'All right,' I says, 'don't mind me.' An' so at five up come the hosses an' the two fellers in uniform an' all. I was lookin' the hosses over when Price come out. 'Wa'al, what do you think of 'em?' he says.

"'Likely pair,' I says, goin' over an' examinin' the nigh one's feet an' legs. 'Sore forr'ed?' I says, lookin' up at the driver.

"'A trifle, sir,' he says, touchin' his hat.

"'What's that?' says Price, comin' up an' examinin' the critter's face an' head. 'I don't see anythin' the matter with his forehead,' he says. I looked up an' give the driver a wink," said David with a chuckle, "an' he give kind of a chokin' gasp, but in a second was lookin' as solemn as ever.

"I can't tell ye jest where we went," the narrator proceeded, "but anyway it was where all the nabobs turned out, an' I seen more style an' git-up in them two hours 'n I ever see in my life, I reckon. The' didn't appear to be no one we run across that, accordin' to Price's tell, was wuth under five million, though we may 'a' passed one without his noticin'; an' the' was a good many that run to fifteen an' twenty an' over, an' most on 'em, it appeared, was f'm New York. Wa'al, fin'ly we got back to the house a little 'fore seven. On the way back Price says, 'The' are goin' to be three four people to dinner to-night in a quiet way, an' the' ain't no reason why you shouldn't stay dressed jest as you are, but if you would feel like puttin' on evenin' clo'es (that's what he called 'em), why I've got an extry suit that'll fit ye to a "tee,"' he says.

"'No,' I says, 'I guess I better not. I reckon I'd better git my grip an' go to the hotel. I sh'd be ruther bashful to wear your swallertail, an' all them folks'll be strangers,' I says. But he insisted on't that I sh'd come to dinner anyway, an' fin'ly I gin in, an' thinkin' I might 's well go the hull hog, I allowed I'd wear his clo'es; 'but if I do anythin' or say anythin' 't you don't like,' says I, 'don't say I didn't warn ye.' What would you 'a' done?" Mr. Harum asked.

"Worn the clothes without the slightest hesitation," replied John. "Nobody gave your costume a thought."

"They didn't appear to, fer a fact," said David, "an' I didn't either, after I'd slipped up once or twice on the matter of pockets. The same feller brought 'em up to me that fetched the stuff in the mornin'; an' the rig was complete--coat, vest, pants, shirt, white necktie, an', by gum! shoes an' silk socks, an', sir, scat my ----! the hull outfit fitted me as if it was made fer me. 'Shell I wait on you, sir?' says the man. 'No,' I says, 'I guess I c'n git into the things; but mebbe you might come up in 'bout quarter of an hour an' put on the finishin' touches, an' here,' I says, 'I guess that brand of eggs you give me this mornin' 's wuth about two dollars apiece.'

"'Thank you, sir,' he says, grinnin', 'I'd like to furnish 'em right along at that rate, sir, an' I'll be up as you say, sir.'"

"You found the way to *his* heart," said John, smiling.

"My experience is," said David dryly, "that most men's hearts is located ruther closter to their britchis pockets than they are to their breast pockets."

"I'm afraid that's so," said John.

"But this feller," Mr. Harum continued, "was a putty decent kind of a chap. He come up after I'd got into my togs an' pulled me here, an' pulled me there, an' fixed my necktie, an' hitched me in gen'ral so'st I wa'n't neither too tight nor too free, an' when he got through, 'You'll do now, sir,' he says.

"'Think I will?' says I.

"'Couldn't nobody look more fit, sir,' he says, an' I'm dum'd," said David, with an assertive nod, "when I looked at myself in the lookin'-glass. I scurcely knowed myself, an' (with a confidential lowering of the voice) when I got back to New York the very fust hard work I done was to go an' buy the hull rig-out--an'," he added with a grin, "strange as it may appear, it ain't wore out *yit*."

CHAPTER XXVII.

"People don't dress for dinner in Homeville, as a rule, then," John said, smiling.

"No," said Mr. Harum, "when they dress fer breakfust that does 'em fer all three meals. I've wore them things two three times when I've ben down to the city, but I never had 'em on but once up here."

"No?" said John.

"No," said David, "I put 'em on *once* to show to Polly how city folks dressed--he, he, he, he!--an' when I come into the room she set forwud on her chair an' stared at me over her specs. 'What on airth!' she says.

"'I bought these clo'es,' I says, 'to wear when bein' ent'tained by the fust fam'lies. How do I look?' I says.

"'Turn 'round,' she says. 'You look f'm behind,' she says, 'like a red-headed snappin' bug, an' in front,' she says, as I turned agin, 'like a reg'lar slinkum. I'll bet,' she says, 'that you hain't throwed away less 'n twenty dollars on that foolishniss.' Polly's a very conserv'tive person," remarked her brother, "and don't never imagine a vain thing, as the Bible says, not when she **knows** it, an' I thought it wa'n't wuth while to argue the point with her."

John laughed and said, "Do you recall that memorable interview between the governors of the two Carolinas?"

"Nothin' in the historical lit'riture of our great an' glorious country," replied Mr. Harum reverently, "sticks closter to my mind--like a burr to a cow's tail," he added, by way of illustration. "Thank you, jest a mouthful."

"How about the dinner?" John asked after a little interlude. "Was it pleasant?"

"Fust rate," declared David. "The young folks was out somewhere else, all but one o' Price's girls. The' was twelve at the table all told. I was int'duced to all of 'em in the parlor, an' putty soon in come one of the fellers an' said somethin' to Mis' Price that meant dinner was ready, an' the girl come up to me an' took holt of my arm. 'You're goin' to take me out,' she says, an' we formed a procession an' marched out to the dinin' room. 'You're to sit by mammer,' she says, showin' me, an' there was my name on a card, sure enough. Wa'al, sir, that table was a show! I couldn't begin to describe it to ye. The' was a hull flower garden in the middle, an' a worked tablecloth; four five glasses of all colors an' sizes at ev'ry plate, an' a nosegay, an' five six diff'rent forks an' a lot o' knives, though fer that matter," remarked the speaker, "the' wa'n't but one knife in the lot that amounted to anythin', the rest on 'em wouldn't hold nothin'; an' the' was three four sort of chiney slates with what they call--the--you 'n me----"

"Menu," suggested John.

"I guess that's it," said David, "but that wa'n't the way it was spelt. Wa'al, I set down an' tucked my napkin into my neck, an' though I noticed none o' the rest on 'em seemed to care, I allowed that 't wa'n't **my** shirt, an' mebbe Price might want to wear it agin 'fore 't was washed."

John put his handkerchief over his face and coughed violently. David looked at him sharply. "Subject to them spells?" he asked.

"Sometimes," said John when he recovered his voice, and then, with as clear an expression of innocence as he could command, but somewhat irrelevantly, asked,

"How did you get on with Mrs. Price?"

"Oh," said David, "nicer 'n a cotton hat. She appeared to be a quiet sort of woman that might 'a' lived anywhere, but she was dressed to kill--an' so was the rest on 'em, fer that matter," he remarked with a laugh. "I tried to tell Polly about 'em afterwuds, an'--he, he, he!--she shut me up mighty quick, an' I thought myself at the time, thinks I, it's a good thing it's warm weather, I says to myself. Oh, yes, Mis' Price made me feel quite to home, but I didn't talk much the fust part of dinner, an' I s'pose she was more or less took up with havin' so many folks at table; but fin'ly she says to me, 'Mr. Price was so annoyed about your breakfust, Mr. Harum.'

"'Was he?' I says. 'I was afraid you'd be the one that 'd be vexed at me.'

"'Vexed with you? I don't understand,' she says.

"''Bout the napkin I sp'iled,' I says. 'Mebbe not actually sp'iled,' I says, 'but it'll have to go into the wash 'fore it c'n be used agin.' She kind o' smiled, an' says, 'Really, Mr. Harum, I don't know what you are talkin' about.'

"'Hain't nobody told ye?' I says. 'Well, if they hain't they will, an' I may 's well make a clean breast on't. I'm awful sorry,' I says, 'but this mornin' when I come to the egg I didn't see no way to eat it 'cept to peel it, an' fust I knew it kind of exploded and daubed ev'rythin' all over creation. Yes'm,' I says, 'it went *off*, 's ye might say, like old Elder Maybee's powder,' I guess," said David, "that I must 'a' ben talkin' ruther louder 'n I thought, fer I looked up an' noticed that putty much ev'ry one on 'em was lookin' our way, an' kind o' laughin', an' Price in pertic'ler was grinnin' straight at me.

"'What's that,' he says, 'about Elder Maybee's powder?'

"'Oh, nuthin' much,' I says, 'jest a little supprise party the elder had up to his house.'

"'Tell us about it,' says Price. 'Oh, yes, do tell us about it,' says Mis' Price.

"'Wa'al,' I says, 'the' ain't much to it in the way of a story, but seein' dinner must be most through,' I says, 'I'll tell ye all the' was of it. The elder had a small farm 'bout two miles out of the village,' I says, 'an' he was great on raisin' chickins an' turkeys. He was a slow, putterin' kind of an ole foozle, but on the hull a putty decent citizen. Wa'al,' I says, 'one year when the poultry was comin' along, a family o' skunks moved onto the premises an' done so well that putty soon, as the elder said, it seemed to him that it was comin' to be a ch'ice between the chickin bus'nis an' the skunk bus'nis, an' though he said he'd heard the' was money in it, if it was done on a big enough scale, he hadn't ben edicated to it, he said, and didn't take to it *any* ways. So,' I says, 'he scratched 'round an' got a lot o' traps an' set 'em, an' the very next mornin' he went out an' found he'd ketched an ole he-one--president of the comp'ny. So he went to git his gun to shoot the critter, an' found he hadn't got no powder. The boys had used it all up on woodchucks, an' the' wa'n't nothin' fer it but to git some more down to the village, an', as he had some more things to git, he hitched up 'long in the forenoon an' drove down.' At this," said David, "one of the ladies, wife to the judge, name o' Pomfort, spoke up an' says, 'Did he leave that poor creature to suffer all that time? Couldn't it have been put out of it's misery some other way?'

"'Wa'al marm,' I says, 'I never happened to know but one feller that set out to kill one o' them things with a club, an' *he* put in most o' *his* time fer a week or two up in the woods *hatin'* himself,' I says. 'He didn't mingle in gen'ral soci'ty, an' in fact,' I says, 'he had the hull road to himself, as ye might say, fer a putty consid'able spell.'"

John threw back his head and laughed. "Did she say any more?" he asked.

"No," said David with a chuckle. "All the men set up a great laugh, an' she colored up in a kind of huff at fust, an' then she begun to laugh too, an' then one o' the waiter fellers put somethin' down in front of me an' I went eatin' agin. But putty soon Price, he says, 'Come,' he says, 'Harum, ain't you goin' on? How about that powder?'

"'Wa'al,' I says, 'mebbe we had ought to put that critter out of his misery. The elder went down an' bought a pound o' powder an' had it done up in a brown paper bundle, an' put it with his other stuff in the bottom of his dem'crat wagin; but it come on to rain some while he was ridin' back, an' the stuff got more or less wet, an' so when he got home he spread it out in a dishpan an' put it under the kitchen stove to dry, an' thinkin' that it wa'n't dryin' fast enough, I s'pose, made out to assist Nature, as the sayin' is, by stirrin' on't up with the kitchin poker. Wa'al,' I says, 'I don't jest know how it happened, an' the elder cert'inly didn't, fer after they'd got him untangled f'm under what was left of the woodshed an' the kitchin stove, an' tied him up in cotton battin', an' set his leg, an' put out the house, an' a few things like that, bom-by he come round a little, an' the fust thing he says was, "Wa'al, wa'al, wa'al!" "What is it, pa?" says Mis' Maybee, bendin' down over him. "That peowder," he says, in almost no voice, "that peowder! I was jest stirrin' on't a little, an' it went *o-f-f*, it went *o-f-f*," he says, "***seemin'ly--in--a--minute!***" an' that,' I says to Mis' Price, 'was what that egg done.'

"'We'll have to forgive you that egg,' she says, laughin' like ev'rything, 'for Elder Maybee's sake'; an' in fact," said David, "they all laughed except one feller. He was an Englishman--I fergit his name. When I got through he looked kind o' puzzled an' says" (Mr. Harum imitated his style as well as he could), "'But ra'ally, Mr. Harum, you kneow that's the way powdah always geoes off, don't you kneow,' an' then," said David, "they laughed harder 'n ever, an' the Englishman got redder 'n a beet."

"What did you say?" asked John.

"Nuthin'," said David. "They was all laughin' so't I couldn't git in a word, an' then the waiter brought me another plateful of somethin'. Scat my ----!" he exclaimed, "I thought that dinner 'd go on till kingdom come. An' wine! Wa'al! I begun to feel somethin' like the old feller did that swallered a full tumbler of white whisky, thinkin' it was water. The old feller was temp'rence, an' the boys put up a job on him one hot day at gen'ral trainin'. Somebody ast him afterwuds how it made him feel, an' he said he felt as if he was sittin' straddle the meetin' house, an' ev'ry shingle was a Jew's-harp. So I kep' mum fer a while. But jest before we fin'ly got through, an' I hadn't said nothin' fer a spell, Mis' Price turned to me an' says, 'Did you have a pleasant drive this afternoon?'

"'Yes'm,' I says, 'I seen the hull show, putty much. I guess poor folks must be 't a premium 'round here. I reckon,' I says, 'that if they'd club together, the folks your husband p'inted out to me to-day could ***almost*** satisfy the requirements of the 'Merican Soci'ty fer For'n Missions.' Mis' Price laughed, an' looked over at her husband. 'Yes,' says Price, 'I told Mr. Harum about some of the people we saw this afternoon, an' I must say he didn't appear to be as much impressed as I thought he would. How's that, Harum?' he says to me.

"'Wa'al,' says I, 'I was thinkin' 't I'd like to bet you two dollars to a last year's bird's nest,' I says, 'that if all them fellers we seen this afternoon, that air over fifty, c'd be got together, an' some one was suddinly to holler "LOW BRIDGE!" that nineteen out o' twenty 'd ***duck their heads***.'"

"And then?" queried John.

"Wa'al," said David, "all on 'em laughed some, but Price--he jest lay back an' roared, and I found out afterwuds," added David, "that ev'ry man at the table, except the Englis'man, know'd what 'low bridge' meant from actial experience. Wa'al, scat my ----!" he exclaimed, as he looked at his watch, "it ain't hardly wuth while undressin'," and started for the door. As he was halfway through it, he turned and said, "Say, I s'pose *you'd* 'a' known what to do with that egg," but he did not wait for a reply.

CHAPTER XXVIII.

It must not be understood that the Harums, Larrabees, Robinsons, Elrights, and sundry who have thus far been mentioned, represented the only types in the prosperous and enterprising village of Homeville, and David perhaps somewhat magnified the one-time importance of the Cullom family, although he was speaking of a period some forty years earlier. Be that as it may, there were now a good many families, most of them descendants of early settlers, who lived in good and even fine houses, and were people of refinement and considerable wealth. These constituted a coterie of their own, though they were on terms of acquaintance and comity with the "village people," as they designated the rank and file of the Homeville population. To these houses came in the summer sons and daughters, nieces, nephews, and grandchildren, and at the period of which I am writing there had been built on the shore of the lake, or in its vicinity, a number of handsome and stately residences by people who had been attracted by the beauty of the situation and the salubrity of the summer climate. And so, for some months in the pleasant season, the village was enlivened by a concourse of visitors who brought with them urban customs, costumes, and equipages, and gave a good deal of life and color to the village streets. Then did Homeville put its best foot forward and money in its pouch.

"I ain't what ye might call an old residenter," said David, "though I was part raised on Buxton Hill, an' I ain't so well 'quainted with the nabobs; but Polly's lived in the village ever sence she got married, an' knows their fam'ly hist'ry, dam, an' sire, an' pedigree gen'ally. Of course," he remarked, "I know all the men folks, an' they know me, but I never ben into none o' their houses except now an' then on a matter of bus'nis, an' I guess," he said with a laugh, "that Polly 'd allow 't she don't spend all her time in that circle. Still," he added, "they all know her, an' ev'ry little while some o' the women folks 'll come in an' see her. She's putty popular, Polly is," he concluded.

"I should think so, indeed," remarked John.

"Yes, sir," said David, "the's worse folks 'n Polly Bixbee, if she don't put on no style; an' the fact is, that some of the folks that lives here the year 'round, an' always have, an' call the rest on us 'village people,' 'r jest as countryfied in their way 's me an' Polly is in our'n--only they don't know it. 'Bout the only diff'rence is the way they talk an' live." John looked at Mr. Harum in some doubt as to the seriousness of the last remark.

"Go to the 'Piscopal church, an' have what they call dinner at six o'clock," said David. "Now, there's the The'dore Verjooses," he continued; "the 'rig'nal Verjoos come an' settled here some time in the thirties, I reckon. He was some kind of a Dutchman, I guess" ["Dutchman" was Mr. Harum's generic name for all people native to the Continent of Europe]; "but he had some money, an' bought land an' morgidges, an' so on, an' havin' money--money was awful scurce in them early days--made more; never spent anythin' to speak of, an' died pinchin' the 'rig'nal cent he started in with."

"He was the father of Mr. Verjoos the other banker here, I suppose?" said John.

"Yes," said David, "the' was two boys an' a sister. The oldest son, Alferd, went into the law an' done bus'nis in Albany, an' afterw'ds moved to New York; but he's always kept up the old place here. The old man left what was a good deal o' propity fer them days, an' Alf he kept his share an' made more. He was in the Assembly two three terms, an' afterw'ds member of Congress, an' they do say," remarked Mr. Harum with a wink, "that he never lost no money by his politics. On the other hand, The'dore made more or less of a muddle on't, an' 'mongst 'em they set him up in the bankin' bus'nis. I say 'them' because the Verjooses, an' the Rogerses, an' the Swaynes, an' a lot of 'em, is all more or less related to each other, but Alf's reely the one at the bottom on't, an' after The 'd lost most of his money it was the easiest way to kind o' keep him on his legs."

"He seems a good-natured, easy-going sort of person," said John by way of comment, and, truth to say, not very much interested.

"Oh, yes," said David rather contemptuously, "you could drive him with a tow string. He don't **know** enough to run away. But what I was gettin' at was this: He an' his wife--he married one of the Tenakers--has lived right here fer the Lord knows how long; born an' brought up here both on 'em, an' somehow we're 'village people' an' they ain't, that's all."

"Rather a fine distinction," remarked his hearer, smiling.

"Yes, sir," said David. "Now, there's old maid Allis, relative of the Rogerses, lives all alone down on Clark Street in an old house that hain't had a coat o' paint or a new shingle sence the three Thayers was hung, an' she talks about the folks next door, both sides, that she's knowed alwus, as 'village people,' and I don't believe," asserted the speaker, "she was ever away f'm Homeville two weeks in the hull course of her life. She's a putty decent sort of a woman too," Mr. Harum admitted. "If the' was a death in the house she'd go in an' help, but she wouldn't never think of askin' one on 'em to tea."

"I suppose you have heard it said," remarked John, laughing, "that it takes all sorts of people to make a world."

"I think I hev heard a rumor to that effect," said David, "an' I guess the' 's about as much human nature in some folks as the' is in others, if not more."

"And I don't fancy that it makes very much difference to you," said John, "whether the Verjooses or Miss Allis call you 'village people' or not."

"Don't cut no figger at all," declared Mr. Harum. "Polly 'n I are too old to set up fer shapes even if we wanted to. A good fair road-gait 's good enough fer me; three square meals, a small portion of the 'filthy weed,' as it's called in po'try, a hoss 'r two, a ten-dollar note where you c'n lay your hand on't, an' once in a while, when your consciunce pricks ye, a little somethin' to permote the cause o' temp'rence, an' make the inwurd moniter quit jerkin' the reins--wa'al, I guess I c'n git along, heh?"

"Yes," said John, by way of making some rejoinder, "if one has all one needs it is enough."

"Wa'al, yes," observed the philosopher, "that's so, as you might say, up to a certain **point**, an' in some **ways**. I s'pose a feller could git along, but at the same time

I've noticed that, gen'ally speakin', a leetle too big 's about the right size."

"I am told," said John, after a pause in which the conversation seemed to be dying out for lack of fuel, and apropos of nothing in particular, "that Homeville is quite a summer resort."

"Quite a consid'able," responded Mr. Harum. "It has ben to some extent fer a good many years, an' it's gettin' more an' more so all the time, only diff'rent. I mean," he said, "that the folks that come now make more show an' most on 'em who ain't visitin' their relations either has places of their own or hires 'em fer the summer. One time some folks used to come an' stay at the hotel. The' was quite a fair one then," he explained; "but it burned up, an' wa'n't never built up agin because it had got not to be thought the fash'nable thing to put up there. Mis' Robinson (Dug's wife), an' Mis' Truman, 'round on Laylock Street, has some fam'lies that come an' board with them ev'ry year, but that's about all the boardin' the' is nowdays." Mr. Harum stopped and looked at his companion thoughtfully for a moment, as if something had just occurred to him.

"The' 'll be more o' your kind o' folk 'round, come summer," he said; and then, on a second thought, "you're 'Piscopal, ain't ye?"

"I have always attended that service," replied John, smiling, "and I have gone to St. James's here nearly every Sunday."

"Hain't they taken any notice of ye?" asked David.

"Mr. Euston, the rector, called upon me," said John, "but I have made no further acquaintances."

"E-um'm!" said David, and, after a moment, in a sort of confidential tone, "Do you like goin' to church?" he asked.

"Well," said John, "that depends--yes, I think I do. I think it is the proper thing," he concluded weakly.

"Depends some on how a feller's ben brought up, don't ye think so?" said David.

"I should think it very likely," John assented, struggling manfully with a yawn.

"I guess that's about my case," remarked Mr. Harum, "an' I sh'd have to admit that I ain't much of a hand fer church-goin'. Polly has the princ'pal charge of that branch of the bus'nis, an' the one I stay away from, when I ***don't*** go," he said with a grin, "'s the Prespyteriun." John laughed.

"No, sir," said David, "I ain't much of a hand for't. Polly used to worry at me about it till I fin'ly says to her, 'Polly,' I says, 'I'll tell ye what I'll do. I'll compermise with ye,' I says. 'I won't undertake to foller right along in your track--I hain't got the req'sit speed,' I says, 'but f'm now on I'll go to church reg'lar on Thanksgivin'.' It was putty near Thanksgivin' time," he remarked, "an' I dunno but she thought if she c'd git me started I'd finish the heat, an' so we fixed it at that."

"Of course," said John with a laugh, "you kept your promise?"

"Wa'al, sir," declared David with the utmost gravity, "fer the next five years I never missed attendin' church on Thanksgivin' day but *four* times; but after that," he added, "I had to beg off. It was too much of a strain," he declared with a chuckle, "an' it took more time 'n Polly c'd really afford to git me ready." And so he rambled on upon such topics as suggested themselves to his mind, or in reply to his auditor's comments and questions, which were, indeed, more perfunctory than otherwise. For the Verjooses, the Rogerses, the Swaynes, and the rest, were people whom John not only did not know, but whom he neither expected nor cared to know; and so his present interest in them was extremely small.

Outside of his regular occupations, and despite the improvement in his domestic environment, life was so dull for him that he could not imagine its ever being otherwise in Homeville. It was a year since the world--his world--had come to an end, and though his sensations of loss and defeat had passed the acute stage, his mind was far from healthy. He had evaded David's question, or only half answered it, when he merely replied that the rector had called upon him. The truth was that some tentative advances had been made to him, and Mr. Euston had presented him to a few of the people in his flock; but beyond the point of mere politeness he had made no response, mainly from indifference, but to a degree because of a suspicion that his connection with Mr. Harum would not, to say the least, enhance his position in the minds of certain of the people of Homeville. As has been intimated, it seemed at the outset of his career in the village as if there had been a combination of circumstance and effort to put him on his guard, and, indeed, rather to prejudice him against his employer; and Mr. Harum, as it now appeared to our friend, had on one or two occasions laid himself open to misjudgment, if no more. No allusion had ever been made to the episode of the counterfeit money by either his employer or himself, and it was not till months afterward that the subject was brought up by Mr. Richard Larrabee, who sauntered into the bank one morning. Finding no one there but John, he leaned over the counter on his elbows, and, twisting one leg about the other in a restful attitude, proceeded to open up a conversation upon various topics of interest to his mind. Dick was Mr. Harum's confidential henchman and factotum, although not regularly so employed. His chief object in life was apparently to get as much amusement as possible out of that experience, and he was quite unhampered by over-nice notions of delicacy or bashfulness. But, withal, Mr. Larrabee was a very honest and loyal person, strong in his likes and dislikes, devoted to David, for whom he had the greatest admiration, and he had taken a fancy to our friend, stoutly maintaining that he "wa'n't no more stuck-up 'n you be," only, as he remarked to Bill Perkins, "he hain't had the advantigis of your bringin' up."

After some preliminary talk--"Say," he said to John, "got stuck with any more countyfit money lately?"

John's face reddened a little and Dick laughed.

"The old man told me about it," he said. "Say, you'd ought to done as he told ye to. You'd 'a' saved fifteen dollars," Dick declared, looking at our friend with an expression of the utmost amusement.

"I don't quite understand," said John rather stiffly.

"Didn't he tell ye to charge 'em up to the bank, an' let him take 'em?" asked Dick.

"Well?" said John shortly.

"Oh, yes, I know," said Mr. Larrabee. "He said sumpthin' to make you think he was goin' to pass 'em out, an' you didn't give him no show to explain, but jest marched into the back room an' stuck 'em onto the fire. Ho, ho, ho, ho! He told me all about it," cried Dick. "Say," he declared, "I dunno 's I ever see the old man more kind o' womble-cropped over anythin'. Why, he wouldn't no more 'a' passed them bills 'n he'd 'a' cut his hand off. He, he, he, he! He was jest ticklin' your heels a little," said Mr. Larrabee, "to see if you'd kick, an'," chuckled the speaker, "you *surely* did."

"Perhaps I acted rather hastily," said John, laughing a little from contagion.

"Wa'al," said Dick, "Dave's got ways of his own. I've summered an' wintered with him now for a good many years, an' *I* ain't got to the bottom of him yet, an'," he added, "I don't know nobody that has."

CHAPTER XXIX.

Although, as time went on and John had come to a better insight of the character of the eccentric person whom Dick had failed to fathom, his half-formed prejudices had fallen away, it must be admitted that he ofttimes found him a good deal of a puzzle. The domains of the serious and the facetious in David's mind seemed to have no very well defined boundaries.

The talk had drifted back to the people and gossip of Homeville, but, sooth to say, it had not on this occasion got far away from those topics.

"Yes," said Mr. Harum, "Alf Verjoos is on the hull the best off of any of the lot. As I told ye, he made money on top of what the old man left him, an' he married money. The fam'ly--some on 'em--comes here in the summer, an' he's here part o' the time gen'ally, but the women folks won't stay here winters, an' the house is left in care of Alf's sister who never got married. He don't care a hill o' white beans fer anything in Homeville but the old place, and he don't cal'late to have nobody on his grass, not if he knows it. Him an' me are on putty friendly terms, but the fact is," said David, in a semi-confidential tone, "he's about an even combine of pykery an' viniger, an' about as pop'lar in gen'ral 'round here as a skunk in a hen-house; but Mis' Verjoos is putty well liked; an' one o' the girls, Claricy is her name, is a good deal of a fav'rit. Juliet, the other one, don't mix with the village folks much, an' sometimes don't come with the fam'ly at all. She favors her father," remarked the historian.

"Inherits his popularity, I conclude," remarked John, smiling.

"She does favor him to some extent in that respect," was the reply; "an' she's dark complected like him, but she's a mighty han'some girl, notwithstandin'. Both on 'em is han'some girls," observed Mr. Harum, "an' great fer hosses, an' that's the way I got 'quainted with 'em. They're all fer ridin' hossback when they're up here. Did you ever ride a hoss?" he asked.

"Oh, yes," said John, "I have ridden a good deal one time and another."

"Never c'd see the sense on't," declared David. "I c'n imagine gettin' on to a hoss's back when 't was either that or walkin', but to do it fer the fun o' the thing 's more 'n I c'n understand. There you be," he continued, "stuck up four five feet up in the air like a clo'espin, havin' your backbone chucked up into your skull, an' takin' the skin off in spots an' places, expectin' ev'ry next minute the critter'll git out f'm under ye--no, sir," he protested, "if it come to be that it was either to ride a hossback fer the fun o' the thing or have somebody kick me, an' kick me hard, I'd say, 'Kick away.' It comes to the same thing fur 's enjoyment goes, and it's a dum sight safer."

John laughed outright, while David leaned forward with his hands on his knees, looking at him with a broad though somewhat doubtful smile.

"That being your feeling," remarked John, "I should think saddle horses would be rather out of your line. Was it a saddle horse that the Misses Verjoos were interested in?"

"Wa'al, I didn't buy him fer that," replied David, "an' in fact when the feller that sold him to me told me he'd ben rode, I allowed that ought to knock twenty dollars off 'n the price, but I did have such a hoss, an', outside o' that, he was a nice piece of hoss flesh. I was up to the barn one mornin', mebbe four years ago," he continued, "when in drove the Verjoos carriage with one of the girls, the oldest one, inside, an' the yeller-haired one on a hossback. 'Good mornin'. You're Mr. Harum, ain't you?' she says. 'Good mornin',' I says, 'Harum's the name 't I use when I appear in public. You're Miss Verjoos, I reckon,' I says.

"She laughed a little, an' says, motionin' with her head to'ds the carriage, 'My sister is Miss Verjoos. I'm Miss Claricy.' I took off my cap, an' the other girl jest bowed her head a little.

"'I heard you had a hoss 't I could ride,' says the one on hossback.

"'Wa'al,' I says, lookin' at her hoss, an' he was a good one," remarked David, "'fer a saddle hoss, I shouldn't think you was entirely out o' hosses long's you got that one.' 'Oh,' she says, this is my sister's hoss. Mine has hurt his leg so badly that I am 'fraid I sha'n't be able to ride him this summer.' 'Wa'al,' I says, 'I've got a hoss that's ben rode, so I was told, but I don't know of my own knowin'.'

"'Don't you ride?' she says. 'Hossback?' I says. 'Why, of course,' she says. '*No*, ma'am,' I says, 'not when I c'n raise the money to pay my *fine*' She looked kind o' puzzled at that," remarked David, "but I see the other girl look at her an' give a kind of quiet laugh."

"'Can I see him?' says Miss Claricy. 'Cert'nly,' I says, an' went an' brought him out. 'Oh!' she says to her sister, 'ain't he a beauty? C'n I try him?' she says to me. 'Wa'al,' I says, 'I guess I c'n resk it if you can, but I didn't buy him fer a saddle hoss, an' if I'm to own him fer any len'th of time I'd ruther he'd fergit the saddle bus'nis, an' in any case,' I says, 'I wouldn't like him to git a sore back, an' then agin,' I says, 'I hain't got no saddle.'

"'Wa'al,' she says, givin' her head a toss, 'if I couldn't sit straight I'd never ride agin. I never made a hoss's back sore in my life,' she says. 'We c'n change the saddle,' she says, an' off she jumps, an', scat my ----!" exclaimed David, "the way she knowed about gettin' that saddle fixed, pads, straps, girt's, an' the hull bus'nis, an' put up her foot fer me to give her a lift, an' wheeled that hoss an' went out o' the yard a-kitin', was as slick a piece o' hoss bus'nis as ever I see. It took fust money, that did," said Mr. Harum with a confirmatory shake of the head. "Wa'al," he resumed, "in about a few minutes back she come, lickity-cut, an' pulled up in front of me. 'C'n you send my sister's hoss home?' she says, 'an' then I sha'n't have to change agin. I'll stay on *my* hoss,' she says, laughin', an' then agin laughin' fit to kill, fer I stood there with my mouth open clear to my back teeth, not bein' used to doin' bus'nis 'ith quite so much neatniss an' dispatch, as the sayin' is.

"'Oh, it's all right,' she says. 'Poppa came home last night an' I'll have him see you this afternoon or to-morro'.' 'But mebbe he 'n I won't agree about the price,' I says. 'Yes, you will,' she says, 'an' if you don't I won't make his back sore'--an' off they went, an' left me standin' there like a stick in the mud. I've bought an' sold hosses to some extent fer a consid'able number o' years," said Mr. Harum reflectively, "but that partic'ler transaction's got a peg all to itself."

John laughed and asked, "How did it come out? I mean, what sort of an interview did you have with the young woman's father, the popular Mr. Verjoos?"

"Oh," said David, "he druv up to the office the next mornin', 'bout ten o'clock, an' come into the back room here, an' after we'd passed the time o' day, he says, clearin' his throat in a way he's got, 'He-uh, he-uh!' he says, 'my daughter tells me that she run off with a hoss of yours yestidy in rather a summery manner, an--he-uh-uh--I have come to see you about payin' fer him. What is the price?' he says.

"'Wa'al,' I says, more 'n anythin' to see what he'd say, 'what would you say he was wuth?' An' with that he kind o' stiffened a little stiffer 'n he was before, if it could be.

"'Really,' he says, 'he-uh-uh, I haven't any idea. I haven't seen the animal, an' I should not consider myself qual'fied to give an opinion upon his value if I had, but,' he says, 'I don't know that that makes any material diff'rence, however, because I am quite--he-uh, he-uh--in your hands--he-uh!--within limits--he-uh-uh!--within limits,' he says. That kind o' riled me," remarked David. "I see in a minute what was passin' in his mind. 'Wa'al,' I says, 'Mr. Verjoos, I guess the fact o' the matter is 't I'm about as much in the mud as you be in the mire--your daughter's got my hoss,' I says. 'Now you ain't dealin' with a hoss jockey,' I says, 'though I don't deny that I buy an' sell hosses, an' once in a while make money at it. You're dealin' with David Harum, Banker, an' I consider 't I'm dealin' with a lady, or the father of one on her account,' I says.

"'He-uh, he-uh! I meant no offense, sir,' he says.

"'None bein' meant, none will be took,' I says. 'Now,' I says,' I was offered one-seventy-five fer that hoss day before yestidy, an' wouldn't take it. I can't sell him fer that,' I says.

"'He-uh, uh! cert'nly not,' he says.

"'Wait a minit,' I says. 'I can't sell him fer that because I *said* I wouldn't; but if you feel like drawin' your check fer one-seventy-*six*,' I says, 'we'll call it a deal,'" The speaker paused with a chuckle.

"Well?" said John.

"Wa'al," said David, "he, he, he, he! That clean took the wind out of him, an' he got redder 'n a beet. 'He-uh-uh-uh-huh! really,' he says, 'I couldn't think of offerin' you less than two hunderd.'

"'All right,' I says, 'I'll send up fer the hoss. One-seventy-six is my price, no more an' no less,' an' I got up out o' my chair."

"And what did he say then?" asked John.

"Wa'al," replied Mr. Harum, "he settled his neck down into his collar an' neck-tie an' cleared his throat a few times, an' says, 'You put me in ruther an embarrassin' position, Mr. Harum. My daughter has set her heart on the hoss, an'--he-uh-uh-uh!--with a kind of a smile like a wrinkle in a boot, 'I can't very well tell her that I wouldn't buy him because you wouldn't accept a higher offer than your own price. I--I think I must accede to your proposition, an'--he-uh-uh--accept the favor,' he says, draggin' the words out by the roots.

"'No favor at all,' I says, 'not a bit on't, not a bit on't. It was the cleanest an' slickist deal I ever had,' I says, 'an' I've had a good many. That girl o' your'n,' I says, 'if you don't mind my sayin' it, comes as near bein' a full team an' a cross dog under the wagin as you c'n git; an' you c'n tell her if you think fit,' I says, 'that if she ever wants anythin' more out o' *my* barn I'll throw off twenty-four dollars ev'ry time, if she'll only do her own buyin'.'

"Wa'al," said Mr. Harum, "I didn't know but what he'd gag a little at that, but he didn't seem to, an' when he went off after givin' me his check, he put out his hand an' shook hands, a thing he never done before."

"That was really very amusing," was John's comment.

"'T wa'n't a bad day's work either," observed Mr. Harum. "I've sold the crowd a good many hosses since then, an' I've laughed a thousan' times over that pertic'ler trade. Me 'n Miss Claricy," he added, "has alwus ben good friends since that time--an' she 'n Polly are reg'lar neetups. She never sees me in the street but what it's 'How dee do, Mr. H-a-rum?' An' I'll say, 'Ain't that ole hoss wore out yet?' or, 'When you comin' 'round to run off with another hoss?' I'll say."

At this point David got out of his chair, yawned, and walked over to the window.

"Did you ever in all your born days," he said, "see such dum'd weather? Jest look out there--no sleighin', no wheelin', an' a barn full wantin' exercise. Wa'al, I guess I'll be moseyin' along." And out he went.

CHAPTER XXX.

If John Lenox had kept a diary for the first year of his life in Homeville most of its pages would have been blank.

The daily routine of the office (he had no assistant but the callow Hopkins) was more exacting than laborious, but it kept him confined seven hours in the twenty-four. Still, there was time in the lengthened days as the year advanced for walking, rowing, and riding or driving about the picturesque country which surrounds Homeville. He and Mr. Harum often drove together after the bank closed, or after "tea," and it was a pleasure in itself to observe David's dexterous handling of his horses, and his content and satisfaction in the enjoyment of his favorite pastime. In pursuit of business he "jogged 'round," as he said, behind the faithful Jinny, but when on pleasure bent, a pair of satin-coated trotters drew him in the latest and "slickest" model of top-buggies.

"Of course," he said, "I'd ruther ride all alone than not to ride at all, but the's twice as much fun in't when you've got somebody along. I ain't much of a talker, unless I happen to git started" (at which assertion John repressed a smile), "but once in a while I like to have somebody to say somethin' to. You like to come along, don't ye?"

"Very much indeed."

"I used to git Polly to come once in a while," said David, "but it wa'n't no pleasure to her. She hadn't never ben used to hosses an' alwus set on the edge of the seat ready to jump, an' if one o' the critters capered a little she'd want to git right out then an' there. I reckon she never went out but what she thanked mercy when she struck the hoss block to git back with hull bones."

"I shouldn't have thought that she would have been nervous with the reins in your hands," said John.

"Wa'al," replied David, "the last time she come along somethin' give the team a little scare an' she reached over an' made a grab at the lines. That," he remarked with a grin, "was quite a good while ago. I says to her when we got home, 'I guess after this you'd better take your airin's on a stun-boat. You won't be so liable to git run away with an' throwed out,' I says."

John laughed a little, but made no comment.

"After all," said David, "I dunno 's I blamed her fer bein' skittish, but I couldn't have her grabbin' the lines. It's curi's," he reflected, "I didn't used to mind what I rode behind, nor who done the drivin', but I'd have to admit that as I git older I prefer to do it myself, I ride ev'ry once in a while with fellers that c'n drive as well, an' mebbe better, 'n I can, an' I know it, but if anythin' turns up, or looks like it, I can't help wishin' 't I had holt o' the lines myself."

The two passed a good many hours together thus beguiling the time. Whatever David's other merits as a companion, he was not exacting of response when engaged in conversation, and rarely made any demands upon his auditor.

*   *   *   *   *

During that first year John made few additions to his social acquaintance, and if in the summer the sight of a gay party of young people caused some stirrings in his breast, they were not strong enough to induce him to make any attempts toward the acquaintance which he might have formed. He was often conscious of glances of curiosity directed toward himself, and Mr. Euston was asked a good many questions about the latest addition to his congregation.

Yes, he had called upon Mr. Lenox and his call had been returned. In fact, they had had several visits together--had met out walking once and had gone on in company. Was Mr. Lenox "nice"? Yes, he had made a pleasant impression upon Mr. Euston, and seemed to be a person of intelligence and good breeding--very gentlemanlike. Why did not people know him? Well, Mr. Euston had made some proffers to that end, but Mr. Lenox had merely expressed his thanks. No, Mr. Euston did not know how he happened to be in Homeville and employed by that queer old Mr. Harum, and living with him and his funny old sister; Mr. Lenox had not confided in him at all, and though very civil and pleasant, did not appear to wish to be communicative.

So our friend did not make his entrance that season into the drawing or dining rooms of any of what David called the "nabobs'" houses. By the middle or latter part of October Homeville was deserted of its visitors and as many of that class of its regular population as had the means to go with and a place to go to.

It was under somewhat different auspices that John entered upon the second winter of his sojourn. It has been made plain that his relations with his employer and the kind and lovable Polly were on a satisfactory and permanent footing.

"I'm dum'd," said David to Dick Larrabee, "if it hain't got putty near to the p'int when if I want to git anythin' out o' the common run out o' Polly, I'll have to ask John to fix it fer me. She's like a cow with a calf," he declared.

"David sets all the store in the world by him," stated Mrs. Bixbee to a friend, "though he don't jest let on to--not in so many words. He's got a kind of a notion that his little boy, if he'd lived, would 'a' ben like him some ways. I never seen the child," she added, with an expression which made her visitor smile, "but as near 's I c'n make out f'm Dave's tell, he must 'a' ben red-headed. Didn't you know 't he'd ever ben married? Wa'al, he was fer a few years, though it's the one thing--wa'al, I don't mean exac'ly that--it's *one* o' the things he don't have much to say about. But once in a while he'll talk about the boy, what he'd be now if he'd lived, an' so on; an' he's the greatest hand fer childern--everlastin'ly pickin' on 'em up when he's ridin' and such as that--an' I seen him once when we was travelin' on the cars go an' take a squawlin' baby away f'm it's mother, who looked ready to drop, an' lay it across that big chest of his, an' the little thing never gave a whimper after he got it into his arms--jest went right off to sleep. No," said Mrs. Bixbee, "I never had no childern, an' I don't know but what I was glad of it at the time; Jim Bixbee was about as much baby as I thought I could manage, but now--"

There was some reason for not concluding the sentence, and so we do not know what was in her mind.

CHAPTER XXXI.

The year that had passed had seemed a very long one to John, but as the months came and went he had in a measure adjusted himself to the change in his fortunes and environment; and so as time went on the poignancy of his sorrow and regret diminished, as it does with all of us. Yet the sight of a gray-haired man still brought a pang to his heart, and there were times of yearning longing to recall every line of the face, every detail of the dress, the voice, the words, of the girl who had been so dear to him, and who had gone out of his life as irrevocably, it seemed to him, as if by death itself. It may be strange, but it is true that for a very long time it never occurred to him that he might communicate with her by mailing a letter to her New York address to be forwarded, and when the thought came to him the impulse to act upon it was very strong, but he did not do so. Perhaps he would have written had he been less in love with her, but also there was mingled with that sentiment something of bitterness which, though he could not quite explain or justify it, did exist. Then, too, he said to himself, "Of what avail would it be? Only to keep alive a longing for the impossible." No, he would forget it all. Men had died and worms had eaten them, but not for love. Many men lived all their lives without it and got on very well too, he was aware. Perhaps some day, when he had become thoroughly affiliated and localized, he would wed a village maiden, and rear a Freeland County brood. Our friend, as may be seen, had a pretty healthy mind, and we need not sympathize with him to the disturbance of our own peace.

Books accumulated in the best bedroom. John's expenses were small, and there was very little temptation, or indeed opportunity, for spending. At the time of his taking possession of his quarters in David's house he had raised the question of his contribution to the household expenses, but Mr. Harum had declined to discuss the matter at all and referred him to Mrs. Bixbee, with whom he compromised on a weekly sum which appeared to him absurdly small, but which she protested she was ashamed to accept. After a while a small upright piano made its appearance, with Aunt Polly's approval.

"Why, of course," she said. "You needn't to hev ast me. I'd like to hev you anyway. I like music ever so much, an' so does David, though I guess it would floor him to try an' raise a tune. I used to sing quite a little when I was younger, an' I gen'ally help at church an' prayer meetin' now. Why, cert'nly. Why not? When would you play if it wa'n't in the evenin'? David sleeps over the wing. Do you hear him snore?"

"Hardly ever," replied John, smiling. "That is to say, not very much--just enough sometimes to know that he is asleep."

"Wa'al," she said decidedly, "if he's fur enough off so 't you can't hear *him*, I guess he won't hear *you* much, an' he sure won't hear you after he gits to sleep."

So the piano came, and was a great comfort and resource. Indeed, before long it became the regular order of things for David and his sister to spend an hour or so on Sunday evenings listening to his music and their own as well--that is, the music of their choice--which latter was mostly to be found in "Carmina Sacra" and "Moody and Sankey"; and Aunt Polly's heart was glad indeed when she and John together made concord of sweet sounds in some familiar hymn tune, to the great edification of Mr. Harum, whose admiration was unbounded.

       *   *   *   *   *

"Did I tell you," said David to Dick Larrabee, "what happened the last time me an' John went ridin' together?"

"Not's I remember on," replied Dick.

"Wa'al, we've rode together quite a consid'able," said Mr. Harum, "but I hadn't never said anythin' to him about takin' a turn at the lines. This day we'd got a piece out into the country an' I had the brown colts. I says to him, 'Ever do any drivin'?'"

"'More or less,' he says.

"'Like to take the lines fer a spell?' I says.

"'Yes,' he says, lookin' kind o' pleased, 'if you ain't afraid to trust me with 'em,' he says.

"'Wa'al, I'll be here,' I says, an' handed 'em over. Wa'al, sir, I see jest by the way he took holt on 'em it wa'n't the fust time, an' we went along to where the road turns in through a piece of woods, an' the track is narrer, an' we run slap onto one o' them dum'd road-engines that had got wee-wawed putty near square across the track. Now I tell ye," said Mr. Harum, "them hosses didn't like it fer a cent, an' tell the truth I didn't like it no better. We couldn't go ahead fer we couldn't git by the cussed thing, an' the hosses was 'par'ntly tryin' to git back under the buggy, an', scat my ----! if he didn't straighten 'em out an' back 'em 'round in that narrer road, an' hardly scraped a wheel. Yes, sir," declared Mr. Harum, "I couldn't 'a' done it slicker myself, an' I don't know nobody that could."

"Guess you must 'a' felt a little ticklish yourself," said Dick sympathetically, laughing as usual.

"Wa'al, you better believe," declared the other. "The' was 'bout half a minute when I'd have sold out mighty cheap, an' took a promise fer the money. He's welcome to drive any team in *my* barn," said David, feeling--in which view Mr. Larrabee shared--that encomium was pretty well exhausted in that assertion.

"I don't believe," said Mr. Harum after a moment, in which he and his companion reflected upon the gravity of his last declaration, "that the's any dum thing that feller can't do. The last thing 's a piany. He's got a little one that stands up on it's hind legs in his room, an' he c'n play it with both hands 'thout lookin' on. Yes, sir, we have reg'lar concerts at my house ev'ry Sunday night, admission free, an' childern half price, an'," said David, "you'd ought to hear him an' Polly sing, an'--he, he, he! you'd ought to *see* her singin'--tickleder 'n a little dog with a nosegay tied to his tail."

CHAPTER XXXII.

Our friend's acquaintance with the rector of St. James's church had grown into something like friendship, and the two men were quite often together in the evening. John went sometimes to Mr. Euston's house, and not unfrequently the latter would spend an hour in John's room over a cigar and a chat. On one of the latter occasions, late in the autumn, Mr. Euston went to the piano after sitting a few minutes and looked over some of the music, among which were two or three hymnals. "You are musical," he said.

"In a modest way," was the reply.

"I am very fond of it," said the clergyman, "but have little knowledge of it. I wish I had more," he added in a tone of so much regret as to cause his hearer to look curiously at him. "Yes," he said, "I wish I knew more--or less. It's the bane of my existence," declared the rector with a half laugh. John looked inquiringly at him, but did not respond.

"I mean the music--so called--at St. James's," said Mr. Euston. "I don't wonder you smile," he remarked; "but it's not a matter for smiling with me."

"I beg pardon," said John.

"No, you need not," returned the other, "but really--Well, there are a good many unpleasant and disheartening experiences in a clergyman's life, and I can, I hope, face and endure most of them with patience, but the musical part of my service is a never-ending source of anxiety, perplexity, and annoyance. I think," said Mr. Euston, "that I expend more nerve tissue upon that branch of my responsibilities than upon all the rest of my work. You see we can not afford to pay any of the singers, and indeed my people--some of them, at least--think fifty dollars is a great sum for poor little Miss Knapp, the organist. The rest are volunteers, or rather, I should say, have been pressed into the service. We are supposed to have two sopranos and two altos; but in effect it happens sometimes that neither of a pair will appear, each expecting the other to be on duty. The tenor, Mr. Hubber, who is an elderly man without any voice to speak of, but a very devout and faithful churchman, is to be depended upon to the extent of his abilities; but Mr. Little, the bass--

well," observed Mr. Euston, "the less said about him the better."

"How about the organist?" said John. "I think she does very well, doesn't she?"

"Miss Knapp is the one redeeming feature," replied the rector, "but she has not much courage to interfere. Hubber is nominally the leader, but he knows little of music." Mr. Euston gave a sorry little laugh. "It's trying enough," he said, "one Sunday with another, but on Christmas and Easter, when my people make an unusual effort, and attempt the impossible, it is something deplorable."

John could not forbear a little laugh. "I should think it must be pretty trying," he said.

"It is simply corroding," declared Mr. Euston.

They sat for a while smoking in silence, the contemplation of his woes having apparently driven other topics from the mind of the harassed clergyman. At last he said, turning to our friend:

"I have heard your voice in church."

"Yes?"

"And I noticed that you sang not only the hymns but the chants, and in a way to suggest the idea that you have had experience and training. I did not come here for the purpose," said Mr. Euston, after waiting a moment for John to speak, "though I confess the idea has occurred to me before, but it was suggested again by the sight of your piano and music. I know that it is asking a great deal," he continued, "but do you think you could undertake, for a while at least, to help such a lame dog as I am over the stile? You have no idea," said the rector earnestly, "what a service you would be doing not only to me, but to my people and the church."

John pulled thoughtfully at his mustache for a moment, while Mr. Euston watched his face. "I don't know," he said at last in a doubtful tone. "I am afraid you are taking too much for granted--I don't mean as to my good will, but as to my ability to be of service, for I suppose you mean that I should help in drilling your choir."

"Yes," replied Mr. Euston. "I suppose it would be too much to ask you to sing as well."

"I have had no experience in the way of leading or directing," replied John, ignoring the suggestion, "though I have sung in church more or less, and am familiar with the service, but even admitting my ability to be of use, shouldn't you be afraid that my interposing might make more trouble than it would help? Wouldn't your choir resent it? Such people are sometimes jealous, you know."

"Oh, dear, yes," sighed the rector. "But," he added, "I think I can guarantee that there will be no unpleasant feeling either toward you or about you. Your being from New York will give you a certain prestige, and their curiosity and the element of novelty will make the beginning easy."

There came a knock at the door and Mr. Harum appeared, but, seeing a visitor, was for withdrawing.

"Don't go," said John. "Come in. Of course you know Mr. Euston."

"Glad to see ye," said David, advancing and shaking hands. "You folks talkin' bus'nis?" he asked before sitting down.

"I am trying to persuade Mr. Lenox to do me a great favor," said Mr. Euston.

"Well, I guess he won't want such an awful sight o' persuadin'," said David, taking a chair, "if he's able to do it. What does he want of ye?" he asked, turning to John. Mr. Euston explained, and our friend gave his reasons for hesitating--all but the chief one, which was that he was reluctant to commit himself to an undertaking which he apprehended would be not only laborious but disagreeable.

"Wa'al," said David, "as fur 's the bus'nis itself 's concerned, the hull thing's all nix-cum-rouse to me; but as fur 's gettin' folks to come an' sing, you c'n git a barn full, an' take your pick; an' a feller that c'n git a pair of hosses an' a buggy out of a tight fix the way you done a while ago ought to be able to break in a little team of half a dozen women or so."

"Well," said John, laughing, "*you* could have done what I was lucky enough to do with the horses, but--"

"Yes, yes," David broke in, scratching his cheek, "I guess you got me that time."

Mr. Euston perceived that for some reason he had an ally and advocate in Mr. Harum. He rose and said good-night, and John escorted him downstairs to the door. "Pray think of it as favorably as you can," he said, as they shook hands at parting.

"Putty nice kind of a man," remarked David when John came back; "putty nice kind of a man. 'Bout the only 'quaintance you've made of his kind, ain't he? Wa'al, he's all right fur 's he goes. Comes of good stock, I'm told, an' looks it. Runs a good deal to emptins in his preachin' though, they say. How do you find him?"

"I think I enjoy his conversation more than his sermons," admitted John with a smile.

"Less of it at times, ain't the'?" suggested David. "I may have told ye," he continued, "that I wa'n't a very reg'lar churchgoer, but I've ben more or less in my time, an' when I did listen to the sermon all through, it gen'ally seemed to me that if the preacher 'd put all the' really was in it together he wouldn't need to have took only 'bout quarter the time; but what with scorin' fer a start, an' laggin' on the back stretch, an' ev'ry now an' then breakin' to a stan'still, I gen'ally wanted to come down out o' the stand before the race was over. The's a good many fast quarter hosses," remarked Mr. Harum, "but them that c'n keep it up fer a full mile is scurce. What you goin' to do about the music bus'nis, or hain't ye made up your mind yet?" he asked, changing the subject.

"I like Mr. Euston," said John, "and he seems very much in earnest about this matter; but I am not sure," he added thoughtfully, "that I can do what he wants, and I must say that I am very reluctant to undertake it; still, I don't know but that I ought to make the trial," and he looked up at David.

"I guess I would if I was you," said the latter. "It can't do ye no harm, an' it may do ye some good. The fact is," he continued, "that you ain't out o' danger of runnin' in a rut. It would do you good mebbe to git more acquainted, an' mebbe this'll be the start on't."

"With a little team of half a dozen women, as you called them," said John. "Mr. Euston has offered to introduce me to any one I cared to know."

"I didn't mean the singin' folks," responded Mr. Harum, "I meant the church folks in gen'ral, an' it'll come 'round in a natur'l sort of way--not like bein' took 'round by Mr. Euston as if you'd *ast* him to. You can't git along--you may, an' have fer a spell, but not alwus--with nobody to visit with but me an' Polly an' Dick, an' so on, an' once in a while with the parson; you ben used to somethin' diff'rent, an' while I ain't sayin' that Homeville soci'ty, pertic'lerly in the winter, 's the finest in the land, or that me an' Polly ain't all right in our way, you want a change o' feed once in a while, or you *may* git the colic. Now," proceeded the speaker, "if this singin' bus'nis don't do more'n to give ye somethin' new to think about, an' take up an evenin' now an' then, even if it bothers ye some, I think mebbe it'll be a good thing fer ye. They say a reasonable amount o' fleas is good fer a dog--keeps him from broodin' over ***bein'*** a dog, mebbe," suggested David.

"Perhaps you are right," said John. "Indeed, I don't doubt that you are right, and I will take your advice."

"Thank you," said David a minute or two later on, holding out the glass while John poured, "jest a wisdom toothful. I don't set up to be no Sol'mon, an' if you ever find out how I'm bettin' on a race jest 'copper' me an' you c'n wear di'monds, but I know when a hoss has stood too long in the barn as soon as the next man."

It is possible that even Mr. Euston did not fully appreciate the difficulties of the task which he persuaded our friend John to undertake; and it is certain that had the latter known all that they were to be he would have hardened his heart against both the pleadings of the rector and the advice of David. His efforts were welcomed and seconded by Mr. Hubber the tenor, and Miss Knapp the organist, and there was some earnestness displayed at first by the ladies of the choir; but Mr. Little, the bass, proved a hopeless case, and John, wholly against his intentions, and his inclinations as well, had eventually to take over the basso's duty altogether, as being the easiest way--in fact, the only way--to save his efforts from downright failure.

Without going in detail into the trials and tribulations incident to the bringing of the musical part of the service at Mr. Euston's church up to a respectable if not a high standard, it may be said that with unremitting pains this end was accomplished, to the boundless relief and gratitude of that worthy gentleman, and to a good degree of the members of his congregation.

CHAPTER XXXIII.

On a fine Sunday in summer after the close of the service the exit of the congregation of St. James's church presents an animated and inspiring spectacle. A good many well-dressed ladies of various ages, and not quite so many well-dressed men, mostly (as David would have put it) "runnin' a little younger," come from out the sacred edifice with an expression of relief easily changeable to something gayer. A few drive away in handsome equipages, but most prefer to walk, and there is usually a good deal of smiling talk in groups before parting, in which Mr. Euston likes to join. He leaves matters in the vestry to the care of old Barlow, the sexton, and makes, if one may be permitted the expression, "a quick change."

Things had come about very much as David had desired and anticipated, and our friend had met quite a number of the "summer people," having been waylaid at times by the rector--in whose good graces he stood so high that he might have sung anything short of a comic song during the offertory--and presented willy-nilly. On this particular Sunday he had lingered a while in the gallery after service over some matter connected with the music, and when he came out of the church most of the people had made their way down the front steps and up the street; but standing near the gate was a group of three--the rector and two young women whom John had seen the previous summer, and now recognized as the Misses Verjoos. He raised his hat as he was passing the group, when Mr. Euston detained him: "I want to present you to the Misses Verjoos." A tall girl, dressed in some black material which gave John the impression of lace, recognized his salutation with a slight bow and a rather indifferent survey from a pair of very somber dark eyes, while her sister, in light colors, gave him a smiling glance from a pair of very blue ones, and, rather to his surprise, put out her hand with the usual declaration of pleasure, happiness, or what not.

"We were just speaking of the singing," said the rector, "and I was saying that it was all your doing."

"You really have done wonders," condescended she of the somber eyes. "We have only been here a day or two and this is the first time we have been at church."

The party moved out of the gate and up the street, the rector leading with Miss Verjoos, followed by our friend and the younger sister.

"Indeed you have," said the latter, seconding her sister's remark. "I don't believe even yourself can quite realize what the difference is. My! it is very nice for the rest of us, but it must be a perfect killing bore for you."

"I have found it rather trying at times," said John; "but now--you are so kind--it is beginning to appear to me as the most delightful of pursuits."

"Very pretty," remarked Miss Clara. "Do you say a good deal of that sort of thing?"

"I am rather out of practice," replied John. "I haven't had much opportunity for some time."

"I don't think you need feel discouraged," she returned. "A good method is everything, and I have no doubt you might soon be in form again."

"Thanks for your encouragement," said John, smiling. "I was beginning to feel quite low in my mind about it." She laughed a little.

"I heard quite a good deal about you last year from a very good friend of yours," said Miss Clara after a pause.

John looked at her inquiringly.

"Mrs. Bixbee," she said. "Isn't she an old dear?"

"I have reason to think so, with all my heart," said John stoutly.

"She talked a lot about you to me," said Miss Clara.

"Yes?"

"Yes, and if your ears did not burn you have no sense of gratitude. Isn't Mr. Harum funny?"

"I have sometimes suspected it," said John, laughing. "He once told me rather an amusing thing about a young woman's running off with one of his horses."

"Did he tell you that? Really? I wonder what you must have thought of me?"

"Something of what Mr. Harum did, I fancy," said John.

"What was that?"

"Pardon me," was the reply, "but I have been snubbed once this morning." She gave a little laugh.

"Mr. Harum and I are great 'neetups,' as he says. Is 'neetups' a nice word?" she asked, looking at her companion.

"I should think so if I were in Mr. Harum's place," said John. "It means 'cronies,' I believe, in his dictionary."

They had come to where Freeland Street terminates in the Lake Road, which follows the border of the lake to the north and winds around the foot of it to the south and west.

"Why!" exclaimed Miss Clara, "there comes David. I haven't seen him this summer."

They halted and David drew up, winding the reins about the whipstock and pulling off his buckskin glove.

"How do you do, Mr. Harum?" said the girl, putting her hand in his.

"How air ye, Miss Claricy? Glad to see ye agin," he said. "I'm settin' up a little ev'ry day now, an' you don't look as if you was off your feed much, eh?"

"No," she replied, laughing, "I'm in what you call pretty fair condition, I think."

"Wa'al, I reckon," he said, looking at her smiling face with the frankest admiration. "Guess you come out a little finer ev'ry season, don't ye? Hard work to keep ye out o' the 'free-fer-all' class, I guess. How's all the folks?"

"Nicely, thanks," she replied.

"That's right," said David.

"How is Mrs. Bixbee?" she inquired.

"Wa'al," said David with a grin, "I ben a little down in the mouth lately 'bout Polly--seems to be fallin' away some--don't weigh much more 'n I do, I guess;" but Miss Clara only laughed at this gloomy report.

"How is my horse Kirby?" she asked.

"Wa'al, the ole bag-o'-bones is breathin' yet," said David, chuckling, "but he's putty well wore out--has to lean up agin the shed to whicker. Guess I'll have to sell ye another putty soon now. Still, what the' is left of him 's 's good 's ever 't will be, an' I'll send him up in the mornin'." He looked from Miss Clara to John, whose salutation he had acknowledged with the briefest of nods.

"How'd you ketch *him*?" he asked, indicating our friend with a motion of his head. "Had to go after him with a four-quart measure, didn't ye? or did he let ye corner him?"

"Mr. Euston caught him for me," she said, laughing, but coloring perceptibly, while John's face grew very red. "I think I will run on and join my sister, and Mr. Lenox can drive home with you. Good bye, Mr. Harum. I shall be glad to have Kirby whenever it is convenient. We shall be glad to see you at Lakelawn," she said to John cordially, "whenever you can come;" and taking her prayer book and hymnal from him, she sped away.

"Look at her git over the ground," said David, turning to watch her while John got into the buggy. "Ain't that a gait?"

"She is a charming girl," said John as old Jinny started off.

"She's the one I told you about that run off with my hoss," remarked David, "an' I alwus look after him fer her in the winter."

"Yes, I know," said John. "She was laughing about it to-day, and saying that you and she were great friends."

"She was, was she?" said David, highly pleased. "Yes, sir, that's the girl, an', scat my ----! if I was thirty years younger she c'd run off with me jest as easy--an' I dunno but what she could anyway," he added.

"Charming girl," repeated John rather thoughtfully.

"Wa'al," said David, "I don't know as much about girls as I do about some things; my experience hain't laid much in that line, but I wouldn't like to take a contract to match *her* on any *limit*. I guess," he added softly, "that the consideration in that deal 'd have to be 'love an' affection.' Git up, old lady," he exclaimed, and drew the whip along old Jinny's back like a caress. The mare quickened her pace, and in a few minutes they drove into the barn.

CHAPTER XXXIV.

"Where you ben?" asked Mrs. Bixbee of her brother as the three sat at the one o'clock dinner. "I see you drivin' off somewheres."

"Ben up the Lake Road to 'Lizer Howe's," replied David. "He's got a hoss 't I've some notion o' buyin'."

"Ain't the' week-days enough," she asked, "to do your horse-tradin' in 'ithout breakin' the Sabbath?"

David threw back his head and lowered a stalk of the last asparagus of the year into his mouth.

"Some o' the best deals I ever made," he said, "was made on a Sunday. Hain't you never heard the sayin', 'The better the day, the better the deal'?"

"Wa'al," declared Mrs. Bixbee, "the' can't be no blessin' on money that's made in that way, an' you'd be better off without it."

"I dunno," remarked her brother, "but Deakin Perkins might ask a blessin' on a hoss trade, but I never heard of it's bein' done, an' I don't know jest how the deakin 'd put it; it'd be two fer the deakin an' one fer the other feller, though, somehow, you c'n bet."

"Humph!" she ejaculated. "I guess nobody ever did; an' I sh'd think you had money enough an' horses enough an' time enough to keep out o' that bus'nis on

Sunday, anyhow."

"Wa'al, wa'al," said David, "mebbe I'll swear off before long, an' anyway the' wa'n't no blessin' needed on this trade, fer if you'll ask 'Lizer he'll tell ye the' wa'n't none made. 'Lizer 's o' your way o' thinkin' on the subjict."

"That's to his credit, anyway," she asserted.

"Jes' so," observed her brother; "I've gen'ally noticed that folks who was of your way o' thinkin' never made no mistakes, an' 'Lizer 's a very consistent believer;" whereupon he laughed in a way to arouse both Mrs. Bixbee's curiosity and suspicion.

"I don't see anythin' in that to laugh at," she declared.

"He, he, he, he!" chuckled David.

"Wa'al, you may 's well tell it one time 's another. That's the way," she said, turning to John with a smile trembling on her lips, "'t he picks at me the hull time."

"I've noticed it," said John. "It's shameful."

"I do it hully fer her good," asserted David with a grin. "If it wa'n't fer me she'd git in time as narrer as them seven-day Babtists over to Peeble--they call 'em the 'narrer Babtists.' You've heard on 'em, hain't you, Polly?"

"No," she said, without looking up from her plate, "I never heard on 'em, an' I don't much believe you ever did neither."

"What!" exclaimed David, "You lived here goin' on seventy year an' never heard on 'em?"

"David Harum!" she cried, "I ain't within ten year----"

"Hold on," he protested, "don't throw that teacup. I didn't say you *was*, I only said you was *goin' on*--an' about them people over to Peeble, they've got the name of the 'narrer Babtists' because they're so narrer in their views that fourteen on 'em c'n sit, side an' side, in a buggy." This astonishing statement elicited a laugh even from Aunt Polly, but presently she said:

"Wa'al, I'm glad you found one man that would stan' you off on Sunday."

"Yes'm," said her brother, "'Lizer 's jest your kind. I knew 't he'd hurt his foot, an' prob'ly couldn't go to meetin', an' sure enough, he was settin' on the stoop, an' I drove in an' pulled up in the lane alongside. We said good mornin' an' all that, an' I ast after the folks an' how his foot was gettin' 'long, an' so on, an' fin'ly I says, 'I see your boy drivin' a hoss the other day that looked a little--f'm the middle o' the road--as if he might match one I've got, an' I thought I'd drive up this mornin' an' see if we couldn't git up a dicker.' Wa'al, he give a kind of a hitch in his chair as if his foot hurt him, an' then he says, 'I guess I can't deal with ye to-day. I don't never do no bus'nis on Sunday,' he says.

"'I've heard you was putty pertic'ler,' I says, 'but I'm putty busy jest about now, an' I thought that mebbe once in a way, an' seein' that you couldn't go to meetin' anyway, an' that I've come quite a ways an' don't know when I c'n see you agin, an' so on, that mebbe you'd think, under all the circumstances, the' wouldn't be no great harm in't--long 's I don't pay over no money, at cetery,' I says.

"'No,' he says, shakin' his head in a sort o' mournful way, 'I'm glad to see ye, an' I'm sorry you've took all that trouble fer nuthin', but my conscience won't allow me,' he says, 'to do no bus'nis on Sunday.'

"'Wa'al,' I says, 'I don't ask no man to go agin his conscience, but it wouldn't be no very glarin' transgression on your part, would it, if I was to go up to the barn all alone by myself an' look at the hoss?' I c'd see," continued Mr. Harum, "that his face kind o' brightened up at that, but he took his time to answer. 'Wa'al,' he says fin'ly, 'I don't want to lay down no law fer *you*, an' if *you* don't see no harm in't, I guess the' ain't nuthin' to prevent ye.' So I got down an' started fer the barn, an'--he, he, he!--when I'd got about a rod he hollered after me, 'He's in the end stall,' he says.

"Wa'al," the narrator proceeded, "I looked the critter over an' made up my mind about what he was wuth to me, an' went back an' got in, an' drove into the yard, an' turned 'round, an' drew up agin 'longside the stoop. 'Lizer looked up at me in an askin' kind of a way, but he didn't say anythin'.

"'I s'pose,' I says, 'that you wouldn't want me to say anythin' more to ye, an' I may 's well jog along back.'

"'Wa'al,' he says, 'I can't very well help hearin' ye, kin I, if you got anythin' to say?'

"'Wa'al,' I says, 'the hoss ain't exac'ly what I expected to find, nor jest what I'm lookin' fer; but I don't say I wouldn't 'a' made a deal with ye if the price had ben right, an' it hadn't ben Sunday.' I reckon," said David with a wink at John, "that that there foot o' his'n must 'a' give him an extry twinge the way he wriggled in his chair; but I couldn't break his lockjaw yit. So I gathered up the lines an' took out the whip, an' made all the motions to go, an' then I kind o' stopped an' says, 'I don't want you to go agin your princ'ples nor the law an' gosp'l on my account, but the' can't be no harm in s'posin' a case, can the'?' No, he allowed that s'posin' wa'n't jest the same as doin'. 'Wa'al,' says I, 'now s'posin' I'd come up here yestidy as I have to-day, an' looked your hoss over, an' said to you, "What price do you put on him?" what do you s'pose you'd 'a' said?'

"'Wa'al,' he said, 'puttin' it that way, I s'pose I'd 'a' said one-seventy.'

"'Yes,' I says, 'an' then agin, if I'd said that he wa'n't wuth that money to me, not bein' jest what I wanted--an' so he ain't--but that I'd give one-forty, *cash*, what do you s'pose you'd 'a' said?'

"'Wa'al,' he says, givin' a hitch, 'of course I don't know jest what I would have said, but I *guess*,' he says, ''t I'd 'a' said if you'll make it one-fifty you c'n have the hoss.'

"'Wa'al, now,' I says, 's'posin' I was to send Dick Larrabee up here in the mornin' with the money, what do you s'pose you'd do?'

"'I *s'pose* I'd let him go,' says 'Lizer.

"'All right,' I says, an' off I put. That conscience o' 'Lizer's," remarked Mr. Harum in conclusion, "is wuth its weight in gold, *jest about*."

"David Harum," declared Aunt Polly, "you'd ort to be 'shamed o' yourself."

"Wa'al," said David with an air of meekness, "if I've done anythin' I'm sorry for, I'm willin' to be forgi'n. Now, s'posin'----"

"I've heard enough 'bout s'posin' fer one day," said Mrs. Bixbee decisively, "unless it's s'posin' you finish your dinner so's't Sairy c'n git through her work sometime."

CHAPTER XXXV.

After dinner John went to his room and David and his sister seated themselves on the "verandy." Mr. Harum lighted a cigar and enjoyed his tobacco for a time in silence, while Mrs. Bixbee perused, with rather perfunctory diligence, the columns of her weekly church paper.

"I seen a sight fer sore eyes this mornin'," quoth David presently.

"What was that?" asked Aunt Polly, looking up over her glasses.

"Claricy Verjoos fer one part on't," said David.

"The Verjooses hev come, hev they? Wa'al, that's good. I hope she'll come up an' see me."

David nodded. "An' the other part on't was," he said, "she an' that young feller of our'n was walkin' together, an' a putty slick pair they made too."

"Ain't she purty?" said Mrs. Bixbee.

"They don't make 'em no puttier," affirmed David; "an' they was a nice pair. I couldn't help thinkin'," he remarked, "what a nice hitch up they'd make."

"Guess the' ain't much chance o' that," she observed.

"No, I guess not either," said David.

"He hain't got anythin' to speak of, I s'pose, an' though I reckon she'll hev prop'ty some day, all that set o' folks seems to marry money, an' some one's alwus dyin' an' leavin' some on 'em some more. The' ain't nothin' truer in the Bible," declared Mrs. Bixbee with conviction, "'n that sayin' thet them that has gits."

"That's seemin'ly about the way it runs in gen'ral," said David.

"It don't seem right," said Mrs. Bixbee, with her eyes on her brother's face. "Now there was all that money one o' Mis' Elbert Swayne's relations left her last year, an' Lucy Scramm, that's poorer 'n poverty's back kitchin, an' the same relation to him that Mis' Swayne was, only got a thousan' dollars, an' the Swaynes rich already. Not but what the thousan' was a godsend to the Scramms, but he might jest as well 'a' left 'em comf'tibly off as not, 'stid of pilin' more onto the Swaynes that didn't need it."

"Does seem kind o' tough," David observed, leaning forward to drop his cigar ash clear of the veranda floor, "but that's the way things goes, an' I've often had to notice that a man'll sometimes do the foolishist thing or the meanest thing in his hull life after he's dead."

"You never told me," said Mrs. Bixbee, after a minute or two, in which she appeared to be following up a train of reflection, "much of anythin' about John's matters. Hain't he ever told you anythin' more 'n what you've told me? or don't ye want me to know? Didn't his father leave anythin'?"

"The' was a little money," replied her brother, blowing out a cloud of smoke, "an' a lot of unlikely chances, but nothin' to live on."

"An' the' wa'n't nothin' for 't but he had to come up here?" she queried.

"He'd 'a' had to work on a salary somewhere, I reckon," was the reply. "The' was one thing," added David thoughtfully after a moment, "that'll mebbe come to somethin' some time, but it may be a good while fust, an' don't you ever let on to him nor nobody else 't I ever said anythin' about it."

"I won't open my head to a livin' soul," she declared. "What was it?"

"Wa'al, I don't know 's I ever told ye," he said, "but a good many years ago I took some little hand in the oil bus'nis, but though I didn't git in as deep as I wish now 't I had, I've alwus kept up a kind of int'rist in what goes on in that line."

"No, I guess you never told me," she said. "Where you goin'?" as he got out of his chair.

"Goin' to git my cap," he answered. "Dum the dum things! I don't believe the's a fly in Freeland County that hain't danced the wild kachuky on my head sence we set here. Be I much specked?" he asked, as he bent his bald poll for her inspection.

"Oh, go 'long!" she cried, as she gave him a laughing push.

"'Mongst other-things," he resumed, when he had returned to his chair and relighted his cigar, "the' was a piece of about ten or twelve hunderd acres of land down in Pennsylvany havin' some coal on it, he told me he understood, but all the timber, ten inch an' over, 'd ben sold off. He told me that his father's head clerk told him that the old gentleman had tried fer a long time to dispose of it; but it called fer too much to develop it, I guess; 't any rate he couldn't, an' John's got it to pay taxes on."

"I shouldn't think it was wuth anythin' to him but jest a bill of expense," observed Mrs. Bixbee.

"Tain't now," said David, "an' mebbe won't be fer a good while; still, it's wuth somethin', an' I advised him to hold onto it on gen'ral princ'ples. I don't know the pertic'ler prop'ty, of course," he continued, "but I do know somethin' of that section of country, fer I done a little prospectin' 'round there myself once on a time. But it wa'n't in the oil territory them days, or wa'n't known to be, anyway."

"But it's eatin' itself up with taxes, ain't it?" objected Mrs. Bixbee.

"Wa'al," he replied, "it's free an' clear, an' the taxes ain't so very much--though they do stick it to an outside owner down there--an' the p'int is here: I've alwus thought they didn't drill deep enough in that section. The' was some little traces of oil the time I told ye of, an' I've heard lately that the's some talk of a move to test the territory agin, an', if anythin' was to be found, the young feller's prop'ty might be wuth somethin', but," he added, "of course the' ain't no tellin'."

CHAPTER XXXVI.

"Well," said Miss Verjoos, when her sister overtook her, Mr. Euston having stopped at his own gate, "you and your latest discovery seemed to be getting on pretty well from the occasional sounds which came to my ears. What is he like?"

"He's charming," declared Miss Clara.

"Indeed," remarked her sister, lifting her eyebrows. "You seem to have come to a pretty broad conclusion in a very short period of time. 'Charming' doesn't leave very much to be added on longer acquaintance, does it?"

"Oh, yes it does," said Miss Clara, laughing. "There are all degrees: Charming, very charming, most charming, and *perfectly* charming."

"To be sure," replied the other. "And there is the descending scale: Perfectly charming, most charming, very charming, charming, very pleasant, quite nice, and, oh, yes, well enough. Of course you have asked him to call."

"Yes, I have," said Miss Clara.

"Don't you think that mamma----"

"No, I don't," declared the girl with decision. "I know from what Mr. Euston said, and I know from the little talk I had with him this morning, from his manner and--*je ne sais quoi*--that he will be a welcome addition to a set of people in which every single one knows just what every other one will say on any given subject and on any occasion. You know how it is."

"Well," said the elder sister, smiling and half shutting her eyes with a musing look, "I think myself that we all know each other a little too well to make our affairs very exciting. Let us hope the new man will be all you anticipate, and," she added with a little laugh, and a side glance at her sister, "that there will be enough of him to go 'round."

It hardly needs to be said that the aristocracy of Homeville and all the summer visitors and residents devoted their time to getting as much pleasure and amusement out of their life as was to be afforded by the opportunities at hand: Boating, tennis, riding, driving; an occasional picnic, by invitation, at one or the other of two very pretty waterfalls, far enough away to make the drive there and back a feature; as much dancing in an informal way as could be managed by the younger people; and a certain amount of flirtation, of course (but of a very harmless sort), to supply zest to all the rest. But it is not intended to give a minute account of the life, nor to describe in detail all the pursuits and festivities which prevailed during the season. Enough to say that our friend soon had opportunity to partake in them as much and often as was compatible with his duties. His first call at Lakelawn happened to be on an evening when the ladies were not at home, and it is quite certain that upon this, the occasion of his first essay of the sort, he experienced a strong feeling of relief to be able to leave cards instead of meeting a number of strange people, as he had thought would be likely.

One morning, some days later, Peleg Hopkins came in with a grin and said, "The's some folks eout in front wants you to come eout an' see 'em."

"Who are they?" asked John, who for the moment was in the back room and had not seen the carriage drive up.

"The two Verjoos gals," said Peleg with another distortion of his freckled countenance. "One on 'em hailed me as I was comin' in and ast me to ast you to come eout." John laughed a little as he wondered what their feeling would be were they aware that they were denominated as the "Verjoos gals" by people of Peleg's standing in the community.

"We were so sorry to miss your visit the other evening," said Miss Clara, after the usual salutations.

John said something about the loss having been his own, and after a few remarks of no special moment the young woman proceeded to set forth her errand.

"Do you know the Bensons from Syrchester?" she asked.

John replied that he knew who they were but had not the pleasure of their acquaintance.

"Well," said Miss Clara, "they are extremely nice people, and Mrs. Benson is very musical; in fact, Mr. Benson does something in that line himself. They have with them for a few days a violinist, Fairman I think his name is, from Boston, and a pianist--what was it, Juliet?"

"Schlitz, I think," said Miss Verjoos.

"Oh, yes, that is it, and they are coming to the house to-night, and we are going to have some music in an informal sort of way. We shall be glad to have you come if you can."

"I shall be delighted," said John sincerely. "At what time?"

"Any time you like," she said; "but the Bensons will probably get there about half-past eight or nine o'clock."

"Thank you very much, and I shall be delighted," he repeated.

Miss Clara looked at him for a moment with a hesitating air.

"There is another thing," she said.

"Yes?"

"Yes," she replied, "I may as well tell you that you will surely be asked to sing. Quite a good many people who have heard you in the quartette in church are anxious to hear you sing alone, Mrs. Benson among them."

John's face fell a little.

"You do sing other than church music, do you not?" she asked.

"Yes," he admitted, "I know some other music."

"Do you think it would be a bore to you."

"No," said John, who indeed saw no way out of it; "I will bring some music, with pleasure, if you wish."

"That's very nice of you," said Miss Clara, "and you will give us all a great deal of pleasure."

He looked at her with a smile.

"That will depend," he said, and after a moment, "Who will play for me?"

"I had not thought of that," was the reply. "I think I rather took it for granted that you could play for yourself. Can't you?"

"After a fashion, and simple things," he said, "but on an occasion I would rather not attempt it."

The girl looked at her sister in some perplexity.

"I should think," suggested Miss Verjoos, speaking for the second time, "that Mr. or Herr Schlitz would play your accompaniments, particularly if Mrs. Benson were to ask him, and if he can play for the violin I should fancy he can for the voice."

"Very well," said John, "we will let it go at that." As he spoke David came round the corner of the bank and up to the carriage.

"How d'y' do, Miss Verjoos? How air ye, Miss Claricy?" he asked, taking off his straw hat and mopping his face and head with his handkerchief. "Guess we're goin' to lose our sleighin', ain't we?"

"It seems to be going pretty fast," replied Miss Clara, laughing.

"Yes'm," he remarked, "we sh'll be scrapin' bare ground putty soon now if this weather holds on. How's the old hoss now you got him agin?" he asked. "Seem to 've wintered putty well? Putty chipper, is he?"

"Better than ever," she affirmed. "He seems to grow younger every year."

"Come, now," said David, "that ain't a-goin' to do. I cal'lated to sell ye another hoss *this* summer anyway. Ben dependin' on't in fact, to pay a dividend. The bankin' bus'nis has been so neglected since this feller come that it don't amount to much any more," and he laid his hand on John's shoulder, who colored a little as he caught a look of demure amusement in the somber eyes of the elder sister.

"After that," he said, "I think I had better get back to my neglected duties," and he bowed his adieus.

"No, sir," said Miss Clara to David, "you must get your dividend out of some one else this summer."

"Wa'al," said he, "I see I made a mistake takin' such good care on him. Guess I'll have to turn him over to Dug Robinson to winter next year. Ben havin' a little visit with John?" he asked. Miss Clara colored a little, with something of the same look which John had seen in her sister's face.

"We are going to have some music at the house to-night, and Mr. Lenox has kindly promised to sing for us," she replied.

"He has, has he?" said David, full of interest. "Wa'al, he's the feller c'n do it if anybody can. We have singin' an' music up t' the house ev'ry Sunday night--me an' Polly an' him--an' it's fine. Yes, ma'am, I don't know much about music myself, but I c'n beat time, an' he's got a stack o' music more'n a mile high, an' one o' the songs he sings 'll jest make the windows rattle. That's my fav'rit," averred Mr. Harum.

"Do you remember the name of it?" asked Miss Clara.

"No," he said; "John told me, an' I guess I'd know it if I heard it; but it's about a feller sittin' one day by the org'n an' not feelin' exac'ly right--kind o' tired an' out o' sorts an' not knowin' jest where he was drivin' at--jest joggin' 'long with a loose rein fer quite a piece, an' so on; an' then, by an' by, strikin' right into his gait an' goin' on stronger 'n stronger, an' fin'ly finishin' up with an A--men that carries him quarter way round the track 'fore he c'n pull up. That's my fav'rit," Mr. Harum repeated, "'cept when him an' Polly sings together, an' if that ain't a show--pertic'lerly Polly--I don't want a cent. No, ma'am, when him an' Polly gits good an' goin' you can't see 'em fer dust."

"I should like to hear them," said Miss Clara, laughing, "and I should particularly like to hear your favorite, the one which ends with the Amen--the very *large* A--men."

"Seventeen hands," declared Mr. Harum. "Must you be goin'? Wa'al, glad to have seen ye. Polly's hopin' you'll come an' see her putty soon."

"I will," she promised. "Give her my love, and tell her so, please."

They drove away and David sauntered in, went behind the desks, and perched himself up on a stool near the teller's counter as he often did when in the office, and John was not particularly engaged.

"Got you roped in, have they?" he said, using his hat as a fan. "Scat my ----! but ain't this a ring-tail squealer?"

"It is very hot," responded John.

"Miss Claricy says you're goin' to sing fer 'em up to their house to-night."

"Yes," said John, with a slight shrug of the shoulders, as he pinned a paper strap around a pile of bills and began to count out another.

"Don't feel very fierce for it, I guess, do ye?" said David, looking shrewdly at him.

"Not very," said John, with a short laugh.

"Feel a little skittish 'bout it, eh?" suggested Mr. Harum. "Don't see why ye should--anybody that c'n put up a tune the way you kin."

"It's rather different," observed the younger man, "singing for you and Mrs. Bixbee and standing up before a lot of strange people."

"H-m, h-m," said David with a nod; "diff'rence 'tween joggin' along on the road an' drivin' a fust heat on the track; in one case the' ain't nothin' up, an' ye don't care whether you git there a little more previously or a little less; an' in the other the's the crowd, an' the judges, an' the stake, an' your record, an' mebbe the pool box into the barg'in, that's all got to be considered. Feller don't mind it so much after he gits fairly off, but thinkin' on't beforehand 's fidgity bus'nis."

"You have illustrated it exactly," said John, laughing, and much amused at David's very characteristic, as well as accurate, illustration.

*   *   *   *   *

"My!" exclaimed Aunt Polly, when John came into the sitting room after dinner dressed to go out. "My, don't he look nice? I never see you in them clo'es. Come here a minute," and she picked a thread off his sleeve and took the opportunity to turn him round for the purpose of giving him a thorough inspection.

"That wa'n't what you said when you see me in *my* gold-plated harniss," remarked David, with a grin. "You didn't say nothin' putty to me."

"Humph! I guess the's some diff'rence," observed Mrs. Bixbee with scorn, and her brother laughed.

"How was you cal'latin' to git there?" he asked, looking at our friend's evening shoes.

"I thought at first I would walk," was the reply, "but I rather think I will stop at Robinson's and get him to send me over."

"I guess you won't do nothin' o' the sort," declared David. "Tom's all hitched to take you over, an' when you're ready jest ring the bell."

"You're awfully kind," said John gratefully, "but I don't know when I shall be coming home."

"Come back when you git a good ready," said Mr. Harum. "If you keep him an' the hoss waitin' a spell, I guess they won't take cold this weather."

CHAPTER XXXVII.

The Verjoos house, of old red brick, stands about a hundred feet back from the north side of the Lake Road, on the south shore of the lake. Since its original construction a *porte cochere* has been built upon the front. A very broad hall, from which rises the stairway with a double turn and landing, divides the main body of the house through the middle. On the left, as one enters, is the great drawing room; on the right a parlor opening into a library; and beyond, the dining room, which looks out over the lake. The hall opens in the rear upon a broad, covered veranda, facing the lake, with a flight of steps to a lawn which slopes down to the lake shore, a distance of some hundred and fifty yards.

John had to pass through a little flock of young people who stood near and about the entrance to the drawing room, and having given his package of music to the maid in waiting, with a request that it be put upon the piano, he mounted the stairs to deposit his hat and coat, and then went down.

In the south end of the drawing room were some twenty people sitting and standing about, most of them the elders of the families who constituted society in Homeville, many of whom John had met, and nearly all of whom he knew by sight and name. On the edge of the group, and halfway down the room, were Mrs. Verjoos and her younger daughter, who gave him a cordial greeting; and the elder lady was kind enough to repeat her daughter's morning assurances of regret that they were out on the occasion of his call.

"I trust you have been as good as your word," said Miss Clara, "and brought some music."

"Yes, it is on the piano," he replied, looking across the room to where the instrument stood.

The girl laughed. "I wish," she said, "you could have heard what Mr. Harum said this morning about your singing, particularly his description of The Lost Chord, and I wish that I could repeat it just as he gave it."

"It's about a feller sittin' one day by the org'n," came a voice from behind John's shoulder, so like David's as fairly to startle him, "an' not feelin' exac'ly right--kind o' tired an' out o' sorts, an' not knowin' jest where he was drivin' at--jest joggin' along with a loose rein fer quite a piece, an' so on; an' then, by an' by, strikin' right into his gait an' goin' on stronger an' stronger, an' fin'ly finishin' up with an A--men that carries him quarter way 'round the track 'fore he c'n pull up." They all laughed except Miss Verjoos, whose gravity was unbroken, save that behind the dusky windows of her eyes, as she looked at John, there was for an instant a gleam of mischievous drollery.

"Good evening, Mr. Lenox," she said. "I am very glad to see you," and hardly waiting for his response, she turned and walked away.

"That is Juliet all over," said her sister. "You would not think to see her ordinarily that she was given to that sort of thing, but once in a while, when she feels like it--well--pranks! She is the funniest creature that ever lived, I believe, and can mimic and imitate any mortal creature. She sat in the carriage this morning, and one might have fancied from her expression that she hardly heard a word, but I haven't a doubt that she could repeat every syllable that was uttered. Oh, here come the Bensons and their musicians."

John stepped back a pace or two toward the end of the room, but was presently recalled and presented to the newcomers. After a little talk the Bensons settled themselves in the corner at the lower end of the room, where seats were placed for the two musicians, and our friend took a seat near where he had been standing. The violinist adjusted his folding music rest. Miss Clara stepped over to the entrance door and put up her finger at the young people in the hall. "After the music begins," she said, with a shake of the head, "if I hear one sound of giggling or chattering, I will send every one of you young heathen home. Remember now! This isn't your party at all."

"But, Clara, dear," said Sue Tenaker (aged fifteen), "if we are very good and quiet do you think they would play for us to dance a little by and by?"

"Impudence!" exclaimed Miss Clara, giving the girl's cheek a playful slap and going back to her place. Miss Verjoos came in and took a chair by her sister. Mrs. Benson leaned forward and raised her eyebrows at Miss Clara, who took a quick survey of the room and nodded in return. Herr Schlitz seated himself on the piano chair, pushed it a little back, drew it a little forward to the original place, looked under the piano at the pedals, took out his handkerchief and wiped his face and hands, and after arpeggioing up and down the key-board, swung into a waltz of Chopin's (Opus 34, Number 1), a favorite of our friend's, and which he would have thoroughly enjoyed--for it was splendidly played--if he had not been uneasily apprehensive that he might be asked to sing after it. And while on some accounts he would have been glad of the opportunity to "have it over," he felt a cowardly sense of relief when the violinist came forward for the next number. There had been enthusiastic applause at the north end of the room, and more or less clapping of hands at the south end, but not enough to impel the pianist to supplement his performance at the time. The violin number was so well received that Mr. Fairman added a little minuet of Boccherini's without accompaniment, and then John felt that his time had surely come. But he had to sit, drawing long breaths, through a

Liszt fantasie on themes from Faust before his suspense was ended by Miss Clara, who was apparently mistress of ceremonies and who said to him, "Will you sing now, Mr. Lenox?"

He rose and went to the end of the room where the pianist was sitting. "I have been asked to sing," he said to that gentleman. "Can I induce you to be so kind as to play for me?"

"I am sure he will," said Mrs. Benson, looking at Herr Schlitz.

"Oh, yes, I blay for you if you vant," he said. "Vhere is your moosic?" They went over to the piano. "Oh, ho! Jensen, Lassen, Helmund, Grieg--you zing dem?"

"Some of them," said John. The pianist opened the Jensen album.

"You want to zing one of dese?" he asked.

"As well as anything," replied John, who had changed his mind a dozen times in the last ten minutes and was ready to accept any suggestion.

"Ver' goot," said the other. "Ve dry dis: Lehn deine wang' an meine Wang'." His face brightened as John began to sing the German words. In a measure or two the singer and player were in perfect accord, and as the former found his voice the ends of his fingers grew warm again. At the end of the song the applause was distributed about as after the Chopin waltz.

"Sehr schoen!" exclaimed Herr Schlitz, looking up and nodding; "you must zing zome more," and he played the first bars of Marie, am Fenster sitzest du, humming the words under his breath, and quite oblivious of any one but himself and the singer.

"Zierlich," he said when the song was done, reaching for the collection of Lassen. "Mit deinen blauen Augen," he hummed, keeping time with his hands, but at this point Miss Clara came across the room, followed by her sister.

"Mrs. Tenaker," she said, laughing, "asked me to ask you, Mr. Lenox, if you wouldn't please sing something they could understand."

"I have a song I should like to hear you sing," said Miss Verjoos. "There is an obligato for violin and we have a violinist here. It is a beautiful song--Tosti's Beauty's Eyes. Do you know it?"

"Yes," he replied.

"Will you sing it for me?" she asked.

"With the greatest pleasure," he answered.

Once, as he sang the lines of the song, he looked up. Miss Verjoos was sitting with her elbows on the arm of her chair, her cheek resting upon her clasped hands and her dusky eyes were fastened upon his face. As the song concluded she rose and walked away. Mrs. Tenaker came over to the piano and put out her hand.

"Thank you so much for your singing, Mr. Lenox," she said. "Would you like to do an old woman a favor?"

"Very much so," said John, smiling and looking first at Mrs. Tenaker and then about the room, "but there are no old women here as far as I can see."

"Very pretty, sir, very pretty," she said, looking very graciously at him. "Will you sing Annie Laurie for me?"

"With all my heart," he said, bowing. He looked at Herr Schlitz, who shook his head.

"Let me play it for you," said Mrs. Benson, coming over to the piano.

"Where do you want it?" she asked, modulating softly from one key to another.

"I think D flat will be about right," he replied. "Kindly play a little bit of it."

The sound of the symphony brought most of even the young people into the drawing room. At the end of the first verse there was a subdued rustle of applause, a little more after the second, and at the end of the song so much of a burst of approval as could be produced by the audience. Mrs. Benson looked up into John's face and smiled.

"We appear to have scored the success of the evening," she said with a touch of sarcasm. Miss Clara joined them.

"What a dear old song that is!" she said. "Did you see Aunt Charlie (Mrs. Tenaker) wiping her eyes?--and that lovely thing of Tosti's! We are ever so much obliged to you, Mr. Lenox."

John bowed his acknowledgments.

"Will you take Mrs. Benson out to supper? There is a special table for you musical people at the east end of the veranda."

"Is this merely a segregation or a distinction?" said John as they sat down.

"We shall have to wait developments to decide that point, I should say," replied Mrs. Benson. "I suppose that fifth place was put on the off chance that Mr. Benson might be of our party, but," she said, with a short laugh, "he is probably nine fathoms deep in a flirtation with Sue Tenaker. He shares Artemas Ward's tastes, who said, you may remember, that he liked little girls--big ones too."

A maid appeared with a tray of eatables, and presently another with a tray on which were glasses and a bottle of Pommery *sec.* "Miss Clara's compliments," she said.

"What do you think now?" asked Mrs. Benson, laughing.

"Distinctly a distinction, I should say," he replied.

"Das ist nicht so schlecht," grunted Herr Schlitz as he put half a *pate* into his mouth, "bot I vould brefer beer."

"The music has been a great treat to me," remarked John. "I have heard nothing of the sort for two years."

"You have quite contributed your share of the entertainment," said Mrs. Benson.

"You and I together," he responded, smiling.

"You have got a be-oodifool woice," said Herr Schlitz, speaking with a mouthful of salad, "und you zing ligh a moosician, und you bronounce your vorts very goot."

"Thank you," said John.

After supper there was more singing in the drawing room, but it was not of a very classical order. Something short and taking for violin and piano was followed by an announcement from Herr Schlitz.

"I zing you a zong," he said. The worthy man "breferred beer," but had, perhaps, found the wine quicker in effect, and in a tremendous bass voice he roared out, Im tiefen Keller sitz' ich hier, auf einem Fass voll Reben, which, if not wholly understood by the audience, had some of its purport conveyed by the threefold repetition of "trinke" at the end of each verse. Then a deputation waited upon John, to ask in behalf of the girls and boys if he knew and could sing Solomon Levi.

"Yes," he said, sitting down at the piano, "if you'll all sing with me," and it came to pass that that classic, followed by Bring Back my Bonnie to Me, Paddy Duffy's Cart, There's Music in the Air, and sundry other ditties dear to all hearts, was given by "the full strength of the company" with such enthusiasm that even Mr. Fairman was moved to join in with his violin; and when the Soldier's Farewell was given, Herr Schlitz would have sung the windows out of their frames had they not been open. Altogether, the evening's programme was brought to an end with a grand climax.

"Thank you very much," said John as he said good night to Mrs. Verjoos. "I don't know when I have enjoyed an evening so much."

"Thank *you* very much," she returned graciously. "You have given us all a great deal of pleasure."

"Yes," said Miss Verjoos, giving her hand with a mischievous gleam in her half-shut eyes, "I was enchanted with Solomon Levi."

CHAPTER XXXVIII.

David and John had been driving for some time in silence. The elder man was apparently musing upon something which had been suggested to his mind. The horses slackened their gait to a walk as they began the ascent of a long hill. Presently the silence was broken by a sound which caused John to turn his head with a look of surprised amusement--Mr. Harum was singing. The tune, if it could be so called, was scaleless, and these were the words:

"*Mon*day *mor*nin' I *mar*ried me a *wife*,
*Think*in' to *lead* a *more* contented *life*;
*Fid*dlin' an' *danc*in' *the*' was *played*,
To *see* how un*happy* poor *I* was *made*.
"*Tues*day *mor*nin', *'bout* break o' *day*,
While my *head* on the *pil*ler did *lay*,
She *tuned* up her *clack*, an' *scold*ed *more*
Than I *ever* heard be*fore*."

"Never heard me sing before, did ye?" he said, looking with a grin at his companion, who laughed and said that he had never had that pleasure. "Wa'al, that's all 't I remember on't," said David, "an' I dunno 's I've thought about it in thirty year. The' was a number o' verses which carried 'em through the rest o' the week, an' ended up in a case of 'sault an' battery, I rec'lect, but I don't remember jest how.

Somethin' we ben sayin' put the thing into my head, I guess."

"I should like to hear the rest of it," said John, smiling.

David made no reply to this, and seemed to be turning something over in his mind. At last he said:

"Mebbe Polly's told ye that I'm a wid'wer."

John admitted that Mrs. Bixbee had said as much as that.

"Yes, sir," said David, "I'm a wid'wer of long standin'."

No appropriate comment suggesting itself to his listener, none was made.

"I hain't never cared to say much about it to Polly," he remarked, "though fer that matter Jim Bixbee, f'm all accounts, was about as poor a shack as ever was turned out, I guess, an'--"

John took advantage of the slight hesitation to interpose against what he apprehended might be a lengthy digression on the subject of the deceased Bixbee by saying:

"You were quite a young fellow when you were married, I infer."

"Two or three years younger 'n you be, I guess," said David, looking at him, "an' a putty green colt too in some ways," he added, handing over the reins and whip while he got out his silver tobacco box and helped himself to a liberal portion of its contents. It was plain that he was in the mood for personal reminiscences.

"As I look back on't now," he began, "it kind o' seems as if it must 'a' ben some other feller, an' yet I remember it all putty dum'd well too--all but one thing, an' that the biggist part on't, an' that is how I ever come to git married at all. She was a widdo' at the time, an' kep' the boardin' house where I was livin'. It was up to Syrchester. I was better lookin' them days 'n I be now--had more hair at any rate--though," he remarked with a grin, "I was alwus a better goer than I was a looker. I was doin' fairly well," he continued, "but mebbe not so well as was thought by some.

"Wa'al, she was a good-lookin' woman, some older 'n I was. She seemed to take some shine to me. I'd roughed it putty much alwus, an' she was putty clever to me. She was a good talker, liked a joke an' a laugh, an' had some education, an' it come about that I got to beauin' her 'round quite a consid'able, and used to go an' set in her room or the parlor with her sometimes evenin's an' all that, an' I wouldn't deny that I liked it putty well."

It was some minutes before Mr. Harum resumed his narrative. The reins were sagging over the dashboard, held loosely between the first two fingers and thumb of his left hand, while with his right he had been making abstracted cuts at the thistles and other eligible marks along the roadside.

"Wa'al," he said at last, "we was married, an' our wheels tracked putty well fer quite a consid'able spell. I got to thinkin' more of her all the time, an' she me, seemin'ly. We took a few days off together two three times that summer, to Niag'ry, an' Saratogy, an' 'round, an' had real good times. I got to thinkin' that the state of matrimony was a putty good institution. When it come along fall, I was doin' well enough so 't she could give up bus'nis, an' I hired a house an' we set up housekeepin'. It was really more on my account than her'n, fer I got to kind o' feelin' that when the meat was tough or the pie wa'n't done on the bottom that I was 'sociated with it, an' gen'ally I wanted a place of my own. But," he added, "I guess it was a mistake, fur 's she was concerned."

"Why?" said John, feeling that some show of interest was incumbent.

"I reckon," said David, "'t she kind o' missed the comp'ny an' the talk at table, an' the goin's on gen'ally, an' mebbe the work of runnin' the place--she was a great worker--an' it got to be some diff'rent, I s'pose, after a spell, settin' down to three meals a day with jest only me 'stid of a tableful, to say nothin' of the evenin's. I was glad enough to have a place of my own, but at the same time I hadn't ben used to settin' 'round with nothin' pertic'ler to do or say, with somebody else that hadn't neither, an' I wa'n't then nor ain't now, fer that matter, any great hand fer readin'. Then, too, we'd moved into a diff'rent part o' the town where my wife wa'n't acquainted. Wa'al, anyway, fust things begun to drag some--she begun to have spells of not speakin', an' then she begun to git notions about me. Once in a while I'd have to go down town on some bus'nis in the evenin'. She didn't seem to mind it at fust, but bom-by she got it into her head that the' wa'n't so much bus'nis goin' on as I made out, an' though along that time she'd set sometimes mebbe the hull evenin' without sayin' anythin' more 'n yes or no, an' putty often not that, yet if I went out there'd be a flare-up; an' as things went on the'd be spells fer a fortni't together when I couldn't any time of day git a word out of her hardly, unless it was to go fer me 'bout somethin' that mebbe I'd done an' mebbe I hadn't--it didn't make no diff'rence. An' when them spells was on, what she didn't take out o' me she did out o' the house--diggin' an' scrubbin', takin' up carpits, layin' down carpits, shiftin' the furniture, eatin' one day in the kitchin an' another in the settin' room, an' sleepin' most anywhere. She wa'n't real well after a while, an' the wuss she seemed to feel, the fiercer she was fer scrubbin' an' diggin' an' upsettin' things in gen'ral, an' bomby she got so she couldn't keep a hired girl in the house more 'n a day or two at a time. She either wouldn't have 'em, or they wouldn't stay, an' more 'n half the time we was without one. This can't int'rist you much, can it?" said Mr. Harum, turning to his companion.

"On the contrary," replied John, "it interests me very much. I was thinking," he added, "that probably the state of your wife's health had a good deal to do with her actions and views of things, but it must have been pretty hard on you all the same."

"Wa'al, yes," said David, "I guess that's so. Her health wa'n't jest right, an' she showed it in her looks. I noticed that she'd pined an' pindled some, but I thought the' was some natural criss-crossedniss mixed up into it too. But I tried to make allow'nces an' the best o' things, an' git along 's well 's I could; but things kind o' got wuss an' wuss. I told ye that she begun to have notions about me, an' 't ain't hardly nec'sary to say what shape they took, an' after a while, mebbe a year 'n a half, she got so 't she wa'n't satisfied to know where I was *nights*--she wanted to know where I was *daytimes*. Kind o' makes me laugh now," he observed, "it seems so redic'lous; but it wa'n't no laughin' matter then. If I looked out o' winder she'd hint it up to me that I was watchin' some woman. She grudged me even to look at a picture paper; an' one day when we happened to be walkin' together she showed feelin' about one o' them wooden Injun women outside a cigar store."

"Oh, come now, Mr. Harum," said John, laughing.

"Wa'al," said David with a short laugh, "mebbe I did stretch that a little; but 's I told ye, she wanted to know where I was daytimes well 's nights, an' ev'ry once 'n a while she'd turn up at my bus'nis place, an' if I wa'n't there she'd set an' wait fer me, an' I'd either have to go home with her or have it out in the office. I don't mean to say that all the sort of thing I'm tellin' ye of kep' up all the time. It kind o' run in streaks; but the streaks kep' comin' oftener an' oftener, an' you couldn't never tell when the' was goin' to appear. Matters 'd go along putty well fer a while, an' then, all of a sudden, an' fer nothin' 't I could see, the' 'd come on a thunder shower 'fore you c'd git in out o' the wet."

"Singular," said John thoughtfully.

"Yes, sir," said David. "Wa'al, it come along to the second spring, 'bout the first of May. She'd ben more like folks fer about a week mebbe 'n she had fer a long spell, an' I begun to chirk up some. I don't remember jest how I got the idee, but f'm somethin' she let drop I gathered that she was thinkin' of havin' a new bunnit. I will say this for her," remarked David, "that she was an economical woman, an' never spent no money jest fer the sake o' spendin' it. Wa'al, we'd got along so nice fer a while that I felt more 'n usual like pleasin' her, an' I allowed to myself that if she wanted a new bunnit, money shouldn't stand in the way, an' I set out to give her a supprise."

They had reached the level at the top of the long hill and the horses had broken into a trot, when Mr. Harum's narrative was interrupted and his equanimity upset by the onslaught of an excessively shrill, active, and conscientious dog of the "yellow" variety, which barked and sprang about in front of the mares with such frantic assiduity as at last to communicate enough of its excitement to them to cause them to bolt forward on a run, passing the yellow nuisance, which, with the facility of long practice, dodged the cut which David made at it in passing. It was with some little trouble that the horses were brought back to a sober pace.

"Dum that dum'd dog!" exclaimed David with fervor, looking back to where the object of his execrations was still discharging convulsive yelps at the retreating vehicle, "I'd give a five-dollar note to git one good lick at him. I'd make him holler 'pen-an'-ink' *once*! Why anybody's willin' to have such a dum'd, wuthless, pestiferous varmint as that 'round 's more 'n I c'n understand. I'll bet that the days they churn, that critter, unless they ketch him an' tie him up the night before, 'll be under the barn all day, an' he's jest blowed off steam enough to run a dog churn a hull forenoon."

Whether or not the episode of the dog had diverted Mr. Harum's mind from his previous topic, he did not resume it until John ventured to remind him of it, with "You were saying something about the surprise for your wife."

"That's so," said David. "Yes, wa'al, when I went home that night I stopped into a mil'nery store, an' after I'd stood 'round a minute, a girl come up an' ast me if she c'd show me anythin'.

"'I want to buy a bunnit,' I says, an' she kind o' laughed. 'No,' I says, 'it ain't fer me, it's fer a lady,' I says; an' then we both laughed.

"'What sort of a bunnit do you want?' she says.

"'Wa'al, I dunno,' I says, 'this is the fust time I ever done anythin' in the bun- nit line.' So she went over to a glass case an' took one out an' held it up, turnin' it 'round on her hand.

"'Wa'al,' I says, 'I guess it's putty enough fur 's it goes, but the' don't seem to be much of anythin' *to* it. Hain't you got somethin' a little bit bigger an'--'

"'Showier?' she says. 'How is this?' she says, doin' the same trick with another.

"'Wa'al,' I says, 'that looks more like it, but I had an idee that the A 1, trible- extry fine article had more traps on't, an' most any one might have on either one o' them you've showed me an' not attrac' no attention at all. You needn't mind expense,' I says.

"'Oh, very well,' she says, 'I guess I know what you want,' an' goes over to an- other case an' fetches out another bunnit twice as big as either the others, an' with more notions on't than you c'd shake a stick at--flowers, an' gard'n stuff, an' fruit, an' glass beads, an' feathers, an' all that, till you couldn't see what they was fixed on to. She took holt on't with both hands, the girl did, an' put it onto her head, an' kind o' smiled an' turned 'round slow so 't I c'd git a gen'ral view on't.

"'Style all right?' I says.

"'The very best of its kind,' she says.

"'How 'bout the *kind*?' I says.

"'The very best of its style,' she says."

John laughed outright. David looked at him for a moment with a doubtful grin.

"She *was* a slick one, wa'n't she?" he said. "What a hoss trader she would 'a' made. I didn't ketch on at the time, but I rec'lected afterward. Wa'al," he resumed, after this brief digression, "'how much is it?' I says.

"'Fifteen dollars,' she says.

"'What?' I says. 'Scat my ----! I c'd buy head rigging enough to last me ten years fer that.'

"'We couldn't sell it for less,' she says.

"'S'posin' the lady 't I'm buyin' it fer don't jest like it,' I says, 'can you alter it or swap somethin' else for it?'

"'Cert'nly, within a reasonable time,' she says.

"'Wa'al, all right,' I says, 'do her up.' An' so she wrapped the thing 'round with soft paper an' put it in a box, an' I paid for't an' moseyed along up home, feelin' that ev'ry man, woman, an' child had their eyes on my parcel, but thinkin' how tickled my wife would be."

CHAPTER XXXIX.

The road they were on was a favorite drive with the two men, and at the point where they had now arrived David always halted for a look back and down upon the scene below them--to the south, beyond the intervening fields, bright with maturing crops, lay the village; to the west the blue lake, winding its length like a broad river, and the river itself a silver ribbon, till it was lost beneath the southern hills.

Neither spoke. For a few minutes John took in the scene with the pleasure it always afforded him, and then glanced at his companion, who usually had some comment to make upon anything which stirred his admiration or interest. He was gazing, not at the landscape, but apparently at the top of the dashboard. "Ho, hum," he said, straightening the reins, with a "clk" to the horses, and they drove along for a while in silence--so long, in fact, that our friend, while aware that the elder man did not usually abandon a topic until he had "had his say out," was moved to suggest a continuance of the narrative which had been rather abruptly broken off, and in which he had become considerably interested.

"Was your wife pleased?" he asked at last.

"Where was I?" asked the other in return.

"You were on your way home with your purchase," was the reply.

"Oh, yes," Mr. Harum resumed. "It was a little after tea time when I got to the house, an' I thought prob'ly I'd find her in the settin' room waitin' fer me; but she wa'n't, an' I went up to the bedroom to find her, feelin' a little less sure o' things. She was settin' lookin' out o' winder when I come in, an' when I spoke to her she didn't give me no answer except to say, lookin' up at the clock, 'What's kept ye like this?'

"'Little matter o' bus'nis,' I says, lookin' as smilin' 's I knew how, an' holdin' the box behind me.

"'What you got there?' she says, slewin' her head 'round to git a sight at it.

"'Little matter o' bus'nis,' I says agin, bringin' the box to the front an' feelin' my face straighten out 's if you'd run a flat iron over it. She seen the name on the paper.

"'You ben spendin' your time there, have ye?' she says, settin' up in her chair an' pointin' with her finger at the box. '*That's* where you ben the last half hour, hangin' 'round with them minxes in Mis' Shoolbred's. What's in that box?' she says, with her face a-blazin'.

"'Now, Lizy,' I says, 'I wa'n't there ten minutes if I was that, an' I ben buyin' you a bunnit.'

"'*You--ben--buyin'--me--a--bunnit*?' she says, stifnin' up stiffer 'n a stake.

"'Yes,' I says, 'I heard you say somethin' 'bout a spring bunnit, an' I thought, seein' how economicle you was, that I'd buy you a nicer one 'n mebbe you'd feel like yourself. I thought it would please ye,' I says, tryin' to rub her the right way.

"'Let me see it,' she says, in a voice dryer 'n a lime-burner's hat, pressin' her lips together an' reachin' out fer the box. Wa'al, sir, she snapped the string with a jerk an' sent the cover skimmin' across the room, an' then, as she hauled the parcel out of the box, she got up onto her feet. Then she tore the paper off on't an' looked at it a minute, an' then took it 'tween her thumb an' finger, like you hold up a dead rat by the tail, an' held it off at the end of her reach, an' looked it all over, with her face gettin' even redder if it could. Fin'ly she says, in a voice 'tween a whisper 'n a choke:

"'What'd you pay fer the thing?'

"'Fifteen dollars,' I says.

"'Fifteen *dollars*?' she says.

"'Yes,' I says, 'don't ye like it?' Wa'al," said David, "she never said a word. She drawed in her arm an' took holt of the bunnit with her left hand, an' fust she pulled off one thing an' dropped it on the floor, fur off as she c'd reach, an' then another, an' then another, an' then, by gum! she went at it with both hands jest as fast as she could work 'em, an' in less time 'n I'm tellin' it to ye she picked the thing cleaner 'n any chicken you ever see, an' when she got down to the carkis she squeezed it up between her two hands, give it a wring an' a twist like it was a wet dish towel, an' flung it slap in my face. Then she made a half turn, throwin' back her head an' grabbin' into her hair, an' give the awfullest screechin' laugh--one screech after another that you c'd 'a' heard a mile--an' then throwed herself face down on the bed, screamin' an' kickin'. Wa'al, sir, if I wa'n't at my wits' end, you c'n have my watch an' chain.

"She wouldn't let me touch her no way, but, as luck had it, it was one o' the times when we had a hired girl, an' hearin' the noise she come gallopin' up the stairs. She wa'n't a young girl, an' she had a face humbly 'nough to keep her awake nights, but she had some sense, an'--'You'd bether run fer the docther,' she says, when she see the state my wife was in. You better believe I done the heat of my life," said David, "an' more luck, the doctor was home an' jest finishin' his tea. His house an' office wa'n't but two three blocks off, an' in about a few minutes me an' him an' his bag was leggin' it fer my house, though I noticed he didn't seem to be 'n as much of a twitter 's I was. He ast me more or less questions, an' jest as we got to the house he says:

"'Has your wife had any thin' to 'larm or shock her this evenin'?'

"'Nothin' 't I know on,' I says, ''cept I bought her a new bunnit that didn't seem to come quite up to her idees.' At that," remarked Mr. Harum, "he give me a funny look, an' we went in an' upstairs.

"The hired girl," he proceeded, "had got her quieted down some, but when we went in she looked up, an' seein' me, set up another screech, an' he told me to go downstairs an' he'd come down putty soon, an' after a while he did.

"'Wa'al?' I says.

"'She's quiet fer the present,' he says, takin' a pad o' paper out o' his pocket, an' writin' on it.

"'Do you know Mis' Jones, your next-door neighbor?' he says. I allowed 't I had a speakin' acquaintance with her.

"'Wa'al,' he says, 'fust, you step in an' tell her I'm here an' want to see her, and ast her if she won't come right along; an' then you go down to my office an' have these things sent up; an' then,' he says, 'you go down town an' send this'--handin' me a note that he'd wrote an' put in an envelope--'up to the hospital--better send it up with a hack, or, better yet, go yourself,' he says, 'an' hurry. You can't be no use here,' he says. 'I'll stay, but I want a nurse here in an hour, an' less if possible.' I was putty well scared," said David, "by all that, an' I says, 'Lord,' I says, 'is she as bad off as that? What is it ails her?'

"'Don't you know?' says the doc, givin' me a queer look.

"'No,' I says, 'she hain't ben fust rate fer a spell back, but I couldn't git nothin' out of her what was the matter, an' don't know what pertic'ler thing ails her now, unless it's that dum'd bunnit,' I says.

"At that the doctor laughed a little, kind as if he couldn't help it.

"'I don't think that was hully to blame,' he says; 'may have hurried matters up a little--somethin' that was liable to happen any time in the next two months.'

"'You don't mean it?' I says.

"'Yes,' he says. 'Now you git out as fast as you can. Wait a minute,' he says. 'How old is your wife?'

"'F'm what she told me 'fore we was married,' I says, 'she's thirty-one.'

"'Oh!' he says, raisin' his eyebrows. 'All right; hurry up, now,'

"I dusted around putty lively, an' inside of an hour was back with the nurse, an 'jest after we got inside the door--" David paused thoughtfully for a moment and then, lowering his tone a little, "jest as we got inside the front door, a door upstairs opened an' I heard a little 'Waa! waa!' like it was the leetlist kind of a new lamb--an' I tell you," said David, with a little quaver in his voice, and looking straight over the off horse's ears, "nothin' 't I ever heard before nor since ever fetched me, right where I *lived*, as that did. The nurse, she made a dive fer the stairs, wavin' me back with her hand, an' I--wa'al--I went into the settin' room, an--wa'al--ne' mind.

"I dunno how long I set there list'nin' to 'em movin' 'round overhead, an' wonderin' what was goin' on; but fin'ly I heard a step on the stair an' I went out into the entry, an' it was Mis' Jones. 'How be they?' I says.

"'We don't quite know yet,' she says. 'The little boy is a nice formed little feller,' she says, 'an' them childern very often grow up, but he is *very little*,' she says.

"'An' how 'bout my wife?' I says.

"'Wa'al,' she says, 'we don't know jest yet, but she is quiet now, an' we'll hope fer the best. If you want me,' she says, 'I'll come any time, night or day, but I must go now. The doctor will stay all night, an' the nurse will stay till you c'n git some one to take her place,' an' she went home, an',' declared David, "you've hearn tell of the 'salt of the earth,' an' if that woman wa'n't more on't than a hoss c'n draw down hill, the' ain't no such thing."

"Did they live?" asked John after a brief silence, conscious of the bluntness of his question, but curious as to the sequel.

"The child did," replied David; "not to grow up, but till he was 'twixt six an' seven; but my wife never left her bed, though she lived three four weeks. She never seemed to take no int'rist in the little feller, nor nothin' else much; but one day--it was Sunday, long to the last--she seemed a little more chipper 'n usual. I was settin' with her, an' I said to her how much better she seemed to be, tryin' to chirk her up.

"'No,' she says, 'I ain't goin' to live.'

"'Don't ye say that,' I says.

"'No,' she says, 'I ain't, an' I don't care.'

"I didn't know jest what to say, an' she spoke agin:

"'I want to tell you, Dave,' she says, 'that you've ben good an' kind to me.'

"'I've tried to,' I says, 'an' Lizy,' I says, 'I'll never fergive myself about that bunnit, long 's I live.'

"'That hadn't really nothin' to do with it,' she says, 'an' you meant all right, though,' she says, almost in a whisper, an' the' came across her face, not a smile exac'ly, but somethin' like a little riffle on a piece o' still water, 'that bunnit *was* enough to kill most *any*body.'"

CHAPTER XL.

John leaned out of the buggy and looked back along the road, as if deeply interested in observing something which had attracted his attention, and David's face worked oddly for a moment.

Turning south in the direction of the village, they began the descent of a steep hill, and Mr. Harum, careful of loose stones, gave all his attention to his driving. Our friend, respecting his vigilance, forebore to say anything which might distract his attention until they reached level ground, and then, "You never married again?"

he queried.

"No," was, the reply. "My matrymonial experience was 'brief an' to the p'int,' as the sayin' is."

"And yet," urged John, "you were a young man, and I should have sup-posed----"

"Wa'al," said David, breaking in and emitting his chuckling laugh, "I allow 't mebbe I sometimes thought on't, an' once, about ten year after what I ben tellin' ye, I putty much made up my mind to try another hitch-up. The' was a woman that I seen quite a good deal of, an' liked putty well, an' I had some grounds fer thinkin' 't she wouldn't show me the door if I was to ask her. In fact, I made up my mind I would take the chances, an' one night I put on my best bib an' tucker an' started fer her house. I had to go 'cross the town to where she lived, an' the farther I walked the fiercer I got--havin' made up my mind--so 't putty soon I was travelin' 's if I was 'fraid some other feller'd git there 'head o' me. Wa'al, it was Sat'day night, an' the stores was all open, an' the streets was full o' people, an' I had to pull up in the crowd a little, an' I don't know how it happened in pertic'ler, but fust thing I knew I run slap into a woman with a ban'box, an' when I looked 'round, there was a mil'nery store in full blast an' winders full o' bunnits. Wa'al, sir, do you know what I done? Ye don't. Wa'al, the' was a hoss car passin' that run three mile out in the country in a diff'rent direction f'm where I started fer, an' I up an' got onto that car, an' rode the length o' that road, an' got off an' **walked back**--an' I never went near her house f'm that day to this, an' that," said David, "was the nearest I ever come to havin' another pardner to my joys an' sorro's."

"That was pretty near, though," said John, laughing.

"Wa'al," said David, "mebbe Prov'dence might 'a' had some other plan fer stop-pin' me 'fore I smashed the hull rig, if I hadn't run into the mil'nery shop, but as it was, that fetched me to a stan'still, an' I never started to run agin."

They drove on for a few minutes in silence, which John broke at last by saying, "I have been wondering how you got on after your wife died and left you with a little child."

"That was where Mis' Jones come in," said David. "Of course I got the best nurse I could, an' Mis' Jones 'd run in two three times ev'ry day an' see 't things was goin' on as right 's they could; but it come on that I had to be away f'm home a good deal, an' fin'ly, come fall, I got the Joneses to move into a bigger house, where I could have a room, an' fixed it up with Mis' Jones to take charge o' the little feller right along. She hadn't but one child, a girl of about thirteen, an' had lost two little ones, an' so between havin' took to my little mite of a thing f'm the fust, an' my makin' it wuth her while, she was willin', an' we went on that way till--the' wa'n't no further occasion fur 's he was concerned, though I lived with them a spell longer when I was at home, which wa'n't very often, an' after he died I was gone fer a good while. But before that time, when I was at home, I had him with me all the time I could manage. With good care he'd growed up nice an' bright, an' as big as the average, an' smarter 'n a steel trap. He liked bein' with me better 'n anybody else, and when I c'd manage to have him I couldn't bear to have him out o' my sight. Wa'al, as I told you, he got to be most seven year old. I'd had to go out to Chicago, an' one day I got a telegraph sayin' he was putty sick--an' I took the fust train East. It was 'long in March, an' we had a breakdown, an' run into an awful snowstorm, an' one thing another, an' I lost twelve or fifteen hours. It seemed to me that them two days was longer 'n my hull life, but I fin'ly did git home about nine o'clock in the mornin'. When I got to the house Mis' Jones was on the lookout fer me, an' the door opened as I run up the stoop, an' I see by her face that I was too late. 'Oh, David, David!' she says (she'd never called me David before), puttin' her hands on my shoulders.

"'When?' I says.

"''Bout midnight,' she says.

"'Did he suffer much?' I says.

"'No,' she says, 'I don't think so; but he was out of his head most of the time after the fust day, an' I guess all the time the last twenty-four hours.'

"'Do you think he'd 'a' knowed me?' I says. 'Did he say anythin'?' an' at that," said David, "she looked at me. She wa'n't cryin' when I come in, though she had ben; but at that her face all broke up. 'I don't know,' she says. 'He kept sayin' things, an' 'bout all we could understand was "Daddy, daddy,"' an' then she throwed her apern over her face, an'----"

David tipped his hat a little farther over his eyes, though, like many if not most "horsey" men, he usually wore it rather far down, and leaning over, twirled the whip in the socket between his two fingers and thumb. John studied the stitched ornamentation of the dashboard until the reins were pushed into his hands. But it was not for long. David straightened himself, and, without turning his head, resumed them as if that were a matter of course.

"Day after the fun'ral," he went on, "I says to Mis' Jones, 'I'm goin' back out West,' I says, 'an' I can't say how long I shall be gone--long enough, anyway,' I says, 'to git it into my head that when I come back the' won't be no little feller to jump up an' 'round my neck when I come into the house; but, long or short, I'll come back some time, an' meanwhile, as fur 's things between you an' me air, they're to go on jest the same, an' more 'n that, do you think you'll remember him some?' I says.

"'As long as I live,' she says, 'jest like my own.'

"'Wa'al,' I says, 'long 's you remember him, he'll be, in a way, livin' to ye, an' as long 's that I allow to pay fer his keep an' tendin' jest the same as I have, **an'**,' I says, 'if you don't let me you ain't no friend o' mine, an' you **ben** a **good** one.' Wa'al, she squimmidged some, but I wouldn't let her say 'No.' 'I've 'ranged it all with my pardner an' other ways,' I says, 'an' more 'n that, if you git into any kind of a scrape an' I don't happen to be got at, you go to him an' git what you want.'"

"I hope she lived and prospered," said John fervently.

"She lived twenty year," said David, "an' I wish she was livin' now. I never drawed a check on her account without feelin' 't I was doin' somethin' for my little boy.

"The's a good many diff'rent sorts an' kinds o' sorro'," he said, after a moment, "that's in some ways kind o' kin to each other, but I guess losin' a child 's a specie by itself. Of course I passed the achin', smartin' point years ago, but it's somethin' you can't fergit--that is, you can't help feelin' about it, because it ain't only what the child **was** to you, but what you keep thinkin' he'd 'a' ben growin' more an' more to **be** to you. When I lost my little boy I didn't only lose him as he was, but I ben losin' him over an' agin all these years. What he'd 'a' ben when he was **so** old; an' what when he'd got to be a big boy; an' what he'd 'a' ben when he went mebbe to collidge; an' what he'd 'a' ben afterward, an' up to **now**. Of course the times when a man stuffs his face down into the pillers nights, passes, after a while; but while the's some sorro's that the happenin' o' things helps ye to fergit, I guess the's some that the happenin' o' things keeps ye rememberin', an' losin' a child 's one on 'em."

CHAPTER XLI.

It was the latter part of John's fifth winter in Homeville. The business of the office had largely increased. The new manufactories which had been established did their banking with Mr. Harum, and the older concerns, including nearly all the merchants in the village, had transferred their accounts from Syrchester banks to David's. The callow Hopkins had fledged and developed into a competent all-'round man, able to do anything in the office, and there was a new "skeezicks" discharging Peleg's former functions. Considerable impetus had been given to the business of the town by the new road whose rails had been laid the previous summer. There had been a strong and acrimonious controversy over the route which the road should take into and through the village. There was the party of the "nabobs" (as they were characterized by Mr. Harum) and their following, and the party of the "village people," and the former had carried their point; but now the road was an accomplished fact, and most of the bitterness which had been engendered had died away. Yet the struggle was still matter for talk.

"Did I ever tell you," said David, as he and his cashier were sitting in the rear room of the bank, "how Lawyer Staples come to switch round in that there railroad jangle last spring?"

"I remember," said John, "that you told me he had deserted his party, and you laughed a little at the time, but you did not tell me how it came about."

"I kind o' thought I told ye," said David.

"No," said John, "I am quite sure you did not."

"Wa'al," said Mr. Harum, "the' was, as you know, the Tenaker-Rogers crowd wantin' one thing, an' the Purse-Babbit lot bound to have the other, an' run the road under the other fellers' noses. Staples was workin' tooth an' nail fer the Purse crowd, an' bein' a good deal of a politician, he was helpin' 'em a good deal. In fact, he was about their best card. I wa'n't takin' much hand in the matter either way, though my feelin's was with the Tenaker party. I know 't would come to a point where some money 'd prob'ly have to be used, an' I made up my mind I wouldn't do much drivin' myself unless I had to, an' not then till the last quarter of the heat.

Wa'al, it got to lookin' like a putty even thing. What little show I had made was if anythin' on the Purse side. One day Tenaker come in to see me an' wanted to know flat-footed which side the fence I was on. 'Wa'al,' I says, 'I've ben settin' up fer shapes to be kind o' on the fence, but I don't mind sayin', betwixt you an' me, that the bulk o' my heft is a-saggin' your way; but I hain't took no active part, an' Purse an' them thinks I'm goin' to be on their side when it comes to a pinch.'

"'Wa'al,' he says, 'it's goin' to be a putty close thing, an' we're goin' to need all the help we c'n git.'

"'Wa'al,' I says, 'I guess that's so, but fer the present I reckon I c'n do ye more good by keepin' in the shade. Are you folks prepared to spend a little money?' I says.

"'Yes,' he says, 'if it comes to that.'

"'Wa'al,' I says, 'it putty most gen'ally does come to that, don't it? Now, the's one feller that's doin' ye more harm than some others.'

"'You mean Staples?' he says.

"'Yes,' I says, 'I mean Staples. He don't really care a hill o' white beans which way the road comes in, but he thinks he's on the pop'lar side. Now,' I says, 'I don't know as it'll be nec'sary to use money with him, an' I don't say 't you could, anyway, but mebbe his yawp c'n be stopped. I'll have a quiet word with him,' I says, 'an' see you agin.' So," continued Mr. Harum, "the next night the' was quite a lot of 'em in the bar of the new hotel, an' Staples was haranguin' away the best he knowed how, an' bime by I nodded him off to one side, an' we went across the hall into the settin' room.

"'I see you feel putty strong 'bout this bus'nis,' I says.

"'Yes, sir, it's a matter of princ'ple with me,' he says, knockin' his fist down onto the table.

"'How does the outcome on't look to ye?' I says. 'Goin' to be a putty close race, ain't it?'

"'Wa'al,' he says, ''tween you an' me, I reckon it is.'

"'That's the way it looks to me,' I says, 'an' more'n that, the other fellers are ready to spend some money at a pinch.'

"'They be, be they?' he says.

"'Yes, sir,' I says, 'an' we've got to meet 'em halfway. Now,' I says, takin' a paper out o' my pocket, 'what I wanted to say to you is this: You ben ruther more prom'nent in this matter than most anybody--fur's talkin' goes--but I'm consid'ably int'risted. The's got to be some money raised, an' I'm ready,' I says, 'to put down as much as you be up to a couple o' hunderd, an' I'll take the paper 'round to the rest; but,' I says, unfoldin' it, 'I think you'd ought to head the list, an' I'll come next.' Wa'al," said David with a chuckle and a shake of the head, "you'd ought to have seen his jaw go down. He wriggled 'round in his chair, an' looked ten diff'rent ways fer Sunday.

"'What do you say?' I says, lookin' square at him, ''ll you make it a couple a hunderd?'

"'Wa'al,' he says, 'I guess I couldn't go 's fur 's that, an' I wouldn't like to head the list anyway.'

"'All right,' I says, 'I'll head it. Will you say one-fifty?'

"'No,' he says, pullin' his whiskers, 'I guess not.'

"'A hunderd?' I says, an' he shook his head.

"'Fifty,' I says, 'an' I'll go a hunderd,' an at that he got out his hank'chif an' blowed his nose, an' took his time to it. 'Wa'al,' I says, 'what *do* ye say?'

"'Wa'al,' he says, 'I ain't quite prepared to give ye 'n answer to-night. Fact on't is,' he says, 'it don't make a cent's wuth o' diff'rence to me person'ly which way the dum'd road comes in, an' I don't jest this minute see why I should spend any money in it.'

"'There's the *princ'ple* o' the thing,' I says.

"'Yes,' he says, gettin' out of his chair, 'of course, there's the princ'ple of the thing, an'--wa'al, I'll think it over an' see you agin,' he says, lookin' at his watch. 'I got to go now.'

"Wa'al, the next night," proceeded Mr. Harum, "I went down to the hotel agin, an' the' was about the same crowd, but no Staples. The' wa'n't much goin' on, an' Purse, in pertic'ler, was lookin' putty down in the mouth. 'Where's Staples?' I says.

"'Wa'al,' says Purse, 'he said mebbe he'd come to-night, an' mebbe he couldn't. Said it wouldn't make much diff'rence; an' anyhow he was goin' out o' town up to Syrchester fer a few days. I don't know what's come over the feller,' says Purse. 'I told him the time was gittin' short an' we'd have to git in our best licks, an' he said he guessed he'd done about all 't he could, an' in fact,' says Purse, 'he seemed to 'a' lost int'rist in the hull thing.'"

"What did you say?" John asked.

"Wa'al," said David with a grin, "Purse went on to allow 't he guessed some-body's pocketbook had ben talkin', but I didn't say much of anythin', an' putty soon come away. Two three days after," he continued, "I see Tenaker agin. 'I hear Staples has gone out o' town,' he says, 'an' I hear, too,' he says, 'that he's kind o' soured on the hull thing--didn't care much how it did come out.'

"'Wa'al,' I says, 'when he comes back you c'n use your own judgment about havin' a little interview with him. Mebbe somethin' 's made him think the's two sides to this thing. But anyway,' I says, 'I guess he won't do no more hollerin'.'

"'How's that?' says Tenaker.

"'Wa'al,' I says, 'I guess I'll have to tell ye a little story. Mebbe you've heard it before, but it seems to be to the point. Once on a time,' I says, 'the' was a big church meetin' that had lasted three days, an' the last evenin' the' was consid'able excite-ment. The prayin' an' singin' had warmed most on 'em up putty well, an' one o' the most movin' of the speakers was tellin' 'em what was what. The' was a big crowd, an' while most on 'em come to be edified, the' was quite a lot in the back part of the place that was ready fer anythin'. Wa'al, it happened that standin' mixed up in that lot was a feller named--we'll call him Smith, to be sure of him--an' Smith was jest runnin' over with power, an' ev'ry little while when somethin' the speaker said touched him on the funny bone he'd out with an "A--men! **Yes**, Lord!" in a voice like a fact'ry whistle. Wa'al, after a little the' was some snickerin' an' gigglin' an' scroughin' an' hustlin' in the back part, an' even some of the serioustest up in front would kind o' smile, an' the moderator leaned over an' says to one of the bretherin on the platform, "Brother Jones," he says, "can't you git down to the back of the hall an' say somethin' to quiet Brother Smith? Smith's a good man, an' a pious man," the moderator says, "but he's very excitable, an' I'm 'fraid he'll git the boys to goin' back there an' disturb the meetin'." So Jones he worked his way back to where Smith was, an' the moderator watched him go up to Smith and jest speak to him 'bout ten seconds; an' after that Smith never peeped once. After the meetin' was over, the moderator says to Jones, "Brother Jones," he says, "what did you say to Brother Smith to-night that shut him up so quick?" "I ast him fer a dollar for For'n

Missions," says Brother Jones, 'an', wa'al,' I says to Tenaker, 'that's what I done to Staples.'"

"Did Mr. Tenaker see the point?" asked John, laughing.

"He laughed a little," said David, "but didn't quite ketch on till I told him about the subscription paper, an' then he like to split."

"Suppose Staples had taken you up," suggested John.

"Wa'al," said David, "I didn't think I was takin' many chances. If, in the fust place, I hadn't knowed Staples as well 's I did, the Smith fam'ly, so fur 's my experience goes, has got more members 'n any other fam'ly on top of the earth." At this point a boy brought in a telegram. David opened it, gave a side glance at his companion, and, taking out his pocketbook, put the dispatch therein.

CHAPTER XLII.

The next morning David called John into the rear room. "Busy?" he asked.

"No," said John. "Nothing that can't wait."

"Set down," said Mr. Harum, drawing a chair to the fire. He looked up with his characteristic grin. "Ever own a hog?" he said.

"No," said John, smiling.

"Ever feel like ownin' one?"

"I don't remember ever having any cravings in that direction."

"Like pork?" asked Mr. Harum.

"In moderation," was the reply. David produced from his pocketbook the dispatch received the day before and handed it to the young man at his side. "Read that," he said.

John looked at it and handed it back.

"It doesn't convey any idea to my mind," he said.

"What?" said David, "you don't know what 'Bangs Galilee' means? nor who 'Raisin' is?"

"You'll have to ask me an easier one," said John, smiling.

David sat for a moment in silence, and then, "How much money have you got?" he asked.

"Well," was the reply, "with what I had and what I have saved since I came I could get together about five thousand dollars, I think."

"Is it where you c'n put your hands on't?"

John took some slips of paper from his pocketbook and handed them to David.

"H'm, h'm," said the latter. "Wa'al, I owe ye quite a little bunch o' money, don't I? Forty-five hunderd! Wa'al! Couldn't you 'a' done better 'n to keep this here at four per cent?"

"Well," said John, "perhaps so, and perhaps not. I preferred to do this at all events."

"Thought the old man was *safe* anyway, didn't ye?" said David in a tone which showed that he was highly pleased.

"Yes," said John.

"Is this all?" asked David.

"There is some interest on those certificates, and I have some balance in my account," was the reply; "and then, you know, I have some very valuable securities--a beautiful line of mining stocks, and that promising Pennsylvania property."

At the mention of the last-named asset David looked at him for an instant as if about to speak, but if so he changed his mind. He sat for a moment fingering the yellow paper which carried the mystic words. Presently he said, opening the message out, "That's from an old friend of mine out to Chicago. He come from this part of the country, an' we was young fellers together thirty years ago. I've had a good many deals with him and through him, an' he never give me a wrong steer, fur 's I know. That is, I never done as he told me without comin' out all right, though he's give me a good many pointers I never did nothin' about. 'Tain't nec'sary to name no names, but 'Bangs Galilee' means 'buy pork,' an' as I've ben watchin' the market fer quite a spell myself, an' standard pork 's a good deal lower 'n it costs to pack it, I've made up my mind to buy a few thousan' barrels fer fam'ly use. It's a handy thing to have in the house," declared Mr. Harum, "an' I thought mebbe it wouldn't be a bad thing fer you to have a little. It looks cheap to me," he added, "an' mebbe bime-by what you don't eat you c'n sell."

"Well," said John, laughing, "you see me at table every day and know what my appetite is like. How much pork do you think I could take care of?"

"Wa'al, at the present price," said David, "I think about four thousan' barrels would give ye enough to eat fer a spell, an' mebbe leave ye a few barrels to dispose of if you should happen to strike a feller later on that wanted it wuss 'n you did."

John opened his eyes a little. "I should only have a margin of a dollar and a quarter," he said.

"Wa'al, I've got a notion that that'll carry ye," said David. "It may go lower 'n what it is now. I never bought anythin' yet that didn't drop some, an' I guess nobody but a fool ever did buy at the bottom more'n once; but I've had an idee for some time that it was about bottom, an' this here telegraph wouldn't 'a' ben sent if the feller that sent it didn't think so too, an' I've had some other cor'spondence with him." Mr. Harum paused and laughed a little.

"I was jest thinkin'," he continued, "of what the Irishman said about Stofford. Never ben there, have ye? Wa'al, it's a place eight nine mile f'm here, an' the hills 'round are so steep that when you're goin' up you c'n look right back under the buggy by jest leanin' over the edge of the dash. I was drivin' 'round there once, an' I met an Irishman with a big drove o' hogs.

"'Hello, Pat!' I says, 'where 'd all them hogs come from?'

"'Stofford,' he says.

"'Wa'al,' I says, 'I wouldn't 'a' thought the' was so many hogs *in* Stofford.'

"'Oh, be gobs!' he says, 'sure they're *all* hogs in Stofford;' an'," declared David, "the bears ben sellin' that pork up in Chicago as if the hull everlastin' West was *all* hogs."

"It's very tempting," said John thoughtfully.

"Wa'al," said David, "I don't want to tempt ye exac'ly, an' certain I don't want to urge ye. The' ain't no sure things but death an' taxes, as the sayin' is, but buyin' pork at these prices is buyin' somethin' that's got value, an' you can't wipe it out. In other words, it's buyin' a warranted article at a price consid'ably lower 'n it c'n be produced for, an' though it may go lower, if a man c'n *stick*, it's bound to level up in the long run."

Our friend sat for some minutes apparently looking into the fire, but he was not conscious of seeing anything at all. Finally he rose, went over to Mr. Harum's desk, figured the interest on the certificates up to the first of January, indorsed them, and filling up a check for the balance of the amount in question, handed the check and certificate to David.

"Think you'll go it, eh?" said the latter.

"Yes," said John; "but if I take the quantity you suggest, I shall have nothing to remargin the trade in case the market goes below a certain point."

"I've thought of that," replied David, "an' was goin' to say to you that I'd carry the trade down as fur as your money would go, in case more margins had to be called."

"Very well," said John. "And will you look after the whole matter for me?"

"All right," said David.

John thanked him and returned to the front room.

    *   *   *   *   *

There were times in the months which followed when our friend had reason to wish that all swine had perished with those whom Shylock said "your prophet the Nazarite conjured the devil into;" and the news of the world in general was of secondary importance compared with the market reports. After the purchase pork dropped off a little, and hung about the lower figure for some time. Then it began to advance by degrees until the quotation was a dollar above the purchase price.

John's impulse was to sell, but David made no sign. The market held firm for a while, even going a little higher. Then it began to drop rather more rapidly than it had advanced, to about what the pork had cost, and for a long period fluctuated only a few cents one way or the other. This was followed by a steady decline to the extent of half-a-dollar, and, as the reports came, it "looked like going lower," which it did. In fact, there came a day when it was so "low," and so much more "looked like going lower" than ever (as such things usually do when the "bottom" is pretty nearly reached), that our friend had not the courage to examine the market reports for the next two days, and simply tried to keep the subject out of his mind. On the morning of the third day the Syrchester paper was brought in about ten o'clock, as usual, and laid on Mr. Harum's desk. John shivered a little, and for some time refrained from looking at it. At last, more by impulse than intention, he went into the back room and glanced at the first page without taking the paper in his hands. One of the press dispatches was headed: "Great Excitement on Chicago Board of Trade: Pork Market reported Cornered: Bears on the Run," and more of the same sort, which struck our friend as being the most profitable, instructive, and delightful literature that he had ever come across. David had been in Syrchester the two days previous, returning the evening before. Just then he came into the office, and John handed him the paper.

"Wa'al," he said, holding it off at arm's length, and then putting on his glasses, "them fellers that thought they was *all* hogs up West, are havin' a change of heart, are they? I reckoned they would 'fore they got through with it. It's ben ruther a long pull, though, eh?" he said, looking at John with a grin.

"Yes," said our friend, with a slight shrug of the shoulders.

"Things looked ruther colicky the last two three days, eh?" suggested David. "Did you think 'the jig was up an' the monkey was in the box?'"

"Rather," said John. "The fact is," he admitted, "I am ashamed to say that for a few days back I haven't looked at a quotation. I suppose you must have carried me to some extent. How much was it?"

"Wa'al," said David, "I kept the trade margined, of course, an' if we'd sold out at the bottom you'd have owed me somewhere along a thousan' or fifteen hunderd; but," he added, "it was only in the slump, an' didn't last long, an' anyway I cal'lated to carry that pork to where it would 'a' ketched fire. I wa'n't worried none, an' you didn't let on to be, an' so I didn't say anythin'."

"What do you think about it now?" asked John.

"My opinion is now," replied Mr. Harum, "that it's goin' to putty near where it belongs, an' mebbe higher, an' them 's my advices. We can sell now at some profit, an' of course the bears 'll jump on agin as it goes up, an' the other fellers 'll take the profits f'm time to time. If I was where I could watch the market, I'd mebbe try to make a turn in 't 'casionally, but I guess as 't is we'd better set down an' let her take her own gait. I don't mean to try an' git the top price--I'm alwus willin' to let the other feller make a little--but we've waited fer quite a spell, an' as it's goin' our way, we might 's well wait a little longer."

"All right," said John, "and I'm very much obliged to you."

"Sho, sho!" said David.

It was not until August, however, that the deal was finally closed out.

CHAPTER XLIII.

The summer was drawing to a close. The season, so far as the social part of it was concerned, had been what John had grown accustomed to in previous years, and there were few changes in or among the people whom he had come to know very well, save those which a few years make in young people: some increase of importance in demeanor on the part of the young men whose razors were coming into requisition; and the changes from short to long skirts, from braids, pig-tails, and flowing-manes to more elaborate coiffures on the part of the young women. The most notable event had been the reopening of the Verjoos house, which had been closed for two summers, and the return of the family, followed by the appearance of a young man whom Miss Clara had met abroad, and who represented himself as the acknowledged *fiance* of that young woman. It need hardly be said that discussions of the event, and upon the appearance, manners, prospects, etc., of that fortunate gentleman had formed a very considerable part of the talk of the season among the summer people; and, indeed, interest in the affair had permeated all grades and classes of society.

*   *   *   *   *

It was some six weeks after the settlement of the transaction in "pork" that David and John were driving together in the afternoon as they had so often done in the last five years. They had got to that point of understanding where neither felt constrained to talk for the purpose of keeping up conversation, and often in their long drives there was little said by either of them. The young man was never what is called "a great talker," and Mr. Harum did not always "git goin'." On this occasion they had gone along for some time, smoking in silence, each man absorbed in his thoughts. Finally David turned to his companion.

"Do you know that Dutchman Claricy Verjoos is goin' to marry?" he asked.

"Yes," replied John, laughing; "I have met him a number of times. But he isn't a Dutchman. What gave you that idea?"

"I heard it was over in Germany she run across him," said David.

"I believe that is so, but he isn't a German. He is from Philadelphia, and is a friend of the Bradways."

"What kind of a feller is he? Good enough for her?"

"Well," said John, smiling, "in the sense in which that question is usually taken, I should say yes. He has good looks, good manners, a good deal of money, I am told, and it is said that Miss Clara--which is the main point, after all--is very much in love with him."

"H'm," said David after a moment. "How do you git along with the Verjoos girls? Was Claricy's ears pointed all right when you seen her fust after she come home?"

"Oh, yes!" replied John, smiling, "she and her sister were perfectly pleasant and cordial, and Miss Verjoos and I are on very friendly terms."

"I was thinkin'," said David, "that you an' Claricy might be got to likin' each other, an' mebbe--"

"I don't think there could ever have been the smallest chance of it," declared John hastily.

"Take the lines a minute," said David, handing them to his companion after stopping the horses. "The nigh one's picked up a stone, I guess," and he got out to investigate. "The river road," he remarked as he climbed back into the buggy after removing the stone from the horse's foot, "is about the puttiest road 'round here, but I don't drive it oftener jest on account of them dum'd loose stuns." He sucked the air through his pursed-up lips, producing a little squeaking sound, and the horses started forward. Presently he turned to John:

"Did you ever think of gettin' married?" he asked.

"Well," said our friend with a little hesitation, "I don't remember that I ever did, very definitely."

"Somebody 't you knew 'fore you come up here?" said David, jumping at a conclusion.

"Yes," said John, smiling a little at the question.

"Wouldn't she have ye?" queried David, who stuck at no trifles when in pursuit of information.

John laughed. "I never asked her," he replied, in truth a little surprised at his own willingness to be questioned.

"Did ye cal'late to when the time come right?" pursued Mr. Harum.

Of this part of his history John had, of course, never spoken to David. There had been a time when, if not resenting the attempt upon his confidence, he would have made it plain that he did not wish to discuss the matter, and the old wound still gave him twinges. But he had not only come to know his questioner very well, but to be much attached to him. He knew, too, that the elder man would ask him nothing save in the way of kindness, for he had had a hundred proofs of that; and now, so far from feeling reluctant to take his companion into his confidence, he rather welcomed the idea. He was, withal, a bit curious to ascertain the drift of the inquiry, knowing that David, though sometimes working in devious ways, rarely started without an intention. And so he answered the question and what followed as he might have told his story to a woman.

"An' didn't you never git no note, nor message, nor word of any kind?" asked David.

"No."

"Nor hain't ever heard a word about her f'm that day to this?"

"No."

"Nor hain't ever tried to?"

"No," said John. "What would have been the use?"

"Prov'dence seemed to 've made a putty clean sweep in your matters that spring, didn't it?"

"It seemed so to me," said John.

Nothing more was said for a minute or two. Mr. Harum appeared to have abandoned the pursuit of the subject of his questions. At last he said:

"You ben here most five years."

"Very nearly," John replied.

"Ben putty contented, on the hull?"

"I have grown to be," said John. "Indeed, it's hard to realize at times that I haven't always lived in Homeville. I remember my former life as if it were something I have read in a book. There was a John Lenox in it, but he seems to me sometimes more like a character in a story than myself."

"An' yet," said David, turning toward him, "if you was to go back to it, this last five years 'd git to be that way to ye a good deal quicker. Don't ye think so?"

"Perhaps so," replied John. "Yes," he added thoughtfully, "it is possible."

"I guess on the hull, though," remarked Mr. Harum, "you done better up here in the country 'n you might some 'ers else--"

"Oh, yes," said John sincerely, "thanks to you, I have indeed, and--"

"--an'--ne' mind about me--you got quite a little bunch o' money together now. I was thinkin' 't mebbe you might feel 't you needn't to stay here no longer if you didn't want to."

The young man turned to the speaker inquiringly, but Mr. Harum's face was straight to the front, and betrayed nothing.

"It wouldn't be no more 'n natural," he went on, "an' mebbe it would be best for ye. You're too good a man to spend all your days workin' fer Dave Harum, an' I've had it in my mind fer some time--somethin' like that pork deal--to make you a little independent in case anythin' should happen, an'--gen'ally. I couldn't give ye no money 'cause you wouldn't 'a' took it even if I'd wanted to, but now you got it, why----"

"I feel very much as if you had given it to me," protested the young man.

David put up his hand. "No, no," he said, "all 't I did was to propose the thing to ye, an' to put up a little money fer two three days. I didn't take no chances, an' it's all right, an' it's your'n, an' it makes ye to a certain extent independent of Homeville."

"I don't quite see it so," said John.

"Wa'al," said David, turning to him, "if you'd had as much five years ago you wouldn't 'a' come here, would ye?"

John was silent.

"What I was leadin' up to," resumed Mr. Harum after a moment, "is this: I ben thinkin' about it fer some time, but I haven't wanted to speak to ye about it before. In fact, I might 'a' put it off some longer if things wa'n't as they are, but the fact o' the matter is that I'm goin' to take down my sign."

John looked at him in undisguised amazement, not unmixed with consternation.

"Yes," said David, obviously avoiding the other's eye, "'David Harum, Banker,' is goin' to come down. I'm gettin' to be an' old man," he went on, "an' what with some investments I've got, an' a hoss-trade once in a while, I guess I c'n manage to keep the fire goin' in the kitchin stove fer Polly an' me, an' the' ain't no reason why I sh'd keep my sign up much of any longer. Of course," he said, "if I was to go on as I be now I'd want ye to stay jest as you are; but, as I was sayin', you're to a consid'able extent independent. You hain't no speciul ties to keep ye, an' you ought anyway, as I said before, to be doin' better for yourself than jest drawin' pay in a country bank."

One of the most impressive morals drawn from the fairy tales of our childhood, and indeed from the literature and experience of our later periods of life, is that the fulfilment of wishes is often attended by the most unwelcome results. There had been a great many times when to our friend the possibility of being able to bid farewell to Homeville had seemed the most desirable of things, but confronted with the idea as a reality--for what other construction could he put upon David's words except that they amounted practically to a dismissal, though a most kind one?--he found himself simply in dismay.

"I suppose," he said after a few moments, "that by 'taking down your sign' you mean going out of business--"

"Figger o' speech," explained David.

"--and your determination is not only a great surprise to me, but grieves me very much. I am very sorry to hear it--more sorry than I can tell you. As you remind me, if I leave Homeville I shall not go almost penniless as I came, but I shall leave with great regret, and, indeed--Ah, well--" he broke off with a wave of his hands.

"What was you goin' to say?" asked David, after a moment, his eyes on the horizon.

"I can't say very much more," replied the young man, "than that I am very sorry. There have been times," he added, "as you may understand, when I have been restless and discouraged for a while, particularly at first; but I can see now that, on the whole, I have been far from unhappy here. Your house has grown to be more a real home than any I have ever known, and you and your sister are like my own people. What you say, that I ought not to look forward to spending my life behind the counter of a village bank on a salary, may be true; but I am not, at present at least, a very ambitious person, nor, I am afraid, a very clever one in the way of getting on in the world; and the idea of breaking out for myself, even if that were all to be considered, is not a cheerful one. I am afraid all this sounds rather selfish to you, when, as I can see, you have deferred your plans for my sake, and after all else that you have done for me."

"I guess I sha'n't lay it up agin ye," said David quietly.

They drove along in silence for a while.

"May I ask," said John, at length, "when you intend to 'take down your sign,' as you put it?"

"Whenever you say the word," declared David, with a chuckle and a side glance at his companion. John turned in bewilderment.

"What do you mean?" he asked.

"Wa'al," said David with another short laugh, "fur 's the sign 's concerned, I s'pose we *could* stick a new one over it, but I guess it might 's well come down; but we'll settle that matter later on."

John still looked at the speaker in utter perplexity, until the latter broke out into a laugh.

"Got any idee what's goin' onto the new sign?" he asked.

"You don't mean----"

"Yes, I do," declared Mr. Harum, "an' my notion 's this, an' don't you say aye, yes, nor no till I git through," and he laid his left hand restrainingly on John's knee.

"The new sign 'll read 'Harum & Comp'ny,' or 'Harum & Lenox,' jest as you elect. You c'n put in what money you got an' I'll put in as much more, which 'll make cap'tal enough in gen'ral, an' any extry money that's needed--wa'al, up to a certain point, I guess I c'n manage. Now putty much all the new bus'nis has come in through you, an' practically you got the hull thing in your hands. You'll do the work about 's you're doin' now, an' you'll draw the same sal'ry; an' after that's paid we'll go snucks on anythin' that's left--that *is*," added David with a chuckle, "if you feel that you c'n *stan'* it in Homeville."

*   *   *   *   *

"I wish you was married to one of our Homeville girls, though," declared Mr. Harum later on as they drove homeward.

CHAPTER XLIV.

Since the whooping-cough and measles of childhood the junior partner of Harum & Company had never to his recollection had a day's illness in his life, and he fought the attack which came upon him about the first week in December with a sort of incredulous disgust, until one morning when he did not appear at breakfast. He spent the next week in bed, and at the end of that time, while he was able to be about, it was in a languid and spiritless fashion, and he was shaken and exasperated by a persistent cough. The season was and had been unusually inclement even for that region, where the thermometer sometimes changes fifty degrees in thirty-six hours; and at the time of his release from his room there was a period of successive changes of temperature from thawing to zero and below, a characteristic of the winter climate of Homeville and its vicinity. Dr. Hayes exhibited the inevitable quinine, iron, and all the tonics in his pharmacopoeia, with cough mixtures and sundry, but in vain. Aunt Polly pressed bottles of sovereign decoctions and infusions upon him--which were received with thanks and neglected with the blackest ingratitude--and exhausted not only the markets of Homeville, but her own and Sairy's culinary resources (no mean ones, by the way) to tempt the appetite which would not respond. One week followed another without any improvement in his condition; and indeed as time went on he fell into a condition of irritable listlessness which filled his partner with concern.

"What's the matter with him, Doc?" said David to the physician. "He don't seem to take no more int'rist than a foundered hoss. Can't ye do nothin' for him?"

"Not much use dosin' him," replied the doctor. "Pull out all right, may be, come warm weather. Big strong fellow, but this cussed influenzy, or grip, as they call it, sometimes hits them hardest."

"Wa'al, warm weather 's some way off," remarked Mr. Harum, "an' he coughs enough to tear his head off sometimes."

The doctor nodded. "Ought to clear out somewhere," he said. "Don't like that cough myself."

"What do you mean?" asked David.

"Ought to go 'way for a spell," said the doctor; "quit working, and get a change of climate."

"Have you told him so?" asked Mr. Harum.

"Yes," replied the doctor; "said he couldn't get away."

"H'm'm!" said David thoughtfully, pinching his lower lip between his thumb and finger.

A day or two after the foregoing interview, John came in and laid an open letter in front of David, who was at his desk, and dropped languidly into a chair without speaking. Mr. Harum read the letter, smiled a little, and turning in his chair, took off his glasses and looked at the young man, who was staring abstractedly at the floor.

"I ben rather expectin' you'd git somethin' like this. What be you goin' to do about it?"

"I don't know," replied John. "I don't like the idea of leasing the property in any case, and certainly not on the terms they offer; but it is lying idle, and I'm paying taxes on it----"

"Wa'al, as I said, I ben expectin' fer some time they'd be after ye in some shape. You got this this mornin'?"

"Yes."

"I expect you'd sell the prop'ty if you got a good chance, wouldn't ye?"

"With the utmost pleasure," said John emphatically.

"Wa'al, I've got a notion they'll buy it of ye," said David, "if it's handled right. I wouldn't lease it if it was mine an' I wanted to sell it, an' yet, in the long run, you might git more out of it--an' then agin you mightn't," he added.

"I don't know anything about it," said John, putting his handkerchief to his mouth in a fit of coughing. David looked at him with a frown.

"I ben aware fer some time that the' was a movement on foot in your direction," he said. "You know I told ye that I'd ben int'ristid in the oil bus'nis once on a time; an' I hain't never quite lost my int'rist, though it hain't ben a very active one lately, an' some fellers down there have kep' me posted some. The' 's ben oil found near where you're located, an' the prospectin' points your way. The hull thing has ben kep' as close as possible, an' the holes has ben plugged, but the oil is there somewhere. Now it's like this: If you lease on shares an' they strike the oil on your prop'ty, mebbe it'll bring you more money; but they might strike, an' agin they mightn't. Sometimes you git a payin' well an' a dry hole only a few hunderd feet apart. Nevertheless they want to drill your prop'ty. I know who the parties is. These fellers that wrote this letter are simply actin' for 'em."

The speaker was interrupted by another fit of coughing, which left the sufferer very red in the face, and elicited from him the word which is always greeted with laughter in a theater.

"Say," said David, after a moment, in which he looked anxiously at his companion, "I don't like that cough o' your'n."

"I don't thoroughly enjoy it myself," was the rejoinder.

"Seems to be kind o' growin' on ye, don't it?"

"I don't know," said John.

"I was talkin' with Doc Hayes about ye," said David, "an' he allowed you'd ought to have your shoes off an' run loose a spell."

John smiled a little, but did not reply.

"Spoke to you about it, didn't he?" continued David.

"Yes."

"An' you told him you couldn't git away?"

"Yes."

"Didn't tell him you wouldn't go if you could, did ye?"

"I only told him I couldn't go," said John.

David sat for a moment thoughtfully tapping the desk with his eyeglasses, and then said with his characteristic chuckle:

"I had a letter f'm Chet Timson yestidy."

John looked up at him, failing to see the connection.

"Yes," said David, "he's out fer a job, an' the way he writes I guess the dander's putty well out of him. I reckon the' hain't ben nothin' much but hay in *his* manger fer quite a spell," remarked Mr. Harum.

"H'm!" said John, raising his brows, conscious of a humane but very faint interest in Mr. Timson's affairs. Mr. Harum got out a cigar, and, lighting it, gave a puff or two, and continued with what struck the younger man as a perfectly irrelevant question. It really seemed to him as if his senior were making conversation.

"How's Peleg doin' these days?" was the query.

"Very well," was the reply.

"C'n do most anythin' 't's nec'sary, can't he?"

A brief interruption followed upon the entrance of a man, who, after saying good-morning, laid a note on David's desk, asking for the money on it. Mr. Harum handed it back, indicating John with a motion of his thumb.

The latter took it, looked at the face and back, marked his initials on it with a pencil, and the man went out to the counter.

"If you was fixed so 't you could git away fer a spell," said David a moment or two after the customer's departure, "where would you like to go?"

"I have not thought about it," said John rather listlessly.

"Wa'al, s'pose you think about it a little now, if you hain't got no pressin' engagement. Bus'nis don't seem to be very rushin' this mornin'."

"Why?" said John.

"Because," said David impressively, "you're goin' somewhere right off, quick 's you c'n git ready, an' you may 's well be makin' up your mind where."

John looked up in surprise. "I don't want to go away," he said, "and if I did, how could I leave the office?"

"No," responded Mr. Harum, "you don't want to make a move of any kind that you don't actually have to, an' that's the reason fer makin' one. F'm what the doc said, an' f'm what I c'n see, you got to git out o' this dum'd climate," waving his hand toward the window, against which the sleet was beating, "fer a spell; an' as fur 's the office goes, Chet Timson 'd be tickled to death to come on an' help out while you're away, an' I guess 'mongst us we c'n mosey along some gait. I ain't *quite* to the bone-yard yet myself," he added with a grin.

The younger man sat for a moment or two with brows contracted, and pulling thoughtfully at his moustache.

"There is that matter," he said, pointing to the letter on the desk.

"Wa'al," said David, "the' ain't no tearin' hurry 'bout that; an' any way, I was goin' to make you a suggestion to put the matter into my hands to some extent."

"Will you take it?" said John quickly. "That is exactly what I should wish in any case."

"If you want I should," replied Mr. Harum. "Would you want to give full power attorney, or jest have me say 't I was instructed to act for ye?"

"I think a better way would be to put the property in your name altogether," said John. "Don't you think so?"

"Wa'al," said David, thoughtfully, after a moment, "I hadn't thought of that, but mebbe I *could* handle the matter better if you was to do that. I know the parties, an' if the' was any bluffin' to be done either side, mebbe it would be better if they thought I was playin' my own hand."

At that point Peleg appeared and asked Mr. Lenox a question which took the latter to the teller's counter. David sat for some time drumming on his desk with the fingers of both hands. A succession of violent coughs came from the front room. His mouth and brows contracted in a wince, and rising, he put on his coat and hat and went slowly out of the bank.

CHAPTER XLV.

The Vaterland was advertised to sail at one o'clock, and it wanted but fifteen or twenty minutes of the hour. After assuring himself that his belongings were all together in his state-room, John made his way to the upper deck and leaning against the rail, watched the bustle of embarkation, somewhat interested in the people standing about, among whom it was difficult in instances to distinguish the passengers from those who were present to say farewell. Near him at the moment were two people, apparently man and wife, of middle age and rather distinguished appearance, to whom presently approached, with some evidence of hurry and with outstretched hand, a very well dressed and pleasant looking man.

"Ah, here you are, Mrs. Ruggles," John heard him say as he shook hands.

Then followed some commonplaces of good wishes and farewells, and in reply to a question which John did not catch, he heard the lady addressed as Mrs. Ruggles say, "Oh, didn't you see her? We left her on the lower deck a few minutes ago. Ah, here she comes."

The man turned and advanced a step to meet the person in question. John's eyes involuntarily followed the movement, and as he saw her approach his heart contracted sharply: it was Mary Blake. He turned away quickly, and as the collar of his ulster was about his face, for the air of the January day was very keen, he thought that she had not recognized him. A moment later he went aft around the deck-house, and going forward to the smoking-room, seated himself therein, and took the passenger list out of his pocket. He had already scanned it rather cursorily, having but the smallest expectation of coming upon a familiar name, yet feeling sure that, had hers been there, it could not have escaped him. Nevertheless, he now ran his eye over the columns with eager scrutiny, and the hands which held the paper shook a little.

There was no name in the least like Blake. It occurred to him that by some chance or error hers might have been omitted, when his eye caught the following:

William Ruggles
New York.

Mrs. Ruggles
"

"

Mrs. Edward Ruggles "
"

It was plain to him then. She was obviously traveling with the people whom she had just joined on deck, and it was equally plain that she was Mrs. Edward Ruggles. When he looked up the ship was out in the river.

CHAPTER XLVI.

John had been late in applying for his passage, and in consequence, the ship being very full, had had to take what berth he could get, which happened to be in the second cabin. The occupants of these quarters, however, were not rated as second-class passengers. The Vaterland took none such on her outward voyages, and all were on the same footing as to the fare and the freedom of the ship. The captain and the orchestra appeared at dinner in the second saloon on alternate nights, and the only disadvantage in the location was that it was very far aft; unless it could be considered a drawback that the furnishings were of plain wood and plush instead of carving, gilding, and stamped leather. In fact, as the voyage proceeded, our friend decided that the after-deck was pleasanter than the one amidships, and the cozy second-class smoking-room more agreeable than the large and gorgeous one forward.

Consequently, for a while he rarely went across the bridge which spanned the opening between the two decks. It may be that he had a certain amount of reluctance to encounter Mrs. Edward Ruggles.

The roof of the second cabin deck-house was, when there was not too much wind, a favorite place with him. It was not much frequented, as most of those who spent their time on deck apparently preferred a place nearer amidships. He was sitting there on the morning of the fifth day out, looking idly over the sea, with an occasional glance at the people who were walking on the promenade-deck below, or leaning on the rail which bounded it. He turned at a slight sound behind him, and rose with his hat in his hand. The flush in his face, as he took the hand which was offered him, reflected the color in the face of the owner, but the grayish brown eyes, which he remembered so well, looked into his, a little curiously, perhaps, but frankly and kindly. She was the first to speak.

"How do you do, Mr. Lenox?" she said.

"How do you do, Mrs. Ruggles?" said John, throwing up his hand as, at the moment of his reply, a puff of wind blew the cape of his mackintosh over his head. They both laughed a little (this was their greeting after nearly six years), and sat down.

"What a nice place!" she said, looking about her.

"Yes," said John; "I sit here a good deal when it isn't too windy."

"I have been wondering why I did not get a sight of you," she said. "I saw your name in the passenger list. Have you been ill?"

"I'm in the second cabin," he said, smiling.

She looked at him a little incredulously, and he explained.

"Ah, yes," she said, "I saw your name, but as you did not appear in the dining saloon, I thought you must either be ill or that you did not sail. Did you know that I was on board?" she asked.

It was rather an embarrassing question.

"I have been intending," he replied rather lamely, "to make myself known to you--that is, to--well, make my presence on board known to you. I got just a glimpse of you before we sailed, when you came up to speak to a man who had been saying good-bye to Mr. and Mrs. Ruggles. I heard him speak their name, and looking over the passenger list I identified you as Mrs. Edward Ruggles."

"Ah," she said, looking away for an instant, "I did not know that you had seen me, and I wondered how you came to address me as Mrs. Ruggles just now."

"That was how," said John; and then, after a moment, "it seems rather odd, doesn't it, that we should be renewing an acquaintance on an ocean steamer as we did once before, so many years ago? and that the first bit of intelligence that I have had of you in all the years since I saw you last should come to me through the passenger list?"

"Did you ever try to get any?" she asked. "I have always thought it very strange that we should never have heard anything about you."

"I went to the house once, some weeks after you had gone," said John, "but the man in charge was out, and the maid could tell me nothing."

"A note I wrote you at the time of your father's death," she said, "we found in my small nephew's overcoat pocket after we had been some time in California; but I wrote a second one before we left New York, telling you of our intended departure, and where we were going."

"I never received it," he said. Neither spoke for a while, and then:

"Tell me of your sister and brother-in-law," he said.

"My sister is at present living in Cambridge, where Jack is at college," was the reply; "but poor Julius died two years ago."

"Ah," said John, "I am grieved to hear of Mr. Carling's death. I liked him very much."

"He liked you very much," she said, "and often spoke of you."

There was another period of silence, so long, indeed, as to be somewhat embarrassing. None of the thoughts which followed each other in John's mind was of the sort which he felt like broaching. He realized that the situation was getting awkward, and that consciousness added to the confusion of his ideas. But if his companion shared his embarrassment, neither her face nor her manner betrayed it as at last she said, turning, and looking frankly at him:

"You seem very little changed. Tell me about yourself. Tell me something of your life in the last six years."

During the rest of the voyage they were together for a part of every day, sometimes with the company of Mrs. William Ruggles, but more often without it, as her husband claimed much of her attention and rarely came on deck; and John, from time to time, gave his companion pretty much the whole history of his later career. But with regard to her own life, and, as he noticed, especially the two years since the death of her brother-in-law, she was distinctly reticent. She never spoke of her marriage or her husband, and after one or two faintly tentative allusions, John forebore to touch upon those subjects, and was driven to conclude that her experience had not been a happy one. Indeed, in their intercourse there were times when she appeared distrait and even moody; but on the whole she seemed to him to be just as he had known and loved her years ago; and all the feeling that he had had for her then broke forth afresh in spite of himself--in spite of the fact that, as he told himself, it was more hopeless than ever: absolutely so, indeed.

It was the last night of their voyage together. The Ruggleses were to leave the ship the next morning at Algiers, where they intended to remain for some time.

"Would you mind going to the after-deck?" he asked. "These people walking about fidget me," he added rather irritably.

She rose, and they made their way aft. John drew a couple of chairs near to the rail. "I don't care to sit down for the present," she said, and they stood looking out at sea for a while in silence.

"Do you remember," said John at last, "a night six years ago when we stood together, at the end of the voyage, leaning over the rail like this?"

"Yes," she said.

"Does this remind you of it?" he asked.

"I was thinking of it," she said.

"Do you remember the last night I was at your house?" he asked, looking straight out over the moonlit water.

"Yes," she said again.

"Did you know that night what was in my heart to say to you?"

There was no answer.

"May I tell you now?" he asked, giving a side glance at her profile, which in the moonlight showed very white.

"Do you think you ought?" she answered in a low voice, "or that I ought to listen to you?"

"I know," he exclaimed. "You think that as a married woman you should not listen, and that knowing you to be one I should not speak. If it were to ask anything of you I would not. It is for the first and last time. To-morrow we part again, and for all time, I suppose. I have carried the words that were on my lips that night all these years in my heart. I know I can have no response--I expect none; but it can not harm you if I tell you that I loved you then, and have----"

She put up her hand in protest.

"You must not go on, Mr. Lenox," she said, turning to him, "and I must leave you."

"Are you very angry with me?" he asked humbly.

She turned her face to the sea again and gave a sad little laugh.

"Not so much as I ought to be," she answered; "but you yourself have given the reason why you should not say such things, and why I should not listen, and why I ought to say good-night."

"Ah, yes," he said bitterly; "of course you are right, and this is to be the end."

She turned and looked at him for a moment. "You will never again speak to me as you have to-night, will you?" she asked.

"I should not have said what I did had I not thought I should never see you again after to-morrow," said John, "and I am not likely to do that, am I?"

"If I could be sure," she said hesitatingly, and as if to herself.

"Well," said John eagerly. She stood with her eyes downcast for a moment, one hand resting on the rail, and then she looked up.

"We expect to stay in Algiers about two months," she said, "and then we are going to Naples to visit some friends for a few days, about the time you told me you thought you might be there. Perhaps it would be better if we said good-bye to-night; but if after we get home you are to spend your days in Homeville and I mine in New York, we shall not be likely to meet, and, except on this side of the ocean, we may, as you say, never see each other again. So, if you wish, you may come to see me in Naples if you happen to be there when we are. I am sure after to-night that I may trust you, may I not? But," she added, "perhaps you would not care. I am treating you very frankly; but from your standpoint you would expect or excuse more frankness than if I were a young girl."

"I care very much," he declared, "and it will be a happiness to me to see you on any footing, and you may trust me never to break bounds again." She made a motion as if to depart.

"Don't go just yet," he said pleadingly; "there is now no reason why you should for a while, is there? Let us sit here in this gorgeous night a little longer, and let me smoke a cigar."

At the moment he was undergoing a revulsion of feeling. His state of mind was like that of an improvident debtor who, while knowing that the note must be paid some time, does not quite realize it for a while after an extension. At last the cigar was finished. There had been but little said between them.

"I really must go," she said, and he walked with her across the hanging bridge and down the deck to the gangway door.

"Where shall I address you to let you know when we shall be in Naples?" she asked as they were about to separate.

"Care of Cook & Son," he said. "You will find the address in Baedeker."

He saw her the next morning long enough for a touch of the hand and a good-bye before the bobbing, tubby little boat with its Arab crew took the Ruggleses on board.

CHAPTER XLVII.

How John Lenox tried to kill time during the following two months, and how time retaliated during the process, it is needless to set forth. It may not, however, be wholly irrelevant to note that his cough had gradually disappeared, and that his appetite had become good enough to carry him through the average table d'hote dinner. On the morning after his arrival at Naples he found a cable dispatch at the office of Cook & Son, as follows: "Sixty cash, forty stock. Stock good. Harum."

"God bless the dear old boy!" said John fervently. The Pennsylvania property was sold at last; and if "stock good" was true, the dispatch informed him that he was, if not a rich man for modern days, still, as David would have put it, "wuth consid'able." No man, I take it, is very likely to receive such a piece of news without satisfaction; but if our friend's first sensation was one of gratification, the thought which followed had a drop of bitterness in it. "If I could only have had it before!" he said to himself; and indeed many of the disappointments of life, if not the greater part, come because events are unpunctual. They have a way of arriving sometimes too early, or worse, too late.

Another circumstance detracted from his satisfaction: a note he expected did not appear among the other communications waiting him at the bankers, and his mind was occupied for the while with various conjectures as to the reason, none of which was satisfactory. Perhaps she had changed her mind. Perhaps--a score of things! Well, there was nothing for it but to be as patient as possible and await events. He remembered that she had said she was to visit some friends by the name of Hartleigh, and she had told him the name of their villa, but for the moment he did not remember it. In any case he did not know the Hartleighs, and if she had changed her mind--as was possibly indicated by the omission to send him word-- well----! He shrugged his shoulders, mechanically lighted a cigarette, and strolled down and out of the Piazza Martiri and across to the Largo della Vittoria. He had a half-formed idea of walking back through the Villa Nazionale, spending an hour at the Aquarium, and then to his hotel for luncheon. It occurred to him at the moment that there was a steamer from Genoa on the Monday following, that he was tired of wandering about aimlessly and alone, and that there was really no reason why he should not take the said steamer and go home. Occupied with these reflections, he absently observed, just opposite to him across the way, a pair of large bay horses in front of a handsome landau. A coachman in livery was on the box, and a small foot-man, very much coated and silk-hatted, was standing about; and, as he looked, two ladies came out of the arched entrance to the court of the building before which the equipage was halted, and the small footman sprang to the carriage door.

One of the ladies was a stranger to him, but the other was Mrs. William Ruggles; and John, seeing that he had been recognized, at once crossed over to the carriage; and presently, having accepted an invitation to breakfast, found himself sitting opposite them on his way to the Villa Violante. The conversation during the drive up to the Vomero need not be detailed. Mrs. Hartleigh arrived at the opinion that our friend was rather a dull person. Mrs. Ruggles, as he had found out, was usually rather taciturn. Neither is it necessary to say very much of the breakfast, nor of the people assembled.

It appeared that several guests had departed the previous day, and the people at table consisted only of Mr. and Mrs. Ruggles, Mary, Mr. and Mrs. Hartleigh and their two daughters, and John, whose conversation was mostly with his host, and was rather desultory. In fact, there was during the meal a perceptible air of something like disquietude. Mr. Ruggles in particular said almost nothing, and wore an appearance of what seemed like anxiety. Once he turned to his host: "When ought I to get an answer to that cable, Hartleigh? to-day, do you think?"

"Yes, I should say so without doubt," was the reply, "if it's answered promptly, and in fact there's plenty of time. Remember that we are about six hours earlier than New York by the clock, and it's only about seven in the morning over there."

 *   *   *   *   *

Coffee was served on the balustraded platform of the flight of marble steps leading down to the grounds below.

"Mary," said Mrs. Hartleigh, when cigarettes had been offered, "don't you want to show Mr. Lenox something of La Violante?"

"I shall take you to my favorite place," she said, as they descended the steps together.

The southern front of the grounds of the Villa Violante is bounded and upheld by a wall of tufa fifty feet in height and some four hundred feet long. About midway of its length a semicircular bench of marble, with a rail, is built out over one of the buttresses. From this point is visible the whole bay and harbor of Naples, and about one third of the city lies in sight, five hundred feet below. To the left one sees Vesuvius and the Sant' Angelo chain, which the eye follows to Sorrento. Straight out in front stands Capri, and to the right the curve of the bay, ending at Posilipo. The two, John and his companion, halted near the bench, and leaned upon the parapet of the wall for a while in silence. From the streets below rose no rumble of traffic, no sound of hoof or wheel; but up through three thousand feet of distance came from here and there the voices of street-venders, the clang of a bell, and ever and anon the pathetic supplication of a donkey. Absolute quiet prevailed where they stood, save for these upcoming sounds. The April sun, deliciously warm, drew a smoky odor from the hedge of box with which the parapet walk was bordered, in and out of which darted small green lizards with the quickness of little fishes.

John drew a long breath.

"I don't believe there is another such view in the world," he said. "I do not wonder that this is your favorite spot."

"Yes," she said, "you should see the grounds--the whole place is superb--but this is the glory of it all, and I have brought you straight here because I wanted to see it with you, and this may be the only opportunity."

"What do you mean?" he asked apprehensively.

"You heard Mr. Ruggles's question about the cable dispatch?" she said.

"Yes."

"Well," she said, "our plans have been very much upset by some things he has heard from home. We came on from Algiers ten days earlier than we had intended, and if the reply to Mr. Ruggles's cable is unfavorable, we are likely to depart for Genoa to-morrow and take the steamer for home on Monday. The reason why I did not send a note to your bankers," she added, "was that we came on the same boat that I intended to write by; and Mr. Hartleigh's man has inquired for you every day at Cook's so that Mr. Hartleigh might know of your coming and call upon you."

John gave a little exclamation of dismay. Her face was very still as she gazed out over the sea with half-closed eyes. He caught the scent of the violets in the bosom of her white dress.

"Let us sit down," she said at last. "I have something I wish to say to you."

He made no rejoinder as they seated themselves, and during the moment or two of silence in which she seemed to be meditating how to begin, he sat bending forward, holding his stick with both hands between his knees, absently prodding holes in the gravel.

"I think," she began, "that if I did not believe the chances were for our going to-morrow, I would not say it to-day." John bit his lip and gave the gravel a more vigorous punch. "But I have felt that I must say it to you some time before we saw the last of each other, whenever that time should be."

"Is it anything about what happened on board ship?" he asked in a low voice.

"Yes," she replied, "it concerns all that took place on board ship, or nearly all, and I have had many misgivings about it. I am afraid that I did wrong, and I am afraid, too, that in your secret heart you would admit it."

"No, never!" he exclaimed. "If there was any wrong done, it was wholly of my own doing. I was alone to blame. I ought to have remembered that you were married, and perhaps--yes, I did remember it in a way, but I could not realize it. I had never seen or heard of your husband, or heard of your marriage. He was a perfectly unreal person to me, and you--you seemed only the Mary Blake that I had known, and as I had known you. I said what I did that night upon an impulse which was as unpremeditated as it was sudden. I don't see how you were wrong. You couldn't have foreseen what took place--and----"

"Have you not been sorry for what took place?" she asked, with her eyes on the ground. "Have you not thought the less of me since?"

He turned and looked at her. There was a little smile upon her lips and on her downcast eyes.

"No, by Heaven!" he exclaimed desperately, "I have not, and I am not sorry. Whether I ought to have said what I did or not, it was true, and I wanted you to know----"

He broke off as she turned to him with a smile and a blush. The smile was almost a laugh.

"But, John," she said, "I am not Mrs. Edward Ruggles. I am Mary Blake."

     *   *   *   *   *

The parapet was fifty feet above the terrace. The hedge of box was an impervious screen.

     *   *   *   *   *

Well, and then, after a little of that sort of thing, they both began hurriedly to admire the view again, for some one was coming. But it was only one of the gardeners, who did not understand English; and confidence being once more restored, they fell to discussing--everything.

"Do you think you could live in Homeville, dear?" asked John after a while.

"I suppose I shall have to, shall I not?" said Mary. "And are you, too, really happy, John?"

John instantly proved to her that he was. "But it almost makes me unhappy," he added, "to think how nearly we have missed each other. If I had only known in the beginning that you were not Mrs. Edward Ruggles!"

Mary laughed joyously. The mistake which a moment before had seemed almost tragic now appeared delightfully funny.

"The explanation is painfully simple," she answered. "Mrs. Edward Ruggles--the real one--did expect to come on the Vaterland, whereas I did not. But the day before the steamer sailed she was summoned to Andover by the serious illness of her only son, who is at school there. I took her ticket, got ready overnight--I like to start on these unpremeditated journeys--and here I am." John put his arm about her to make sure of this, and kept it there--lest he should forget. "When we met on the steamer and I saw the error you had made I was tempted--and yielded--to let you go on uncorrected. But," she added, looking lovingly up into John's eyes, "I'm glad you found out your mistake at last."

CHAPTER XLVIII.

A fortnight later Mr. Harum sat at his desk in the office of Harum & Co. There were a number of letters for him, but the one he opened first bore a foreign stamp, and was postmarked "Napoli." That he was deeply interested in the contents of this epistle was manifest from the beginning, not only from the expression of his face, but from the frequent "wa'al, wa'als" which were elicited as he went on; but interest grew into excitement as he neared the close, and culminated as he read the last few lines.

"Scat my CATS!" he cried, and, grabbing his hat and the letter, he bolted out of the back door in the direction of the house, leaving the rest of his correspondence to be digested--any time.

EPILOGUE.

I might, in conclusion, tell how John's further life in Homeville was of comparatively short duration; how David died of injuries received in a runaway accident; how John found himself the sole executor of his late partner's estate, and, save for a life provision for Mrs. Bixbee, the only legatee, and rich enough (if indeed with his own and his wife's money he had not been so before) to live wherever he pleased. But as heretofore I have confined myself strictly to facts, I am, to be consistent, constrained to abide by them now. Indeed, I am too conscientious to do otherwise, notwithstanding the temptation to make what might be a more artistic ending to my story. David is not only living, but appears almost no older than when we first knew him, and is still just as likely to "git goin'" on occasion. Even "old Jinny" is still with us, though her master does most of his "joggin' 'round" behind a younger horse. Whatever Mr. Harum's testamentary intentions may be, or even whether he has made a will or not, nobody knows but himself and his attorney. Aunt Polly--well, there is a little more of her than when we first made her acquaintance, say twenty pounds.

John and his wife live in a house which they built on the shore of the lake. It is a settled thing that David and his sister dine with them every Sunday. Mrs. Bixbee at first looked a little askance at the wine on the table, but she does not object to it now. Being a "son o' temp'rence," she has never been induced to taste any champagne, but on one occasion she was persuaded to take the smallest sip of claret. "Wa'al," she remarked with a wry face, "I guess the' can't be much sin or danger 'n drinkin' anythin' 't tastes the way *that* does."

She and Mrs. Lenox took to each other from the first, and the latter has quite supplanted (and more) Miss Claricy (Mrs. Elton) with David. In fact, he said to our friend one day during the first year of the marriage, "Say, John, I ain't sure but what we'll have to hitch that wife o' your'n on the off side."

I had nearly forgotten one person whose conversation has yet to be recorded in print, but which is considered very interesting by at least four people. His name is David Lenox.

I think that's all.

The Codes Of Hammurabi And Moses
W. W. Davies

QTY

The discovery of the Hammurabi Code is one of the greatest achievements of archaeology, and is of paramount interest, not only to the student of the Bible, but also to all those interested in ancient history...

Religion   **ISBN:** *1-59462-338-4*   **Pages:132**
MSRP $12.95

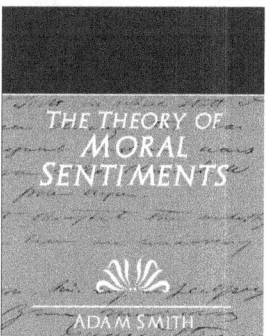

The Theory of Moral Sentiments
Adam Smith

QTY

This work from 1749. contains original theories of conscience amd moral judgment and it is the foundation for systemof morals.

Philosophy **ISBN:** *1-59462-777-0*   **Pages:536**
MSRP $19.95

Jessica's First Prayer
Hesba Stretton

QTY

In a screened and secluded corner of one of the many railway-bridges which span the streets of London there could be seen a few years ago, from five o'clock every morning until half past eight, a tidily set-out coffee-stall, consisting of a trestle and board, upon which stood two large tin cans, with a small fire of charcoal burning under each so as to keep the coffee boiling during the early hours of the morning when the work-people were thronging into the city on their way to their daily toil...

Pages:84

Childrens   **ISBN:** *1-59462-373-2*   *MSRP $9.95*

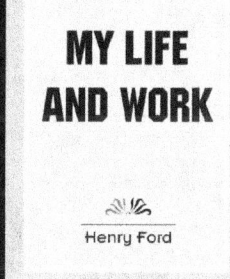

My Life and Work
Henry Ford

QTY

Henry Ford revolutionized the world with his implementation of mass production for the Model T automobile. Gain valuable business insight into his life and work with his own auto-biography... "We have only started on our development of our country we have not as yet, with all our talk of wonderful progress, done more than scratch the surface. The progress has been wonderful enough but..."

Pages:300

Biographies/   **ISBN:** *1-59462-198-5*   *MSRP $21.95*

The Art of Cross-Examination
Francis Wellman

QTY

I presume it is the experience of every author, after his first book is published upon an important subject, to be almost overwhelmed with a wealth of ideas and illustrations which could readily have been included in his book, and which to his own mind, at least, seem to make a second edition inevitable. Such certainly was the case with me; and when the first edition had reached its sixth impression in five months, I rejoiced to learn that it seemed to my publishers that the book had met with a sufficiently favorable reception to justify a second and considerably enlarged edition. ...

Pages:412

Reference   **ISBN:** *1-59462-647-2*   *MSRP $19.95*

On the Duty of Civil Disobedience
Henry David Thoreau

QTY

Thoreau wrote his famous essay, On the Duty of Civil Disobedience, as a protest against an unjust but popular war and the immoral but popular institution of slave-owning. He did more than write—he declined to pay his taxes, and was hauled off to gaol in consequence. Who can say how much this refusal of his hastened the end of the war and of slavery ?

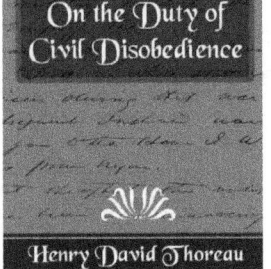

Law   **ISBN:** *1-59462-747-9*   **Pages:48**

MSRP $7.45

Dream Psychology Psychoanalysis for Beginners
Sigmund Freud

QTY

Sigmund Freud, born Sigismund Schlomo Freud (May 6, 1856 - September 23, 1939), was a Jewish-Austrian neurologist and psychiatrist who co-founded the psychoanalytic school of psychology. Freud is best known for his theories of the unconscious mind, especially involving the mechanism of repression; his redefinition of sexual desire as mobile and directed towards a wide variety of objects; and his therapeutic techniques, especially his understanding of transference in the therapeutic relationship and the presumed value of dreams as sources of insight into unconscious desires.

Dream Psychology
Psychoanalysis for Beginners

Sigmund Freud

Pages:196

Psychology   **ISBN:** *1-59462-905-6*   *MSRP $15.45*

The Miracle of Right Thought
Orison Swett Marden

QTY

Believe with all of your heart that you will do what you were made to do. When the mind has once formed the habit of holding cheerful, happy, prosperous pictures, it will not be easy to form the opposite habit. It does not matter how improbable or how far away this realization may see, or how dark the prospects may be, if we visualize them as best we can, as vividly as possible, hold tenaciously to them and vigorously struggle to attain them, they will gradually become actualized, realized in the life. But a desire, a longing without endeavor, a yearning abandoned or held indifferently will vanish without realization.

Pages:360

Self Help   **ISBN:** *1-59462-644-8*   *MSRP $25.45*

QTY

The Rosicrucian Cosmo-Conception Mystic Christianity by *Max Heindel*　ISBN: *1-59462-188-8*　**$38.95**
The Rosicrucian Cosmo-conception is not dogmatic, neither does it appeal to any other authority than the reason of the student. It is: not controversial, but is: sent forth in the, hope that it may help to clear...　New Age/Religion Pages 646

Abandonment To Divine Providence by *Jean-Pierre de Caussade*　ISBN: *1-59462-228-0*　**$25.95**
"The Rev. Jean Pierre de Caussade was one of the most remarkable spiritual writers of the Society of Jesus in France in the 18th Century. His death took place at Toulouse in 1751. His works have gone through many editions and have been republished...　Inspirational/Religion Pages 400

Mental Chemistry by *Charles Haanel*　ISBN: *1-59462-192-6*　**$23.95**
Mental Chemistry allows the change of material conditions by combining and appropriately utilizing the power of the mind. Much like applied chemistry creates something new and unique out of careful combinations of chemicals the mastery of mental chemistry...　New Age Pages 354

The Letters of Robert Browning and Elizabeth Barret Barrett 1845-1846 vol II　ISBN: *1-59462-193-4*　**$35.95**
by *Robert Browning* and *Elizabeth Barrett*　Biographies Pages 596

Gleanings In Genesis (volume I) by *Arthur W. Pink*　ISBN: *1-59462-130-6*　**$27.45**
Appropriately has Genesis been termed "the seed plot of the Bible" for in it we have, in germ form, almost all of the great doctrines which are afterwards fully developed in the books of Scripture which follow...　Religion/Inspirational Pages 420

The Master Key by *L. W. de Laurence*　ISBN: *1-59462-001-6*　**$30.95**
In no branch of human knowledge has there been a more lively increase of the spirit of research during the past few years than in the study of Psychology, Concentration and Mental Discipline. The requests for authentic lessons in Thought Control, Mental Discipline and...　New Age/Business Pages 422

The Lesser Key Of Solomon Goetia by *L. W. de Laurence*　ISBN: *1-59462-092-X*　**$9.95**
This translation of the first book of the "Lernegton" which is now for the first time made accessible to students of Talismanic Magic was done, after careful collation and edition, from numerous Ancient Manuscripts in Hebrew, Latin, and French...　New Age/Occult Pages 92

Rubaiyat Of Omar Khayyam by *Edward Fitzgerald*　ISBN:*1-59462-332-5*　**$13.95**
Edward Fitzgerald, whom the world has already learned, in spite of his own efforts to remain within the shadow of anonymity, to look upon as one of the rarest poets of the century, was born at Bredfield, in Suffolk, on the 31st of March, 1809. He was the third son of John Purcell...　Music Pages 172

Ancient Law by *Henry Maine*　ISBN: *1-59462-128-4*　**$29.95**
The chief object of the following pages is to indicate some of the earliest ideas of mankind, as they are reflected in Ancient Law, and to point out the relation of those ideas to modern thought.　Religion/History Pages 452

Far-Away Stories by *William J. Locke*　ISBN: *1-59462-129-2*　**$19.45**
"Good wine needs no bush,' but a collection of mixed vintages does. And this book is just such a collection. Some of the stories I do not want to remain buried for ever in the museum files of dead magazine-numbers an author's not unpardonable vanity..."　Fiction Pages 272

Life of David Crockett by *David Crockett*　ISBN: *1-59462-250-7*　**$27.45**
"Colonel David Crockett was one of the most remarkable men of the times in which he lived. Born in humble life, but gifted with a strong will, an indomitable courage, and unremitting perseverance...　Biographies/New Age Pages 424

Lip-Reading by *Edward Nitchie*　ISBN: *1-59462-206-X*　**$25.95**
Edward B. Nitchie, founder of the New York School for the Hard of Hearing, now the Nitchie School of Lip-Reading, Inc, wrote "LIP-READING Principles and Practice". The development and perfecting of this meritorious work on lip-reading was an undertaking...　How-to Pages 400

A Handbook of Suggestive Therapeutics, Applied Hypnotism, Psychic Science　ISBN: *1-59462-214-0*　**$24.95**
by *Henry Munro*　Health/New Age/Health/Self-help Pages 376

A Doll's House: and Two Other Plays by *Henrik Ibsen*　ISBN: *1-59462-112-8*　**$19.95**
Henrik Ibsen created this classic when in revolutionary 1848 Rome. Introducing some striking concepts in playwriting for the realist genre, this play has been studied the world over.　Fiction/Classics/Plays 308

The Light of Asia by *sir Edwin Arnold*　ISBN: *1-59462-204-3*　**$13.95**
In this poetic masterpiece, Edwin Arnold describes the life and teachings of Buddha. The man who was to become known as Buddha to the world was born as Prince Gautama of India but he rejected the worldly riches and abandoned the reigns of power when...　Religion/History/Biographies Pages 170

The Complete Works of Guy de Maupassant by *Guy de Maupassant*　ISBN: *1-59462-157-8*　**$16.95**
"For days and days, nights and nights, I had dreamed of that first kiss which was to consecrate our engagement, and I knew not on what spot I should put my lips..."　Fiction/Classics Pages 240

The Art of Cross-Examination by *Francis L. Wellman*　ISBN: *1-59462-309-0*　**$26.95**
Written by a renowned trial lawyer, Wellman imparts his experience and uses case studies to explain how to use psychology to extract desired information through questioning.　How-to/Science/Reference Pages 408

Answered or Unanswered? by *Louisa Vaughan*　ISBN: *1-59462-248-5*　**$10.95**
Miracles of Faith in China　Religion Pages 112

The Edinburgh Lectures on Mental Science (1909) by *Thomas*　ISBN: *1-59462-008-3*　**$11.95**
This book contains the substance of a course of lectures recently given by the writer in the Queen Street Hall, Edinburgh. Its purpose is to indicate the Natural Principles governing the relation between Mental Action and Material Conditions...　New Age/Psychology Pages 148

Ayesha by *H. Rider Haggard*　ISBN: *1-59462-301-5*　**$24.95**
Verily and indeed it is the unexpected that happens! Probably if there was one person upon the earth from whom the Editor of this, and of a certain previous history, did not expect to hear again...　Classics Pages 380

Ayala's Angel by *Anthony Trollope*　ISBN: *1-59462-352-X*　**$29.95**
The two girls were both pretty, but Lucy who was twenty-one who supposed to be simple and comparatively unattractive, whereas Ayala was credited, as her Bombwhat romantic name might show, with poetic charm and a taste for romance. Ayala when her father died was nineteen...　Fiction Pages 484

The American Commonwealth by *James Bryce*　ISBN: *1-59462-286-8*　**$34.45**
An interpretation of American democratic political theory. It examines political mechanics and society from the perspective of Scotsman James Bryce　Politics Pages 572

Stories of the Pilgrims by *Margaret P. Pumphrey*　ISBN: *1-59462-116-0*　**$17.95**
This book explores pilgrims religious oppression in England as well as their escape to Holland and eventual crossing to America on the Mayflower, and their early days in New England...　History Pages 268

QTY

The Fasting Cure *by Sinclair Upton*   ISBN: *1-59462-222-1*   **$13.95**
In the Cosmopolitan Magazine for May, 1910, and in the Contemporary Review (London) for April, 1910, I published an article dealing with my experiences in fasting. I have written a great many magazine articles, but never one which attracted so much attention... New Age/Self Help/Health Pages 164

Hebrew Astrology *by Sepharial*   ISBN: *1-59462-308-2*   **$13.45**
In these days of advanced thinking it is a matter of common observation that we have left many of the old landmarks behind and that we are now pressing forward to greater heights and to a wider horizon than that which represented the mind-content of our progenitors... Astrology Pages 144

Thought Vibration or The Law of Attraction in the Thought World   ISBN: *1-59462-127-6*   **$12.95**
by William Walker Atkinson   Psychology/Religion Pages 144

Optimism *by Helen Keller*   ISBN: *1-59462-108-X*   **$15.95**
Helen Keller was blind, deaf, and mute since 19 months old, yet famously learned how to overcome these handicaps, communicate with the world, and spread her lectures promoting optimism. An inspiring read for everyone... Biographies/Inspirational Pages 84

Sara Crewe *by Frances Burnett*   ISBN: *1-59462-360-0*   **$9.45**
In the first place, Miss Minchin lived in London. Her home was a large, dull, tall one, in a large, dull square, where all the houses were alike, and all the sparrows were alike, and where all the door-knockers made the same heavy sound... Childrens/Classic Pages 88

The Autobiography of Benjamin Franklin *by Benjamin Franklin*   ISBN: *1-59462-135-7*   **$24.95**
The Autobiography of Benjamin Franklin has probably been more extensively read than any other American historical work, and no other book of its kind has had such ups and downs of fortune. Franklin lived for many years in England, where he was agent... Biographies/History Pages 332

Name	
Email	
Telephone	
Address	
City, State ZIP	

☐ **Credit Card**   ☐ **Check / Money Order**

Credit Card Number	
Expiration Date	
Signature	

Please Mail to: Book Jungle
PO Box 2226
Champaign, IL 61825
or Fax to: 630-214-0564

ORDERING INFORMATION

web: *www.bookjungle.com*
email: *sales@bookjungle.com*
fax: *630-214-0564*
mail: *Book Jungle PO Box 2226 Champaign, IL 61825*
or PayPal *to sales@bookjungle.com*

Please contact us for bulk discounts

DIRECT-ORDER TERMS

**20% Discount if You Order
Two or More Books**
Free Domestic Shipping!
Accepted: Master Card, Visa,
Discover, American Express